The Shoeshine Boy

The Shoeshine Boy

Melvin Sterne

LITERARY PRESS
LAMAR UNIVERSITY

ISBN: 978-1-942956-38-9
Library of Congress Control Number: 2017940688

Manufactured in the United States of America

Lamar University Literary Press
Beaumont, Texas

This book is dedicated to you. Yes, you. The person holding it open in your hands right now. So why, you ask, would a perfect stranger dedicate a book to me? Good question. Nobody's perfect. But if you read it, I think you'll understand.

Recent Fiction from Lamar University Literary Press

Robert Bonazzi, *Awakened by Surprise*
David Bowles, *Border Lore*
Kevin Casey, *Four Peace*
Terry Dalrymple, *Love Stories, Sort Of*
Gerald Duff, *Memphis Mojo*
Britt Haraway, *Early Men*
Lynn Hoggard, *Motherland: Stories and Poems of Louisiana*
Michael Howarth, *Fair Weather Ninjas*
Gretchen Johnson, *The Joy of Deception*
Christopher Linforth, *When You Find Us We Will Be Gone*
Tom Mack and Andrew Geyer, editors, *A Shared Voice*
Moumin Quazi, *Migratory Words*
Harold Raley, *Louisiana Rogue*
Jim Sanderson, *Trashy Behavior*
Jan Seale, *Appearances*
Melvin Sterne, *The Number You Have Reached*
John Wegner, *Love is not a Dirty Word and Other Stories*
Robert Wexelblatt, *The Artist Wears Rough Clothing*

For more information about these and other books, go to
www.lamar.edu/literarypress

Acknowledgments

Thanks to Jerry Craven and Katherine Hoerth of Lamar University Literary Press for their faith and encouragement and support (and editing). I thank Phoebe, from the Starbucks at Bugis Junction, for her killer lattes, without which this book might not have happened (for most of it was written there). And I thank Pan Yuling, my wife, for her incredible love and patience. How many women would marry a man who quits his job and empties his savings to write a book? You're one in a billion, sweetie. And most of all, I'd like to thank Gus, wherever you are.

Prologue

When I was a boy, I woke every morning at dawn and crossed the bridge from Juarez, Mexico, where I stayed, to El Paso, Texas. I worked in El Paso as a shoeshine boy. I couldn't have been more than six when I started. This would have been in late 1930, although the older I get the harder it is to keep dates and times straight in this old memory of mine. And as a boy, I would not have been as aware of time. I couldn't have told you much more than morning, noon, or night, or what the weather was that day. I couldn't have named the seasons or the holidays. I never knew my real birthdate or how old I was. I did not even know my family name.

I worked like this all through what people today call The Depression. An appropriate name, I think. At the time, people just thought times were bad. They had never seen anything like it, so there was nothing for them to compare it to. They had no name for it. Funny how a thing happens and people invent a name for it later on. For me, I had never known anything but bad times. What else was there? And it was certainly depressing.

One morning, on my way to work, I ran into some teenage white boys. Bullies. They wore nice checkered shirts and blue jeans. New boots or shoes. They carried leather or canvas bags with their books and things. They stopped me on the sidewalk and made a circle around me. One of the boys, speaking Spanish, told me to sing this song. He made me repeat the words until I had them right, and then they made me sing and dance while they clapped and laughed:

> *My name is Pancho,*
> *I live on a Rancho,*
> *I work for two pesos a day.*
> *I visit my Lucy,*
> *I play with her pussy,*
> *she takes my two pesos away.*

I did not know what the words meant, but these were the first words I learned in English. And the little bits of broken English I spoke in those distant and difficult days I learned on the street and under the most difficult of circumstances. But who knows? Perhaps repeating this silly, vulgar rhyme showed me that there were other ways of speaking and thinking. Maybe it put the idea into my head that I could learn English. Sometimes something good can be made from something bad. Even by accident.

I never went to school. Not a single day. Not until I went to college. So when people ask about my childhood, I don't tell them that I lived on the streets and struggled to survive. Nobody wants to hear that, anyway. I tell them I spent my childhood *learning*. It was just a different kind of school. I suppose it depends on how you look at things.

My name is Pablo, not Pancho, but that didn't matter to the boys who bullied me that day. They gave me a nickel for singing and that was, to me, a lot of money. I was so frightened of them that I would have sung for nothing, just for the relief of knowing they weren't going to beat me. But they didn't beat me. They gave me a nickel. And every time this same group of boys saw me on the street they stopped me and made me sing it again, just to see if I remembered. I did. But they didn't give me any more nickels. A nickel was a lot of money in those days. Especially to a poor boy from Mexico. I would have remembered that. And besides, that nickel bought my lunch *and* dinner. That's how poor I was back then. Before I learned to read. Before I went to college and learned *proper* English. Before I married and got a good job. Before, well, lots of things, the most important of which I'm sure you won't believe. Maybe you won't believe any of it. Who knows? Doesn't matter. People believe what they want to believe and ignore the rest. Why let a few facts stand in the way? On the other hand, what would happen if you believed me? What would happen then?

I learned about words in college. I like how English has so many words, and sometimes these words have more than one meaning. Take the words *fantastic* and *fabulous*. They can mean something extremely wonderful and good. But they can also mean something unbelievable or invented—like a fantasy. But that's how life seems to me. A little of both. Sometimes I wonder if these *fantastic, fabulous* things happened like I remember them. Perhaps one morning I will wake to find this whole thing was just a long, bad dream. On the bad days, I wish that was the case, though I know that what I am about to tell you is true. Every word. If I misremember some small detail here or there I assure you, the substance is true. Any error is only due to the crumbling walls in the vaults of my memory. And let me tell you, sometimes it's no fun even to revisit these events.

So why bother writing this all down? Because I think it's important that I share my whole story with somebody. Please don't get me wrong. It's not that *I'm* important. I think my *story* is important. I'm just one of seven billion people alive on the planet today. Nothing special about me. I'm just a shoeshine boy. But my story, well, read it and judge for yourself.

How convinced am I that my story is important? Let me tell you, friend, I'm willing to die for my words. And the truth is, there are still people around who would kill me to keep me from telling you what I know. Who is the boy buried under the catclaw tree? Who killed him? And why? Who killed the people buried on the abandoned ranch outside of Juarez? Who cut the soldier's throat in the clinic at Walker Air Force Base? Who was the stranger in the Colonel's uniform and was he really a Russian spy? What really happened on July 7, 1947? The answers to those questions could get me killed in a hurry. And you might add to the list of questions this question of your own: If the answers to those questions could get you killed, *Why are you telling me?* I'll get to that.

Back when I was young, I was known as the quiet one. For a boy who started out in life meaning no harm to anyone, I learned a lot about harm in a very short time. As my friend Gus asked me one day, "What *is* the matter with you people?"

So I was a shoeshine boy and never went to school, but today I have a Master's Degree in Psychology and am a retired high school guidance counselor. Really. And I have a house and a vacation cabin and two cars and all the clothes and furniture and tools and junk a man could ask for. And I draw a pension from the State of California. In between those jobs—a shoeshine boy and guidance counselor—I've been a smuggler, a gangster, a construction worker, shipyard worker, cook, dishwasher, busboy, and agricultural laborer. Not much of a career path.

And I'm a U.S. citizen, too. Imagine that. Until I took my oath, I was an illegal alien. Illegal and alien. Two other interesting words.

That day, though, the day the boys made me sing, I was barefoot. I owned one pair of dirty pants, one tattered shirt, and a chipped blue marble I'd found in the back room of a vacant house. All I had in the world. I wouldn't learn what underpants were until I was a teenager. Even my shoeshine box was rented. I paid every night for its use.

My family came from central Mexico. Near Torreón, I believe. I said this because I love caramels and had a vague memory of eating them on some special occasion when I was small. Torreón is famous for its caramel. And I remember once walking with my mother on a hot afternoon in a town by a river. I held a balloon but let it slip and cried when it floated away. That could be Torreón. There's a river there. But it doesn't matter. One name is as good as another, and I can call Torreón home if I want. My past, such as it was, is like a *fantasy*. Words to write on a line in some paperwork. A name, a place, a date. I could be anyone from anywhere. So I'm from Torreón. I like the sound of that. It's a sweet-sounding name. It's as if I got off to a good start in life.

I have no memory of my father. I must have had one. I had a little brother, Marco, so I must have seen my father sometime. Or perhaps we had different fathers, or even many fathers. Who knows? My mother was—how do I say this gracefully?—*una puta*. A whore. I did not understand what that meant at the time, though it was a word I learned young and heard often.

We lived in a one-room shack of gray boards out on the edge of town, beyond the police checkpoint, beyond the petrol station, beyond even the little roadside *taquerias* and cantinas that fed the hungry truckers and travelers passing up and down the highway. Ours was a little house in a little collection of houses surrounded by cotton and watermelon and bean fields. I suppose all of the women there were *putas*. I remember a few other children. No fathers, only mothers.

Our house had a tin roof, a long, low front window of grimy, white glass. There was a mattress on the floor in one corner. We did not have a toilet, electric lights, or running water. We shit and peed in the fields across the road or behind the house. I remember clouds of dust in the air and chickens clucking and flapping in the dirt. Roosters crowing in the morning. I remember the summer heat and the cold in winter, the music of water dripping into rusty steel buckets when it rained, and drinking the irony-tasting water from those buckets. I remember the rumble of trucks at every hour of the day and night.

But my most vivid memory—and the most outstanding feature of that house—was a great big galvanized steel toolbox that sat right in the middle of the room. I hated that box. During the daytime my mother covered it with a worn red blanket and we used it for a table. At night she folded the blanket inside the box and it served as a hiding place and bed for my brother and me so that her customers wouldn't know that we were there. Marco and I had to keep very quiet and sleep inside it. If we made any noise, or came out when there was a customer in the house, she would beat us, or they would beat us. Or worse. I never knew who was going to be passed out on the floor when we crept out of our hiding place in the early hours of the morning. Sometimes my mother was alone on her mattress. Sometimes there was a man with her. Sometimes there were three or four.

Things went on like this for several years until one night a customer beat my mother to death. Marco and I huddled in the box until she stopped screaming and the man ransacked the house. It wasn't the first time we'd heard her beaten or raped. I don't know what happened. Perhaps it was robbery. Maybe he was *loco*, crazy. The man wrecked the house, smashed what furniture we had, broke the window, kicked the door off the hinges. Nobody came to help. Maybe such events were common in that neighborhood. Who knows?

Eventually the man opened the box and found Marco and me. He dragged me out first and beat me. After he reduced me to a sobbing, bleeding pile of shit, he locked me back in the box and set fire to the house—I would see this later on—but the fire didn't take. If it had, I wouldn't be telling you this story. That was the first time I almost died in a fire.

I lay in that little box and screamed until I lost my voice, but nobody came to help me. I lay in that box until I wet and soiled myself. I have never again felt so frightened and alone—even years later when I was kidnapped by a rival gang and almost murdered. Eventually I kicked so hard that I flipped the box onto its side. The latch came loose and I crawled out to find the man gone, my brother gone, the house full of smoke, and my mother on the floor in a puddle of blood and brains. The blanket lay smoldering on the bed, the ashes falling and glowing faintly in the dark. I lit a match to see. I took one look at my mother and knew that this was what death looked like. I was afraid to touch her, even to cover up her naked body. I was standing by her feet. One leg was broken sideways below the knee. Her eyes were open, her mouth full of broken, bloody teeth. Her throat crushed, her head turned at a weird angle.

I remember the smell of my skin burning as I held that match and wondered what to do. I wanted to do something, but what? When you are five or six years old, and your reality (such as it was, even a bad reality) ends like that, there is nothing you can do. The world is a blank stare.

When the match sputtered out, the darkness and fear overwhelmed me. I ran out into the night so frightened I could not even cry. I have only told one person what happened that night: a priest in whom I confided. I never told my wives or my children. I didn't know what happened to my brother, Marco, whether he was dead or alive. I thought that the man who killed our mother took him, and I was tortured by the knowledge that I had failed him. He was my brother. I should have protected him, but I didn't. I should have gone for help, but instead I ran away.

That night I ran until I could run no more, and then I limped along until dawn. At first light I laid down, exhausted. I know, now, that I traveled north, though I had no destination in mind. I just walked. Perhaps it was fate. The old priest said that God was looking after me. I can't imagine that this is what being looked after by God looks like. Maybe. Like I said, sometimes good things happen by accident, even when that wasn't the intention.

So early that morning I took shelter in an abandoned farmhouse and slept. When I awoke, I found a pump and drank cold, clean water from a well. I plucked a few stunted ears of green corn and a handful of dry, dying string beans from the fields surrounding the house. Green corn and raw beans aren't much for breakfast, but at least it was something.

I set out again, following the single-lane paved road that served as the main highway north. It was probably the only paved road running north in all of Mexico. That was my life for the rest of that spring and summer. Life was a road that ran north through an endless desert.

I did not speak to anyone for days. If I really am from Torreón, then I traveled nearly 1000 kilometers to reach Juarez. Perhaps I was from somewhere closer to the border, but either way, I walked most of it.

I remember bits and pieces of farmhouses and ranches, towns, one large, most small, some just tiny clusters of adobe huts. I remember eating from piles of garbage or stealing more raw vegetables from gardens or fields. I remember a sweet yellow melon. I slept under bridges, in barns, under mesquites in dry arroyos, in natural caves scooped from the hills by the wind—wherever I thought I might spend a few hours and not be found. And my sleep was haunted by dreams of my house, my mother, her blood, her brains, my brother calling to me from the surrounding darkness, a galvanized steel box that hovered in the air above me. If you said I was crazy, I wouldn't argue. How could I *not* be?

My memories of this journey are not coherent like a manuscript. I think that perhaps I was too traumatized to order my thoughts that way. But then, too, I was so young. Do the young look at their life in the logical order of a story? Or do they look at certain moments as more important than the actual sequence of events? I think my memory works by the order of importance, rather than the sequence. So my memory of this journey is like old postcards pulled from a box and out of order. A shade tree by a river on hot afternoon. A stray kitten I carried for a few days until I woke and found it cold and stiff, its fur moving with the breeze. An old woman who gave me a glass of something sweet. A bucket of fresh milk left for no reason I could tell in the shady corner of a barn. A chipped blue marble I found in the back room in a broken-down house. A courtyard with a bright green pond full of fat orange fish.

I was alone and terrified, but if there is a God, and this God was looking after me like the priest said, then He kept me alive with small doses of wonder. And perhaps it was because that was all I had—this sense of wonder—that I have held onto this all these years. I am still astonished by the beauty that I find in life: sunrises, sunsets, snowflakes, shooting stars, dahlias, the delicate lines like lace that frost makes freezing on a window, the sweet taste of Bing cherries, beignets and coffee, the way that children laugh and play and are so innocent and real. Much of my life was not easy and most of my life I was very poor, but the sense of wonder costs nothing and it kept me alive. It gave me something to live for.

I think it was spring when I began my journey and then full Mexican summer. I remember shimmering heat that rippled the purple mountains on the horizon. I remember sleeping out under stars. I remember a storm and meeting hailstones for the first time. Imagine—stones of ice falling from the sky! I remember a night sky full of shooting stars at what must have been the Perseids Shower in August. There were so many! Somewhere in the desert, on an especially hot afternoon, the kind of suffocating heat that kills if you're not careful, I met a man with a long black car who was fixing a flat tire by the side of the road. This was in the middle of nowhere and he must have known that I was in trouble. This man was a gringo—the first gringo I ever met. He had a large round face, blue eyes, the whitest skin I had ever seen, and red hair. Red. I couldn't take my eyes off it.

I don't think he spoke much Spanish. Only a couple of words. *A dónde vas? Hambre? Sediento?* Where are you going? Hungry? Thirsty? He gave me a ride all the way to Juarez and he bought me a meal at a *taqueria* along the way. He let me out on a corner across the street from a church and gave me a shiny silver coin which I now know was a silver dollar. I spent it on tortillas with a vendor who took the coin and gave me no change. It was the first American money I ever saw. How was I to know what it was worth? I could barely count pesos.

Imagine a boy of six making a journey alone like that today? I read once, in college, about a boy of four who traveled alone from Russia to the United States. His family had left him behind with a grandmother who then died. When the family, knowing nothing of this, sent money for their fare to America, the villagers pinned a note to the boy's coat, put the money in his

14

pocket, and set him on a train. From there he passed in the care of strangers, from stranger to stranger, on trains and across borders, all the way to Le Harve, France, where still more strangers saw him safely boarded on a ship to America and then delivered to his family in New York. Four months after leaving his home village he arrived in New York City. Imagine that.

I had neither money nor relatives. I was just a little boy alone and frightened and hoping only to eat and sleep and be left undisturbed. My real memories, like this story, begin when I met Don Pablo and began shining shoes. Sometimes it seems I was born a fully-formed boy of six with a shoeshine box in my hand.

I say *seems* because even now, many years since, there is no sensation regarding that experience that I can describe in terms as concrete as a *feeling*. I reach back into the past and find only the numbness of a scar. It is as though in my youth a bullet passed through the exact spot in my heart that registered feelings, and I have spent most of my life relearning what it was I lost, what I was supposed to possess from the beginning. I have spent my whole life learning how to feel. The irony is that now, at the end of my life, I have succeeded.

Act I Scene 1

Don Pablo lived upstairs over a café and cantina and hotel on Juarez Avenue. He occupied the whole fourth floor of the building, but spent most of his time at a table kept especially for him on the verandah. It was a big, rectangular wood-and-stone building in the middle of the block, painted red-and-white, and hung with signs showing pretty girls with plunging necklines and advertising *Dos Equis* and *Tecate* and *Negro Modelo*. The hotel might have been nice for a little while back in the late 1800's. It wasn't bad for a hotel in a border town, but it had seen better days. You could tell that. The sag in the floor. The tattered curtains and linens. The tarnished and bent silverware. Chairs and tables that didn't sit level, the woodwork fading to gray. That kind of thing.

I knew the moment Don Pablo saw me, and I knew that he knew that I knew he saw me. It was as if he looked inside me and saw what was broken there. This was perhaps six months after I'd fled my home and brother and dead mother. It was only a few weeks after I'd arrived in Juarez, so it must have been in the fall of 1930. I was walking down an alley that morning and looking in bins behind restaurants for something to eat. I came out from the alley onto Juarez Avenue clutching half a beef-and-bean burrito, and not even a little bit spoiled. Don Pablo was sitting at his table under a big green umbrella on the gray wooden deck in front of the cantina.

The café served meals, and the food was not bad, but Don Pablo's business was pleasure, not food, and he was drinking a whiskey—I know that now from the small glass of brownish liquid he rolled between his forefinger and his thumb—and he was smoking a fat cigar. Perhaps he had been up all night. That would not have been unusual for him. He was leaning back in the chair with his feet on the table. He whistled for me from across the street and I looked at him. He pointed at the table meaning that I should come to him.

There was something about Don Pablo that when he gestured or spoke, there was no will to resist, only the thought that one should obey him. This was not pleasant. I have seen grown men answer Don Pablo's call knowing that they were going to die but coming anyway, subserviently, as though the way they answered might make some difference in their fate.

Don Pablo wore a pale blue suit with a wide lapel, but no tie. His shirt was white and open at the throat. His chest was matted with black hair. He wore a heavy gold chain around his fat neck and gold rings on all his fat fingers. On the back of the chair beside him hung a round, white hat. His face was wide and his jaw square, his hair black and perfect, parted from the right side to the left, his skin not light, but not dark, either. Across his upper lip was drawn the pencil-thin line of a Hollywood mustache. The Clark Gable of Ciudad Juarez. He was, perhaps, forty, and when he smiled he had one big gold tooth. His top right canine. *"Tienes hambre?"* he asked. Are you hungry? It was not a question. It was his way of striking up a conversation—to ask a question to which all parties already knew the answer.

A half a burrito is better than nothing, but it doesn't make breakfast for a growing boy. *"Siéntate,"* he said. Sit down. He pointed at the seat beside him and put on his hat. "And throw that trash away." He pointed into the street.

I sat down opposite him but clutched the burrito.

A waiter was instantly at his side.

"What would you like?" Don Pablo asked. When I made no reply, he said to the waiter, *"Huevos rancheros con tortillas."*

The waiter returned in a short while with a plate of eggs and pork and tomato and onion and chili and beans and cheese, with two fat, thick, hot, homemade tortillas with a ball of fresh sour cream. He also poured me a glass of orange juice. I don't believe I had ever seen so much food on a single plate. I stared in disbelief until Don Pablo insisted for the third time that I eat.

Don Pablo stretched and slouched in his chair while I stuffed myself. He drank whiskey from this tiny glass that was never empty, and smoked a cigar that seemed like it would burn forever. When I had eaten all that I could he said, *"Necessitas trabajo?"* You need a job? His words posed as a question, or an observation, perhaps, but were really a statement. He knew.

I did not then know what he meant when he said, "a job."

"Necessitas dinero?" Do you need money?

That I understood. I nodded.

"*Y yo tambien,*" he replied, and laughed. So do I.

I said nothing.

He narrowed his eyes and said, "Would you like to be a shoeshine boy?"

I shrugged. I had no idea what a shoeshine boy was. I had never even worn shoes.

"*Tienes los aperos?*" Do you have tools?

I shook my head.

He leaned forward and his eyes looked right through me. The smoke from his cigar drifted into my face and I choked a cough. "Do you think you can learn, *Señor Hablador?*" Mr. talks-too-much.

I nodded.

"*Cómo se llama?*" he asked. What's your name?

"Pablo," I said.

He flashed a broad, gold-toothed smile. "That's my name, too!" He stood up and clapped his hands. "Come with me, Pablo. I have all the equipment you need." I followed Pablo to the back of the bar and then up three flights of steps to the fourth floor.

The second floor was nothing but a ring of small, narrow rooms with doors facing a big open space that looked out over the dance floor below. The third floor was a hallway with larger rooms. There were fewer doors. The hallway was carpeted in dusty blue. I would find out all about these floors in a few weeks. It was quiet in the upper floors. Nobody stirred. Not even the cleaners were about yet.

The fourth floor was Don Pablo's. All of it. And it looked to me like the presidential palace. The entrance was in a little alcove at the top of the stairs. Inside was a living room that would have held twenty of the little wooden shacks like I grew up in. And beyond that was a kitchen and beside that, a hallway that led to the back of the apartment. The hallway, what I could see of it, was lined with still more doors. A palace.

Don Pablo sat down on a red velvet sofa. He patted the cushion that I should sit beside him. "I will give you the equipment," he said, "and you will give me half of what you make every day."*Cada día,*" he said. He stretched out the word *cada*, making it last a long, long time. Then he ruffled my hair, paused, parted it and checked me for lice. I did not have any at the time, though I remembered my mother putting turpentine on my brother and me one time when we came home with an itching rash.

"Half of what you make will be at least three pesos, do you understand? At least three. And don't lie to me because every morning I will know exactly how much polish is in your kit, and I know exactly how much polish it takes to shine a shoe, and if" his hand tightened around the back of my neck and he turned my face to look at him, "and if you cheat me for so much a single *centavo*, do you know what I will do to you?" He held me in a grasp so tight I could not move my head.

"No," I stammered.

He sighed and let me go. "I'll show you sometime. Next time somebody is stupid enough to lie to me."

In exactly one month, I would be in a car with Don Pablo and some other boys when he would show me what he meant, but then, that morning, sitting in his apartment, it was only an abstract threat.

He patted me on the head to show that all was forgiven. He leaned forward close to my face. "I started out as a shoeshine boy, too, you know." He winked and pressed a finger to his lips as if it were a secret he was sharing. As if it was the promise of a bright future. He smiled. "Now do you want your equipment? His hand had drifted to the small of my back.

I nodded, looking around the room and wondering what was equipment.

I have never told anyone what I had to do to get that little box with a few rags, a worn wooden horsehair brush, and an assortment of little tins of *El Oso* shoe polish. I suppose I never will. To this day, the smell of shoe polish sickens me, and indeed, as soon as I was out of sight of the hotel I vomited all of my breakfast. After giving me the box, though, Don Pablo showed me how to shine shoes, and when I left his apartment, I clung to that little box as though my life depended on it, even though I wanted to throw it into the nearest bin and run. But to where? South across the desert to a Torreón whose memory was already fading? North across the river into the *Los Estados Unidos* of which I knew nothing? I had no options. Only to do the best I could with what I had, and that little box was all I had in the world. Almost ninety years later, would it surprise you to learn I still have it? I could not have guessed for all the world how far it would take me, or what it would open my eyes to see.

Act I Scene 2

Don Pablo was one of a group of criminals operating in Juarez. Today we would call them gangsters. Back then, I'm not sure there was a word for it. It was something, maybe, like the mafia. Don Ricardo was the *jefe,* the chief. He had a half-dozen smaller bosses answering to him, men like Don Pablo. All the small bosses had their own special rackets. They divided Juarez into smaller territories which they guarded like rabid dogs. There was Don Elias' eastside gang (called Sixteenth of September, for the main road there). Don Pablo ran the downtown gang with the border crossing and the bullring. There was a gang organized around the racetrack, and another that operated around the train station. There was the south-side gang and still another in Zaragoza, to the southeast. Sometimes these gangs cooperated with one another. Sometimes not. There was always competition among the smaller bosses, and I suppose Don Ricardo liked it like that. If you keep your underlings weak, if they must be constantly on guard against one another, then they must depend on you for their support. And if they are busy fighting one another, they cannot conspire against you.

Within each of these gangs there was a still smaller pecking order of still smaller bosses with still smaller rackets. All of the gangs had bars, gambling, prostitution, drugs, protection schemes, and so forth. But it seemed there was no vice too small or crime too petty for them not to control. Even beggars and shoeshine boys. And the smallest of all of these was me.

Don Pablo's shoeshine boys had already taken the logical spots in front of the nicer hotels, restaurants, and bars. There were shoeshine boys in the other territories, too; on the platforms at the train station, at the bus station, hanging around the racetrack, and even at the new aerodrome out on the east side of town.

Our value to the gangs was not entirely based on what we could earn shining shoes. They made money off us, of course, but they made money off every one of their ventures. That was expected. We also served as eyes and ears. *The word on the street*, so to speak. And we served as messengers or errand boys. Sometimes we had value for other forms of entertainment. But I think, mostly, that our value was that we were expected to grow up and fill up the ranks of the gangs. We were taken in, all of us, from the streets, and informally trained to serve as loyal soldiers. Our lives were saved, but not for our benefit. Any pleasure we might derive from life was counted as part of our wages. Pleasure was something we earned for what we did for the bosses. I know, now, that most of life works like this. It's called exploitation. Back then, I mistook Don Pablo's actions for kindness.

Don Pablo had other boys downtown besides shoeshine boys. He kept a whole army of them selling newspapers, candy, gum, peanuts. There was, I would learn, both a pecking order and steps for advancement. What you sold and where you sold it depended on your ability to fight for and hold on to your territory. And if a boy got too big, say, for shining shoes, then if he had been good to Don Pablo, he would move up to other enterprises. Don Pablo had a whole host of interests like the bar and whorehouse where I first met him. He owned other bars and dance halls, as well, and distilleries where he made the expensive imported whiskeys he sold. And he ran the men and women who sold the whiskey, and the men and women who sold the other things that Don Pablo managed, including other men and women. I suppose pretty much everything illegal that passed through Juarez in those days—in either direction—involved Don Pablo, or at least, one of the gangs. And during the time of the American Prohibition, many vices flourished in Juarez. It was an especially good time to be in the whiskey business.

That first day I got a bloody nose for trying to shine a man's shoes in another boy's territory. The boy also stole two tins of my polish and I lost another in the ensuing scramble. Don Pablo thrashed me that night when I did not have three pesos and was short on polish.

I figured out right then that I was not going to make three pesos a day shining shoes in Juarez. How I made those pesos was not Don Pablo's concern, but I dared not come back without them. That bloody nose did not teach me to cry—I'd had bloody noses in the past, and would have more in the future—but carrying a box for Don Pablo in the daytime and rummaging through garbage cans at night left me no better off than I was before. Only more tired and more hopeless.

It took me two days to decide that if all the good territories were taken, then I would have to either do something else or find somewhere else to do what I was doing. Or both. And so, on the third morning of my employment, I took my box and instead of looking around downtown for a better street corner, I walked north, up Juarez Avenue, until I came to the bridge that crossed over the Rio Grande and into America. I don't know where I got the idea. Perhaps it was the memory of the gringo I met in the desert. The man had so much money he would just hand me a coin for nothing. Or maybe I had heard talk about the border, or about things being better across the river. Or maybe I just didn't know any better. I was that naíve. I might not have known that *Los Estados Unidos* was another country and El Paso another city. There was a road and a bridge. Why not walk on it?

The bridge was iron, painted dark green, the road concrete and newly-paved. The Mexican guards at the south end paid me no attention at all. They didn't give a shit. There were not many cars in those days, but there was a long line of bicycles and carts and people carrying boxes, and even people riding donkeys and horses and towing behind them carts or strings of goats. I joined the line as proudly as if I were graduating from school, and I would have walked right through the American checkpoint except for the guard in the neat blue uniform. He grabbed me by the back of my shirt and lifted me into the air and asked, in perfect Spanish, "*Y dónde vas tu?*" Where are you going?

I pointed toward the city.

"*Y qué, vas a hacer allí?*" And what will you do there?

I held up my shoeshine box.

The guard laughed. "*Crees que se puede caminar por el puente y en los Estados Unidos, así como así?*" You think you can walk across the bridge just like that?

I nodded. I really thought that I could.

"Well, you can't," he said. He set me down and pushed me back toward Juarez.

I stood for a moment practicing my new wet-eyed and hungry look, and then pointed at a woman riding a bicycle piled high with baskets of chickens. "But you let her past," I said.

"She's delivering chickens."

I pointed to a handful of men carrying canvas bags of tools slung over their shoulders, I said, "And you let them cross."

"They're stone masons. They're working on the church."

"And her?" I asked, pointing at a young woman in a tight sweater and long skirt.

"She is... " he paused and licked his lips. "Shopping."

I looked at the woman, now sashaying in a style familiar to my young eyes. "*No me jodas,*" I said. Don't bullshit me.

The border guard's eyes widened. "What did you say?"

"I said, Am I not working?" I held up my little shoeshine box.

By now the other guards had stopped checking the people in line, and even the people waiting in line craned their necks to see.

"Do people in America not need their shoes shined? Do they not want to look their best to go their place of work? To dine with their friends? To go..." I looked at the backside of the young woman, now standing at the base of the bridge and waving for a taxi, " . . . shopping? Except, of course, for you." I pointed at his boots, which were scruffy and gray, and did not shine at all. The rest of the border guards laughed. The guard's face reddened.

"If I shine your shoes, they will last longer and look better, and people will respect you more."

The guard knelt and looked at me eye-to-eye. "Why don't you go home to your mother and go to school? After you finish school, you can find a real job."

Suddenly, and for the first time I can recall, tears sprang to my eyes. It was like I was standing so close to something so good I could taste it, but I could not reach out to grasp it. I began to sob. There must have been a hundred people watching me, and all I could do was lay my head on the guard's shoulder and weep until I felt the cloth wet beneath my face. I dropped my little box and some of the tins rolled away down the bridge. At last I stammered, *"No tengo madre. No tengo padre. No tengo nada."* I have no mother. I have no father. I have nothing.

"All right, all right," he said, as one of the guards picked up the tins and packed them back in my box. "You can go. But you must come back before dark, and if I hear of you causing any trouble, I'll personally throw you in the river, understand?"

I nodded, wiping my eyes and my nose on the back of my hand. I saw then that the other guard was looking through my little box. There was nothing there but my brush and tins of polish and a few rags. I did not even have a bag of peanuts for a snack. I took the box and walked away, but after a few steps I turned back and asked the guard who had held me up, "What time do you start in the morning?"

"Eh, what?" he said, startled. "Oh, six A.M."

"I will be here early to shine your shoes," I said. And then, without waiting for him to reply, I walked into America.

Act I Scene 3

There was, back then, much difference between the USA and Mexico. There were more cars in America, more motorcycles, more bicycles. And the people hurried—at least, compared to Mexico—and I had to learn to be careful on the roads. And the people were different, especially the teenage boys. In Juarez, I had to watch out that I did not work in a territory belonging to another of Don Pablo's boys. In America, *any* boy or group of boys anywhere was a threat—like the ones who gave me my first English lesson when they taught me that song. But the threat was not about work or territory or money. The threat, I would come to understand, was in my being—my existence. For some reason I could not comprehend, people in America disliked Mexicans. This difference in nationality or heritage or culture disturbs them, but especially it disturbs groups of boys. To this day I cannot understand why. Why should a person who speaks differently, or dresses differently, or prefers different food, or practices a different religion, or any of these other petty things—why should this person be perceived as a threat? I find that idea frightening. My existence does not make me anyone's enemy.

There were shoeshine boys in America, too. I found this out on my first day. I went to the train station and there were two or three boys lounging around, and one old negro, but they didn't seem to care that I was there as long as I did not mingle with them. They might have wanted to earn a few dollars, but they were not, evidently, organized into a gang.

I set my box down at the far end of the station. I sat down on it and watched the boys watching me. They talked, they laughed, they looked, they made noises. But nobody got up and said anything to me. And when a man stopped in front of me and I shined his shoes, nobody said a word. The man gave me a nickel. A nickel for shining his shoes. I found out later that the boys in America charged a dime but I didn't care, and they didn't seem to care. Eventually, the boys disappeared and there was nobody left but the old negro and me. And when he vanished, I had all the shoes I could shine. Sometimes men even paid me a dime.

Every morning I shined the guards' shoes at the border crossing, and every night I trudged across the bridge to Juarez and down the road to Don Pablo's cantina. Before I got there, I changed my nickels and dimes into pesos. A dollar made three pesos. Twenty or thirty shoeshines. At the cantina, Don Pablo ruffled my hair and asked me where I was working even though he must have known. Every night I shrugged my shoulders and said nothing. "My quiet one," he would say. But I had a tobacco pouch with money in it tied to a string around my neck, and even if I still ate out of garbage cans, I had the feeling that despite losing my mother and my brother, things were going to be all right. When you start out life like I did, becoming a shoeshine boy is moving up in the world.

I did not sleep near the cantina. Some of the other boys, including the one who had beaten me, hung around there. I tried to keep away from them. But I also watched them—and more than they knew. I watched them and I thought about them. What they did. Why they did it. How to avoid them. How to beat them if I had to. Sometimes the other boys made a little extra money doing this or that. They carried bags for guests. They fetched taxis. They ran errands. I never learned where they stayed. A few might even have had proper homes. I don't know.

There was, in those days, a race track and a bull ring downtown, and I usually slept on bales of straw in one of the barns, or sometimes on the roof of one of the sheds or buildings there. They were big buildings, and quiet on week nights, with just the sighing of the animals and the scamper of mice, the occasional footsteps of a night watchman. And there were spigots there with water where I could wash in the morning if I was careful and quick.

There were often other vagrants, too, in those days. Usually these were men, but sometimes women. Sometimes even families, thin and frightened. They seldom caused me any trouble. Sometimes they joined in little groups to drink. Most often they kept to themselves, as I kept to myself. Like me, they wanted only to be left alone. None of us needed any more trouble in our lives. I learned young to make no noise. Sound invites scrutiny.

Juarez is a high desert, and the heat was more of a problem than the cold. It sometimes gets very cold in the winter, but such spells are short. The fall faded into winter, and even then it was fine to sleep on the roof under the stars. In those days there were not so many electric lights, and you could see the Milky Way, even in the city at night. I would lay on my back with burlap potato sacks rolled up for a pillow, and I would look up at the stars and feel the night breeze on my skin, and it was cool and nice, but still somehow dark, and sad, and lonely, all at the same time. And it was more beautiful than anything I had ever seen, or have ever seen since. I loved looking at the stars, and I would lay on my back and look up and wonder if there were other worlds out there, and if there were, were they better than this one. And for some reason it seemed to me that there *had* to be other worlds, and that we were not as alone as it seemed. I don't know what put that idea into my head. Maybe I saw it in a comic book or something. I read a lot of comics back then. I say read, but looked was more like it. I would look at the pictures and look at the words, run my fingers down the lines of letters as though they were braille. I wondered what messages they contained, and more than once I wished that I could go to school and learn.

23

My mother was Catholic in her own vague kind of way. I must have learned something about God from her because at night I would lay awake and talk to this thing, this sort of spirit that I felt was there, or had been told was there, or thought ought to be there, for it made no sense to me that we should all be alone even though I was terrified of being around other people. And sometimes at night my thoughts went to Marco, and I would talk to him and one night, sleeping on a roof under a full moon, I promised my brother that I would find him and make it up to him, if he would forgive me for running away.

This is what it means to be poor: you are always one step away from annihilation. One failed crop, one flood, one storm, one drunken customer, one virus or snakebite or careless driver or lightning or something. Years later, people asked me how I could be so happy. I know a few things. I say nothing about my past, but if they only knew! No warm pork burrito ever tasted as good as those I filched from garbage cans when I was starving. No starry sky has since shined so sweetly as the ones into which I gazed on those lonesome nights. But actually, I think it is not that I am all that happy. People may think that, but the truth is that I learned not to complain. Who would listen, anyway? Who wants to hear somebody else's misery?

If I have a satisfactory life today, it is not because of this house I own, or the comfortable bedding on which I sleep, or that I can go to the market and buy whatever I want for dinner. I have aches and pains in my body and in my heart, the same as everybody else. But a long time ago I learned two simple things which are essential for happiness. I learned that today's troubles are sufficient for today, which is to say, to take care of business and don't worry about what hasn't happened yet. And I learned that one should never lose that sense of wonder like what I felt looking up at the night sky. Having this, what else does one require?

By spring of 1931, I settled into a kind of routine. I crossed the bridge in the morning and shined shoes all day. I returned at night, paid Don Pablo, ate, washed, and slept. I acquired a second pair of pants and a second shirt. I had a bar of soap and a comb. I had a blanket. I was not so hungry. As for the loneliness, there was no cure for that.

Act I Scene 4

One evening, when I arrived at the cantina to make my nightly payment, Don Pablo was waiting at his table with several men. He did not greet me with a smile and ruffle my hair. Instead he sniffed and said, "You. Upstairs, now! Wash, and be quick about it."

I washed upstairs in a basin in the big room in the whorehouse. The big room was where the girls went to wash and dress. All the girls were there and, as it was early, they were adjusting their lingerie and putting on their makeup and oiling their long, black hair. They giggled and pinched my butt as I tried to wash and keep some modesty in the room. One of them squirted me with some perfume which, try as I might, I could not wash off.

Downstairs two other boys and one girl stood against the wall behind the table. Don Pablo motioned for us and we followed him out the back door. There were two cars idling in the alley, and we got into them, two men and two kids in the back seat in each car. In the front was the driver and another man. I rode in the car with Don Pablo and another boy.

"We are going to a party," Don Pablo said to me. He put his arm around me. "We're going to make a movie tonight. Do you want to be in a movie?"

I had a vague notion of what movies were from the posters outside the cinemas. I had no idea what it took to make a movie or what I might do in one. I had never seen a movie.

We drove through town and then south and west from the city toward the mountains. Don Pablo and the other man lit cigars and drank whiskey, which they shared with the men in the front. He made me and the other boy take drinks of the whiskey, too, until our stomachs were hot and heads spinning. We also were supposed to smoke part of the cigar, but I did not inhale the smoke. The other boy did, and while we were stopped by the side of the road so he could vomit, a motorcycle caught up to us and the rider said something to Don Pablo and Don Pablo rubbed his forehead and said, "*Cabrón! Hijola!*" Then he told the driver to turn around and said, to me, "You might as well come and see."

After that, we turned around and drove back toward town, but before we reached the city, we turned off on a dirt road that wound south for perhaps a dozen miles, then west down another road, in even worse condition, a road that wound up and along a narrowing canyon between two arms of a rocky, desert mountain. We eventually turned south again, down a short road that was even worse—just two ruts carved into the rocky ground—and stopped at a ranch house in the middle of nowhere. This house was really old. It was built from adobe and had not been maintained for some time. Much of the plaster had broken away from the walls revealing the adobe bricks, and the roof over the main room sagged so badly in the middle that I was afraid it would fall.

We stopped in front of the house. "Leave the car running," Don Pablo said. And with the headlamps lighting our way, we went inside. Some of the ceiling plaster, in fact, had fallen. It laid in chunks on the tile floor. There was no electricity, only two kerosene lanterns hung from hooks on the walls. There was no proper furniture in the house, only a couple of weathered wooden chairs. Two wooden nail kegs stood in the middle of the room, with two iron stands on top of them. The stands that looked like they came from a blacksmith shop. A length of pipe ran between the stands, and a man hung from the pipe. The man had his hands tied behind his back and the rope then fastened around his waist and between his legs. The pipe passed behind his back and underneath his armpits so that he hung that way, kind of like a chicken on a spit. His feet trailed on the ground and he might have stood except that his legs were broken below the knees. Two men with shotguns sat in chairs watching him and smoking cigarettes. They stood up when Don Pablo came in. The man hanging from the bar sobbed softly. It was as if he had been crying for a long time.

Don Pablo walked to the man and took him by the hair and held his face to the light. "Michaelo," he said, his voice deep and musical. "*Estoy muy decepcionado de ti.*" I am very disappointed in you.

Michaelo mumbled something I could not hear.

Don Pablo shook his head slowly. "*Confié, en ti,*" he said. I trusted you. "And this is how you repay me? I helped you. I took you in. What were you before I found you and gave you a job?" To the man in the front of our car he said, "Fetch us some whiskey." To Michaelo he said, "Will you have a drink and discuss this with me?" He snapped his fingers and one of the men went out to the car. The other took a knife from a sheath on his belt.

Michaelo cried out but Don Pablo said, still speaking in Spanish, "Come, come! What kind of man do you take me for?" And the man with the knife cut Michaelo loose and then helped Don Pablo carry Michaelo to a chair. The other man returned with whiskey and another man came in the room with a tray of glasses and they filled four of them and drank, with Don Pablo himself helping Michaelo to drink. When the whiskey was gone, the man took the tray out of the room, and when he returned there was a single glass which Don Pablo took and twirled in his hand, holding the glass and looking at the lantern through it. Then he swiftly bent Michaelo's head back and poured the contents into his mouth, dropping the glass and covering Michaelo's mouth in one quick motion, holding Michaelo with such force that he tilted the chair back onto its back legs, and then pinching Michaelo's nose shut with his free hand and speaking softly to him until Michaelo at last gulped down the liquid. As soon as Michaelo swallowed, he began to gag. But just as quickly as he had grabbed Michaelo, Don Pablo released him, letting the chair fall forward. Michaelo sprawled on the floor and vomited. Don Pablo lit a match and tossed it into the vomit and Michaelo's whole face exploded into flames. Michaelo opened his mouth and a ball of flame erupted from his throat. In a moment, the room was filled with the stench of vomit and burnt flesh. The other boy from our car passed smooth out and collapsed on the floor. Don Pablo looked at him and snorted. Then he looked at me and raised an eyebrow.

Michaelo thrashed and rolled over, then lay on the floor on his back, his body quivering, smoke rising from his mouth. He looked like he would scream, but no noise came out. Don Pablo kicked Michaelo and bent over him. "Do you have anything to say to me? Any last words? No? I wouldn't even dirty my hands beating your sorry ass, you worthless piece of shit. But I promise you this: Tonight, before your body is cold, I'm going to fuck that sweet little wife of yours, and when I'm done, I'm going to kill her too." He spit on Michaelo and then the two men who had been in the room picked Michaelo up and stuffed him head first into one of the nail kegs. "Fill it with sand," Don Pablo said. "And then bury it. Bury it deep so the dogs won't dig it up."

In the car Don Pablo scratched the back of his hands and looked annoyed. He looked at his watch and then at me and shook his head. "What do you think?" he said. "You think it is easy, this business? You think I just sit around all day and let people bring me money? You think it is that easy? I told you I would show you what I did to people who cross me. Now do you believe me?"

I nodded, and for the first time in an hour, he smiled. "My quiet boy." He nodded. "But you stood there and took it.

"*You!*" He turned and punched the other boy in the ribs. "What's the matter with you? Haven't you seen a man die before? No, not a man." He spit. "A rat. A filthy lying, good-for-nothing rat. Bastard. But that's finished. We can close the book on that one." He looked at his watch, then looked at me. "The less you say and the less other people know about you, the better off you are. Let them gossip, let them guess, but let them be wrong." He wagged a finger at me. "Words are like diamonds, boy. The fewer you spread around the more they are worth. And when a man is known for his silence, he can command any price for his words." He paused, then looked at me. "But you have seen a corpse before." It was not a question.

I said nothing.

Don Pablo narrowed his eyes at me, then turned to the driver. "We'll never make the party now. And I have to go back to town. I'm a man of my word, unlike our soon-to-be-buried-alive friend back there." He gestured over his shoulder with his thumb. "I would hate to keep his wife up late worrying about him."

To me and the other boy he said, "Want to watch? No? I don't blame you. We'll have to do the movie another time." We drove back and Don Pablo let us off at the south end of town, far from the cantina. When I opened the door, Don Pablo grabbed my arm and held it, his grip nearly crushing me. "Now if I hear so much as one word about tonight from anybody in this world, I'll track you down and give you the same treatment. You understand?"

I nodded. We stood by the road, the other boy and me, until the tail lights of Don Pablo's car disappeared. When he was gone, the other boy turned and ran across the road and out of sight. I never saw him again. Perhaps he ran all the way to Torreón.

Act I Scene 5

Don Pablo said that watching a man die had no effect on me. And I *had* seen one corpse already. Don Pablo sensed that. But I think what he meant was that I didn't react, and that's not the same thing as *having no effect*. It just means you can't see it on the outside. But all these years I have told no one what happened that night. So clearly it had some effect on me. It must have. I was, what, six years old? Seven? But now I have told you, and now you know. And there was one other thing. Watching Michaelo die got me thinking about people, and what it meant to be good or bad.

With the other boy gone, and Don Pablo gone, I trudged across town to the bullring where I intended to sleep on the roof of the stable. But when I got there it was late and I was out of my routine, and even the watchman was walking up and down, up and down. He seemed agitated. I wondered, Is violence contagious? Does fear poison the air? I knew I couldn't sleep, so instead of climbing the fence into the bullring I walked aimlessly across town, my mind churning. I wanted something else to do, somewhere else to go. I wanted to leave Juarez, but I couldn't run away. I was so young, but at least I had food and a place to sleep and some kind of routine. Routines are important to survive. I know that now.

I walked through one of the nicer neighborhoods. I looked at the houses and wondered what it would be like to live in a normal house with a mother and father and family, to have regular meals, to go to school, to celebrate holidays, to sleep safely in a comfortable bed. Did people really live like that? How, I wondered, *How* does someone acquire these things? And how had my life come to be so different from theirs? Had I done something wrong? Above all, I think (although I had no words to express this), but above all, I wondered what it was like to be loved. These were the homes where the families lived—fathers, mothers, sons, daughters, grandparents. They cared for each other. I had no one. I wondered, standing there, if I could change the circumstances of my life.

That's an interesting thought for a boy so young. Actually it is not so difficult to change one's life, even for the better. What is difficult is to change the way one feels about the life that they have.

One of the things about walking at night in a city is that you have to watch out for dogs because dogs late at night are not the same as dogs in the daytime. The dog that lolls and pants in the shade at two in the afternoon is not the same creature that roams the streets hunting in packs at two in the morning. Perhaps that is where the legend of the werewolf came from. Who would believe that their beloved pet could act like that? So when I saw a pack of wild dogs trotting down the road toward me, I froze. The night was dark and this was not my neighborhood. I did not know which way to run or where to find shelter, and I turned and looked in the dark for a stick, or for a pile of trash where I might find a stick or a bottle or some other heavy object with which to defend myself. But before the dogs reached me, I heard a sharp yelp and I looked up to see a white cat crossing the road between me and the dogs. Spying the cat, one of the dogs barked and the pack sprang. But the cat stood still and gathered, waiting until the dogs were almost upon it before sprinting back the way that it had come, leading the dogs away from me, leaping over a fence at the last instant even as the lead dog dove and snapped at it. The dogs had to go around to the gate. In a moment they were all out of sight down some road or alley or ravine. I ran after them, my curiosity to see the outcome of the hunt overriding my fear. But the dogs were gone, the cat gone, and quickly even the sound of them was gone. I turned and walked back in the direction of what I called home. The night became eerily silent.

Until that moment it seemed to me that there was two kinds of people in the world. There were people like Don Pablo, who had money and power and did whatever they wanted. The man who killed my mother. These were the dogs of the world—the strong. And then there were the weak, like me. How did I come to live on the streets of Juarez? It was not a choice. My mother—her face and voice already fading in my memory—she was murdered and I was alone. The strong win. The weak suffer. We were like *gallinas para el mercado*, as they say. Hens for the market. We existed to be eaten. We were like the cat that walked along only to be set upon for no reason.

But then I thought, *What if there was more to life than just the strong and the weak? What if the cat had done what it did deliberately, just to help me?* Maybe there were three kinds of people in the world: the strong, the weak, and people with something else. That something else, if it existed, was not measured in brute force. It couldn't work that way. It was something that would be present or absent, and that alone would count for something. Perhaps, I thought, there are good people, too. Maybe somewhere, though I was not immediately convinced of this.

My mother had pictures of Jesus, Mary the Mother of God, and Mary Magdalene on her walls, along with some other saints whose names and images I never got straight. So people believed that there were good people in the world, though I could not recall ever meeting one. With the possible exception of the gringo who drove me from the desert into Juarez. Don Pablo might have fed me and given me a shoeshine box, but he was using me, and I understood that. The strong and the weak. Among my mother's best customers were several of the local priests, and once even a Bishop who was passing through, though what a man like a bishop could want with a woman like my mother I still cannot imagine. Surely he could have afforded better. Were these men good, I wondered, or were they also just using the weak? Was it even possible to tell the difference?

I did not know for what reason Don Pablo wanted to take me and the other boy to this party, or what kind of movie he wanted us to make, but I had a feeling that I was lucky not to find out, and that I did not want to know. But I also came to the conclusion that night that if I was going to survive in this world, I was going to have to be like Don Pablo. I was going to be one of the dogs of this world. To do that, I was going to have to find a way to make certain that Don Pablo left me alone. He promised me a lesson in what happened to people who crossed him and I got that. I would have to do the same for him someday, though God knows, at the time, I had no idea how that would happen. Big thoughts for a boy so small. But then, I had so much thrust upon me.

At dawn I climbed up on the roof of the stable and I slept there until almost noon, and I did not shine shoes the next day, but it did not matter, for I had enough money in my tobacco pouch that I could pay Don Pablo and still take the day off. And I remember even now the surprise and sense of relief when I realized that I had enough money that I did not have to work that day. That was at least something to build on, something to look forward to. I looked at the money in my pouch and it was enough for several days, but if I were to fill that pouch with dimes, how many days ahead could I go? And I knew that morning that something changed deep inside me, and that I was not the small boy that I had been the day before. I could never be like that again.

Act I Scene 6

If I changed that night, the change was not manifest straight away. For some time, in fact, nothing changed, at least on the outside. The winter passed, and then spring, summer, fall, and another winter. My existence, such as it was, mattered to nobody but me. But at least I had a routine. Or perhaps, at most I had a routine?

And then one morning I awoke burning with fever and covered with spots, and I was so sick that I could hardly move. I lay alone in the stable for three days until one of Don Pablo's men found me. He came in, looked at me, then left. An hour later two more men came and carried me outside to a car, and then on to Don Pablo's. I was bedded down in a small corner room on the second floor, the last room in the whorehouse, and the girls took turns taking care of me and spooning me chicken soup and rice and jello for another week until I felt better.

Don Pablo himself looked in on me once, and I was terrified that he would be angry. "I'm sorry!" I groaned, as soon as I saw his face in the door. "I will bring you your money tomorrow, I swear."

"Yes," Don Pablo said, "You will bring me my money. Of that I have no doubt. Are you better?"

"A little," I said.

He nodded and tugged on the edge of his moustache. I noticed he was wearing a big black hat and a string tie like the cowboys sometimes wear. It was cinched with a large piece of silver set with sky blue stones. "Take a few more days and get your strength back," he said. "You have earned that." And then he was gone. I knew from the way that Don Pablo looked at me that he was thinking something, but I could not imagine what.

A few months later, after I had returned to work, I stopped one morning as I crossed the bridge and looked behind me. There, in a little line, walking stiff as penguins, were three boys with familiar-looking scuffed-up wooden boxes. I stopped and they stopped so abruptly that the last one bumped into the one in the middle, and he, in turn, into the boy in front. It was funny to see.

I realized, looking at these boys, that the passage of time was having a good effect on me. I was eating better, for one thing, and growing. I was looking down on these boys, physically. They were smaller than me, and it was both a joy and a surprise to realize that I was no longer the smallest boy in the gang. But what did that mean?

I looked at the boys and knew what it meant: I had to confront them. In fact, I wanted to confront them. But a voice in my head whispered, *Not yet. Not here.* I was just leaving the guardhouse, having shined the shoes of the American border guards. I turned toward the American side of the bridge and walked slowly. It would be easy to hit the boys and frighten them away. That was what I wanted—to defend my territory. But at the same time, the voice in my head knew that when I was in their place, I did the same thing. They, too, owed Don Pablo three pesos a day, and would have to shine at least twenty pairs of shoes just to pay the rent on their boxes. They, too, must have made the same mistakes as I had, suffered the same hunger, pain, and humiliation. Perhaps Don Pablo himself pointed me out to them and said, "He pays me every day, no problem! Go and see how he does it." It might have happened like that. But still, I had my territory to defend. And there was something else. Without hurting the boys, I wondered if there was some way that I could turn this problem to my advantage.

The bridge sloped down to the first intersection, where, for some reason, there was an unusually long line of trucks crossing into Mexico that morning. They backed down from the bridge and around the corner and almost to the next intersection. I had never seen so many trucks going to Mexico, and it struck me that there were three boys following me, but tomorrow there might be ten, and twenty a week after that. Certainly this would be the case if I did nothing. No, I had to act.

Ten steps from the intersection I turned and ran straight at the boys. The first turned and fled but I hit the second right on the nose and, running over him, grabbed the third (and smallest boy) and began to beat him, holding his head up by the hair with my left hand, and pounding on his face and shoulder and arms with my right. It was a good spot for a fight—far enough from the guard station that they would not intervene, and far enough from the street that none of the gringos were likely to get involved. The truckers would watch, but they weren't getting out of their trucks—not with that long line in front of them.

After a moment, I threw the smaller boy on top of the other and stood there, between them and their return to Mexico, my hands on my hips. "So you think you can just walk into my territory and set up shop? Just like that?" I asked, addressing them in Spanish. "Without even asking my terms? What kind of man do you think I am?"

Both of the boys were crying, but the one with the bloody nose at least tried to answer. "Don Pablo " he said, over and over again. "Don Pablo "

"Don Pablo *que*?" I replied. What. "What did Don Pablo say? To follow me?"

The older boy nodded. "He said you were doing good in America and that we should follow you."

"*No me jodas*," I replied. Don't bullshit me. "Don Pablo said that you should *ask* me. He did not say that you should *follow* me."

The younger boy stopped his wailing and sat, legs straight out in front of him, on the concrete. The older boy looked at me, confused.

"He said to *ask* me, right?" I continued. "I know what he said because you know what Don Pablo said to me? Do you know what he said to me?"

The boys shook their heads.

"He said that if any boys wanted to work for me in America, I should first make certain that they were up to the task, and that I should make sure they knew who was boss, and that I should instruct them well and that they should *pay me* for the privilege of working in my *territory*. That's what Don Pablo told me."

I was making this up as I went, of course, and I surprised myself with that bit about the privilege of working in my territory. But it sounded good, and the boys, wide-eyed, and with snot and tears running down their faces, nodded at everything. "So are you going to work for me and do everything I tell you and exactly how I tell you to do it?"

They nodded again.

"Okay then," I said. "Get your things and follow me." They took their shoeshine boxes, and I took the box the first boy had dropped, and carrying two, led the boys off the bridge and into America.

Down by the freight yards, on Paisano Street, there was an abandoned feedlot with an office and stables and a blacksmith shop. The whole thing was long gone out of business. There were six wooden buildings—the barns, the forge, two long rows of stalls for horses or cattle, and the office. There had once been a ramp that led to the railroad yard behind it, but the ramp was gone and the hole in the fence boarded over. The place was falling apart, the wood dry and gray and loose with age. It had been looted of anything of value, most of the windows broken, but it hadn't been torn down or burned, not yet, though everybody knew it would happen someday. Sometimes, in the heat of the day, I slept in one of the old stalls, or up in the loft in the big barn. Sometimes there were drifters, hobos they called them, who got off the trains and slept in the place. But most of the time I was alone, and when I wasn't, nobody bothered me. I took the boys here, to the blacksmith shop, and set down the shoeshine boxes.

"What's your name?" I asked the smallest boy.

"Filo," he answered.

"Filo? What kind of a name is that?"

The boy shrugged.

"Okay. Filo it is," I said. I looked at the other boy. "And you?"

"Paco."

"Okay, Paco," I said. "A shoeshine in America costs ten cents if you can get it. A dime. If you can't get ten cents, you can take five, but not less. Five cents is a nickel. Do you know what a nickel is?"

The boys shook their heads.

I took coins out of my pocket and showed them. Pennies, nickels, dimes, quarters. I showed them a silver dollar and a half-dollar. Six nickels make one peso. Three dimes. "How much did Don Pablo say to pay him?"

"Three pesos," they replied.

"That's about ten to twenty shines to pay Don Pablo. The next peso belongs to me. Thirty cents you owe me at the end of the day. You pay me in American money, not pesos. At the end of the day we meet here and you give me my money."

I could see the boys doing the math in their heads. That made twelve shines a day if they got a dime each. And that was just for the privilege of working. "Don't worry," I said. "I'll put you where you will make plenty of shoeshines. Gringos like to have shiny shoes. But they also like to have it done right. If you do it right, they sometimes even pay you extra."

Filo and Paco looked at me wide-eyed. I sniffed and flicked my fingers at their hair. "They also like to have their shoeshine boys clean. Tonight when you finish, you wash. Tomorrow if you don't come to work clean " I flashed my fist under their noses. "And if you don't pay me, I will beat you for real. Got it?"

The boys nodded in unison. I took a rag and wiped their faces the best that I could.

I had learned, by then, a very few words of English, and I told the boys the words that I thought they would need to know. Please. Thank you. Ten cents. Shine your shoes? "If anybody tries to hurt you, you run away and find me here in the afternoon and tell me. If you can point them out to me, I'll take care of them for you."

"How will you do that?" Filo asked.

"That's my business," I said. "If I can't take care of it, I have friends who can." I was making things up again, but how would they know? If something came up, I would figure it out. "One more thing," I said. "You *always* pay me. You *always* pay Don Pablo. If I hear anything bad about you, you're finished. I'll hurt you so bad you'll wish you had never been born. And you don't ever, ever, *ever* say anything to anyone back there about how you do here. You don't tell anybody how much you make or how long you work, what you eat, where you work, nothing. And you never tell anybody they can come over here. Do you understand? If you do that "

The boys shrank from me.

"You'll make good money here. More money than the boys working in Mexico make. But nobody knows this but us. This is *my* territory and *our* secret. So you don't tell anybody, and you don't bring anybody. The less you talk, the better off you are about everything. Understand?"

They understood.

I put Filo at the train station and Paco at the bus station. I went out by the American army base where there were always soldiers who wanted their shoes shiny but were too lazy to do it themselves. Even though I started late, I made more money that day than I had ever made before. And when evening came and I went to the abandoned blacksmith shop, Filo and Paco were waiting, and they each had money for me. Another sixty cents. I made so much money that day that I ate a steak for dinner.

That night I found Don Pablo at his usual table. He was talking to a white man in a cream-colored suit with a straw hat pulled down low over his eyes. The man smoked a cigarette in a long black holder. When he stood up to go, I saw that he walked with a cane. As soon as the stranger was gone, I went to Don Pablo and set the extra shoeshine box on the table. Without looking at me he took it off the table and dropped it on the floor. It landed with a thud, and the people at the tables around us turned to look.

"We need to talk," I said.

Don Pablo tossed the rest of his beer and then whistled and pointed at his glass. He wiped his face with the back of his left hand and then rested his elbow on the table and looked at me. His eyes were red and bleary. He looked like he had been drinking all night and all day. After a minute a bar girl brought him his beer, and he took a long drink. Then he said, "So when did you start telling me we need to talk, little man?"

"Have I not paid you your three pesos every day? Have I not done everything you have asked of me? Do I not bring you back what is yours when I find it lost in my territory? I've done everything you've asked me to do, and now I want you to do something for me."

"You want me to do something for you? What do you want me to do for you, little man?"

"You sent three boys to follow me today. Because you sent them, I taught them how to do their jobs right, so they, too, can pay you every day. And they paid you, right?"

Don Pablo had already finished most of his beer. He swirled what was left in the bottom of his class and watch the foam go round and round. "I saw how well you taught them, at least one of them," he said. "But two of them paid me."

"It was you who taught me about respect, Don Pablo. Or don't you remember?"

He looked at me, and for the first time I thought I saw the hint of a smile. He stuck out his lower lip and said, "*Mi pequeño estudiante.*" My little student.

"What you teach me, I learn. And I will make you more money, Don Pablo. That's the kind of student you want, right?"

Don Pablo nodded, then guzzled the rest of his beer and whistled for another. "So what do you want from me, little man. My suddenly talkative one. My little parrot."

"You sent three boys to follow me. Next time you want to put boys in El Paso, you send them to me. I'll teach them what they need to know, and put them where they can make you money. But you send them to me, not *behind* me."

"And how much are you making on this deal?" Don Pablo asked. He patted the bar girl on the ass as she left the beer on the table.

I opened my mouth and then closed it.

"Don't look at me like that." Don Pablo raised the glass to his lips and drank. When he had drained half the beer, he set the glass on the table with a thud and wiped the foam off his moustache with the back of his hand. "You think I'm stupid? You think I was born yesterday? You come in here with a shitty box and a few pesos and think you can tell me what to do?" He leaned over close to me and gestured that I should come closer. "Power is earned or bought," he said, his voice a low growl. "And you haven't earned any yet. And this shit . . . " He dug some notes from his pants pocket and looked at the bills in his hand. The pesos were gray on one side, red on the other. "This shit isn't worth the paper it's printed on." He threw the bills on the floor and spit at them. Now everybody in the bar was watching us.

"So what does it cost me?" I asked.

Don Pablo laughed. He lit a cigar and leaned back in his chair and laughed a long, deep, belly-laugh. "Sit down," he said. He whistled again and held up two fingers. In a moment, the bar girl appeared with two glasses of beer. She set one in front of me and one in front of Don Pablo. I noticed that she stuck close to my side of the table and kept her rear end as far from Don Pablo as she could. She couldn't have been more than twelve or thirteen. She looked at me just briefly—a quick glance—as she set down my beer. Then she hurried away.

Don Pablo looked at his hands. He looked like he was trying to bring them into focus. I had never seen him this drunk before. He looked across the room at the little bar girl. "She's a good fuck, that one is," he said. Then he took out a silver pocketknife and began cleaning his fingernails.

I took the glass and drank my first beer. How old was I that night? Nine? Ten? The beer was black and bitter. It tasted like the rusty water we got out of buckets at the stables, only worse. But I drank it anyway. In a moment, I felt warm. My vision changed. Dark got darker and light got lighter. My vision was amplified. I heard rushing in my ears. I liked the beer. I liked it better than the whisky I drank in the back of Don Pablo's car. It didn't hurt my stomach.

"Three pesos a day," Don Pablo said. "Three pesos each."

I shook my head. "Two. Two pesos total. One each." And when Don Pablo frowned, I said, "Things are okay, but I'm not getting rich over there."

"I've been to America," Don Pablo said.

"Were you shining shoes?"

Don Pablo scowled. "Who the hell are you that I should argue with you? Shines are a dime in America."

"Not if you're Mexican, they're not," I said. "If I'm lucky, they give me a dime. Sometimes it's a nickel. Sometimes just a penny or two."

"Even so . . . "

"And everything costs more. A taco is a dime. A Coca Cola is a nickel. People spit at me. I have to keep my hands clean. I buy soap now."

"Take it or leave it, little man," Don Pablo said.

"And when I have to watch after the others, I can't shine as many shoes myself. I already give you three pesos. This makes five. And they give you three. That makes eleven." Across the bar I saw two or three bar girls clustered in a little group watching us and whispering.

Don Pablo closed his eyes. "What did I say about power?"

"You said it was bought or earned."

"So you're not buying?"

"Don Pablo," I said. "I'm doing both. I've always brought you your money, right? The boys brought you their money. I told them what would happen if they didn't."

Don Pablo took a long puff on his cigar. The end glowed bright red. He checked his watch. "Five for now," he said. "But when you get more boys, then it goes to ten."

And that was how it started. I finished my beer and stood up, a little unsteady on my feet. "*Gracias*, Don Pablo," I said. Thank you.

Don Pablo was leaning back in his chair, his eyes shut. "*Gracias*, Don Pablo," he growled. "Cross me, you little shit, and I'll cut your fucking nuts off and feed them to the squirrels in the park."

"Why would I cross you, Don Pablo? You take good care of me. And I'm going to make you money." I was unsteady on my feet. The room spun. I leaned against the table until the feeling passed.

I walked to the back of the bar and found the men's room and took a long, hard piss. When I came out I practically ran into the little bar girl. She was leaning against the wall and looking down, her palms pressed flat on her thighs. I had the feeling she was not there by accident. She was there for me to run into her. She looked at me, just briefly, and then she hurried away. She *was* kind of pretty. Thin, black-haired. And something else. This feeling—it was like smoke in the air around us. Something burning.

I remember all this clearly, even all these years since. I remember my conversation with Don Pablo, my first beer, my first long beer piss, and then running into the girl. I remember it like it was last night. It was the first time I ever looked at a girl and thought she was, well, not just a *girl*, but pretty. I understood, in that moment, what it meant to be hungry for a woman. Even though I had seen it plenty, it was not something I had experienced until then. And I understood too, my first pang of jealousy. What had Don Pablo said? I didn't even know her name, but I did not want him to "fuck" this girl.

One other small thing happened that night. As I was walking out, some talk from a table caught my ear. It was in English. There were plenty of gringos who came to Juarez to drink and gamble, but something about these voices was familiar. I looked over and recognized some of the guards from the border crossing. They were watching me and Don Pablo.

So this is how it works, I thought. They knew about me and they knew about him, and they must have known for a long time, maybe from the very beginning. And now I knew, and they knew that I knew.

Act I Scene 7

Looking back now, I think Don Pablo sent more boys to El Paso because he knew prohibition was ending and he worried that his business would decline. Gringos would always come to Juarez for food and girls and cheap liquor. But soon they would drink legally in America, and they would be able to buy the real whiskeys instead of Don Pablo's fakes. He knew this would hurt his income. This was not a small thing. In fact, it was the first in a whole chain of events that would profoundly alter my life, though I had no way of knowing at the time.

Prohibition ended in 1933. By then I had six boys working for me. I wasn't actually making that much more money than when I was just working for myself. What the boys paid me I lost in the shines I couldn't do while I wasted time with them. And I paid Don Pablo more. Perhaps my failure to earn as much as I thought I should, coupled with this change in circumstances, opened my mind to a new way of thinking. Everything presents a challenge and an opportunity. Which will we choose? So in time it came to me one day that maybe there were other things I could do besides shining shoes. Why hadn't I thought of that before?

Customers were always asking me questions: *Where can I buy cigarettes? Chewing gum? Do you have matches? Do you know the way to the Paso Del Norte Hotel? What are the drinks like in that bar? Where can I find a cute girl?* Things like this. Many of the things they asked for were sold on the streets in Juarez, and the products themselves were much cheaper than those sold in the USA. I started with cigarettes and matches and lighters. Soon there were maps and magazines, chewing gum, mini bottles of liquor, keyrings combs, breath mints. Really, anything people might want I could bring from Mexico and sell cheaper than stores in the USA.

I knew Don Pablo would catch onto what I was doing. For this reason, I was careful to buy only from vendors in his territory. And one night he asked. He was playing cards when I came to pay him, and he said, without even looking up, "What's with this cigarette business?" I told him that I was making more money selling crap on the streets than I was shining shoes, but I don't think he believed me. But he did send more boys.

A year later I had fifteen boys working for me and the only shoes I shined were the guards' shoes when I crossed the bridge in the morning. I crossed every morning and every night I came back and paid Don Pablo. In between I checked on my boys, kept them supplied, and walked around stupidly drunk on the little bit of power I enjoyed. By the end of that year I had boys selling Spanish language magazines and papers, girly magazines and playing cards, soap, pocket knives, key chains, tissue paper, condoms, lip balm, all kinds of little things people might want or suddenly remember that they needed. I paid Don Pablo ten pesos a day, a little more than three dollars, and I earned about ten on my own. It was a lot of money for a boy of twelve. Don Pablo watched me and said nothing. But I could tell he was thinking.

I told my boys two things. If anybody hurts you, tell me, and I'll take care of it—provided they didn't hurt you for your own stupidity. The second thing was that if they ever cheated me, I'd hurt them so bad they'd wish they'd never been born. When I said it, we all knew what the game was. I meant it and I'd be mad enough to see it through.

I wasn't expecting any trouble. I said these things only to assert my authority. I didn't know what I would do if someone really hurt one of them. If it happened, I'd think of something. But just before Christmas one of my boys, Oscar, lingered in the stables until the other boys were all gone. Then he told me something was wrong with Filo.

"What's wrong with Filo?" I asked.

Oscar shrugged. "There's a man who takes him every day."

Oscar was *un Indio*, a Taramuhara Indian from the mountains in south

Chihuahua. He didn't even speak good Spanish, and he was an orphan, like me. He was quiet but he watched everything around him, even if he didn't say much. And he learned quickly. He was no dummy, Oscar. He just didn't say much. He had dark skin, long, greasy hair, pockmarks on his face, and his eyes were slanted. His legs were bowed so he just about waddled when he walked. I had him working outside a bar downtown because he looked so bad people would get their shoes shined because they felt sorry for him. He was a quick worker, too.

"Takes him where?" I asked.

"I don't know."

"Do you know who it is?"

"*Es el padre*," Oscar said.

"*Filo no tiene padre, estupido,*" I said. "*El es huerfano.*" He's an orphan.

Oscar shrugged and walked off.

At first I thought Oscar was bullshitting me. I thought maybe he had some disagreement with Filo and was trying to make trouble for him. But there was something about what he said that bothered me, and something about Filo that made me wonder if it might be true. Filo was so small. If anybody was going to get picked on, it would be him.

A few minutes later I walked to the bar where Oscar was working. Oscar was sitting on a little handmade three-legged stool he got from somewhere. Or maybe he made it. Oscar was clever that way. He was huddled up in a blanket with his back against the wall keeping out of the wind and watching the snow pile up on the street. He was whittling a piece of wood into a figure. I looked closely and saw he was carving the figure of a running man. Oscar often made little figures of men or women in long red shirts and white skirts, or animals like bears, turtles, humming birds. He sold these things, too, alongside of his cigarettes and magazines and stuff. Sometimes he would stand them in a little row by where he worked. He told me once he people gave him twenty-five cents each for his carvings. He said he made more money from his carvings than from shoe shines or selling things, but I didn't believe him.

There was nobody out but a few morning drinkers. Salesmen. Drifters. Local bums. Who knows? It was a shitty morning. A few businessmen hurried by on the sidewalks on their way to work. Oscar made most of his money in the evening when the men had a few drinks in them. On days like today, nobody made money—not that it mattered to Don Pablo.

Oscar looked up at me as if he had been expecting me. He must have been thinking about how to explain to me. He made the sign of the cross in the air and then I understood what he meant. "*Ven con migo,*" I said. Come with me.

Filo had been with me the longest but he was small like a Chihuahua, and he had big brown eyes that bulged out of their sockets. I had him working the train station because that was the safest place I could put him. Also, there were lots of women there with time to waste and money in their purses. They fell for his big eyes and tiny body. He didn't just shine shoes. The women often gave him money just because they thought he was cute and felt sorry for him. He always had a stack of pennies when he paid me, and he counted them carefully one-by-one. Filo had never caused me any trouble. He was not the kind of boy to cause trouble. He would have been afraid to complain even if someone was hurting him. That was probably why Oscar came to me. Oscar would have wanted me to know.

I don't know why I gave a shit where Filo worked. Maybe I just thought Filo wasn't like the rest of us. He didn't belong on the streets. He was different somehow. I don't think I would have said that I cared, but maybe I did. There was usually a policeman somewhere around the station, and there would be ticket agents and railroad men, and respectable people, so Filo should have been okay there. Maybe the worst thing that could happen was some kids might bully him, but that was going to happen anywhere. What would a priest want with a little kid?

We found Filo huddled outside behind one of the pillars. He was watching the road and not the platform. He about jumped out if his skin when I walked up behind him.

"You working today?" I asked.

Filo nodded and pointed to his box.

"Oscar says somebody is messing with you," I said.

Filo just looked at me.

"Is this true?"

He shook his head.

"Something about a priest?"

He shook his head even harder.

"Is somebody messing with you, Filo? Because if they are, then tell me and I'll fuck them up. Even a priest."

"No—nobody is messing with me," Filo said. He kind of stammered when he said this. He looked down at his bare feet.

It would be cold tonight, I thought, and colder in the morning. Maybe I should get him a serape and some shoes. But then I thought, *It's his money. Let him buy his own. What does he spend it on, anyway?* I slapped him on top of his head. "Stop wasting my time, okay? If you have a problem, tell me, but I'm not here to play guessing games!"

Filo's lip trembled. He tried to keep it in, but then the tears flowed down his face and onto the front of his shirt while he stifled little who-who-who noises like an owl.

"Who?" I shouted. "Who's messing with you?"

"Nobody," he said again.

"Okay," I said. "Then get to work."

Filo ran to the far end of the platform and spread out his things on a little blanket.

I figured that was the end of that. I didn't know what was going on, but I was pretty sure Filo wouldn't show up in the morning. He'd disappear like the boys sometimes did. But there was something about his crying that made me think Oscar was telling the truth, or something like the truth—though I had no idea how Oscar came to this conclusion. One of the boys must have seen something and talked.

There is real crying and there is fake crying, but there was nothing fake about Filo's tears. Maybe it reminded me of my brother, Marco, and the way he cried when our mother slapped him, or her customers found us and beat us. Marco. He reminded me of Marco.

It was no use asking Oscar anything. He talked even less than I did and if I tried to make him tell me he would only lie, anyway. Oscar went back to his bar and his whittling and I went to buy Filo some cheap shoes even though I was sure he would not show up the next morning. But Filo did show up in the morning.

Act I Scene 8

It was still snowing the next day. Everybody was freezing, even me. Filo had found some crappy sandals somewhere, and some old socks. It wasn't much, but it was better than nothing. I gave him the shoes and he put them right on. After he left, I followed him to the railway station. I figured if he was lucky they would let him inside the station where there was heat, but he wasn't lucky. He was outside by the same pillar and watching the road. I thought that was a bad sign.

I spied on him from inside the old cotton market across the road, and sure enough, right around nine-thirty, a priest came along and went straight to Filo. He squatted down in front of him and rubbed Filo on the head, then opened a parcel and did something I couldn't see, for the priest was between me and Filo. After a minute, Filo stood up, and the priest stood up, and then he took Filo by the hand and they crossed the road making straight for me. I watched through the iron-screened windows as they walked past and then I saw what it was. He had given Filo a jacket and some gloves. I was angry. I wondered, Why hadn't I thought about gloves?

For all I knew, Don Pablo gave Filo the same welcome that he gave me, but that didn't mean that every priest who passed through town could fuck my boys in the ass. I ducked out to stop them but already the priest had flagged a taxi and they were climbing in. There was nothing I could do. They drove off. I stood by the road looking after them. But then I realized, *How hard can it be to find a priest?*

The Sacred Heart Church was downtown, a little bit past the bar where Oscar worked. It was a big, red brick building. So maybe Oscar *had* seen them together. Maybe that was how he knew. I went to the church but it was empty. Nothing but an old woman sweeping the floor and a couple of bums sleeping in the pews. The next mass wasn't until noon. Even the office door was locked. I went around to the rectory but nobody was there, or nobody answered when I knocked. I went back inside the church. At least it was warmer inside than out. Already there was four or five inches of snow, though it was not falling so fast now. The old woman was gone and I wandered around looking at the stained-glass windows. Eventually I saw a door behind the sacrament. I looked around. Still, nobody but the bums. I tried the handle and the door opened. It led to a hallway. I poked around but there was nobody in any of the rooms, and I didn't hear anything, or even see any lights on.

At the end of the hallway was another door. It led into the rectory. This door was also locked, but there was a stairway next to it. I crept up a steep set of worn, creaking, cracked wooden stairs to find another long hall and another set of locked doors. It reminded me of the second floor of Don Pablo's hotel. I wondered who slept in these rooms. The priests? Or did the rooms have some other function? The last door in the hallway was the only one that bore a sign: STUDY.

I could not, in those days, read the sign, but I would eventually learn that English and Spanish were enough alike that I could sound out words—even unfamiliar words—and make sense of them. Study. *Estudiar.* It was a room where people went to take in knowledge. I pressed my ear against the door and heard the low murmur of voices.

I once, some years ago, met a photographer who liked to take pictures of doorways. When I asked him the source of his fascination, he replied that every door was an adventure waiting to happen. "Doors," he said, "take courage to open." I suppose that depends on what one fears.

How old was I that day? Eleven? I am old now and I look back on things in my life and wonder how it was that there were some things I could do—to walk alone across the high desert, to confront Don Pablo, to open a strange door into the adult world—while there were other things I could not do—like speak to a person normally on the street, make a friend, laugh. Funny, isn't it? Why is it that fear makes us *do* the things we don't want to do, and keeps us from doing the things we do want to do? But once in a while, we face our fears, and when we do, usually good things happen.

But perhaps I mistake courage for stupidity, or naivety, or inexperience. If one can't imagine the consequences, then one doesn't know any better than to proceed. I wish I could say I threw open the door in a dramatic made-for-TV entry. I wish I could say I had a nifty one-liner like you see in the movies. *Go ahead, make my day. Consider this a divorce.* But I was neither Clint Eastwood nor Arnold Schwarzenegger. I was a skinny little Mexican kid with no gun and no muscles, and hadn't yet conceived the idea that I might need them. Still, I opened the door.

The priest sat behind a desk with Filo in a chair opposite him. Filo held a book open in his lap. *"Que está sucediendo aquí?"* I asked. What's going on here?

Filo dropped the book. He looked like he might faint from shock.

The priest reached out and placed his hand on Filo's shoulder.

The priest was a gringo, tall, thin, brown-haired. He dressed differently from the proper Mexican friars in their long gray or black robes—the priests I saw in Mexico. This one wore a black shirt and black pants. The shirt had a small square white patch in the middle of the collar. He had a black jacket, too, but the jacket was off and folded over the back of a chair. *"Estoy enseñando al niño a leer,"* the priest replied. I'm teaching the boy to read. His voice was deep, melodious, and calm.

"Bullshit you are," I said, in English.

The priest looked at me. Maybe he searched me with his eyes for a weapon, or to gauge my potential for violence. Nobody moved.

"Filo works for me," I said. "He has a job. And he's not working here."

"He gives you your money every day, and Don Pablo, too," the priest replied.

At that moment I realized what had been happening. Filo paid me every day in nickels and pennies, but every day, when he paid me, he was pushing the money across to me and counting, "One, two, three..." He must have been learning English for some time. How had I missed this? Who knows? Either way, it wasn't going to happen.

"Filo gets paid to shine shoes, not to spend time with you."

"Does it matter where he gets his money?"

"He has a boss to answer to, and I have a boss to answer to, and that's the way it is, and that's how it's going to be." I stared hard at Filo and said, "Go." He was out the door in an instant, leaving the door open and the book on the floor. He left his jacket draped over the back of the chair and his gloves on the desk.

The priest looked angry. "Now what happens to him?" he said. It was more of a statement than a question.

"Nothing. He won't tell Don Pablo, and I won't tell Don Pablo. If you don't tell Don Pablo, then none of us have a problem. If you do " I shrugged.

The priest looked at Filo's things. "Will you take him these?"

"Sure," I said. "Okay."

The priest nodded, then stood up and handed me the jacket and the gloves and the book.

I placed the book on the desk.

"He'd be better off with an education," the priest said.

"So would you," I replied.

The priest smiled. "Not that kind of education," he said. "That won't work with me."

"He's getting plenty."

"The parish has a school. He could take classes for free. I was going to enroll him."

"And who would feed him?"

"I would," the priest said.

I took the jacket and shoes. "And what does he have to do to earn this education?"

"What does that mean?" he asked. He stiffened like he was angry.

I had already reached the door. "Nobody gives anything for free," I said.

The priest looked at me, then said, "Who gave you life?"

"What?"

"Who gave life to you? What did He charge for that? What does He charge for making the sun to shine, or the wind to blow, or the rain or snow to fall? What did He, who gave His only begotten Son that you might have everlasting life, what did He ever ask of you, but that you have faith in Him? Does He charge you for anything? I think you misunderstand me, son. I think you misunderstand a lot of things, but I don't hold that against you. We all have a boss, young man. You. Me. Don Pablo. All of us. And someday you're going to find out that it's the same boss. And like Filo, and you, we all have to do our boss' bidding. We either do it or we don't. And there are consequences for our actions. The important thing is to know which boss matters." He paused and looked at me. He scowled, but then his face softened. "Are you also an orphan?"

I said, "Do you know what Don Pablo would do if he caught Filo studying with you and not working?"

"I know," the priest said.

"Not do to Filo. I mean to you."

"I doubt if he would do anything to me, but even if I knew for certain that he would, I'm not afraid. Tell him Father Sheehy says hello. See what he does."

I looked at the priest.

"So why are you?" he said.

"Why am I what?"

"Why are you afraid?"

"What could frighten me?"

"Besides Don Pablo?"

"I'm not afraid of Don Pablo." I wanted to spit but I was in a church.

"Maybe, maybe not," the priest said. "But you are afraid of something, and I know what it is." When I said nothing, Father Sheehy continued, "You, young man, are afraid of yourself. You. You're afraid of what you might become. Like most young people, you are afraid that if I told you what you could do, then you would have to try to do it. And if you tried, you might fail. And what if you failed? What then? That, young man, is what you are afraid of. Or even worse, What if you succeeded? What would that mean? That your whole life, right up to now, had been a mistake?"

I stared at the priest for a moment in shock. What the hell was he talking about? My life a mistake? "Fuck you," I said. I spit on the floor and left. But a week later I was back, and that was how I learned to read and write properly in English.

Act II Scene 1

Father Sheehy didn't seem surprised when I returned. Neither did he seem pleased. He was sitting in the same office reading a book and making notes as he read. I watched from the door for some time before he asked (without ever looking up), "Are you coming in? Or are you just going to stand there letting the cold air in?"

Though I first thought Father Sheehy was trying to abuse Filo, if so, he never made any advances at me. He only mentioned Filo once or twice, saying that he felt sorry for the little boy shining shoes. He said that he first invited him to the church the winter before, just to get him out of the cold. He began to teach Filo English because he thought that learning might help the boy.

"How could it help him?" I asked.

Father Sheehy leaned back in the chair and looked out the window. He got up and poured himself a cup of coffee from a steel percolator and offered me a cup, which I declined. He added some sugar to the coffee, then opened the window and took a small jar of milk from the windowsill outside and added that to the coffee. He closed the window, stirred the cup, and drank slowly. The sun was shining, though it was still cold outside. It was a bitter-sharp winter morning, breezy, and the snow from a week ago was gone. It was the kind of wind that whips the dry, powdered snow from the ground and carries it away like sand.

"It doesn't matter how smart you are," Father Sheehy said, still looking out the window. "Everybody learns from others. The smartest people take what they learn and then add to it. They build on what they learn. Without education, we're all ignorant. And no matter what kind of good or important ideas you have," he said, turning to look at me now, "if you can't explain them clearly to people, they're worthless. That's why education is important. We learn what others already know and we build on that. We solve problems by applying lessons from the past to our situation today. We anticipate what might happen if we try something new. We combine ideas together into something new, and we learn how to convince other people to help us, or follow us, or use what we create. Education teaches us how to think, and it also teaches us how to express our ideas."

"But Filo doesn't have ideas," I said. "He's just a dumb kid."

"Of course Filo has ideas. And he's not so dumb as you think. You see him as a homeless orphan eeking out an existence shining shoes. But what could he become if he had an education?"

I thought about this. The boys and I talked about things sometimes, at night, when we met in the old blacksmith shop and settled accounts. Mostly we talked about money and food and girls and stuff. How strange our customers were. Sometimes we talked about things we heard. If there was a circus in town, or a rodeo, some movie that people were talking about. Big news, maybe, like if there was an election, or a murder. I never thought about Filo having dreams, or what I might now call *potential*. Why should I? What dreams did I have? What potential could anybody see in me? To be like Don Pablo some day? I wondered if Don Pablo had been to school.

I seldom thought about my life in any way beyond *What am I going to eat today?* or *Where am I going to sleep tonight?* I was driven by what needed to be done, or what others told me to do. What was ambition to someone like me? My ambition was not to be at the bottom of the food chain. Real ambition was a luxury I couldn't afford. But Father Sheehy's words got me thinking. They bothered me. I wondered if I was the only person who did not know this secret. I felt like I was missing something in my life—like I had been cheated, or been too stupid to know what was good for me. He was right. By opening the door to his office—a door clearly labeled STUDY—I had invited the question, and now—like it or not—I had to succeed or fail with the answer. I asked, "Did Filo ever say what he wanted to be?"

"He said he wanted to be a doctor."

"A *doctor*? Him?"

"Sure, why not. Given a chance, he could do anything. So could you, if you wanted, and if someone gave you a chance."

"I didn't mean he couldn't do it. I mean, it's just that Filo never said anything to me about being a doctor. Why would he want to do that?"

"Did he tell you about his brother?"

I shook my head. "I didn't know Filo had a brother." Come to think about it, I didn't know much about Filo at all. Where he stayed. Where he came from. He wasn't a talker about things like that, and I didn't ask. None of us were, really. Some things it's better not to know. The personal things. Especially in personal things. You don't need anybody else's misery on top of your own, and they didn't want to hear yours, either. I hadn't told any of the boys about my past, and didn't ask about theirs.

"Filo has a crippled brother. The boy can't walk, can hardly talk. Filo wanted to know if I could help his brother."

"What's wrong with his brother?" I asked.

Father Sheehy shrugged. "I don't know. I haven't seen him."

"Can you help him?"

"Some things are in God's hands," Father Sheehy said. "And God alone understands why things work out like they do. Filo asked me for money once, but I don't have money to spare. I told him to ask one of the churches across the river. If I was going to help the boy, it would have been by helping Filo first. Perhaps Filo could do more for him then."

I thought about Filo's brother. I've seen sick and lame and crippled children on the sidewalks, crawling through the muck to cross the road. In wheelchairs and on little wheeled carts, or sometimes just lying there. What you can do besides avert your eyes and be thankful that it isn't you?

"But Filo isn't my problem now," Father Sheehy said. "You took care of that. He came back to work, right? And you gave him his gloves and his jacket?"

"He came back. I gave him his things. But you went to check, anyway, right?"

Father Sheehy shook his head. "I have other things to do. If Filo came to me, I would continue to teach him. I would put him in school and find him a home. But Filo has not come to me, and I haven't seen him. I presumed you—or someone—would be watching."

Father Sheehy leaned back in his chair and looked at his notes. Then he looked back at me. "I'm writing an article for a church journal. I'm talking about the importance of being flexible in God's work. We humans—we have these plans and we start thinking they are important. Our plans. And then we start thinking we are important. But only God knows what is best for us, and we have to listen for His Word, and His Word comes to us in surprising ways, and from surprising places. I suppose that's what we mean when we talk about miracles. Do you know what a miracle is?"

"A miracle is something from God," I said. I did not necessarily believe this. I just remembered little bits and pieces of things my mother had said. That was why we had images on the wall of our little shack and sometimes prayed to them and put little decorations before them, or burned candles beside them. We were asking for miracles.

Father Sheehy smiled. "Everything is from God, son. A miracle is when something happens that cannot be explained by natural law."

He might as well have spoken Greek to me. I could hear the words. Even today I can hear Father Sheehy's voice, deep and resonant, with a hint of what I now know is a Scottish accent. I didn't know what he was saying. I think Father Sheehy must have understood. He set his book and paper and pencil aside and looked at me for some time. "What is your name?" he asked.

I thought, *My name is Pancho I live on a Rancho . . .* Names. Why would this old priest care about my name? "My name is Pablo," I said.

He nodded. "Okay, Pablo. What would happen if *you* learned to read and write?"

"What do you mean?" I replied.

I mean, "What do you think you could become if you learned to read and write?"

I shrugged. Who knows?

And then he asked me something I had never been asked before. He said, "What would you like to do?"

I wasn't sure how to feel about the priest's words. What would I *like*? What would happen *if*? I wasn't sure I even knew what it was like to like something. What did I *like*? Ice cream on a hot day? To be warm on a cold night? To have good food in my belly and to be clean in the morning? My likes were pretty simple. Was it possible to have a bigger thing to like? I had a sudden vision of the meteors falling in the desert on a night so long ago. I remembered thinking there had to be something else. Could this be it? But then the fear rose up like a wave inside of me. "I don't have time to worry about things like that," I said.

"Oh really? And will your life get better if you don't do anything about it? If you don't worry about your future, who will? Maybe," Father Sheehy said, "maybe I'm supposed to help you, not Filo. Maybe that's what this is all about." Father Sheehy looked at his watch. "And what's on your agenda for this morning, young man? Do people make appointments to shine shoes these days? How many dimes will you miss if you study a few hours with me? How many dollars might you make *if* you had a real education? Or, at least, if you could read and write a bit?"

English is not so differet from Spanish, not if you think about it. So many words are almost the same. *Especial*. Special. *Tiempo*. Time. *Estudiar*. Study. The letters are the same. The pronunciation is similar. *Similar*. Sometimes *exatemente similar*. In a year, I could read and write well enough. Once you know even a little, all it takes is practice. And I had hours and hours every day with nothing to do but read.

But Father Sheehy gave me something else, something perhaps even more important than literacy. Until I met Father Sheehy, I had met strong people, weak people, and people in the middle, but I had never met anybody I thought of as good. I wasn't sure that such people existed, but after meeting Father Sheehy, I began to think that there might be a few around. I studied with Father Sheehy for a couple of hours a day, five mornings a week, for two years. Father Sheehy was right. Things changed. But again, the changes did not happen quickly, nor were they what I expected. On the surface, my life went on exactly as it had. I walked across the bridge every morning. I looked after my boys. I walked back to Juarez at night. I paid Don Pablo. And then, in the spring of 1937, Don Pablo sent for me.

Act II Scene 2

I was fourteen and growing taller, eating better, but I remained a boy; skinny, all arms and legs. I had yet to find a hair on my chin, though I was old enough to look anytime I found a mirror. I was big enough now to menace the younger boys that I employed, though not big enough that I didn't have to watch out for older teenagers, and some of them still harassed me any chance they had. Some of them. I had, by this time, been in enough scrapes that I was not afraid of being hit, and I had learned how to throw a punch. I knew how to move and to keep my hands up in a fight, to be light and quick on my feet. And my hands were fast. I had balance. I had fought enough that I was no longer afraid. If you were going to hit me, then hit me and let's get it over with. Or if I thought you would hit me, I might just hit you first. I was getting a reputation as a fighter. Some of the boys wanted nothing to do with me. Others? Well, that's just the way it was. There was always somebody who didn't like you, or had something to prove by beating you. There was always something.

So one night I came to the hotel at the regular time but Don Pablo wasn't there. One of his men was taking care of things for him—collecting the money and so forth. I had met the man once or twice, his name was Raul. He was one of Don Pablo's lieutenants. He was a dark-skinned, heavy man. Not fat, just thick all over. Not somebody you want to mess with. I left my money but when I turned to go, Raul called me back and said Don Pablo wanted to see me. He would return late to the hotel. "What does he want?" I asked.

Raul shrugged. Who knows? "He wants you here."

So I waited, and it was close to midnight when Don Pablo returned. It was odd to be in the cantina and not have Don Pablo there. Nobody else was allowed to sit at Don Pablo's table. Not ever. Not even Raul. Certainly not me when I was waiting for Don Pablo. The place seemed a little less crowed, a little less busy, a little less boisterous, even though there was only the one less table filled. The customers might not have noticed, but everybody who worked there breathed a little easier. Or maybe not. Which was more uncertain? Having Don Pablo in his place, or wondering where he was and when he would return, and what kind of mood he might be in?

When he came in it was through the back door, and he hurried upstairs to his room. He came down a few minutes later having left off his coat and changed his shirt. He sat down at his table. A barmaid was instantly by his side. He ordered beer and tequila, a *filet tampequena* with rice and beans and corn tortillas. He looked around for me straight away and signaled me to join him. "Tomorrow morning," he said, "when you cross the bridge, I want you to carry a package for me."

"Okay," I said.

He gave me a piece of paper with an address on it. It was the Conrad Hilton Hotel. I knew the place right away. It was the newest hotel in El Paso, and the finest. Also, it was the tallest building in town. There was a name and a room number.

"Deliver the package at 3:00 in the afternoon, sharp. Understand?"

"What's in the package?" I asked.

"It is better that you do as you are told and don't ask questions, little talker. What you don't know you can't say. Come to my room at five in the morning and pick up the package and put it in your box. Carry it across the bridge. Bring it to the man in the hotel and bring back to me what he gives you. Don't talk to anybody and don't tell anybody. Nobody will look in your box. You still carry your box, don't you?"

"Every day." I looked at him.

"What?"

"Are you paying me for this?"

"I'm already paying you, remember?"

"I pay *you* for the privilege of working, Don Pablo."

"Either way you work for me."

"But what work I do for you, Don Pablo, for which I pay you, that work pays me. I haven't carried packages before, Don Pablo, and I don't see how this will pay me."

Don Pablo finished his beer and snapped his fingers for another. "When I met you, you were eating shit out garbage cans. Now what do you eat? And you want to argue about how much you make?"

"Okay," I said. "I am grateful for all that you have done for me, Don Pablo. And, yes, I eat better than a few years ago. Much better. But I am also getting older and I have to think about my future."

"Your *what*?" Don Pablo said. He slapped his hand on the table and looked at me glassy eyed. I might as well have told him I was saving money for college.

"My future, Don Pablo. Perhaps I won't be a shoeshine boy forever. I have boys working for me now. I have boys doing things besides shining shoes. I make you more money than when I started. A lot more. It seems there are still more things I can do to be useful to you. Don't get me wrong, Don Pablo. I like being useful to you. It's just—what was it you said?—everything is earned or bought? I've been earning for you for seven years now, Don Pablo. I am not a little kid anymore. If you are asking me to deliver a special package, there must be a reason you want me. If I hadn't earned, you wouldn't ask."

Don Pablo ran his fingers through his hair. "Just do it like I tell you. See the man. Deliver the package. The man will give you an envelope. Come straight here in the evening. Don't talk to anybody. And don't tell anybody. What was the room number again?"

"Three one five."

"And the time?"

"Three in the afternoon."

"Three in the afternoon, sharp."

"Sharp," I said.

"And the hotel?"

"The Hilton."

"You know where it is?"

"Of course I know. It's on Mills."

"You have a boy working there already?"

"Two."

Don Pablo looked at me. "Two?"

"One shines shoes and the other sells candy and cigarettes and cards and things."

"And things?"

"Things."

"What things?"

"You know everything, Don Pablo. I buy them from your shops."

Don Pablo nodded. "And the man's name?"

I looked at the paper and pronounced the word slowly, "An-der-son."

"It is important that nobody—and I mean nobody—knows what you are doing. Even you, little man. Just do as I say and I'll take your new responsibilities into consideration."

The barmaid came with Don Pablo's meal. He picked up his knife and fork. I folded the paper and put it in my pocket. I got up to go.

"So it's true, then," Don Pablo said.

"What's true?"

"The priest is teaching you to read and write."

I stared at Don Pablo. He carefully cut his steak, a fine tenderloin hammered thin and then seared on a grill under a split green chili. He took a bite and rolled his eyes.

"He's teaching me."

Don Pablo chewed thoughtfully, the meat making his cheek bulge. He washed it down with more beer.

"Do I have to send somebody to visit this priest?" he asked.

"Why would you do that?"

"The same reason you did. I'm looking after my interests."

"No," I replied. "You don't need to send anyone."

"Good," he said. "Better for all concerned. I'll see you in the morning."

I started to walk away, but then I turned and came back to the table.

"What, my quiet one. Now you want to talk? You want to talk English to me? You want to play games with Don Pablo?"

"Aren't you going to ask me *why*?"

He stuffed a chunk of steak into his mouth. "I don't know and I don't care. I get paid and the work gets done, and nothing comes between us. That's what I care about. So don't go getting ideas. You work for me, and once you work for me you don't quit. You don't quit, you don't talk, and you don't get ideas. I do the thinking." Don Pablo jabbed at his temple with his left index finger for emphasis. Then, with his right hand, he pointed the steak knife at me. "I do the thinking," he said again. He was practically shouting. Everyone in the cantina was watching us. "And don't you forget it."

"You're a smart man, Don Pablo," I said.

He stopped eating, knife and fork suspended in the air. His eyes narrowed and his face darkened.

"It's one of the things I like about you. So when I cross the bridge, you send me because it makes you money. And I'm *happy* to make you money, Don Pablo. Don't get me wrong. You take good care of me and I *like* to work for you. I would not want to do anything else, and I would not want to do anything that caused you any trouble."

"Damn straight you don't," he said. He whistled and pointed at his empty glass, then resumed eating.

"But things are different over there."

Now Don Pablo frowned and leaned back in his chair. He scratched his neck and then unbuttoned his collar. The barmaid came with a pitcher of beer and refilled his glass.

"I have different things to watch out for," I said. "The police, they speak English. The customers, they speak it too. And the taxi drivers, and the people. If I can speak it, I can take better care of your business. That's why I see the priest, Don Pablo. Education gives me ... gives me ... *oportunidad*. Opportunities. I didn't think I would have to explain to you. I thought you would know. I *do* think you know. But I get your point. I know what you are telling me about loyalty. I'm still loyal, Don Pablo. That will never change."

The little barmaid lingered behind Don Pablo. She was looking at me, and she blushed when she saw that I saw. She turned and walked away, but I caught her looking at me again out of the corner of her eye as she passed.

Don Pablo tossed his tequila, then chased it with half a glass of beer. "And what's your point?" he said.

"I'm helping you," I replied. "You gave me a territory and I'm taking good care of it. I just want to do my job the best that I can."

"Okay," he said. "So now you can read and write a little. That's enough. Do I make myself clear?"

I nodded.

"Okay then."

Instead of walking out the front door, I went to the toilet, in the back. When I came out, the bar girl was leaning against the wall by the door. I knew she wasn't there to smoke a cigarette. I looked at her and she looked at me. "Who was it?" I asked.

She peeked around the corner at Don Pablo but he was talking to somebody else. "Filo," she said.

"The little fucker." I spit on the floor. He's getting back at me, I thought. "So that's how it works, eh? Why? Did he tell you?"

The girl brushed a lock of hair back from her forehead. She was thinking. She was pretty, short, with dark brown skin and budding breasts that pressed against the fabric of her blouse. She was wearing simple white cotton over a long green wool skirt. She was barefoot. Her toenails were painted red. "Why don't you ask him?" she said.

"I like Filo but I don't like his going to Don Pablo behind my back."

"He doesn't know any better."

"Then I'll have to teach him."

"That's not what I meant," she said.

I looked at her. "Then what do you mean?"

"He's an orphan."

"So am I."

"Then you should know what it's like not to have a father. Maybe Filo thought you took something from him."

"You mean the priest?"

She shrugged. "You figure it out."

"I get by without a father," I said. "I've got by my whole life like this."

"Everybody needs a father," the girl said. "Even you."

"But that's not why I went to see the priest."

"I don't know why you went to see the priest. Neither does Filo. But things might be one way for you, and look another way to somebody else."

I thought about this. "And how did he find out?" I asked.

"I don't know," she said. "People find out things."

"Then how did you find out? You were watching? You listened?"

She straightened up and wiped her hands on her dress, then pulled at her hair. "Maybe somebody saw you. Maybe you let something slip. Maybe Don Pablo watches you more than you think. You have to be careful who you trust."

"So why should I trust you?"

"You shouldn't."

She looked at me and I saw that she held a softness inside. She was tough on the outside, but inside she wasn't that kind of girl. I remembered seeing Don Pablo grab her ass when she was younger. I wondered how she came to work here, and why she didn't leave. I wondered why she wasn't getting tough and mean like the other girls. I wanted to ask her, but I don't know how to talk to people. How do you ask somebody how they got like they got? "Why are you telling me?" I said.

"I don't want you to be angry."

"Why shouldn't I be?"

"Because Filo is my brother and I don't want you to hurt him."

I stared at her. "I didn't know he had a sister."

"Nobody knows," she said. "But like all secrets, people will figure it out.

Eventually." She pressed a piece of paper into my hand and then walked away. On the paper was a name, *Maria*, and an address. My first thought was that I would go there and beat the crap out of Filo. My second thought was that I couldn't. Not now, not ever. How could I hurt the little brother of the girl I was destined to marry?

Act II Scene 3

A 3:00 *sharp* the next afternoon, I knocked on the door to room 315 of the Conrad Hilton Hotel. The man who opened the door was about twenty-five or thirty, an American, and really big, maybe six-foot five or more. He was blond with a short blond beard. His eyes were blue and cold. He opened the door and looked at me, closed the door, said something I couldn't make out, and then opened the door full wide to let me in. He was wearing dark blue pants and a white shirt, blue canvas suspenders, and white shoes. He carried a short black revolver in a brown leather holster over his heart.

The room was a suite. I know that, now. I did not know what it was back then. At the time, I just knew it was big, like Don Pablo's room. I thought maybe all hotel rooms looked like this. It was big, but I did not know what that size meant. Money, power, those kinds of things. What could I know? I was sleeping in a barn at the bull ring.

In the back of the suite, at a table by a window overlooking Mills Street and with a view of the mountain to the north, sat the pale man with the cane; the same man I had seen some months earlier sitting in the cantina with Don Pablo. He was wearing a pink shirt and white pants, also with suspenders. He did not carry a gun. He was sitting at the table with a blonde woman who was wearing a thin white sleeveless dress. The bright light pouring in from the window turned her dress to something like vapor. I saw every curve, and there was plenty of curve to see. I was, for a moment, paralyzed. She smiled at me. They were eating steak sandwiches on toasted bread, and they had a fruit salad on a plate in between them.

"Anderson?" I asked.

The pale man nodded and gestured for me to come closer.

I approached until I stood at arm's length and then opened my box, took out the parcel and handed it to him. He took the parcel without looking at it, pushed his chair back, got up stiffly and limped into the back bedroom, returning with a parcel of his own, a smaller block wrapped in brown paper and tied with a string. He offered the parcel to me and when I reached for it, withdrew his hand. "I was not expecting Don Pablo to send a boy."

"Don't send a boy to do a man's job," the big man with the pistol said.

He was standing behind me, towering over me.

"I do what Don Pablo tells me," I said, "and Don Pablo trusts me to do his work."

"Do you know what's inside that packet?" the pale man asked, gesturing with his chin to the room behind him.

"No," I said.

"And do you know what is in this package?" he asked, holding it up for me to see.

"No," I said. "And I don't care. My job is to carry it to Don Pablo."

"And how is Don Pablo keeping?"

"He is well, as always," I replied.

Anderson handed me the packaged and I put it in my shoeshine box and then hesitated by the table. The big man was still standing just behind me, by my left shoulder. The woman took a strawberry from the fruit salad and offered it to me. I shook my head. I was sort of hoping they would give me an envelope with some money, or at least something, but after a minute the pale man looked at me and said, "Yes?"

I shrugged.

He looked at the big man, who laid a hand on my shoulder and steered me to the door.

"Wait a minute," Anderson called from the table. "The boy's right. I almost forgot." He got up slowly again and limped into the back room and returned with another parcel, this one a polished wooden box much like a cigar box, only bigger, heavier. "Tell Don Pablo this is a little present from me to him. And make certain that he gets it, right?"

I nodded. The parcel contained a pistol. It didn't take any brains to figure that out. I had seen boxes like it in the windows of gun shops. It was the exact size and weight. Alone in the stable I opened the box—it wasn't locked—and, indeed, there was a fine pistol inside. But it wasn't a revolver like you usually saw. This one was flat, L-shaped, silver in color but with a pearly white inlay on the grip. It was a fine pistol and it took me a while to figure out that it was an army pistol, a .45. Don Pablo said it was better not to know too much, but I was learning that it was necessary to know all I could because every bit of information was another piece of the puzzle. A few years earlier I didn't know there was a puzzle. Now I knew there was, but I still wasn't sure what the big picture was. I was not surprised that Don Pablo had a pistol. I would have been more surprised if he hadn't had one. But giving pistols as presents signified something. It had to. A pistol was a special thing to give. But what this meant, I did not know. I presumed it meant that Anderson and Don Pablo had a close relationship. You would not, I thought, give a pistol to someone you didn't trust. If you gave someone a pistol, it meant you knew they would use it wisely.

Alone in the old blacksmith shop, I held the pistol in my hand and carefully traced the cool metal with my fingers until I knew the lever and safety and slide and understood how they worked. I held it for a long time, practiced holding it steady at arm's length (no easy feat for a skinny boy with a heavy pistol). I practiced its loading action, ejected and inserted the (empty) clip, even pulled the trigger. I smelled the oil and looked down the barrel. I was the first boy I knew who could say that he held a pistol, had I been inclined to say anything. By the time I wiped the pistol down and returned it to its box, I was pretty sure that I could fire it, if I had to. I put the box away and soon my boys began to drift in to make their evening payment. I took their money, and when they were gone I took my things and crossed the bridge.

When I arrived, Don Pablo was talking to some men in cheap blue suits. They were smoking cigarettes and talking very fast. One of the men took out a paper from a briefcase and they cleared away the table and stood over it and looked while the man drew some pictures or diagrams or maps.

When they left, another man was waiting to talk to Don Pablo. He was older, and looked more like a rancher or a politician. He was better dressed in a light blue shirt and dark pants. He wore dark glasses. Their conversation only lasted a minute. The man sat down, and Don Pablo put the envelope into the inside pocket of his coat. The transaction was so smooth that the envelope didn't even hit the table. I barely saw it. They spoke only a few words and then the man got up and left. Don Pablo signaled for a drink, then looked at me and nodded. "Did you bring it?"

"No, Don Pablo," I said.

He practically flew out of his chair. He was up so fast the chair tipped over.

"Of course I have it, Don Pablo!" I hissed, not wanting to shout, but not wanting to get hit, either. "I was just kidding."

Don Pablo looked around, smoothed the front of his jacket, then righted his chair and sat back down. "You little shit, I liked you better when you didn't talk."

"Sorry, Don Pablo."

"So where is it?"

"Here."

Don Pablo took the first parcel without looking and slipped it into his coat pocket. "Tell me that you kept your mouth shut."

"I kept my mouth shut, Don Pablo, just like you said."

"There's another one." I took the wooden box from my shoeshine box.

"What's this?" he asked, and then right away added, "I see. Nice." He opened the box and looked at the pistol but did not take it out. Then he closed the box and set it on the table. "From Anderson?"

"*Si,*" I said. Yes.

He nodded and sat down. From his right coat pocket he took out another, smaller parcel, also wrapped in brown paper. He pushed it across the table to me. "Don't open it here," he said. "Take it with you."

Act II Scene 4

The parcel was only a few inches long, and thin, but heavy. Brown paper tied with string. Something metal. I felt the weight through the wrap. Inside was twenty pesos. About, in those days, six or seven US dollars. It seemed a lot of money for carrying one small package over the bridge. But what the money was wrapped around was even better than the money. A switchblade, almost new, and sharp. It was not very long, only about seven inches when open, but the blade was good German steel stamped BÖCKER. The handle was real bone cut in a fine crisscross pattern so that it was good to grip, and the lock was recessed to make it hard to open accidentally. At the back end was a ring so I could hang the knife on a string around my neck, but it also had a clip on the back side so I could fasten it to a belt (if I had a belt). I lay on my back in on the stable roof and ran my thumb gently down the blade, opened it and closed it, felt just the pressure on the button, worried that the knife might open accidentally. Nothing to do about that but carry it carefully.

Chick snap. Chick snap. Chick snap.

I opened and closed the knife, tossed it from my right to my left and back again. Balanced it on my hand. Nobody had ever given me a present that I could remember. Not in my entire life. My mother, maybe, back when I was little. Maybe. It was almost as good as a gun. Almost.

I lay on my back and stared up at the stars and wondered if there was a God and decided once and for all that there was not, that there was no God and you could trust nothing in this world but the iron in your hand, and I now I had a knife, and someday, I knew, I would have a gun, too, maybe a hard, flat military-style pistol like Don Pablo, and when I finally had that, there would be nothing in this world that would make me afraid.

Chick snap. Chick snap. Chick snap.

In the late hours of the morning I looked up at the sky, and a single falling star streaked green fire above. It broke into two pieces and then they vanished. *Where do they come from?* I wondered. I knew nothing of astronomy. If you had asked me I might have answered that the world was flat. Perhaps the million questions in my head drove me. I was always asking questions like that. It was one of the things that was different about me.

I was thinking about the priest. It was the foolish and the weak who wasted time in church appealing to heaven for things that would never materialize. You only had in this world what money you stashed, and what you could do yourself—your knowledge and skills—to put beans on your plate. You could trust the money in your pocket and the knife in your hand, what you see and hear with your own eyes and ears. Besides that—there is nothing. Trust nobody, and you will never be disappointed. Everything else is just lines written in the sky with bright green ink that fades to nothing. Having concluded this, it did not matter whether I saw the priest again or not. But the next morning I went to see him one last time, even though Don Pablo had told me not to.

Mass was about to begin. I wanted to arrive before my usual time, just in case somebody was watching, and when there were other people coming and going. I was less likely to be seen. It was the first time that I went to *church* church since I was a small boy and my mother took me. I sat in the back and Father Sheehy saw, I am sure, but he made no sign. After the service, I found my way to the study and sat outside on the floor until he appeared. If Father Sheehy knew that something was up, he kept that to himself. He looked tired, but not surprised, nor startled, not anything. He did not ask why I was there early. He unlocked the door and gestured that I should sit in my old chair, the same place where I practiced my English.

"Pablito," he said. "What can I do for you today?"

"Padre, there are some things I need to know and I have nobody that I can ask. I've wanted to ask you for a long time, but I kept waiting for the right time."

"So how can I help you, Pablito?"

"I want to get a proper place to live, and I want to put some money in a bank, but I don't know how to do any of these things, and there is nobody else I can ask."

"I know nothing about these things, Pablito. Mexico is a different country and it has its own rules."

"I mean in El Paso, Father. On this side of the river."

Father Sheehy squinted at me. "Are there not rooms you can rent? Is there not someone—some widow or old person—who has an extra room and might like someone around to help with the chores? I see signs all the time in windows. The word is boarder. You get a room and a bed and meals."

"I'm Mexican, Father. People don't rent rooms to Mexicans over here. And they would ask who I was and where was my family and what I did for money. Nobody would rent to a boy like me. And even if I got a room, I would always be paying for a *room*, and I would never have anything of my own. If I bought a house—or at least rented one—then perhaps I could rent rooms to other people, and make some money that way."

Father Sheehy scratched the back of his head and looked at me for a long time. "It's not so simple, Pablito," he said. Buying a house and renting a room are very different things. A house is an investment and takes a lot of money. More, I think, than what you will have. And even if you had enough money to make a small down payment, how could you secure a loan for the remainder? The banks will want you to have a real job, and you must be of a certain age. And banks expect documentation for things. It's a legal transaction. There are government records. Banks are much more strict than landlords."

"What's doc-u-men-ta-tion?" I pronounced the word very carefully.

"It means proof. Who you are. Where you work. They will want to know about your education, your job, how much money you make. You will also need a bank account."

"How can I get a bank account?"

Father Sheehy shook his head. "It's not that easy. To get a bank account, you have to have a birth certificate. Do you have a birth certificate?"

I shook my head. "What's a birth . . . sir?"

"Cer-tif-i-cate. It means the government gives you a piece of paper that says where and when you were born, and who your parents are. It is proof of your identity."

"Why do I have to prove my identity?"

"So that they know you are really you."

"But why would anyone pretend to be me?"

Father Sheehy laughed. "It's more likely that *you* would pretend to be *someone else*. But they have rules to make it difficult for people to cheat. Do you have a birth certificate?"

I shook my head. "If I ever did, it was lost a long time ago."

"Do you know where you were born?"

"Torreón? I think. Maybe."

"There should be at least a Baptismal certificate or something in the church records there."

"I can't go back to Torreón and ask, can I?"

"I don't see why not, unless you can write a letter or find out in some other way. Do you know anything for certain about where you were born?"

I shook my head.

"And there is nobody who knows?"

"I do not know of anyone."

"What is your last name?"

"Pablo."

"I mean your family name."

I looked at him.

"Most people have two names. A given name and a family name. Your given name is Pablo. Do you know your family name?"

"Pablo is the only name I have ever had, Father."

Father Sheehy leaned back in his chair and folded his hands as if in thought. "God knows who you are," Father Sheehy said. "If you are going to make an honest life for yourself, I think God would forgive a small lie you told to make that change. But at any rate, you are still too young to worry about those things now. You must be at least twenty-one to purchase a house, and probably eighteen even to sign a rental contract or open a bank account without your parents' consent."

It was discouraging to hear that it would be difficult to find a place to stay in El Paso. But then again, if I could walk a thousand kilometers across the desert, if I could stand up to Don Pablo, if I could fend for myself on the streets, fight, carry a knife, it seemed to me that somehow finding a place to live or putting money in a bank could be possible, and should not even be that difficult. Perhaps I could lie about my age. Something. But what I needed to know was how this business worked. "What lie would I have to tell?" I asked.

Father Sheehy sighed. "Perhaps if you could not prove who you were, then *you* might claim to be *someone else*. At least they would have the kind of record the authorities would want to see. If you could find someone and take their identity, and then get those records."

"How could I do that?"

"I don't know how these things happen, Pablo. I'm not even sure if it is the same in Mexico as it is here. The one person who could help you is Don Pablo, but I take it you don't want him to know about this plan of yours."

I shook my head. "Don Pablo would help me only if he had some profit in helping me."

"Then perhaps the best way is to find that reason. Just try not to get too deeply into trouble doing it."

I stood up to go. I had not yet found the words to tell Father Sheehy that I was not coming to see him again.

"By the way," Father Sheehy said. "I'm leaving the diocese. But you know that already, don't you?"

"I didn't know."

"I was called into the office yesterday. I am being sent to our district office in New Orleans. I leave next week."

I watched him watching me.

"My guess is that Don Pablo said something to the Archbishop. Something about me keeping boys in my office."

"I didn't say anything to him, if that's what you're asking."

"I did not mean to imply that *you* said anything. But *someone* said something."

I thought about this. "It is better that Don Pablo said something to the Archbishop than that he said something to you," I said.

"That depends on what he said," Father Sheehy replied. "But either way, I am not afraid of Don Pablo."

"Everybody is afraid of Don Pablo."

"No, not everybody. The worst he could do is to kill me, and I can handle that. They killed our Lord, and God raised him from the dead. If they kill me, I'll put my faith in God to look after my soul."

"I'm not afraid of dying, either," I said. "But Don Pablo can do worse things than killing you, Father."

The priest looked hard at me. "When Peter struck off the ear of the servant of the high priest, who had come to arrest our Lord and Savior, Jesus told him to put his weapon away for those who live by the sword, by the sword will perish.' I don't worry about Don Pablo," Father Sheehy said. "Don Pablo will work out his own destiny, as you will work out yours.'"

"I have seen what Don Pablo does to those who displease him," I said.

"And I have seen what our Lord does for those who please him and for those who displease him. But all that aside, I wanted you to know that I was leaving." Father Sheehy opened his desk drawer. "I want you to know where I am going," he said. "If you ever get in trouble, you will know where I am. You may be an orphan, but you're not alone in the world. I'll be in New Orleans for a while." He stood up and handed me a small book. *Catechism for Youth*. It was in English. "Perhaps this will save your life someday," he said. "If nothing else," he added, "you can practice your English. You will keep practicing?"

I nodded.

The priest looked at me. "How is Filo?"

"He is fine, father."

"Are you *sure* he is fine?"

"He is fine, Father."

"And you won't hurt him?"

"Why would I do that?"

"Perhaps you think it was Filo who told Don Pablo that you were studying with me."

"I don't know how Don Pablo found out."

"Nor do I. But please pass along my best wishes to Filo when you next see him. And even if you think he told Don Pablo, please don't be angry. Filo would not do anything deliberately to hurt you."

I nodded.

"And take care of yourself, Pablito."

I got up and walked to the door but Father Sheehy called to me and I turned.

"Pablo . . . " he faltered. "When I first met you, I didn't like you. That morning when you walked into my office and chased Filo out. My first impression was that you were a bully, a thug. And perhaps you are. Perhaps you have to be. There is darkness inside you, Pablo. But there is also light. I see that. I sense the struggle in the things you do not tell me more than in what you do. Do you know what I mean, darkness and light?"

I shook my head, no.

"Yes," he said, "I think you do. You bullied Filo, but you also bought him shoes. You think I don't know that? He told me before you chased him away. There is both good and evil inside you. One of those is going to win over you. Which will it be? In the end, Pablo, you get to choose. Think well before you do."

I thought about Father Sheehy's words for years after that. I wondered if other people saw things as a choice, and if they struggled between good and evil. I wondered if there was something wrong with me. Was there something I should have been given, been born with, something missing from my DNA? Something that told me what was right and what was wrong? Was it even possible that there was a single right and wrong? Or was what was right for, say, a man like Father Sheehy, and what was right for a boy like me, would these be different things based upon our circumstances? People make rules and they think of right and wrong, good and evil, as absolutes. But in the middle of the problem, nothing is that simple. Things never look black and white, though I wish it was that way. Worse, I think sometimes that we see what we want to see, and disregard everything else. We twist words, twist our memories, twist the truth to justify our actions. In the end, most of us do whatever we want, regardless of good or bad.

Outside I threw the book in the first garbage can I saw. If Don Pablo caught me with that, he would kill me for sure. But then, after walking away, I went back and got it. In my whole life, nobody had ever given me a present. And then, in twelve hours, I had been given two: a switchblade and a book. Isn't that odd? Maybe the priest was right. Perhaps I would have to choose.

Act II Scene 5

Don Pablo expressed his displeasure about my seeing the priest and learning to read, but he didn't *forbid* that I continue reading. He only said to stop seeing Father Sheehy. I could read a little and I had plenty of time with nothing else to do. Left to myself, I practiced. Besides, I enjoyed reading. There was so much interesting stuff out there—so much to know! And I found it exhilarating that I could now look at these words and understand them. I could talk to anyone anywhere through the pages of a book or magazine. I could even talk to people long dead.

I read from newspapers and magazines that people left laying around. I read signs. I read the packaging on things in stores. From time-to-time someone would lose a book at the train station or bus station or the new airport out on the east end of town. I read these, too. Outside the courthouse one day I found a Spanish/English dictionary, and I quickly learned how to look up words I didn't know. The dictionary was great, but the translation especially helped.

Perhaps I had a natural gift for reading, for it did not take long for me to grasp pronunciation and to learn to look for certain parts of words for clues as to what they meant. I enjoyed figuring out what words meant. I began to understand some, though not all, of the harder things I read. It did not matter to me what I read. A newspaper article about Babe Ruth retiring was as interesting to me as a book about mechanical engineering. In fact, it was the things I didn't understand that interested me the most. So if I could not make sense of the mathematical formulas in an article on economics and trade, I would be on the lookout for a book or article that would explain those operations and symbols to me. If I saw an article about the Napoleonic Code, I would watch for a biography of Napoleon or a history of France or an explanation of law. Everything, it seemed, was connected to something else. And deep inside, underlying all of this, I was driven by the certainty that somewhere in the pages of the things I read was this *something* that I had been missing. This something that other people had that I didn't. I was sure that if I read enough, I would find out what it was.

One day I read that there were places called *libraries* that collected books and anybody could come and read them. They even had special books like encyclopedias and textbooks just laying around. People could take them home if they wanted. This astonished me more than anything. At first, I couldn't believe it. Books there for anybody to read? But if a book said it, it *had* to be true, right? And so I, Pablo the Shoeshine Boy, without even a family name, much less a family, asked and found that there was such thing, and El Paso even had one. It was a large building downtown and not very far from the church.

Swallowing my fear again, I marched through another door and was astonished to see shelf after shelf after shelf—a seemingly endless collection. Surely it held every book that had ever been written! I whistled in awe and was immediately silenced by the stern glare of a tall, middle-aged woman who staffed a desk by the front door. I fled to the back shelves and wandered the aisles wide-eyed wondering what was in all these books and which one I should take home first. I began pulling books off the shelves at random and looking inside. At last I found a book that seemed interesting and I thought would be easy to read. It was called *Maggie: A Girl of the Streets*. I would begin with something simple and familiar and then work my way up.

By that time I had acquired, in addition to my shoeshine box, a canvass bag with a single strap which allowed me to sling the bag over my shoulder. I used this bag to carry supplies for my boys—the candy and matches and girly magazines and things they would sell in addition to shining shoes. I put the book in my bag and made it only to the end of that first aisle before the woman from the front door and a young man I had not seen pounced on me. Evidently they had been watching me through the shelves of the adjoining aisles.

The young man was (I know now) college age (though he seemed so much older at the time). He was not much taller than me, but certainly more mature. He grabbed me and pinned my arms, and the old woman shot her hands into my bag and produced the book. She was taller than the young man, but very thin, perhaps fifty, with gray hair and gold metal glasses that perched on the end of her thin nose. She wore a black blouse with a high collar, almost like a priest's collar, and a long black skirt that hung to the tops of her black, pointed shoes.

"And where are you going with this?" she asked, holding the book high above me.

"Home," I said.

She looked at me incredulously, then looked at the book. Her face soured. "Perhaps you can tell me who wrote this book?"

She was still holding it high above me, but I could make out the name, Stephen Crane. I pronounced his name, "Step-hen Cranny."

"And out you go," the young man said. He dragged me to the front door and tossed me down the steps to the sidewalk.

He made a gesture like wiping his hands. "And stay out, you little thief," he added.

From the ground, looking up, I said, "But I thought a library was a place where people could come and take books. I read it in a magazine."

"What did you say?"

"I said, I read in a magazine that people could take books from the library. They could read books. It said they could even take them home, but that people would take them and bring them back. That's all I wanted."

The boy hesitated by the door. "Even if I thought you were telling the truth," he said, "which I don't, you have to have a library card to check out books. We don't just give them to anybody."

"And how do I get a library card?"

"We don't give them to Mexicans," he said.

Until that day I had never stolen anything. I hadn't even thought about it. You didn't take things from people. I might have been a boy on the streets, but I wasn't a thief, unless you count a little bit of food, or perhaps a blanket to stay warm, or something like that. But I don't count those things as stealing, though now that I am older I often give things to people so that they aren't tempted to take them from others who might not understand. Nothing good comes from taking, I think, but much good comes from giving, though I prefer that people not know if I do something like this.

It took me two days of stealing handbags before I found one with a library card. But the little pink card had a woman's given name and an American family name. Virginia Burnhardt. If I knew where to find her today I'd replace her purse and keys. I didn't want those things, or even the little bit of money I found inside (though I kept it). I wanted the library card, but finding one, I realized that nobody was going to mistake me for Virginia Burnhardt, and I was not going to be checking out any books any time soon, whatever that meant. I kept that card for a long time, though. I used it as a page marker in the *Catechism for Youth* Father Sheehy had given me.

Six months or so after being thrown out of the library, on New Year's Day, 1938, El Paso put on a football game in something called a Sun Bowl at Kidd Field. I had been reading about this in the paper and was curious to go, but there was no way for me to purchase a ticket. However, I figured out that if I climbed some rocks near the stadium, I could watch the game from there and not need a ticket at all.

Of course, people played football in Mexico, too, but from the pictures in the paper it was clear that Americans knew nothing about the game. Everything was wrong—they way the dressed, the way they lined up, the way they played. Even the ball was not round, but pointed at the ends. It was weird and I had to show some of the boys pictures from the paper to prove that I was not making this up. And that, of course, created another problem. Now all the boys wanted to come with me up on the rock to watch the game.

Odd, but in all this time, we had never done anything like this before. Don Pablo had not told us not to do anything together just for fun, but neither did I sense that it would please him. I knew that some of the boys hung out, but I never wanted to lose any of my authority by behaving as friends with them. Still, this seemed different. It was something that these boys were looking up to me to do. They wanted me to lead them to this place to watch this game. It was confusing, but I knew that even if I told them not to come, they would come anyway, and if I led them on my own, there might be other things they would do if I asked them. So I said "Okay" and we met before the game and climbed the rock to watch.

But a funny thing happened before the game. There were thousands and thousands of people there. We were just walking around wide-eyed at the spectacle. There was so much to see. There were bands and pretty girls in short dresses and men with carts selling hot dogs and cotton candy and something called sows' ears (we didn't try those). And there were pickles and peanuts and Coca Colas. And even the weather was not too bad for winter. The sun was bright and it was not so cold. Walking around I saw the boy who had thrown me out of the library and I scowled at him even though he didn't remember me. But one of the boys—Julio, I think his name was—he saw me and he said, "Do you know him?"

"No," I said. "Why?"

Julio giggled but said nothing.

"What?" I said. "Out with it!"

"He and his friends sometimes buy magazines from me."

"Magazines?" I said. "From you?" And then it dawned on me. The girly magazines. "Oh," I said.

I don't remember all that much about the game. There was a team from Texas Tech and a team from West Virginia. The game was very rough and both teams lost the ball a lot. It was boring, except for every now and then somebody had a long throw or a long run, or somebody knocked somebody down. The team from Virginia won, but they didn't look very good and nobody liked them. The Americans, I thought, really knew nothing about football. They should call their game something else.

You know, of course, where this is going, right? After that day I began to hang out in the late afternoons by the bar near the university where Julio shined shoes and sold cigarettes and matches and playing cards and girly magazines. And sure enough, it was only a week into January when the boy showed up and bought two. And they were especially good ones. They were in color and some of the girls were totally naked. In those days, there were not so many magazines where women took off all their clothes. I think Don Pablo might have had these printed himself. If not Don Pablo, then certainly it was Don Ricardo, or one of the *jefes*.

So the boy, glancing left and right to make certain nobody was watching, bought the magazines and stuffed them into his school bag, and then he went inside the bar and drank a few beers. When he went back to his room, I followed him.

I did not say anything that night. I wanted to make certain of a few things before I did. But I followed him to where he lived, and then on another day, when it was raining, I stole a yellow rubber raincoat from a man at the train station and slipped inside the library with a group of school children from somewhere. I only needed a few minutes, and I didn't need to confront anybody, although the woman in black sharp-eyed me from her perch by the front door. I don't think she remembered me, but she was suspicious.

So a month after this, the boy bought magazines again, and again went inside the bar for a few beers. But this time I knew where he lived, so I could take my time and wait for him outside of his room. He lived on the campus in a building full of college students. I was sitting in the dark near the front door when he came along, and from the shadows I tossed a magazine at his feet and he stopped, startled.

I stood up and tossed another. "Does your boss know you read these things?" I asked.

"Who the fuck are you?" he replied.

"Me? I'm just a little Mexican who likes to read books."

He stared at me until it came to him.

"But you didn't answer my question," I said.

"What question?"

"Does your boss know you read these things?" I pulled another one from my back pocket and held it open for him to see. "Did you see the tetas on this one? *Aye, caramba!*"

He slapped the magazine out of my hands. "Put that away, you little shit. What do you think you're doing?" He snatched the magazines from the ground and stuffed them in his book bag. Then he stepped toward me. "I oughta..."

"You what?" I replied, stepping back out of reach.

He stopped and looked around. He licked his lips. Perhaps he didn't believe that I would come alone. Why would I? How could I? "What do you want?" he asked.

"I want a library card."

He stared at me with his mouth hanging open like a cow. "A what?"

"A library card. I want a card and you're going to get me one."

"And what if I don't?"

"Then I'm going to show your boss where you keep your stash of nasty magazines."

"I don't have a stash of magazines," he replied.

"You do now," I said.

He looked at me.

"I know 'cause I put it there. But she won't know that. And she won't believe you if I tell her I sold them to you and you didn't pay me for them." I thought, for a moment, that the boy was going to pass out.

He rubbed his face with his left hand and said, "I can't get you a library card."

"*No me jodas*," I said. It required no translation.

"No," he said. "I can't just give you a card. I have to have, you know, documentation. ID. A name. An address. Something."

I thought about this. What was it Father Sheehy said? If you don't have documentation, then find somebody who does. *Forgive me*, Father, I thought, *for the little lie I am about to tell.*

Act II Scene 6

There have been Hispanic families in El Paso since the 1500's, though admittedly, the land north of the river was preferred by Anglo settlers, while the land south of the river, what is known today as Juarez, was preferred by *los Espanoles*. But by the 1930's there were many Hispanic families in El Paso, and I knew that there had to be at least one with enough social standing to command a library card. There had to be. And so the following afternoon, at 2:00 P.M., I looked in the alley behind the library and found, on a ledge outside the bathroom window, a little white envelope holding a pink library card in the name of Pablo Barela.

I was so proud. Not just that I got a library card. For the first time in my life, I had a proper *name*. It's amazing how much you can learn by reading newspapers and magazines. At least, the newspapers and magazines in those days. How much, I wondered, could I learn reading books?

I liked my library card so much that the first thing I did was to go to a print shop Don Pablo favored to see if they could print me more so that it would not matter if I lost the one I had. The shop was a windowless little storefront on *Aveneda Lerdo*. The owner was named Armando and he ran a little four-color offset press that by day was mostly devoted to bullfight and movie posters, along with the occasional wedding announcement, political tract, advertisement flier, or order of business cards. By night he printed mostly magazines—these for Don Pablo—and not the kind of magazine to which nice people subscribed. I imagine that they made most of their money on the night shift.

Armando knew me and smiled when I made my request. He was a tall, light-skinned man with a bald head and a thick black moustache. His fingers were permanently stained reddish brown from all the ink. He looked at the library card and knew right away what was the paper stock, its weight, the type font, even the card's dimensions. He was a smart man. I liked that about him. He said, "Such a large order! Why nine cards under the same name?"

"Why would I want different names?" I replied, but he didn't have to tell me for me to figure that out.

He looked at me closely for a minute, then asked, "What's your birthdate?"

It was another funny question. I mean, I sort of knew about birthdays. I had heard about them. Read about them. But I didn't know mine. How could I? I could count events through the seasons backwards until the fall I came to Juarez, and in that manner I could count up some years, but I didn't know how old I really was, or on what day, or even in which month I had been born. So this was in March of 1937. "Does it matter?" I asked.

He shrugged his shoulders. "Not to me it doesn't."

When I returned to pick up the library cards, he had printed them with six different names in addition to three more in the name of Pablo Barela. He also had a different kind of a card for me, too, long and yellow and very official-looking. This was something new and he had just begun making them. It was called a Texas Driver's License.

"What is this?" I asked.

"I needed the practice," he replied. "They have to have them up north, now. Soon people will be asking for them. You might find it useful."

I looked at the driver's license for about a minute and wondered how it would be useful. I didn't have a car, or plans to buy one. I didn't know how to drive. But then I saw the age and the birthdate on the license. Pablo Barela was born on February 25, 1920. That made him eighteen years old. I don't think I looked eighteen, but so what? Armando knew what he was doing. And February 25th, I suppose, is as good a day as any other.

For a boy with no family, no inheritance, and no education, I was doing pretty well for myself. The next few years are stamped in my memory as the happiest of my boyhood, and among the happiest in my life.

Anderson returned. I knew right away when he came back because Don Pablo sent word for me to come to the hotel at five in the morning. Soon I was delivering packages once a month, dropping them off at the Hilton at 3:00 P.M. sharp. Anderson was always there. Always with a different woman. Always with the blond giant with the pistol in the shoulder holster.

Don Pablo paid me after each successful delivery. Twenty pesos. About six US dollars. That was a lot of money for a boy at that time. A loaf of bread cost six cents. A cup of coffee was a nickel. American cigarettes were fifteen cents a pack. A new cowboy hat cost three dollars. A quart of milk cost a dime. A pair of good, new shoes was six dollars. Of course, all of these things were even cheaper in Juarez. I had my regular income, as well, and I had so much money I began to bury it in mason jars in the old blacksmith shop. I knew that wouldn't work forever, but I was still unsure how to approach a bank about opening an account. But the best thing of all was that I had my first girlfriend. I finally got the courage to go to the address that Maria had given me.

Maria lived on *Calle Acacias*, out on the west side of town. It was an area of nicer homes and walking down the road I pictured the kind of home and family that had always fascinated me. But of course, the actual house would be nothing like that. How could it be? She said that she was Filo's sister and they were orphans. How could they afford a normal home?

From half a block away I could hear the racket—the squawking of chickens and the cries of small children, a crash of dishes and above all, the bellowing of some old cow of an auntie. There would have been no point knocking on the door—who could have heard over all the racket? But while I was standing at the front gate, trying to decide whether to walk in or walk on by, Maria came around the side of the house with a basket of washing. She was going to scrub the clothes in a tub that stood by a spigot in the front yard.

The house had five rooms and nineteen girls living in it. With them came an assortment of children of various ages, along with mothers, aunties, dogs, cats, a one-eyed parrot who bit if you got too close, a goat who wouldn't go away if he thought you carried food, and a desert tortoise they kept in a wooden crate so he wouldn't get trampled. All of them but the tortoise navigated the little paths that wound though the toys, mattresses, tables, chairs, piles of dirty dishes, trash, empty wine and beer bottles, and whatever else had been stacked, dropped, or discarded in the house. What the girls had in common, Maria said, was that they all worked for Don Pablo. Together they cooked and cleaned and wiped noses and changed diapers, the older women looking after the babies at night while the younger girls worked in the bars. "It isn't much of a life," she said. I wondered which was worse—to live alone and homeless and sleep in a barn, or to live in that den of chaos.

I did not tell her that I envied her the walls and the roof, the regularity of at least having a consistent place to lie down. A place of her own, even if it wasn't much. I wondered if we could do better together. I imagined a little house where we could live, just she and I, and perhaps Filo, and their auntie, if they had one. Maybe we could even take in their sick little brother. I imagined coming home at night to a normal family—to a meal and knowing that Maria was there. We could take walks in the evenings. I could work and she could stay home and keep house, and she would not have to endure the endless taunts and gropes and insults from Don Pablo and the drunken customers. Maria woke in me the dream I had confided to Father Sheehy.

I could afford a house if I could figure out how to obtain one. It would be a nice house; not too big, not too small, stucco perhaps, with a flat roof and little courtyard just for us, and a shade tree in the yard. And the water would be sweet and the electricity always on, and we would have a big white canopy bed and we would be happy in love.

But these things, of course, are just the love-struck imaginings of an inexperienced boy. It was all that I could do in those days just to leave flowers for her on the bar, or to steal away for little walks on Sunday afternoons if I had nothing more important pressing across the border, and if she could get free from her chores. But it was Maria's face I imagined when, that warm spring night in 1939, I pulled one of the girls from the second floor of Don Pablo's hotel into a little room and (how shall I say this?) *perdí mi virginidad*. I lost my cherry. I confess my weakness. The temptation was too much.

Unfortunately, when I came out of that room, it was to a loud round of applause. Evidently, the girls and bartenders and bouncers and cleaning boys all had bets riding on when it would finally happen, which girl would be selected, and how long it would take. Everybody in the bar was watching, including Don Pablo. There were toasts and cheers and taunts, and I had beers thrust upon me and my hair mussed. And the girl draped her arm and around me and we were carried in chairs around the bar for everyone to see. I have never been so embarrassed in my life. And I knew, then, that what I had with Maria would end. How could she consent to see me when she was sure to learn what I had done? Wasn't she the one who said secrets could not be kept? But still I felt I had to try.

It was also the day that I discovered that men were supposed to wear underwear.

Never let anyone tell you that guilt is an entirely bad thing. How many great universities were founded, hospitals, libraries, museums, and so forth built because some millionaire felt, at the end of his life, pangs of regret, or fear, or shame over the way he made his fortune?

So with money in one hand and a Texas Driver's License in the other, and driven by guilt and fear, all I needed was to find an owner desperate enough to rent a house to a Mexican. A run-down house on a dead-end street across from a cemetery fit the bill perfectly. It would be the end of my daily border crossings. I entrusted Paco to shine the guards' shoes. The only nights I would spend in Juarez would be the nights before I made deliveries to Anderson.

The advertisement was in the real estate section of the *Herald-Post*. Mr. Winegardner was nearing sixty, a squint-eyed, leathery man with no eyebrows and a bright bald head he concealed under a straw cowboy hat. When

I found the place, he was patching the roof with tar. The house itself wasn't much by American standards. It was built of stone with a flat roof and stone floors throughout. It had a large front room with two windows facing the street, a kitchen with a kerosene stove and no refrigerator, a bathroom with half an iron barrel supported by bricks for a tub. "There's no hot water," Winegardner said, "unless you light a fire under the tub." The stones under the tub were cracked and black with soot. I wouldn't have thought to do that. I had never had a hot bath in my life. Just having water was a luxury to me. There were two tiny bedrooms in the back. One had an old mattress and a three-legged chair. The other just a rug rolled up and standing in a corner.

I knew Winegardner would rent me the house when we went into the kitchen and I met his wife, Lupita. She was making tortillas and beans for lunch. The house rented for twelve dollars a month. For fifteen I got the electricity included. It would be a long time before I slept out-of-doors again.

The evening of the day that I obtained the keys, I went across the road into the cemetery and watched the sky grow dark and the stars ignite in the sky, and I looked at my little house and wept because for the first in my life I had a place and a key and I could come inside and sleep safely and not have to worry about a watchman or vagrants or anything. Even as a boy, the house I lived in was not as grand as this. But at the same time, there was a sinking feeling in my stomach that whispered that no matter what I did, this was not going to be a normal house like a normal family would have. No matter how much I wanted to imagine Christmas dinners and *quinceñeras* all of the things that normal people do, I had no idea how to make that happen.

One of the books I had read from the library was called *Great Expectations*. It was the story of Pip, an orphan boy, like me (only I had no sister and no Joe to "bring me up by hand"). There was a place in the story when Pip discovered that he was common, that he wore thick shoes and did not know to call a jack a knave when he played cards. This was my experience when I dealt with people. They joked and laughed and did things, but I was always watching, always alert for what should be my next move, my next word, and always fearing some misstep. I was navigating a world without being free to live fully in it. The awareness of this fact gnawed me from the inside like termites in a tree.

What things make a house? A mattress? Of course. Chairs? A table? A carpet? Lamps? I would need blankets and sheets. Perhaps a pillow. A towel. Pots and pans? I knew nothing of cooking. The implements were as foreign to me as a surgeon's tools. All the little that I knew I learned from books. But knowing and feeling are quite different. It is one thing to know what to put in a house, and another altogether to be comfortable using them. Plates. Cups. Knives and forks. Curtains. A broom. I would not require a refrigerator. No, I could keep the house simple. I knew it would be more expensive than I thought. The next day I dug up all the money I buried in the blacksmith shop and re-buried it in my back yard.

But if I expected Maria to forgive, forget, and to join me, in that I was mistaken. All of these things I sought and collected were in vain. A few weeks after my indiscretion, Maria and Filo disappeared.

It did not take long for me to find another girl. By the time I was actually seventeen, I'd had three or four. It was not so difficult as I imagined. Walk with a little swagger, some attitude, and the young girls notice. Especially the stupid and insecure ones. Girls are easy to find. What is hard, I would learn, is to find someone worth keeping, and then to keep them when I did.

Act III Scene 1

Thunder announces the arrival of a storm, and wind the change in seasons. If only the events in our lives were as simple to decode. But what boy of sixteen can make sense of the invisible clues that foretell that change is approaching? The world economies were on the mend. The armies of homeless stragglers trudging the roads of Mexico and America dried up. The hobo camps vanished. Men returned to work. The feeling might not have been optimism, but there was certainly a feeling that the worst was behind us.

True, Europeans worried about a man named Hitler. People everywhere worried about communism. But Mexico's revolution had failed. That was settled. Europe's troubles seemed as far away and surreal as the once-upon-a-time of some fairy tale. I rented a house. I opened a bank account. I made more money every month than a schoolteacher with a college degree. I had all the food I could eat and all the beer I could drink. The girls at Don Pablo's hotel fought over which one would sleep with me on Saturday nights. But I never told a soul about the house. I prepared it for one girl and when she left, the house became something else. A tool for my work. Or maybe something like a shrine to my stupidity.

I still met with the boys in the old blacksmith shop. Five P.M., we settled accounts. I had boys working at night now, too. They worked outside the popular bars and restaurants, and these boys did not always cross the bridge home to Mexico. But they still met me in the late afternoon or early evening and paid me. And one Saturday evening in September of 1939, after the boys were gone and I had hidden my money, I was almost to the door of the blacksmith shop when it swung gently open before me and a half-dozen men blocked my way. If the men had been white, I would not have been nearly so alarmed. White men might threaten me, beat me, even rob me, but the men in my line of work would kill me, and these men were dark, like me. The moment I saw them, I bolted across the room.

Beyond the back door was an abandoned stable, and beyond it an abandoned warehouse, and beyond the warehouse was the fence that bordered the freight yard, and I had only to clear the fence to be lost in a jungle of box cars and switching engines, and nobody would catch me there. But I did not clear the back door of the blacksmith shop, did not see the man swinging a length of pipe, nor remember the blow that cut my forehead to the bone and fractured my skull, that left me, so I was told, lying on my back with my legs still running. I remember almost nothing of the next few hours. I was not unconscious, but I was not thinking, either.

I lay on the ground not understanding why I could not get up or move my arms and legs. I remember a grinning face over me asking again and again, "Where is the money?" I remember laughter when I replied, "Don Pablo, what are *you* doing here?" even though I knew I was not speaking to Don Pablo and that he was not even in the room. I remember counting down from ten out loud, but not knowing why.

In the movies, people wake up when you splash water on them. I do not think it works this way in real life. I faded in and out for what must have been several hours. Once—and only briefly—I woke to the splash of urine on my face. Even then, knowing what it was, I could not form the words to express anger, humiliation, anything. I did not ask for mercy. It was as though the part of my brain that dealt in words was not speaking to the rest of me. I could not even summon the thought that my brain was broken.

The men argued about what was wrong with me. They blamed one man, Alfonso, for killing me instead of knocking me out. I did not ask who they were or why they wanted to kill me. I did not plot an escape, or even think of escaping. The lights were on, as they say, but nobody was home. At least I was breathing. I was not dead yet.

The men became agitated. There was some other place they needed to be. There was talk of a plan. Someone said that time was up. "Kill him," he said. "But cut off his balls first."

But then there was something else. Shouting outside. A police car. A spotlight. People running. "Do it quick," a voice said. "No mistakes." There was another splashing and the smell of gasoline.

There was a man standing over me with a knife. I still couldn't move. I wanted to ask him, *Why?* But the man's eyes bulged, his mouth shaped a word without sound. He turned as if to look behind him, leaned to an impossible angle, then dropped from my view. Oscar stood where the man had been. Oscar, his whittling knife in hand.

At that moment, words returned to me. "Oscar," I gasped. "Take me home."

Oscar cut the ropes, pulled me to my feet, draped my arm over his shoulder, rushed me out the back door and left me with my back aganst the wall of the stable. He ran back into the blacksmith shop, but a moment later he was back, resting his hands on his knees, leaning forward and panting. Already the orange light of fire danced on the ground in front of me. Sparks shot from the open windows and flew up into the night sky. He rested only a few seconds, then helped me to my feet again and we stumbled behind the old buildings at the far end of the property, only then to the front, to Paisano Street, crossing the road quickly and snaking between two warehouses. We turned up Durango and down Overland, walking as quickly as we could manage toward downtown.

I would learn, only a few years ago, that the blow fractured my skull. The x-rays showed the break—it had healed—and I had suffered in my life no other injury that could account for it. But that night, the concussion left me disoriented, confused. I was now on my feet. I could walk. I was awake enough to be angry, but I did not yet know at whom my feelings should be directed. I had a four-inch gash across my forehead and my face, my neck, the whole front of my shirt was heavy with blood. The torn skin burned and the bone underneath throbbed like thunder—a pain so overwhelming I *heard* it. The blood stung my eyes and I could not blink it out. I wiped my face and looked stupidly at the clotted mess on my hand. Had Oscar taken me to a hospital, I'm sure they would have kept me. Had the police spotted me, they would have arrested us for vagrancy, suspicion, something, anything. Had we been white, the guards at the bridge would not have let us cross. But being Mexican, we were somebody else's problem. And they knew us. They stared as they waved us through and seemed glad to be rid of us. *Stupid Mexicans. What now?*

Had Oscar not misunderstood, or I been more present, we would not have gone to Don Pablo's. That's not the *home* I had in mind. But Oscar didn't know because I hadn't told anyone.

We heard the gunfire before we saw the hotel. We weaved through a crowd running the opposite direction and looked around the corner. A dozen men crouching behind cars fired into Don Pablo's hotel. From inside, other men fired back.

We doubled back to the alley. We thought we might get in through the back door, but the alley was blocked by a long, black car. Looking past it, we saw that the other end of the alley was blocked, as well. Both drivers stood by the cars, pistols ready, facing the hotel and watching another group of men trying to break the back door down. A scuffle broke out. The blast of a shotgun. A volley of shots. Shouting. A scream. The driver of the nearest car still faced the hotel. He was watching the fight, his back toward us. Oscar slit his throat, and I pulled the revolver from his dying hand. More shots. Four. Five. Six. The pounding blasts of a shotgun, not the pop-pop-pop of a pistol. The knot of men by the door exploded. Three or four fell. Two ran toward us. I raised the pistol at arm's length, closed my eyes, and emptied the revolver. When I opened my eyes, both men lay still.

Behind them, another man approached, shotgun at his shoulder. Raul. I shouted and waved. He lowered the shotgun and I ran to him. In a moment three other men appeared in the doorway. More shots rang out. The men in the doorway fired at the driver of the car blocking the other end of the alley. Two more men emerged from the hotel. They carried Don Pablo between them. Like me, he was drenched in blood.

We stuffed Don Pablo into the back seat of the car whose driver Oscar had killed. We all piled in—six, seven, eight of us. Raul dove behind the wheel and slammed the car into reverse, out of the alley, into the street, tires burning and squealing, men hanging out the still-open doors. He slammed the stick shift into first and in an instant, we were gone.

The men in front shouted. *To the hospital. The house. Hospital. House. Hospital. To the ranch. Raul's. That's the first place they'll look. The hospital. He won't make it.* The road ahead was jammed. We swerved down a side street, hopping the curb and driving half on the road, half on the sidewalk. Pedestrians scattered. We crushed a bicycle but the rider jumped off just in time. Two blocks and we hit another intersection. "I have a house," I said.

Raul looked back at me. "You? A house? Where?"

"In America. And nobody knows but me. He'll be safe there."

And we drove like that—guns, blood, all of it—back across the bridge and into El Paso. The guards took one look at Don Pablo and let us through without a word.

Act III Scene 2

It is amazing what you can learn on the streets. Especially if you have eyes and ears and business interests like mine. I knew exactly in which bar we could find a surgeon at two A.M.. He was an army doctor, and even drunk he knew what to do with a bullet wound. He took one look at Don Pablo and said, "I saw lots of fellas shot up worse than this in Belleau Wood."

When he was done with Don Pablo, I lay on the kitchen counter and he stitched the gash in my forehead. The shock and adrenalin had worn off, the pure hell of the pain set in. The pain was like nothing I felt before or since. It was like having my head sawed open. The pain roared in my ears like an engine.

Morphine put me to sleep and morphine quieted the pain again when I awoke. A second doctor—a customer of Don Pablo's—arrived at dawn, one of Don Pablo's men traveling to Mexico in the night to fetch him. The doctor checked up on Don Pablo and changed the bandages, swore at the drunken doctor and complained about the stitching, though there was little he could do to improve things. He checked up on me, as well, changed my bandages, and went to fetch us all a supply of alcohol, bandages, antibiotics, morphine, and syringes.

Overnight, my little house had become an armed camp. A thin, flint-eyed man with a Springfield rifle sat on a crate and drank coffee all morning, peering through a blanket hung over one the front window. Four of Don Pablo's men smoked endless cigarettes in a car parked across the road. A half-dozen other men wandered the house, pistols sticking at odd angles from their belts, or carried in leather holsters over their hearts. Two of Don Pablo's favorite girls appeared as nurses. Two more turned the kitchen into a canteen. I have no idea who brought them, or when. There were eggs and cheese and tortillas and beans, but I was not hungry.

The Mexican doctor returned with a real nurse in a white uniform. I have no idea where she came from. The doctor passed his time smoking and drinking coffee with whiskey in it and gossiping with the men. They recited the names of the dead with something like reverence. The nurse never left Don Pablo's side.

Someone brought a new mattress with clean sheets and a couple of feather pillows, and Don Pablo lay in the front room, propped up in bed, his chest swathed in bandages. He looked at me, my eyelids purple and heavy with blood, and the hint of a smile crossed his face. Someone must have told him where he was and how he got there, but for now he wasn't speaking.

The noise and smoke and pain drove me out of the house and into the back yard. A high stone fence separated my house from the neighbors. There was nothing there but dirt, rock, and cactus. A single thorny catclaw tree filled the southeast corner and cast a thin pool of noontime shade. Oscar was sitting in that shade with his back against the wall.

I had forgotten all about Oscar. I went to him and he pointed at a small desert tortoise peeking from beneath a large stone beside the tree. I sat down. The morphine dimmed the drumming in my head. My memory of the day before was still muddled.

Oscar must have read my mind. He said, "I was sitting across the road in the shade when three cars turned the corner driving slow. One of them stopped on this side of the shop. The other two parked a little ways down the road. I knew something was wrong so I got behind a fence where they couldn't see me. I wanted to warn you, but they were between me and the shop. I didn't know what to do. Some of them went to the front door. Some others went around back. They opened the door and went inside. After a while I got close enough to see what they did to you—what they were going to do. I hope you are not mad."

"Why would I be mad?"

"I got the police, Pablo. I didn't want to get them, but I didn't know what else to do. I told them some men had you inside but they acted like they didn't care. I think they thought it was just some teenager stuff, you know, like some kids were hanging out in the shop or something. They drove by and frightened them off, but they didn't go in. But I knew you were still in there, so I went in."

"You saved my life, Oscar."

"The men," he said, "they ran when they saw the police. All but one. He was going—" Oscar was pale, tired. Tiny beads of sweat formed on his upper lip. His hair was wet and hanging down into his eyes. "I found your knife," he said. "I found it by the gasoline can when I lit the fire."

I looked down and in his open hand he held my switchblade. The blade was open and locked. I took it from him. There was blood on the handle. I looked at Oscar. There was blood on his palm, his fingers, all the way down to his nails. A black stripe of dried blood. For a moment I thought it was from the man he'd stabbed.

"They were going to..."

"I know," I said. "What happened to your arm?"

"I think I killed the boy who was going to kill you. I stabbed him and then I set the fire so nobody would know."

"Oscar," I said, lifting the poncho he wore. "Oh, Oscar. What happened?"

I don't know when Oscar got shot. Maybe it was standing by the car in the alley behind Don Pablo's hotel, or when we carried Don Pablo to the car. The whole night he had said nothing. Nothing in the car. Nothing to the men in the house. Why? What was he thinking? I suppose, when you grow up an orphan, that sometimes there's just nothing to say. He always was quiet. We buried him under the catclaw tree.

In the afternoon someone suggested that we get a paper. I went down to the market and bought an *El Paso Times*. I came back and read the news to Don Pablo. The fighting in Juarez was all over the front page. Bullets broke windows on the American side of the border. An old man looking out from his room had been cut by flying glass. A car was hit.

The article said the fighting was between rival gangs and this happened from time-to-time. The writer condemned Mexico for its general lawlessness. The writer reminded El Pasoans that there had been fighting during the revolution and again when Pancho Villa was around. This time, he wrote, it was just criminals acting up. But Don Ricardo was dead, and a dozen other men had been killed and who knows how many sent to the hospital. People in Juarez were afraid to leave their homes. So it said.

The fire that burned the old blacksmith shop was on page five. It took out the shop, but the stables, the old office, and the warehouse survived. The police thought the fire had been set by kids or vagrants. The article said the cops had investigated a disturbance there earlier that day. A body was found inside. Probably a drunk, they said. Maybe he started the fire. Nobody seemed to care. The property had been falling apart for years. It was about time. Now somebody would take over the property and tear the whole thing down.

I translated all this for Don Pablo. Afterwards he whispered instructions to two of his men. When they left, he motioned for me to come.

I sat on the floor beside him. He looked at the bandage and the bruising on my face. "Why did you come to my hotel?" he asked.

I always came to the hotel to pay Don Pablo, but he wouldn't want to hear that. I wondered if he asked because I was late, or maybe because he knew that I was hurt, too. I didn't know what to say. I told Oscar to take me home, and Oscar took me to Don Pablo's by mistake, but Don Pablo would not want to hear that, either. "I came to warn you," I said.

"And what were you doing in the alley by that car?"

"I was trying to get in the back door."

"You killed the driver?"

"Yes, Don Pablo."

"I heard you killed two others."

"I don't know. There was a lot of shooting."

He grunted, almost a laugh. "So they tried to kill you, too."

I nodded. "They almost did."

"Do you know why they wanted to kill you?"

"No, Don Pablo."

"Some of the *jefes* thought it was not fair that I had made the whole of El Paso my territory."

I listened.

"But I did not make the whole of El Paso my territory, my quiet one." Don Pablo looked at me. "You did."

My eyes bulged. "I didn't mean to cause trouble, Don Pablo."

"It was not your fault. And it was bound to happen. Do you think if one of their shoeshine boys had crossed the bridge first, they would have shared their territory with me?"

"Probably not, Don Pablo."

"Of course not. But you did well, my quiet one. I knew you would. Remember when we killed Michaelo and you didn't flinch? Another boy would have run away, but not you. And remember when you were sick and I took care of you? Remember that? I brought you into my house and we nursed you for weeks. And now you have repaid me. You are not a boy anymore, Pablo, and I will not forget. I'm going to kill the bastard who shot me and you and killed Don Ricardo, and when I do, I'll be the next *jefe*. You watch."

Don Pablo once told me that power was either earned or bought. I had believed that, tried to live my life that way, but at that moment, in my house, listening to Don Pablo, I realized that he was wrong. I had *not* killed the driver of the car that blocked the alley. Oscar did. I could barely stand. Oscar saved my life. And I had *not* saved Don Pablo's life. Oscar, much more than I, saved Don Pablo. And if I shot anyone else that night, it was by accident and with my eyes closed. I would have been as likely to have shot one of Don Pablo's men as I would one of his enemies. The only way that I earned anything was the line of little insignificant events going all the way back to that morning when I crossed the bridge into El Paso for the first time. Perhaps I created the opportunity. But Oscar did the earning, and now he was buried in my back yard. All that I was, was lucky. And what would people think of me if I told them that?

I was not yet seventeen and I had learned one of life's most important lessons. Power is no illusion, but the stories we tell of how we obtain power are. And it does not matter what mover and shaker I see on TV, read about in the paper, whose words or pictures are blasted over the internet, I know that these men and women benefit as much from luck as skill. Maybe more. And every one of them has an Oscar buried in his or her backyard somewhere, too. Life is random. We tell ourselves that we are strong or brave or smart or good-looking, but really, it's just like all the other lies we tell ourselves. We see what we want to see, and ignore what we want to ignore. And for the life of me, I don't know why. But that's how people are.

Don Pablo should have been on his back in bed for at least two weeks, but the next morning he chafed at the window as though he were in prison. He rested much of the afternoon, but in three days he was up and pacing the floor. Neither the doctor nor the nurse nor his girlfriends could restrain him.

I left the house four times. Twice Don Pablo entrusted me with an envelope and I walked into Mexico to deliver a message. He whispered that I should be vigilant and I carried the revolver that I had taken from the dead driver.

Twice I went to the market for food and beer. The remainder of the time Don Pablo wanted me close by his side. At first I thought this was because I could speak English, but then I watched Don Pablo watching the men who watched over him. Don Pablo and I shared the same unuttered question: Who in the gang had betrayed us? Don Pablo had been ambushed sitting at his table. Don Ricardo had been shot outside his home. I had been kidnapped where I met with my boys. Who knew the hours of our coming and going? Don Pablo knew that I, for certain, had not betrayed him. He believed that my loyalty was such that I came to warn him. That was why he wanted me near. As for the rest— I also searched their faces and wondered which one of them had turned Judas.

The basic story was obvious, if not the details. Don Elias and the Sixteenth of September gang shot Don Ricardo and Don Pablo. There had been an argument among the *jefes* that Don Pablo had no right to El Paso, but it happened that way and Don Pablo saw no reason to relinquish his advantage. Don Ricardo backed him. Perhaps Don Elias thought that the other gangs would join with him, and they might have, had he killed Don Pablo and taken over in a single swift stroke. Who knows what backroom promises he made? You want the east side? West side? Downtown? Okay. You run the girls and I'll sell the liquor? Let's do it. But it hadn't happened that way, and now things got complicated. The bosses tested each other out circumspectly, diplomatically, cautiously. Deals were cheaper to make than bullets to buy or bodies to bury. Nobody wanted a long war.

The fighting in Mexico broke out again every few days for most of another week. Then one evening Don Pablo got up, changed into his suit, two cars arrived, and the whole gang piled in and drove away. A truce had been negotiated.

Don Pablo returned to his hotel. Repairs were made. The doors reopened. Liquor and girls returned, and soon after, the customers. If anything, the notoriety brought even more customers. And then one morning I woke to read in the *Times* that Don Elias had been shot dead. Nobody needed to explain that to me. I would have been more surprised if he had lived.

Act III Scene 3

Back then I used to say that for two weeks nobody in El Paso got their shoes shined. Actually, some of the boys worked, at least for a few days. I figured they would. How else would they eat? But with the truce, things returned to normal. My boys returned to work, though we met now in the evenings in a little courtyard behind a bar that Don Pablo acquired on Ochoa Street. They all paid me—even for the days they didn't see me. I wasn't going to ask, but I respected their loyalty.

A few days after I read about Don Elias, Don Pablo summoned me to his hotel. When I arrived, he pointed to his driver and said, "Go with him." We headed west, and then south, then west again, following an old road through a canyon between two mountains. I remembered the road and recognized—even in the dark—the ranch to which it led. By now the roof to the front room had completely caved in, but around the side of the house was a long, low wing of smaller rooms that was still okay. The driver led me to a side door where two of Don Pablo's men sat bored and bleary-eyed in steel folding chairs. They were drinking tequila from tin cups. They gestured with their thumbs that I should go inside. The room was dark and I had to light a kerosene lantern to see the small bundle wrapped and tied in a tarp in the corner. The bundle moved when I pulled on the rope. I heard a low moan. I knew right away who was inside the tarp, and why he was there. I took my knife and cut the ropes. I kicked the tarp until it unrolled. Filo lay on his back, hands and feet tied, lips bloody, face swollen, one eye blacked and shut. "Why?" I asked. He looked at me. There were no tears, no plea for sympathy, no sign of remorse. He never said a word. I guess I was supposed to know.

I once bought a box of breakfast cereal in my dreams and saw Filo on the front of the box. In my dream I complained to the clerk at the checkout that the box was wrong, that Filo could not possibly know how to pole vault. Sometimes I would turn a corner and see him for an instant in the face of a stranger. I used to catch glimpses of him as doors slid shut. For years Filo haunted me.

In my dreams, as in real life, Filo had the wet, bulging eyes of a Chihuahua. That night, though, in the pale yellow light of the lantern, I saw in Filo's one undamaged eye the flat, soulless stare of a crocodile. This was not the poor orphan boy on the bridge—the boy I slapped to instill obedience. This was an assassin who calculated, wagered, and lost. He was not large and he was not strong, but he was smart enough to know what he wanted, what tools he had to work with, and how to use them to his advantage. When Filo disappeared, it was because he went over to Don Elias. I can picture their conversation. A bar, a table, a man much like Don Pablo, a boy much like myself. It was Filo who told Don Elias what was happening in El Paso, and how much money could be made there. Filo told Don Elias where to find me, and when. Filo told Don Elias of Don Pablo's routines, and where Don Pablo would be on the night of the attack. Perhaps Don Ricardo, as well. Filo chose his path, and now he knew he would pay the price. Were I tied and on the floor, Filo, the gentle boy who wanted to save his crippled brother, would have shown me no mercy. I knew that, and he knew that, and he knew that I knew. He knew what the gang would do to me when they came to the blacksmith shop. He knew because it was his idea. *Before you kill him, cut off his balls.* That's what I saw in his eyes.

The understanding would come gradually to me. For some months after this I was wildly paranoid—frightened that some additional calamity would befall me. Yes, you say, Who wouldn't be paranoid after all that? But this was irrational fear. I saw enemies everywhere. No place was safe. I felt watched, followed, haunted. I carried my pistol all the time. I ate with it out on the table. When I washed, it was on the basin and within reach. I slept with it under my pillow.

Worse, for some time I felt that all of this chaos came to pass because I crossed a bridge to shine shoes in another country. It was my fault. But I ask you—does that make sense? Was there enough money in shoe shines and cigarettes and girly magazines to justify a gang war? Of course not. And as 1939 melted into 1940, and 1941, I began to see the big picture. The war that mattered was not fought on the streets of Juarez, but on the steppes of Poland; the lowlands of Belgium; the outskirts of Paris; in the skies over England; at the siege of Leningrad and the defense of Moscow; in the deep, cold waters of the Atlantic; and over the air waves of Mexico's border blaster radio stations.

Mexico wanted no part of that war. Let me rephrase that. Mexico wanted no part of the *shooting*. As for America, there were not enough trucks for all the goods moving across the bridge. At first America supplied England. Then she prepared her own invasions. America needed cattle for leather and meat. Coal, timber, and oil. Nitrates for explosives and gunpowder. Iron and copper. Chrome. Chickens. Cotton. Chocolate. Coffee. Buttons. Rope. Paper. Boxes. Horses. Zippers. Men themselves commodified. They entered the service. Their absence from the workplace opened up employment for women, Negroes, Mexicans. America became a giant vacuum consuming everything. This was what Don Elias saw coming. But Don Pablo had the toehold. He had boys on the ground including one who spoke English. And so long as Don Pablo paid his percentage to Don Ricardo, nothing was going to change. And for this, I almost died. And for a long time I thought it was my fault.

Act III Scene 4

The day that Don Pablo returned to Mexico I knew that I, also, had to move. I liked Winegardner, but I was afraid to ask him if he owned or knew of another house. I thought that maybe it would be best for everybody if I just disappeared. I looked in the newspaper. It took me less than a day to find another house in even worse condition. It was far to the west of town in what people call the upper valley, out near Canutillo. It had once been the home of a small-time pecan farmer who had sold his land to a larger pecan farmer who wanted the trees but had no use for the house. It stood at the end of a long dirt road in the middle of the orchard.

This orchard was owned by Mr. Perkins, a skinny, salty old man, and when he saw that I was Mexican he asked right away if I was interested in working for him—at least during the harvest, if not to help with pruning and irrigation and pesticide so forth. I told Mr. Perkins that I represented a printing press from Juarez, and that my job was to find customers for them in the USA. "A sales rep," he said. It took me a week to figure out what "rep" meant. I promised him free labels for his pecans, but Perkins said that he shipped in bulk in burlap sacks. Could I print on burlap? I said that I would find out, but I never did, and he never asked again.

The day that I rented the house from Perkins, I took the car—the same bullet-riddled and bloodstained car in which we carried Don Pablo from the alley behind his hotel—and I drove it around and around the cemetery until I was certain that I could make it across town. Then I loaded up everything it would carry and drove off, leaving the keys and a note for Winegardner on the kitchen counter.

I had a driver's license, but that was the first time I drove a car. Don Pablo did not take it. None of his men took it, and nobody thought to ask me about it. It was as easy to obtain a receipt for its purchase and a new title as it was to obtain the license which allowed me to drive it. I suppose it was stolen to begin with. Who knows? One thing for sure, Don Elias and his driver never asked about it.

Now I owned an automobile. In 1940 I bought a truck, as well. By 1945 I owned four trucks, two cars, and brand-new Indian motorcycle. But I'm getting ahead of myself.

I did not manage—could not have managed—all of Don Pablo's wartime interests. But we became much closer, and I helped him in as many ways as he asked and I could oblige. I read contracts and negotiated leases. If Don Pablo needed something bought in the USA, I bought it. If he needed something stolen, I did that, too, or saw to it. I carried bribes to public officials and directed workers for remodeling, for loading and unloading trucks, as warehouse workers, even some small assembly jobs. For every warehouse and loading dock and factory shop, there was its equivalent in titty bars and counterfeit whiskey and cigarettes and gambling and prostitutes and whatever. The soldiers needed boots and bread and beans and coffee, but they wanted girls and tequila and beer and cigarettes. And there were still monthly packages to Anderson—and these no longer fit in a shoeshine box. I did not carry anything over the bridge. My boys did, and I paid them well, as Don Pablo paid me. And by this time, Don Pablo was paying me *very* well. And Don Pablo grew fat, and I grew tall. You could say that I had it made. But that wasn't exactly true.

This prosperity did not bring me to a second episode of happiness. The urgency of my paranoia faded, but the knowledge that I could be killed—might even have enemies I did not know about—that knowledge could not be erased. I now wore a colt .45 of my own in a shoulder holster under a sports coat or jacket, and sometimes carried another tucked into the waistband of my jeans. There was always a round in the chamber. Always.

The only moments in which I forgot my fears were those alcohol-laced late night sessions with the girls from Don Pablo's bars. I could be tempted to call those moments happy, but distraction and loss of memory from exhaustion and alcohol are not the same thing as a pleasant state of existence. I could seek diversions, but I was not at peace. And then one night in the spring of 1942, as I wheeled a handcart of cases of tequila into one of Don Pablo's bars on Copia Street, I felt a soft hand on my shoulder.

It had been five years since I last saw Maria. She was no longer the lithe teenage girl who left me love struck. She was now much more of a woman, a little more filled out, a little wiser and more confident in the eye, her skin still soft but not possessing the softness of a girl. She wore makeup now, but she still had that dimple.

I was struck stone stupid. I had not thought of Maria in ages, but the instant I saw her face I was just as lovesick as ever. I was also, at the same instant, seized with a heart-stabbing fear. "What are you doing here?" I blurted. A stupid question if ever there was one. But when she looked at me and made no reply, I realized that I had addressed her in English. *"Qué, estás haciendo aquí?"* I repeated.

"Un poco de esto, un poco de aquello," she replied. A little of this, a little of that. A graceful deflection of the obvious.

I wished I hadn't asked. For a moment, I said nothing, I just drank her in—not just her beauty but her energy. Her intentions. But if there was anger, I could make out none of it. She seemed as innocent and out-of-place as a flower bursting through a crack in a highway. And probably just as doomed. The thought of asking her out on a date didn't occur to me.

I knew that the life of a prostitute was not good. The girls who worked for Don Pablo began much as mine had, as children, selling this and that, or cooking and cleaning, running errands for the older girls. When they began to bud breasts, they drifted, as Maria had, into working as waitresses or barmaids. There they would learn about men—the wandering hands, the lascivious stares, the crude jokes. And from the older girls upstairs they would hear stories. They would learn of the acts long before they performed them. They probably reacted (on the outside) with revulsion, or at least prudish disdain. But inside—who knows? What the young girls would hear from the older was the money they made, the good times they had, the interesting men, the exotic vacations. They would see the presents: jewelry, clothes, perfumes, knickknacks. They would hear the laughter.

I'm not saying that these positive-sounding things are genuine or good. They're not. Who wants to admit their failures, humiliation, weakness, fear, defeat, self-loathing, and shame? For every man who treated the girls well there must have been a dozen who treated them poorly. For every handsome and interesting man there were a dozen drunken, rutting pigs. But no one talks about those things. People see what they want to see and ignore the rest. Perhaps the older girls brag to keep their sanity. I think now that the lies wither their features and corrupt their hearts. But the younger girls would hear enough of the gilded version to overcome their fear and revulsion. And they, too, were trying to survive. Maybe they thought, *just for a little while.* Who knows? Once they were in the game, there was no way out. I knew this even then.

And yet, Maria did not have the hard face, the cynical face, the desperate face, the thousand false faces that I watched the women paint on upstairs when I was just a boy who sometimes washed up in the dressing room they shared.

And while many of the girls pushed the limits of fashion by raising or slitting their hemlines to flash a little thigh, or cropping necklines to show off the tops of their breasts, or cinching their waists to agony with binding girdles, or displaying careless bits of lingerie or lace, Maria did none of these things, and needed none. She wore a simple, short-sleeved dress of dark blue rayon with a little pink trim on the shoulders and sleeves. The dress hugged her slim figure but, if anything, was long for the time, reaching down to caress the backs of her calves. If the neckline plunged a little it was in a careless way, it did not look contrived. It looked like a dress a new secretary might wear to work. A schoolteacher. A young mother. The little bit of breast-flesh exposed was all the more enticing for its innocence. She still had that innocence. Or, at least, I chose to see that and ignore the rest. But what I wanted more than anything in that moment was for her to stay just like that. I did not want to see her corrupted. I wanted Maria to be a decent woman. I remembered the passion I felt to protect her and to have a proper family.

Of course, I knew less-than-nothing of how to talk to decent women. "*Y cuando llegaste a El Paso,*" I asked. When did you come to El Paso?

"*Solamente unos días,*" she replied. Only a few days. When I stammered and could make no reply she continued, "*Le pregunté, acerca de usted.*" I asked about you. "*Escuché, que estabas todavía aquí.*" I heard you were still here.

Still here?

Maria turned and looked anxiously around the bar.

"Are you expecting someone?" I asked. I meant, Did she have a customer?

"No," she replied. "*Yo sólo no quiero meterme en problemas por hablar con usted.*" I only don't want to make trouble by talking to you. "*Te puedo cumplir en el momento del cierre.*" I can meet you at closing time. "*Si tu quieres,*" she added. If you want.

"Where do you stay," I asked.

"*No tengo lugar,*" she replied. I have no place. She glanced up the staircase that led to the rooms on the second floor, then looked back at me.

For a moment, I saw Filo's large brown eyes in hers. The resemblance was frightening. I looked around at the customers—soldiers, mostly, a few other men, travelers, perhaps. Nobody paid us any attention. I looked at the bartender, a heavyset man of nearly fifty. He had worked for Don Pablo for years. He was watching us. Perhaps he remembered rumors of our romance from years ago. Perhaps not. He might not recognize Maria as I had. Why would he? He had already put away the first cases I wheeled in. I looked at the back door, standing open, my truck idling in the alley. I wanted to tell Maria that I was busy, that I had to work early in the morning, that I had several hours of work still to do. I wanted to lie and say that I had a woman at home, a family, anything. It would be the smart thing to do. The safe thing. "Okay," I said. I finished my delivery and drove to the next one, cursing myself the whole way. But at two in the morning I was back. I had rented a hotel room, washed, and bought flowers and a bottle of wine.

Maria walked out at closing time with the last group of customers. One man in particular hung all over her. I did not have to hear to know he was trying to talk her into going home with him. For a moment my anger flared and my hand went to the pistol on the seat beside me. But Maria had already pushed the man away, was walking toward me, looking to see if I was in the truck. I slipped the pistol into the waistband of my jeans as she climbed in. She accepted the flowers with a simple "*Gracias*" and held them to her face and inhaled. "*Dónde encontrar estos?*" she asked. Where did you find these?

"I know this city now," I replied.

She did not sit close to me, did not kiss me. She sat straight up clasping her purse and the flowers on her lap like a lady. She did not ask where we were going. She did not even look left or right.

The hotel was not far. Ordinarily they would not have let a room to a Mexican but they knew me. Don Pablo and I had arranged for them not to ask questions if we steered customers their way, and I had arranged for some carpenters and laborers to make some repairs for them on the cheap. Even then, though, it was a small room on the second floor at the very end of a long hall and on the back side of the building.

In the room Maria set the flowers in a glass of water and said, "*Necessitos un momento.*" I'll need a moment. She went into the bathroom and I heard water running. I took off my clothes and stretched out on the bed. I hid the pistol under the mattress. I worried whether I should unload it, but with it under the mattress, what were the chances she would discover it? I listened to the water running and stared at the stains on the ceiling until she came out.

She wore a white towel wrapped tight and covering her breasts and her thighs. She turned off the lamp and the towel fell away. She slid under the sheets beside me. When we were done, I lay on my back and Maria nestled her head on my chest. "*Sola soñar con esto,*" she said." I used to dream about this.

"Me, too," I replied.

"Why didn't we?"

"I never knew you wanted to," I said. "And where would we have gone?"

"I would have gone anywhere with you," she replied.

I thought about this.

"*Siempre fuiste tan callado.*" You were always so quiet. "Is that why they called you '*Señor Hablador*' behind your back?"

"I suppose."

Maria ran her fingers through my hair and sighed. "*Fue muy fácil cuando éramos niños.*" It was so easy back when we were children.

I could not remember anything being easy when I was a child. Perhaps I was lucky that way. Now my life was better. I wondered how it was different to start off well and then watch things fall apart. Maybe it's harder to take like that. Maybe we lose the optimism that comes with a good start in childhood. Maybe we lose our flexibility. Maybe we just give up. Maria relaxed and sank deeper onto my body. If life starts out bad, but then it gets better, maybe it is easier. Maybe we appreciate what have a little more. I fell asleep thinking about this.

I saw Maria every night for the next two weeks. Sometimes we went late for dinner—all night cafes, truck stops. Once to a *taqueria* that was open all night across the street from the bus station. Sometimes we just went to the hotel. The second night Maria had a bottle of wine for me, and every night thereafter she brought beer or wine, a little food, a trinket, a gift. A piece of cake. A pair of new ray-ban aviator sunglasses. Some pilot must have lost the sunglasses in the bar. Two weeks later I took her out of the bar and moved her into my house. A month after that, we were married.

When I drove Maria to the house, she sat as she always sat, straight up, looking like a lady beside me in the car. She didn't ask where we were going and I didn't say. When we walked inside, she looked around and sniffed, ran her finger delicately along the kitchen counter and looked at the dust accumulated there. "*Necesitamos cortinas*," she said. We need curtains.

We. I think it was the most beautiful word I have ever heard. Outside there was nothing but orchard and darkness. "Why?" I asked.

"Because if we have a house I want it to be a proper home," she replied. And a proper home we had. Sort of. For a little while.

Act III Scene 5

Once, a few years ago, when my wife and I were on vacation in Hong Kong, we went to a beach that was famous for its strong current. We saw a man swimming there. He was swimming forward but moving backwards. It was a thought-provoking moment. The man left from a point on the beach and swam steadily as the current carried him half a mile downstream until he turned and swam to shore. Later that morning we saw him again in line at Starbucks. I recognized him right away—an older man, lean, his head shaved, his arms sinewy. I asked him, "Why do you swim against the current?" He replied, "You should see me when I swim and there is no current." Much of my life has felt like that.

Curtains and coffee cups, a colander to wash vegetables and drain pasta. Silverware and bed sheets. Lamps. A coffee pot. A stainless steel toaster. Spatulas and bread knives. A welcome mat. A crucifix on the wall flanked by small framed portraits of Saint Nicholas and Saint Teresa of Avila. There were brushes for scrubbing in the tub, and a separate brush to scrub the tub. There was a closet now, bought new, with women's clothes all on hangars. A chest of drawers for my things. Things. Plural.

In short order there was a garden in the yard and flowers in pots by the front door. A clothes line sprang between two trees. And every single thing that Maria placed so perfectly in the house added to my anxiety.

All my life, I'd had nothing. What had I possessed that was worth worrying about? A shoeshine box? A marble? A switchblade? A copy of

Catechism for Youth? A pistol? Now I had everything I could imagine. Now, I had something to lose. And having lost Maria before, the terror of losing her again grew from nothing, appeared like morning frost in my heart, and the pain and the fear were killing me. I suggested we move into the city where Maria would at least have neighbors to watch after her while I was away.

Maria wouldn't hear of it. *"No recuerdas la casa donde viví cuando me conociste?"* she said. Don't you remember the house where I lived when you met me? *"El silencio es el paraiso."* Silence is heaven. It would be an appropriate epithet for our relationship. In time it would be destroyed by the things we said. Where were you last night? Why do you drink so much? Where does all the money go? Why do I smell perfume in the truck? Whose button is this? But what stands out in my memory now, all these years later, is not what was shouted in the angry hours of the early morning, but what was never said at all.

Only once in five years did Maria mention Filo. So far as I know, Maria's knowledge of Filo ended when he was grabbed from the sidewalk, forced into a black car, and driven away. There were rumors, of course, that Don Pablo kidnapped Filo. There were even rumors that I killed him. No witnesses, only gossip. If Maria had heard, she never said so to me. Twice a year, on what had been Filo's birthday, and about the anniversary of his disappearance, Maria put on a black dress and went to church. But late at night, on the good nights, in the candlelight in our room, when I looked into her eyes, I saw the resemblance. The eyes of the boy I murdered stared back at me in what should have been the most tender moments of the night. Death and sex do not belong in the same bed, and I could not purge the vision with drink nor scrub it away with soap or time. There was no amount of love and no accumulation of things that could soothe my pain, for everything that Maria did only reminded me of what I had done.

Did I say rumors that I killed him? There was nobody in that room that night but Filo and me. There were two men at the door. I never saw either of them before and never saw either of them again. Nobody saw me do anything. Alone I wrapped his body in the tarp and alone dragged him far into the desert that night. Alone I dug his grave, scraping away the dirt and rock with my bare hands. I returned alone. I never said a word to anyone, and there is nobody on the planet can say that they saw. And if my reputation as a killer was made among Don Pablo's men, if it was said that I killed the man who was going to kill me in the old blacksmith's shop, that I stabbed Don Elias' driver and rushed the back door of the hotel, pistol blazing, to rescue Don Pablo, if it was said that I still crept at night with my knife and my pistol, a hired assassin to do Don Pablo's bidding, if this was whispered, the truth is that the only life I took was Filo's on that black night alone in a room on an abandoned ranch in the mountains west of Juarez. Nobody saw me stab Filo again and again, making hamburger of his heart, long after the gasp of pain had frozen in his throat. I don't know what made me angrier: that Filo tried to have me killed, or that I was forced to kill him.

Everything I wanted had arrived—the girl I adored, the home I craved, prosperity, respect, all of it—but in the moment this was given to me it was simultaneously taken away. I cannot describe the pain I felt when I made love to Maria. When I looked into her eyes, all this rushed back at me. And the better that Maria treated me, the more that Filo haunted my dreams, the more that I drank, the worse I treated her in return, and the more that I stayed away.

The one time that we spoke of Filo, Maria asked, "*Has mirado por mi cuando me fui?*" Did you look for me when I went away?

"Look for you? How could I? I was only a boy."

"I thought of you often. I hoped that you would."

We were standing in the kitchen. It was spring, 1947. I had been out all night and Maria, in a rage, had broken every dish in the house and some of the windows. Now the storm had passed and we were sweeping up the broken glass.

"Where did you go?" I asked.

"My auntie was dying and there was nobody to take care of her. Filo insisted that I go. He said he was getting a better job."

"A better job?" I asked. I wondered if he meant Don Elias. I wondered how much Filo had planned by then, and how much Maria knew.

"Perhaps he knew there was going to be trouble. Perhaps that was his way of protecting me."

I thought about this. If this had been Filo's plan, then perhaps he had plotted for his sister's safety, as well. "You have another brother," I said. "How is he?"

Maria looked at me. "Another brother?"

"A smaller brother. A cripple. Filo told the priest about him."

"We had no brother. There were only the two of us. And my auntie died. And Filo died. And now there is only me, and all that I have is you. And I'm not even sure of that anymore."

I could never have left Maria, no matter how often I strayed nor how much I wanted to run, no matter how severe the recriminations for my behavior. I wish I could say it was love that bound us. People say that love is the strongest thing in the universe. But guilt and shame are powerful, too. If love has its rival, its opposite, its Achilles heel, then these negative emotions are love's undoing.

However, I told you that something happened to me, something so extraordinary that I am sure you will not believe me. In the early summer of 1947 this thing happened that changed my life forever, and in this, Maria and I parted for the last time.

Act III Scene 6

Don Pablo summoned me to the bar on a windy night in March of 1947. I had already seen to Anderson's monthly delivery. I was expecting to be told to oversee another, or that the deliveries would now be made more frequently. I was in an especially good mood when I arrived. I was in heat over one of the new bar girls. I ordered beer and tequila and sat at the bar while Don Pablo sat at the table with another of his associates, Nixon, an American, one of the ones he had incorporated into the gang after he expanded into El Paso during the war years.

The bar girl I was in heat over was named— don't laugh—Lucy. Really. She was tall and big-breasted, with wide hips and a great ass. She wore a tight, green wool sweater with a neckline that dived almost to her belly button, a black dress that hugged her skin tight. She gave me a lime with my tequila and rolled her tongue at me before she walked away. Lick me.

Nixon had been in the Army during the war. Something called the Quartermaster Corps. Supplies. Sometimes we sold stuff to him. Sometimes he sold stuff to us. He was one of our guys at Fort Bliss. And he had hooked up—or we had hooked him up—with one of the strippers who danced in a club out Chelsea Street near the base. Now they were married and Nixon retired from the army. But he made a little extra income, as Maria would say, doing "this and that." I never liked him. I never disliked him, either, but I was not going to get close enough to him to find out. He struck me as a weasel. He played both sides of the deck, and people like that can't be trusted. He was useful when the war was on and he was a big-shot at Fort Bliss. Now? I wished he'd retired to California or somewhere. Don Pablo motioned that I should join them.

Odd, but it was nice to see Don Pablo again in Juarez. How many years had we met at that table? Almost eighteen? How time flies. But looking at him that night, I was aware of the passing of time. Don Pablo's hair and moustache were streaked with gray. He flashed four gold teeth when he smiled. The skin around the eyes crinkled like old leather, and the thunder was gone from his voice. Don Pablo kept a steady woman now, Angelina. A slightly older version of Lucy. Rumor had it he was faithful to her. Either that, or impotent. Being shot had aged him. But being the *jefe* of *jefes* had changed him, too. He was quieter, now. He seemed more sure of himself.

When I sat down Don Pablo gestured to Nixon and said, "*Dile.*" Tell him.

This, Nixon, he was a tall man, maybe fifty, almost bald with just a thin bush of gray hair up around his ears. He had a narrow face like a meat cleaver and close-set eyes, a hawk's nose, a tight and thin-lipped mouth of crooked teeth. He was the only soldier I knew who walked bent like a spoon. Most of them walked straight as a fence post, but this guy was a hunchback. And he rubbed his hands together when he talked. But he spoke good Spanish.

"So there's this guy," Nixon said, "Varney Hall. He used to do some work for me around the base. He's a medic. An x-ray tech. After the war he re-upped and they shipped him up to Roswell. So he came down few months ago and asked me for some things." Nixon shot a glance at Don Pablo. Don Pablo shrugged. Nixon continued, "The guys get bored up there, you know. It's hard passing time in the middle of nowhere. So I set him up with a little reefer. Some magazines. Some movies. Guy stuff. And he makes a few trips up and down, and then he asks me for credit."

Don Pablo winced and I knew right away what the problem was. "So he won't pay you," I said.

"So he don't pay me."

"How much does he owe?"

"Maybe a grand."

"Maybe?"

"Maybe a little more, it don't matter."

I looked at Don Pablo. He was fooling with a cigar. He didn't look like he was even listening. "So what do you want with me?" I asked.

Nixon licked his lips and rubbed his hands together. He leaned over the table waiting for Don Pablo.

"*Dile*," Don Pablo said. He made a pushing gesture with the back of his hand like *go on* or *go away*.

Nixon lowered his voice. "I just want to find out where he lives. I know where he works—at the clinic on the base. But I don't know where he *stays*." He fumbled in his jeans pocket and produced a sheet of paper. He thrust it across the table to me. A map of the base. "Here's the clinic," he said, stabbing the paper with his finger. "It's in front of this parts warehouse. You can't miss it. And here's his office. It's on the ground floor. He drives a red-and-black Chevy hot rod. A truck. You'll spot it easy enough. Only one like it. Got an oversized chrome grill and painted yellow fire coming out from under the hood. You can hear it a mile away. Follow him. Get me an address so I can pay him a visit."

I looked at Don Pablo and he nodded.

"So why don't you go?" I asked. "What's the deal? You can't spot him?"

"Too many people know me. Hell, they *all* know me. Half that crew used to work for me. I can't be seen around there. And I don't want Varney to know that I know where he lives."

"What do you pay me?"

"Fifty bucks?"

I laughed. "Fifty bucks to help you catch a thousand? I make fifty bucks before I eat breakfast. And this is a day up and a day back, any way you scratch it. I don't think so. I got better things to do." I stood up so fast I almost knocked my chair over.

"Seventy-five?"

"Look," I said. I leaned over the table close to Nixon. "I don't know what you're after, but you don't need me to spot this guy. Send your own loser and leave me out of it." The word I used for loser was *pendejo*.

"You don't get it," Nixon said. "You know how this is likely to end. For now, I just want to find him, see if I can right the ship before things get that bad. But if I can't get my money, I can't have nothing to do with this. I can't be seen. I gotta be airtight. All I want is an address, but I can't go snooping around. I need somebody outside of my guys, you know what I mean?"

I picked up a toothpick and set to work on my teeth with it. After a minute I said, "Five hundred."

Act III Scene 7

I told you I had this Indian motorcycle. They don't make them anymore. Well, they *do* make them, but not like the originals. I loved that bike. There's nothing like laying out on the road with the sun on your back and the wind in your hair, and you open it up and hit the curves and for a while, you and the bike and the world are just one sweet, easy thing: one sound, one motion, and nothing else matters. It feels like there isn't even a thing called time. I miss riding.

Roswell is north and east of El Paso. There were two ways to get there, both about two hundred miles. The easy way is east first, then north, through Carlsbad, where the big cave is, the one with all the bats. The other way—the pretty way—is a little longer, but not much. You go west first, over to Las Cruces, then north, through the mountains to Ruidoso, then east. I went the pretty way.

There were no interstates in those days, so it was slower travel than today. But that day the traffic was light and the road fine. I remember thinking how good it felt just to be alive, how nice it was to break my routine. I was thinking, too, how different things were from when I was boy walking that long, dusty road from central Mexico. Now I was on the road and the weather was good and I had this fine bike roaring under me.

I got to Roswell and checked out the base. It was south of town. Not much going on. Main Street ran right down to the main gate. I thought about going in but instead I hung out in a bar up the road where I could watch the gate. Sure enough, the Chevy came by a little after five. I followed Hall into town but he didn't go home, he went to a bar for a couple of hours, and then another, and then another, and it was almost 1:00 A.M. when he left that one, and he had a woman with him. They drove to what might or might not be his house. You know how that is. They left the truck in the drive and went inside. The lights came on. The lights went off. I said fuck it and left.

I camped out on the highway outside of town that night. I was cranky. It was nice to camp out, but I wanted to settle things and go home. I got up at dawn, went back to the house. The truck was still there. Around 6:45 Hall came out and drove away. I followed him to the base. I wanted to go back to El Paso, but something said I better stick around for another day just to make sure. If I do a job, I do it right. Maybe it was his house. Maybe it was hers. Who knows?

That evening I followed Hall around until almost 1:00 A.M. again. He went to same bars and came out late with the same woman. They went back to the same house. I figured that was good enough and I rode all night, this time the easy way, rolling through the badlands down to Carlsbad and onto El Paso.

I got some sleep, and the next evening I went to see Don Pablo. I wasn't in a good mood. Maria gave me a hard time about being gone so long and didn't want to hear about me following some guy around in Roswell. She didn't believe a word of it. I hadn't slept well and the five hundred bucks, which was damn good money in those days, was now pretty much divided by three and wasn't such good money. I had other stuff to do and I didn't want anything to do with Nixon or his problems. I knew I shouldn't have got involved, but then, when you work for Don Pablo, sometimes things work out like that. You do what you gotta do. I gave Don Pablo the address and he gave me the money. I went home and that was that. Except that it wasn't.

A couple of days later Don Pablo sent for me. "That's not the house," he said.

"What do you mean it's not the house?" I replied.

"He doesn't live there. Somebody went looking for him and it's not his place."

"Whose place is it?"

"How the hell should I know?" Don Pablo snapped. "Some woman. She claims she doesn't know him. That's not his house."

"I followed him two nights," I said. "What do you want? I should ask for his rent receipts?"

"I don't know," Don Pablo said. He was pissed off, too. "Go back and ask around. Do something. Find out where he lives so I can put this shit to rest."

This time I rode up Friday and, sure enough, when I followed Hall around, he came out with a different woman and spent the night in a different house. Fucking two-timer. And I followed him Saturday, and then Sunday. Hell, every night he went home with a different chick. He was okay looking, but he wasn't *that* good looking. I wondered what the fuck was his deal?

I didn't know much about cocaine back then. I'd seen it around. It might even have been what I was carrying across to Anderson. I was never so rich or so important that I could afford it or somebody might give me some. I think, now, that's what this guy's deal was. I think he was pushing coke. Probably Nixon, too. But nobody was going to tell me that. *This and that* my

93

ass.

By then people were starting to notice me. I mean, how many Mexicans are there riding around Roswell on a new Indian? And if this guy was dealing dope, I didn't want to be seen asking questions. Somebody might think I was a cop, and that was the worst thing that could happen. But then it hit me. *The fucker didn't have a place of his own.* He lived on the base. He was just off tomcatting around all the time, that's all. I wondered if Nixon didn't know that. He had to know! So what was the deal? Something didn't smell right. Maybe he knew it was like impossible to kill somebody on an army base. Maybe he just wanted to know where this guy hung out. But even then, couldn't he have just followed him and killed him somewhere? I thought about this for a while and it hit me. *He wants to know where this fucker keeps his stash.* And that opened up a whole bunch more questions. Like, for instance, where was Hall getting that stash? Like, was he two-timing Nixon and buying from somebody else? All of sudden, this easy money was a can of worms.

So I went back and told Don Pablo that this Hall guy slept on the base and Nixon knew it, that Nixon was fucking with us all. I told him what I thought about the stash and I gave him a half-dozen addresses where Hall had stayed. "This is not my fucking problem," I said. "And if Nixon wants his fucking money back, give it to him."

I went home and tried to make it up to Maria, who was sure that I had set up another woman somewhere. I had. Lucy. But she wasn't in Roswell. I told Maria I was doing some work out-of-town for Don Pablo and still she didn't believe me. I promised that the job was done and it would not happen again. Except that the job wasn't done and it happened again.

Don Pablo called me right before the Fourth of July. The Fourth of July is the American version of the Sixteenth of September, except that Americans don't drink as much or play as much music. But they still like the holiday, and the weather is fine for picnics and parades.

I knew as soon as Don Pablo called that I was going back to Roswell and that I was going to be told to kill this guy. By this time I was so mad that I didn't care—it was worth killing the son-of-a-bitch just to be done with it. Don Pablo was mad, too. He called me straight to his table, dismissing a man I knew to be a Juarez banker just so he could talk to me. And then he ordered a bottle of *Camarena* and we went upstairs to his room.

The décor was still red but the couch was different. His woman was there, but she left the room so we could talk. Don Pablo lit a cigar and poured shots of tequila.

"I know," I said.

"You know what?"

"What you want."

Don Pablo leaned forward on the couch. "How long have you worked for me, my suddenly knowledgeable one? How many years?"

"Seventeen? Eighteen?"

"This is not for Nixon, Pablo. This is for me. For us. I need someone I can trust to do this. The money is not important," he said. "Haven't I always taken care of you? We'll deal with Nixon later. Right now, I need you to drive up to Roswell and take care of this shit up there." He poured another shot. "First you pluck the weed," he said, "and then you dig the roots. You understand?"

I looked at him. I did not understand. And then I did.

"This just became a problem for all of us," Don Pablo said. *Todos nosotros.* He emphasized the word all. He said, "If this guy goes to the cops, we're fucked. We're fucked in El Paso and we're fucked here. This is army stuff and they got *Federales* in America, too, and I don't want no trouble with them. So I need somebody I can trust to take care of this. And I don't need anybody else involved."

"I'll take care of it," I said.

"I can rely on you?"

"Always, Don Pablo." I stood up and Don Pablo grabbed my arm.

"This has to be done with the utmost delicacy," he said. "And finality." The words he used were *fragilidad* and *finalidad*. He meant that the situation was breakable and should be handled as such. *Finalidad* needs no translation. "This is why I need you to do this," he said. "You're smart, Pablito. You have learned much. I cannot send one of my butchers. This is an American problem on an army base. You speak good English. You know these people. I can't trust my boys from this side of the river."

I don't think I knew as much as Don Pablo gave me credit for but I said, "Okay, Don Pablo. It's done."

"And you have a good pistol?"

"Of course, Don Pablo."

"Be careful," he said. He raised his shot glass to me and drank the tequila down.

Act III Scene 8

It was Midsummer Texas desert hot that weekend. A hundred. A hundred-and-one. I rode up to Roswell July 3rd because I figured it would be impossible to find Hall on the holiday. It's too big a deal. I figured I'd follow him as before, and sometime late in the night, when he drove from one bar to another, or from the bar to his woman's house, I'd pull alongside his car and put a bullet in his head. People would mistake the sound for fireworks. It was the best time of the year to kill somebody. I waited at the bar where I could watch the street.

I was reading that night—if you can believe this—*Crime and Punishment*. I grabbed the book from the library the day before. Raskolnikov was concerned about finding blood on his clothes. I took his paranoia for a warning. You can learn a lot reading books.

But Hall never left the base that night. Or if he left, it was early—before I got there. By 7:00 P.M. I gave up and racked my brain to remember the bars where he hung out. I searched them one after the other and found nothing. I tried other bars, just to see if I could get lucky. Roswell wasn't that big. I didn't see him anywhere. I drove past the houses where his girlfriends lived, but the truck was not there. Had he found another ride? Was he gone for the holiday? Was he in some sort of trouble on the base? Who knew? I was mad.

I slept out in the desert that night, angry that this stranger could come into my life and cause me so much trouble. And for what? For nothing. I'd never met him, hadn't spoken a word to him. He hadn't worked for me, stolen from me, lied to me, slept with my woman, done me any wrong that I should want to kill him. There might be a dozen men who had good reason to kill him, but not me. He'd threatened my job. There was that. Why should he rat me out to the cops? At least, I thought, nobody will suspect me. I suppose some good comes of everything. Some years later, when I read Camus, I was thinking how weird it was that somebody would kill a stranger. But there I was, in Roswell, about to do just that. At least this guy was in a line of work where that kind of thing happened. He should have known what was coming. You fuck around, you get fucked around. What was it Father Sheehy said? Those who live by the sword?

I lay on my back and looked up at the stars. Overhead, a streak of light. I remembered watching the meteor shower—the Perseids—in the Chihuahua desert so long ago. Every August I would look for the shooting stars and remember the loneliness, the desolation I felt at night in those months on the highway. Did I know then that I was going to be all right? Was God, as the old priest said, really looking after me? And now for some reason, just the opposite seemed to be true. Now I was all right, should have felt all right, but I was being slowly consumed by the fear that I wasn't. I wasn't being looked after. I kept telling myself that I *had* to be all right. What could go wrong?

I made a small fire and from time to time, as it died, it would hiss and pop and shoot little stars of its own toward the sky. The smell of the wood smoke was comforting and I remembered, for some reason, the smell of my mother's tiny kitchen. I remembered playing games with my brother, Marco, and how we would hang around outside our shack, hungry, smelling the cooking and the smoke from my mother's stove. And once in a while, when it was summer and the weather was fine, me and Marco would hide outside and we wouldn't answer our mother's call. We'd sleep out in the bean fields so we wouldn't have to sleep in that galvanized box. I hadn't thought about that box in a long time, and the memory of it made my blood run cold. An odd thing to remember.

I thought about Maria and knew she would be angry that I was gone again. I thought about Lucy and how easy it was to take her to bed, how large and firm her breasts were, how warm and wet she was, how little she asked of me. I thought about the difference between them. Lucy knew what she wanted. A house. And she had that. She'd have been happy with that from anybody. I was just convenient to her, as she made herself convenient to me.

Maria knew what she wanted, too. She wanted *me*. She didn't give a damn about the house. Yeah, she liked it, but she wouldn't have lived in it with anybody else. And that made my absence more painful. The problem was, I knew that she could never have me, even though there was nothing that I would have so gladly given her. If only I could. And what stood between us was what Dostoevsky had called a "desperate deed."

And here I was, desperate to commit another. How did I get myself into this? One day I was a little boy walking the streets and eating garbage, and a few years later I'm carrying a .45 and looking to kill a stranger. Yet it happened so easily that, for a moment, it almost made sense. And then it didn't.

I looked for Hall on July 4th and didn't find him. I took a room in a shitty little hotel downtown. The kind of place that didn't ask questions. The kind of place that would rent a room to a Mexican on a motorcycle who arrived with no bags. I needed a bath. I was tired of sleeping on the stones. I had to buy a change of clothes. They gave me the last room down the hall. It looked out over the alley in back. Some things never change.

I looked Saturday and Sunday, too. I thought about giving up but I dared not return to Don Pablo without accomplishing this thing I was sent to do. By Sunday I had reached the boiling point. I was desperate. I had to do something. I sat in a bar drinking until I conceived a new plan. It wasn't much, but what do you expect when you've been drinking all day?

There was a dry-cleaning shop across the alley behind the hotel. I could look down from my room and see the back door. The shop was closed for the holiday, and there wasn't much going on in the alley. I thought, *They have to have a uniform in there.* I jimmied the door without breaking the lock. There were all kinds of clothes waiting for pickup. The laundry wrapped them in butcher paper and tied them with string. Each parcel had a little pink receipt taped to the top with a name and address and a pick-up date. I looked all through the stack. Nothing looked like army stuff. I tore a corner on a dozen packages and looked inside. Regular clothes.

But then I saw, in the corner, a rolling canvas cart stacked full of packages. I had seen carts like that before at Fort Bliss. I tried one and right away found a uniform. I held the shirt to my chest but it was too big. I tried another too small. The third packet I opened was just my size. But then I saw, hanging on a hangar from a hook on the wall right fucking in front of me, one lonely something wrapped in paper. It looked special. I tore it open. A green dress uniform—shirt, pants, jacket, tie. All the ribbons and pins. Everything. And it fit. A little big, but not too bad. Best of all, it looked like an officer's uniform. There was even a name tag. *Campana*. Perfect! I cleaned up my mess and shut the door behind me.

In the hotel I tried the uniform on and admired myself in the mirror. The jacket and pants were green, the shirt and tie, tan. I didn't know anything about the uniform. There were some ribbons on the front and a pair of eagles on a strap on the shoulders. I thought it looked fine. Maybe nobody would ask my business. Monday morning I bought a pair of black shoes from a second-hand store. Wouldn't have looked good walking onto the base in cowboy boots.

I'd been on the army base at Fort Bliss lots of times. I'd seen soldiers around in the bars, heard their *lingo*. Still, when it came to it, I didn't know much about being a soldier. I knew how to salute. That was about it. But as I was only going to be on the base for a few minutes, I thought that would be enough. Still, I dared not pass through the main gate. There were too many things that could go wrong. Too many questions I might not know how to answer. And I had no ID. Just the name tag. There must have been a hundred things that could give me away. But I knew where I was going, and if I could just get on the base, and move fast, who would stop me?

Act III Scene 9

So Monday, July 7, 1947, I checked out of the hotel, tied my gear to the back of my bike, and rode out of town. I headed west out 380, but turned south and rolled through the ranch land west of the base, stopping at the dead end of a little farm lane out of sight from the perimeter. I ditched my bike in a dry arroyo. I waited in the shade until just past 4:00. Then, armed with my Colt .45 and a set of wire cutters, I walked to the fence, picked a spot where the wind had gathered a pile of tumbleweeds, and cut the chain links horizontally and low to the ground so that nobody would see right away. I looked left and right—made sure nobody had seen—and crawled through the cut. Once through I dusted off my uniform and carefully noted the surroundings. If I needed, I could find the place in a hurry. Using the little map Nixon gave me, I made my way across the base.

The clinic was open, and Hall's truck was right in front. That was good. But there were a lot of people inside. It was, after all, a clinic. I should have thought of that. The crowd was not good. But there was a door around the side of the building, and it was open. Good. I found an office that said x-ray. It was in the area that Nixon marked. I rattled the door, but it was locked. Bad. I tried another and it, also, was locked. There was one door standing open. I looked in. A soldier behind a desk stood to attention and snapped a salute. That was good. I returned his salute and hoped I got it right. "I'm looking for Hall," I said.

"Sergeant Hall is out, sir," the soldier replied. He looked at me funny, his eyebrows knitted.

"When will he be back?"

"I don't know sir." After a pause, he added, "Everybody's looking for him today, sir."

"And are they finding him?"

"I suppose so, sir."

"Then where are they finding him?"

"I don't know, sir. He left in a rush and didn't say where. Hasn't been back since. There's been all kinds of people in and out all day. It's crazy. Something's going on. Something big. I have no idea what. Sir."

"When did he leave?"

"This morning."

"That's his office, right?" I gestured with my thumb.

"Yes, sir."

"But you don't know where he went?"

"No sir."

"He's on base?"

The young man squinted at me. He was still standing. He rubbed one arm and then the other. "So far as I know, sir. Nobody said anything to me at all."

"And what do you do here?" I asked.

"Pharmacology, sir."

"I see. Thanks." I turned to go. Behind me, the soldier said, "You might try upstairs, Colonel sir."

"And what's upstairs?"

The young man's face flushed red. "I don't know, sir."

"Then why should I try upstairs?"

He stammered. "That's where everybody's been, sir. All day. I thought maybe that's where you were from, sir, or where you were headed."

"Of course," I said. "Upstairs."

The stairway was at the end of the hall. Two MP's blocked my way. They were big men, with helmets and pistols on their hips. Out of habit I looked at their boots. "Your shoes," I said. The men looked down. "Those are filthy. Do you shine shoes here?"

"Yes sir," the guards replied in unison.

"Take better care of those."

"We've been up since midnight, sir," one said.

"We never had the chance," the other added. "They got us out on the double, sir."

"Don't let it happen again," I said. "You should be ready for things like this."

"Yes sir." They looked at each other, then stepped aside and let me pass.

I was starting to like this army business. It was not so bad, I thought. At the top of the stairs was a long hall with a half-dozen doors on each side. I had no idea whether the place should have been full of doctors or totally deserted, or really, what went on there at all. It looked like there should be people but it was totally deserted. I mean completely empty. Too empty. Suddenly it felt wrong. It felt dead. This was a clinic. Shouldn't there be doctors and nurses and patients running around? The first soldier I talked to said something was up. The guards at the bottom of the stairs were jumpy. Something *was* up. It wasn't just me. Something was up and I would be the last person in the world to know what it was. Even the hall lights were out.

I walked to the end of the hall and turned right. More hall. More doors. The hall ended at another door where two big MPs stood. These were even bigger and more grim-faced than the first ones. They blocked the door and carried rifles. I approached. They did not salute and they did not stand aside.

"No admittance, sir," they said, in unison.

"I'm looking for Sergeant Hall."

"No admittance, sir," they replied.

"Is he here?"

The guards looked at each other.

"He is here," I said. "I was sent for him."

"Wait here," one said, and he went inside. The other glared at me.

"Been up all night?" I asked.

"No admittance, sir," he replied.

"I see."

A minute later the other guard came out. "Come with me," he said. I followed him two doors back down the hall and he took from his pocket a ring of keys. He tried several until he found one that opened the door. "Wait here," he said.

"How long?" I asked.

The guard shrugged. "Until they're finished, sir."

"And how long will that be?"

"I don't know, sir. Soon, I hope. Sir."

"Tired?"

"Yes, sir."

Believe it or not, I had *never been in a doctor's office before.* Not once. Not even after I'd had my skull fractured. But I'd seen enough in magazines and movies to know that this was some kind of examination room. There was a bed in the middle with a big lamp hanging over it. Along one wall was a counter with a cabinet and a sink and a number of jars of medical supplies. Cotton balls.

Alcohol. Iodine. Thin, flat strips of wood. A thermometer. Some other things I had no idea what to call. On the opposite side of the room was another counter and cabinet, but these were bare. There was a flat scale on the floor beside a gray steel desk with a plain gray metal chair. A pen. A pad of paper.

When the guard left, I opened some of the drawers and found, and examined, a variety of gleaming silver instruments whose purpose I could not begin to make out. The only one I could recognize for sure was a knife, but it was not like any knife I'd seen before. The handle was silver and round and about six inches long, and machined with a diamond pattern (to take a firm grip, I supposed). The blade itself was very short and thin, perhaps only an inch long, and very, very sharp. I wanted to put the knife in my pocket but there was no sheath for it. I thought it might make Don Pablo a fine gift, and I settled for wrapping it in a small white cotton towel and stuffing it into the inside pocket of my jacket. And then, standing alone in this room, I became aware of a sound, barely audible. It was like a deep, slow melodious groan. I could as much *feel* the sound as hear it. It came through the walls and the floor. I felt it in my hands and feet and hair. It sounded like it came from the adjoining room. I touched the wall and felt vibrations. The sound rolled endlessly, like music, like water, with some notes that I heard repeated, but in no pattern that I could make out.

Years later I heard, on television, whales singing underwater, and the sound would raise me from my chair, stunned to silence, and bring tears to my eyes, standing with my arms limp by my side in my brother-in-law's house. It was just like that.

I listened to the sound, and though they had no rational translation into words, what I felt was utter despair. I panicked. What was I thinking? Coming to an army base to kill a soldier? What if I got caught? Would they shoot me for a spy? What would I say? What defense could I offer for being here? I thought: *I should leave.* I felt like Rascal, standing in the police station and hearing about the murder he committed but for which he was not yet a suspect. I had to get away *right now*. How many people had seen me? How long would it take a clever police officer to associate my face with the man at the bar, the man on the motorcycle, the room in the hotel, a uniform that was bound to turn up as stolen and not mislaid? *Shit*, I thought.

Don Pablo said this was *delicate*. He sent me because he said I was smart, but I had the feeling that I was into something over my head, and whatever was up with this Hall person, I needed to clear out and let somebody else take care of it—or, at least, come back another day, find another place. Something. I couldn't kill this guy here, not in a clinic, not on an army base, not with guards outside the door and guards at the bottom of the stairs and patients in the lobby and soldiers all over. What was I thinking?

On the other hand, I had already seen Don Pablo angry. I knew how he felt about loyalty and following instructions, and what the price could be for disobedience. What would Don Pablo say if I came back with my assignment incomplete? What would he do then?

My heart beat like cannon fire and the strange music from the next room drummed in my ears. The sound was urgent and I turned to the wall, but there was no door connecting the rooms, no way out but the door to the hall, and there were guards outside watching, guards with rifles, and evidently all of these rooms were locked, or so I presumed. Maybe even the room I was in. Even the window was locked but this was a clinic, not a prison. It was easy to unlock a window, and if I was going to escape it would be through the window, and I unfastened the latch and slid it open, and it and was bright outside, summertime, late afternoon, and locusts droned, and birds chirped, but this was the back side of the clinic, and there was nothing but a warehouse next to it, and another warehouse behind it, and there was nobody walking between the buildings, nobody looking. And I looked out the window and the glass throbbed to this strange music, the panes rattled faintly in the frame, I could feel it in my fingernails. Even my teeth picked up the vibrations.

What the hell is going on here? I wondered. I looked out the window and I could maybe jump without alerting anyone or injuring myself, but running down the outside wall between the window from this room and the window to the next room, the room from which this strange music throbbed, was a pipe—a drain pipe, perhaps, or a water main. I don't know. It was painted dark green. But the pipe ran from the roof down and it was bolted to the outside wall and if I could reach it from my window I wouldn't have to jump, and climbing was safer than jumping.

I opened the window and reached out. I could reach the pipe, all right. Climbing out to it was scary, but not so scary as waiting around wondering whether I could kill Hall and get away with it, and wondering what was that strange music. I jerked on the pipe and it was solid to the wall. I climbed out, latched onto it, hung there for just a moment, making certain it was secure. I started to shimmy down but my coat caught up on a bolt in the bracket that fastened the pipe to the wall. The fabric ripped and I was—quite stupidly—angry that I had torn this nice jacket, but also instantly alarmed that I would be stuck hanging from the pipe on the second floor, and somebody was bound to come along and see me. Worse, the window back to the room from which I had just climbed slid shut. Damn. I held onto the pipe with one hand and with the other clawed at my jacket. I hefted myself up a foot or so and the jacket came free. I looked at the window from which I had climbed and then I looked at the window to the room next door.

I wanted to slide down the pipe. I know it sounds crazy, but I couldn't. More than I wanted to get away, more than anything, I wanted to know what was making that unearthly noise from the next room. It was right there. I leaned over to the window and I could see a little bit. There was a wall with a cabinet like the room from which I had just climbed, and I could see the same kind of light hanging down in the middle of the room, but that was all I could see.

I reached out and touched the window, tried to open it, but it was locked. I looked at it. The building was old and the wood shrunk from the sun and the dry desert wind. It reminded me of every abandoned shack and barn and shop that I had ever broken into, and I wondered if I could push the window in enough to free the latch. I could. I could even lift the window a few inches, but when I let go, the window slid shut.

I clung to the pipe and looked at the window. I wanted to go, knew I should go, but the boy in me was caught. I wanted to know, *What is making that sound?* If I could get in, it would only take a second to find out. And who knew what I might find? That in itself might prove useful to me, to Don Pablo. I pushed open the window as far as I could with my right hand, and let go of the drain with my left. I stabbed at the window ledge with my free left hand and grasped it, fell from the drain pipe, the window dropping onto my arm, but I now dangled by my left hand from below the window, and that left hand was inside the room and holding on to the ledge, and it kept the window from shutting, and I pushed the window open with my free right hand and hoisted myself up. I got my head in the window. I wriggled my shoulders in, both arms, I scraped and dragged and shimmied and shook my chest, hips, butt, and then I dropped hands-first onto the floor and the window clunked shut behind me.

The noise in the room stopped. My heart practically stopped. I could feel the blood pulsing on the inside of my ears. I could not hear a sound. And then, from outside, a car horn. Reality. Okay. I was all right.

The room was exactly like the one from which I'd just escaped except that the bed had been shoved to one side and in the middle of the room sat a big, galvanized steel box. The box bore no markings. A handle on each end and a latch on the lid. The latch was padlocked.

I sprang to my feet and backed against the door to the hallway. I pulled the pistol from the holster inside my jacket and shut my eyes and prayed, fool that I was, that nobody outside had heard. I held my breath and counted to ten. No key turned in the lock. I went to the window and looked outside. Nothing stirred. I could see a sliver of the main road off to my left, and while I watched a truck backed into my field of view and a crew began unloading something onto the dock at the front of the warehouse. Nobody saw me.

I studied the box on the floor. I touched it and— thump—something tapped the lid from inside. I about jumped out of my skin. And then there was a scraping sound and someone—or some*thing*—rattled the lid. My lips trembled and my stomach churned. The lid rattled again and then a voice said, in clear, plain English, "Please don't kill me."

God help me, I thought. And I would have jumped out the window right then except that, of all the people in the world, I might be the only man on the planet who could not walk away from somebody locked alone and about to die in a galvanized steel box.

Act IV Scene 1

Imagine, for a moment, that one afternoon Jesus walked into your house. It doesn't matter whether you believe or don't believe, just ask yourself, for a moment, What would happen if? Or take your pick. Mohammed. Buddha. Brahma, Shiva, Vishnu. Moses. Abraham. Lau Tze. Gandhi. Tolstoy. Martin Luther, Martin Luther King. Brigham Young. Whoever founded the Parsis or the Sikhs or the Seventh Day Adventists. Whatever. Choose your prophet. Saint. Deliverer. Guide. He or she walked into your living room. How would you feel? How would you react? How might it change your life? Who could you tell? *Who would believe you?*

You might conclude, as I did, that nothing that happened in your life right up until that moment made any difference at all. It didn't matter who you were or what you had done—or not done. You were a millionaire. A beggar. A priest. A thief. A saint. A murderer. A president. A peasant. What difference would it make? None. The sum total of your life—nothing. All you believed: nothing. All you were taught: nothing. All you rejected: nothing. All the reality you created in your own mind: nothing. The world as you knew it ended. There are seven billion people on our planet, most of whom put faith in something, and most of those *somethings* began eons ago with people or events so lost in time as to be little better than fairy tales. I'm not saying that faith is bad. It isn't. But what would happen if one of those *somethings* happened to you? You can stand in the sanctuary of your choice for a thousand years and hear the stories, but when you stand face-to-face with reality, everything changes.

For the second time in my life, the world was a blank stare. To the best of my knowledge, nobody has invented a word for that kind of experience. The closest I can come is *alienated*. I don't expect you to believe a word of what I say. Sometimes—even now, I ask myself, Did this really happen? Am I crazy? Was this a hallucination? Am I schizophrenic? Did fear or pressure or guilt destroy my capacity to reason? I would settle for any of these. But what I know now is the scariest thing in the whole wide world. What I know is the truth. According to legend, all the world's troubles began when Pandora opened a box. Now it was my turn.

This box was padlocked, but it wasn't made to be secure. It was a tool box. The latch was fastened with screws. All I needed was a screwdriver. I didn't have one. But then I remembered the little knife in my coat pocket. I took it out and, working carefully, loosened the screws. The latch fell away. I opened it.

My first impression was that, inside the box, on his back, lay a boy no bigger than my brother. "Marco," I gasped, but it was not Marco. The being that rose from the box was like a boy: slender; with two long, skinny arms; each punctuated in a long, graceful hand; each hand bearing four long, thin, slightly flattened fingers. It stood on two thin legs. Peered at me with two large, dark, glistening eyes. The eyes were set horizontally like ours, and a few inches apart, but in a decidedly triangular face. The face itself was set in a large, somewhat diamond-shaped, head. The pupils were vertical, not round. The lids were almost transparent. The lips were thin, the mouth small and placed low on the face. The skin was smooth and hairless. And the being before me was bright neon green. He looked at me, blinked, and said, again, "Please don't kill me."

"I'm not here to kill you," I said. He pointed at the pistol in my hand and I hastily tucked it back into its holster. "I'm here to kill somebody else." I bit my tongue and wished I'd said that differently. "I'm not here to kill you."

He—it—for I did not yet know what this thing was, but I'll call him a *he*—he looked at me with an expression I took be bewilderment. He looked like I hadn't understood his question.

"I'm not going to kill you," I said again. "I'm looking for some fucker named Hall."

He cocked his head to one side. "Hall?"

"Hall."

"You want to kill Hall?"

"I want to kill Hall," I said, wishing I could think clearly enough to lie. I thought I should change the subject. "Why do they want to kill *you?*"

"It's a long story," he replied. "Why do you want to kill Hall?"

"It's a long story."

"I see," he said. "Are you sure you're not going to kill me?"

"Yes," I said. "I mean, I'm sure I'm not going to kill you. Why? Should I?"

"No!" he said. "Please don't kill me. You asked us to come so we came. We came to help. Now you want to kill us."

"I told you I don't want to kill anyone," I said.

"Except Hall," he corrected me.

"Except Hall. I'm supposed to kill him." We looked at each other. "What happened to you?" I asked.

"We came just like you asked and then you shot us down."

"I mean, your skin. What happened to it?"

"What do you mean?" He looked at his hands, then down at his feet, then back at me.

"You're green."

"We're green. Yes. That's our color. We're green."

"What are you?"

He paused, looking me up and down. "We're your guests. You asked us to come."

"I didn't ask anybody," I said.

"But you are with the government, correct? In the army?"

I shook my head.

He pointed a long, green finger at me. "But that's what people in your army wear."

I looked down, then up. I saw that I had torn a triangular flap loose in my jacket and touched it, out of habit, and said, "Shit. Look, I'm not in the army. I'm in disguise."

He seemed confused. "You're in the *skies*?"

Now I was confused. "*Disguise*," I said. "It means I don't want anybody to know who I am."

"Oh," he said. "Disguise. I misheard. Why don't you want anybody to know who you are?"

"So I can kill Hall. He's in the army and this is the only way I can get in here." But when the creature's eyes bulged I added, "But not you. I'm not here to kill you. I'm looking for Hall."

"Hall?"

"Yes. But you didn't answer my question."
"What question? I don't know what's going on. You asked us to come and now you want to kill us. Why?"

"I didn't ask you to come and I said I didn't want to kill you. And you still didn't answer my question. What are you?"

"We come from up there," he said. He pointed up.

"Up there?" I looked up. I don't know what I was expecting. A hole in the ceiling? "Up where?"

"Up there. In the skies. I'm from . . . we're from another . . . another place. We're not from your planet."

"From another planet?" I had read about the planets, but the only people from other planets I had read about were in comic books they called science fiction. I had read *War of the Worlds* and once heard it broadcast on the radio in Spanish. I thought about this. It's not every day you meet somebody from another planet. It's pretty unbelievable, though it helps if the person from another planet is green and climbs out of a box on a military base. But then I knew *he was lying to me.* "Hey, if you're from another planet, how come you speak English?"

"I speak many languages."

"Can you speak Spanish?"

"*Por supuesto*," he replied. Of course.

"Can you speak . . . Chinese?"

"*Shi*," he replied.

I supposed that meant yes.

"Please," he said, looking around, "if you're not going to kill me, help me escape."

"Fuck," I said, "they'll probably kill *me* too, if they catch me here."

"Then you *have* to help me."

"I don't have to do jack shit," I said. "What can I do to help you? I got problems of my own." I went to the window and the little green man climbed out of the box and followed me.

"Maybe I can help *you*," he said.

"To kill Hall?"

"I don't want to kill anybody. What's the matter with you people? What is it with your kind and killing each other? Don't you get that it's wrong? That's why we're here. We want to help you before you kill yourselves all off."

"What the fuck are you talking about?"

"I'm talking about wars, bombs, and disease. I'm talking about poverty and pollution. Your kind is killing yourselves off, and you don't even have sense enough to know?" He looked at me, and I looked back at him. "Maybe I should ask if *you* speak English," he said.

"I grew up speaking Spanish," I replied.

He looked at me like he was going to blow up. "*Eres estupido*?" he asked. Are you stupid?

"*No soy*," I replied.

"Then *ayudame*? Help me. Maybe I can help you, too."

"Why do they want to kill you?" I asked again. "You keep not answering my question."

"I don't know why. Killing seems to be your species' favorite pastime. You asked us to come, then you killed my brother." He stopped talking and seemed to shrink. He climbed back into the box and sat down, looked at his feet. "Whoever you are, you're my only hope. But if you're not going to help me, then close the lid and I'll wait until they come and kill me. I don't want to cause you any trouble."

My voice fell to a whisper. "Your *brother?*"

"They took him," he said. "I heard his screams from the other room. He told me what they were doing. He was hurt when we crashed. I thought maybe they were going to help him. Instead they tied him to a table and cut him to pieces. I've been calling, but he doesn't answer now. They killed my brother, and soon they'll come for me." He looked at me. "You're all I have."

"Your brother?"

"They killed him." He looked at me. "If you help me just a little, I can get away. But I have to get to Mexico."

"Mexico? Why Mexico?"

"There's a radio there."

"There are radios here."

"But this one is big." He stood up in the box again. "You can hear it all the way up there." He pointed up. "My friends are waiting. We have an emergency plan. I can call for help. But the army people took all my things away. My radio. My clothing. Everything. Never mind that we might kill you."

"Kill me!" I said. "I thought you didn't like killing? Now you want to kill us?"

"Not on purpose, you idiot. Don't you know anything? *Diseases*. We may have germs that can kill you. You plural, as in, your kind. Not you *personally*. And you have germs that can kill us. Me. Goodness. For a species that calls itself intelligent, you sure are stupid."

"You tell me you can kill me, but now you want me to help you?"

"All the more reason. The clock, as your kind says, is ticking. But you're more likely to kill me than I am to kill you. I was carefully inspected before I came down. You'll probably be all right. If I get sick, and I will if I don't get out of here, but if I get sick, I'll die. You can't do anything for me. But if you got sick, at least I could help you. Provided I don't die first. But I'll die if I don't get back to my ship. And to get back, I have to find a really big radio and then I can call them. They'll come for me. But I need your help."

Off his rocker, lost his marbles, hit his head hard, not dealing with a full deck, a few bricks shy of a load, one toke over the line, bat-shit crazy. Cuckoo. Crackers. Bananas. I know what you're thinking. And I'd be thinking the same thing, too, if I were you. Just keep telling yourself, *It's only a movie. It's only a movie.*

I wanted to run away worse than anything, from his troubles, my troubles, from the insanity, all of it. But at that moment, all I could think of was the nights I spent shut up in a box with my brother, and how I once ran away and left my brother behind. He wasn't in the box. But he was my brother, and I was supposed to help him. But I didn't. I looked outside. There were three or four hours of daylight left. Not good. I looked at the little man—our guest he said he was—now standing in the box. "Okay," I said. "I'll try." I opened the window as high as it would go. "Quick," I said. "Jump." And now that I was going to help, the spoiled little thing stood his ground.

"I can't," he said.

"Why not?"

"It's too far."

"It's not far. You can do it."

"It is far. I'm not big like you."

"It's not far."

"It is. I'm not built like you."

"Shit," I said. I reached out and patted the pipe. "Can you climb?"

He came to the window and stood on tiptoe to look. "I don't think so."

"But the door is locked," I said. "There are guards on the other side. With rifles. There's no other way."

"I cannot."

"It's not far."

He said, "Gravity is different here. My planet is not so dense. My bones are more fragile than yours. Our kind is not as strong. And I have not eaten in many hours. I cannot do it."

"What the fuck?" I said. I grabbed the sheet from the bed and tried to rip it, but the cloth was too strong. I picked up the knife and nicked the edge of the sheet, then tore a long strip six inches wide almost all the way to the other end, then nicked it again, on the opposite side, six inches over, and tore another strip in the opposite direction almost all the way back. I nicked it again, tore it again, repeated the process twice more, then knotted the ends so the fabric could not tear all the way through. I now held a cloth rope perhaps thirty feet long with knots every five feet or so holding it together. I tied a quick loop in the end and said, "Get in."

The little creature grasped right away what I was doing. He wedged himself in the loop and I pushed him through the window and lowered him to the ground.

Someone tried a key in the door. I froze. They tried again.

I threw the rope out the window, shut the lid on the box, grabbed the knife, and jumped behind the door just as it opened. The same guard who'd put me in the other room stepped into this room. In one quick move I caught him in a headlock, banged the door shut with my hip, and cut his throat all the way around. It wasn't deep but I got the arteries and the windpipe. The blood spurted like a fountain. He sank to his hands and knees, eyes wide, mouth open, making no sound, bleeding as from a spigot. I wrenched the keys from his hand and locked the door from the inside, crossed the room in two steps and jumped. I almost landed on the little man. He was looking up at the window with what must have been, among his kind, absolute confusion.

I hit ground, rolled, grabbed my ankle in pain, swore, stood, grabbed him under my arm like a football, and sprinted the length of the warehouse and around to the back fence. I ran down the fence line until I found the cut I'd made earlier that afternoon. I pushed the little green man through and followed, grabbed him again, and sprinted across the field to the road, the arroyo, and to my motorcycle. I set him on the seat in front of me like I would a child, swung my leg over, kicked the starter, and we roared the hell out of there as fast as I could go and still keep it on the road. Once we were moving, the little alien screamed the whole way. How can you fly a billion miles across the universe, I wondered, and be scared to death on a motorcycle?

Act IV Scene 2

Take 380 to Hondo, 70 through Ruidoso and onto Tularosa, then turn south on 54 and it's a straight shot to El Paso. Maybe 200 miles. There was no way we'd make it. Not a snowball's chance in hell. Me in a bloody stolen army uniform on a brand-new Indian bike with a naked green alien riding in front of me and screaming his lungs out? In broad daylight? That won't attract any attention.

Just before Hondo I spied a state trooper coming in the other direction and hung a hard left, screeching off the highway onto a narrow, rutted dirt road that wound through an orchard, then an arroyo, and then another orchard before finally dead-ending in a cottonwood grove by a wide spot on the river. A fishing hole. I set the alien down and climbed off the bike, took my pistol and swore, hiding behind a tree and watching back up the path to see if the cop followed us. He hadn't. As soon as I was sure, I tore off the uniform, took my jeans and tee shirt and boots from my bag, and changed. I stuffed the uniform and shoes in my bag, filled it up with rocks, and threw it as far as I could out into the water. It sank out of sight. The little man watched everything panting and wide-eyed, still standing beside the motorcycle.

I tucked the pistol into my belt. "What's your name?" I asked.

He said, "Our kind does not have names in the same way that your kind does. We begin with a name which is given us, but our history and our name become intertwined in a way that our name changes as we grow older, and it would take some time to explain."

"But you do have a name?"

"Of course. But my name wouldn't translate into your language."

"Then what would you like me to call you?"

After a moment of reflection he replied, "You can call me Visitor. No, wait, call me Guest. That has a nicer connotation. Anyone can visit, but a guest is invited and welcome."

"But Guest isn't a name."

"Why not? Why can't Guest be a name?"

"It just isn't. We have names and we have words, and they don't get mixed up. Our names are simple. If I don't give you something that sounds like a name, how will I remember?"

"I don't know," he said. "I don't see how it makes a difference."

"Well it does." I imagined calling him *Guest*. It didn't sound right. "How about if I call you *Gus*?" I said. "That sounds like guest but it's a name."

"Is it a good name?"

"How would I know? It's a name. One name's as good as another. Except for male or female. You know what that means?"

"Of course."

"So which are you? A boy or a girl? Cause if you're a girl, Gus won't work."

"It's complicated."

"What do you mean?"

"Our kind doesn't do things the same way you do. We're different like that." He looked at me. "But you can call me Gus if you want," Gus said. "I don't mind." After a minute he added, "What's your name?"

"Pablo," I replied.

"Pablo?" Gus said.

"Pablo."

"That's not what it said on your uniform."

"That wasn't my uniform."

"But you were wearing it."

"I told you. I was in disguise. My name is Pablo."

"Just Pablo?"

"Well you could call me Pablo Barela," I said, "but it's complicated."

"I thought you said your names were simple."

"I did say that. And they are. I mean, they're supposed to be. But in my case, it got complicated."

"Do your names change over time?"

"No," I said. "Well, sometimes. But they're not supposed to. Unless you're a woman and you get married."

"Did you get married?"

"I did, but I'm not a woman so my name didn't change."

"So why did you change your name?"

"It's complicated."

"Was it a good name?"

"Look, just call me Pablo, okay?"

"Okay," Gus said. "Pablo it is. You don't have to be so sensitive about it. I was just trying to be friendly." Gus rubbed his chin with as if thinking. "Is Pablo a boy or a girl name?"

"A boy," I said.

"I see," he said. "I believe that in your society we are supposed to say, It's nice to meet you.' Is that correct?"

"Sometimes."

"Sometimes?"

"Yeah, sometimes. Sometimes it's nice to meet people, and sometimes it isn't."

Gus looked confused. Maybe even a little bit hurt.

"Okay, this might be one of those times," I said. I offered him my hand. "Nice to meet you, Gus."

He shook my hand. "Thank you for helping me, Pablo."

I looked at him. "Why are you green?"

"We are partly photosynthetic, like plants," Gus said. "Do you know what that means?"

I had no idea photosynthetic meant, or why Gus liked plants. But he seemed friendly enough. "Yes," I said.

"Usually I am darker, but we turn brighter green after a period of darkness. Our skin darkens again when we are in the sunlight."

"So does mine," I said.

"Oh," Gus said. "I didn't know that."

"Well it does." I looked at him. "Look. I can't carry you all the way to Mexico like this."

"Well you can't leave me here," Gus said. "I told you. I have to find a radio."

"That's not what I mean," I said. "I mean I can't carry you around all green and naked. I won't leave you, but I have to get you some clothes. And we can't ride any more today. They'll be looking for us. For you, anyway. You stay here. I'm going back to town for little while. Can I bring you something to eat?"

"Tomatoes," Gus said. "We have an emergency plan and we felt there were six common items it was safe for me to eat."

"Six items?"

"We're pretty sure they're safe, if they're clean. The germs might kill me, but the food I should be able to eat."

"Tomatoes," I said. "What else? Just in case I can't find any tomatoes."

Gus looked up and counted on his fingers. "Peaches, bell peppers, oranges, grapefruit, and lemons." He had a funny way of counting. He had four fingers on each hand. Or should I say two fingers and two thumbs? Both his outer fingers folded like our thumbs, so he could hold things in either direction. But when he counted, he counted one-two-three-four on the fingers of his right hand. Five was one finger on this left hand. Six was one finger on each hand. I picked up on that right away. I looked at my hands. Later on I would work out that I could count to thirty-five on the fingers of both hands. Why didn't somebody on our planet think of that? I looked up at Gus and he was looking at me like he was expecting me to do something. "You eat lemons?" I asked.

"I never had one, but we think it would be safe. You asked. And I need lots of water. Boiled water."

"The river has good water," I said.

"It has to be boiled. Your germs will kill me. That's why I need to get to Mexico. The germs."

"I don't have any germs," I said.

"Yes, you do, but I don't mean to offend you. Maybe you don't understand."

"There's a lot about this I don't understand."

"Perhaps I can help. Maybe I can explain some things to you. Is there something you'd like to know?"

I thought about all I didn't know. "There's probably a lot," I said. "But I better get you some clothes and us some food before it gets dark."

"I'll die," Gus said, "if I don't get help soon. That's why I have to get to Mexico. It's not that I don't like you. I do. And it's not that I wouldn't like to talk with you. I would. I mean, we came a long way to talk with you, but then you shot down our ship and took my things, and if I don't get help soon, I'll die."

"I think I got that," I said. "Except that I didn't shoot down any ship or take any of your stuff."

"I mean, your *kind*. Your government," Gus said. "But that's why I have to get to Mexico. There's a radio there."

"There's a radio there," I said.

"A radio, yes."

"And you can call for help?"

"I can call."

"And your friends will come?"

"That's our plan."

"And if you don't get help you'll die?"

"I'll die."

"How long will that take?"

"A few days, at most."

"Wait here," I said. "I'll be back. And I'll just be a little while."

Gus looked at me. "Tomatoes?"

"I'll try."

"But you'll come back?"

"I promise," I said. "Trust me. And I'll try to find some boiled water."

I rode into Hondo and came back an hour-and-a-half later. Gus was sitting in the shade looking out over the river. He had made a little shelter from branches and grass and leaves. He looked frightened. "Here," I said. I handed Gus a white kitchen towel; red underpants; blue jeans; a long-sleeved, red-and-white checkered western shirt; a green-and-gold John Deere cap; white socks; and brown shoes. He held up the underpants and looked puzzled. "I also got you a bag of tomatoes, a lemon, and a canteen of boiled water. But before you get dressed, there's one thing we gotta to do first." I handed Gus a tin of black shoe polish.

Act IV Scene 3

Demented. Crazed. Gaga. Whacked. Nutso. Bonkers. Off my rocker. Ready for the fruit factory. Insane in the mem-brain. Did I say "*loco*" yet? I get it, okay. But what if I told you that everything—and I mean *everything*—you have ever heard about life on this planet or on other planets is wrong?

Think for a minute. Would scientists and the government spend billions of perfectly good dollars looking for something that isn't there? Does that make any sense? I mean, think about it, wouldn't they spend their money on something—anything—more practical than (pardon the expression) *little green men?* Things, for example, that might benefit the people who vote for them. Things like roads and bridges and schools and jobs and hospitals and such?

But just a minute, you say. Wouldn't the point be to discover life on other planets?

No. Why would you think that? We can't get governments to spend money on useful things *right here on our own planet*. Why would they search the skies for something that would not be useful at all? And the odds of finding life in space with telescopes and radar would be less than zero, if such thing was possible. And even if we did find intelligent life in space, it might take us a few thousand million years to get there *if we could travel at the speed of light*, so there's less than zero chance we'd ever meet them. No, our government wouldn't waste a bent nickel looking for life in outer space. Unless they already knew it was there.

Okay, you say, but Why look for something if you already know it's there?

That's my point *exactly*. You don't look for something that isn't there. But if you have reason, you look for something you know exists. *Especially* if you worry it might not be too happy with you. I'm not talking about some *Invasion of the Body Snatchers* kind of thing. That's our fucked-up human thinking. Actually, they're not coming back. Gus told me that. But the people who know what really happened on July 7th, 1947, outside of Roswell, New Mexico, USA (a few generals, the president maybe) the people who know what happened aren't talking. And they probably don't know what I know because I talked to Gus and they didn't. But I can tell you for certain that they know there's life on other planets, and they are very afraid that someday Gus (and maybe a whole fleet of his friends) will return. And that's why they're *watching for signs of life in space*. They know there is other life out there in the universe—and they also know that alien society is much more advanced than ours.

But could the government announce this to the world? Could they tell us what they had done? Dear world, by the way, we shot down a UFO last week and pissed off a superior species, and they might come back and kill or enslave us all. Would they admit that? Could they tell the public that they were on high alert for an invasion? You don't like to hear from me that I met a space alien in 1947. You don't have to believe me. But what would people think if the *government* announced that we had not only *met* space aliens, we had *shot down their ship and killed* one? That we had lied to, betrayed, insulted, and pissed off the whole alien species? What would be the result of that? Anarchy? Chaos? Mass suicide?

And what would the religions of the world do if we told them for sure that the Biblical account of creation was wrong? I mean, I'm still Catholic. I have nothing against the Biblical account of creation. I think that, given what they had to work with about seven thousand years ago, they came up with a pretty good story. It served its purpose. And many—if not most—of the teachings of the great religions are just fine. The world would be wonderful if we just practiced them. And Gus would be the first to encourage that. But that doesn't mean that everything we've been told is divine, immutable truth. God, I was told, gave us brains to use. That's one of the things that sets us apart from the rest of the animals. And maybe that was what the writer of Genesis meant when he (or she) said that man was made in God's image.

But what would happen if the whole world woke up one day and found out that everything it had ever known was wrong? People used to swear that the earth was flat. We have people today who deny global warming, for goodness sake! What would people think if they learned for sure that there was such a thing as life on other planets? What if they heard that not only were humans NOT the most import living things in the universe, but that the rest of intelligent creation thinks of us as a *borderline species*? And if they didn't think too much of us, how did God really feel about us? So you see, the cleverest thing the government ever did was to *fund a search* for extraterrestrial intelligence, by which they meant, watch the skies 24/7. Yes, they're looking all the time. But it's not what you think.

Standing in this cottonwood grove, by the Rio Bonito, outside of Hondo, New Mexico, rubbing black shoe polish all over Gus, I said, "We gotta push on tonight."

"Push on?" Gus asked. "Push on what?"

"I mean, we can't stay here."

"I thought you said we had to stay here."

"I did but I changed my mind."

"Why?"

"They're gonna be looking for us. For you. I think the farther we get from the base, the better. And it's safer to ride when it's dark than to wait light until tomorrow. Who knows how many people they'll have out looking by daylight?"

"Good," Gus said. "I don't like it here. There are dangerous insects. And I bet wild animals, too. No telling how they will act. So you'll take me to Mexico?"

"If we get that far," I said. "But it's not that easy. You can't just walk across the bridge."

"Have you been to Mexico?"

"Many times. I told you. I came from Mexico."

"How did you get there?"

"I walked across the bridge."

"You just said you couldn't walk across the bridge."

"I can walk across the bridge. You can't. It's different for me."

"How is it different?"

"It's complicated."

"I don't see how," Gus said.

"I'm tall and I'm not green," I said. "And the guards all know me. I've been crossing that bridge for years. They wouldn't pay me any attention, but they'd want to talk to you. By tomorrow, they might even be looking for you."

"Will they look here?" Gus asked. He looked all around, somewhat anxiously, as if soldiers might rush out of the trees at any moment.

I stopped with the shoe polish and looked at him. It darkened him up a lot. He wasn't quite brown, but he wasn't so obviously green anymore. Kind of a dark yellow. In the fading light he wasn't too bad. He looked like a skinny little kid, unless you noticed the hands with four fingers. "I don't know what they'll do," I said. "It depends on whether they know about me or not. If they know about the bike, they'll block the highway and we're fucked. If they think you escaped by yourself, maybe not. They'll look all over the base for you. But if they know about me . . . "Do you mind?" I asked. I offered him the polish. I had not polished his, well, you know, the places in the middle.

"I told you we're not like your kind," Gus said.

"It's still a little weird," I said.

Gus took the shoe polish and scooped some into his hand. He held it to his face and sniffed it. "I believe the expression is, this *stinks*."

"You smell things?" I asked. "Like we do?"

"More or less," he replied. "The basic environmental senses are universal to life. Light. Color. Sound. Touch. Temperature. Taste and smell. Electromagnetism. Geolocation. Most intelligent species have all or most of these. Some have a kind of sense, too, to judge obstacles and the boundaries of their environment. These are common to life everywhere, but the intelligent species are all limited in some way."

"Limited? Why?"

"Weakness forces the development of the mind, and of interdependent social skills. Cooperation. When ten can accomplish what one cannot, it facilitates the development of society."

"I see," I said, even though I didn't.

Gus rubbed the polish on and wiped down with the towel. He put the underpants on backwards but I didn't say anything. What difference would it make? His skinny little legs stuck through like straws. When he was dressed, he said, "How do I look?"

"All cats look brown in the dark," I said. "Where in Mexico do you want to go?"

"Juarez," he replied. When I made a face he said, "Do you know the city?"

"I used to live there."

"Good," Gus said.

"Why is that good?" I asked. "Have you ever been there?"

"No. But I presume since you lived there that you know your way around. Right?"

"I know it pretty good," I said.

"Okay," Gus said. "There is a radio station there. XAMO. They send signals so powerful you can hear them in orbit. You know about this radio, yes?"

I had no idea whether the station was powerful or not, or if you could hear it from space, but I knew where the station was. The transmitter was on a mountain south of the city. You could see it for miles. "I know where it is," I said, "but that doesn't mean we can just walk right in and start talking on the air."

"Why not?"

"It just doesn't work that way," I said.

"Would they let me if we asked?"

"I doubt it."

"Then we'll have to go in *disguise*."

"I don't think that will work," I said.

"You got into the army base that way."

"That was different," I said.

"Is that your excuse for everything? Everything is different? Your kind is not very consistent. I think that's something you should work on. You shouldn't have thrown the uniform in the water. We could use it."

"Mexico is a different country. They wouldn't care shit about an American uniform. But if I got caught with it, we'd be fucked for sure."

"Well what do you suggest?"

"I don't know," I said. "I have to think about it."

Gus shook his head. "I'm beginning to think your kind isn't as smart as we thought you were." He drank some of the water and took a tentative bite out of the tomato. "You know about germs, right?" he said. He spit the tomato out.

"I know they are little and they can get inside you and make you sick."

"Right. And when different life forms meet—like people from different parts of the earth, or like yours and mine—we have to be very careful. I had equipment to protect both your kind and mine, but the men took everything."

"You wear clothes?"

"Of course we wear clothes," Gus said. "You think we run around naked? All intelligent kinds clothe themselves. It's a response to their weakness. It's also part of their learning process. You could call it a step in evolution. We need protection from the environment— radiation, heat and cold, insects, and so forth. Caustic substances. Abrasions. So, yes, we wear clothes."

"What do your clothes look like?"

Gus looked down at his jeans, his shoes. He took off the John Deere hat and looked at the deer jumping on the front. "Better than this," he said.

"So why did they take them away?"

"I don't know," Gus said. "They probably took them to find out what I had and how it worked."

"So why didn't you just tell them?"

117

"I would have, but they shut me up in that box."

"You said they shot your plane down?"

"We don't have planes," Gus said.

"But you fly?"

"We can fly. We move around. It's not quite like your flying."

"So what do you call it?"

"It's complicated. I don't think you'd understand. We have machines that move us around. They said they were going to show us where to land and instead they shot us down with a rocket. It happened too quick to stop it. We shouldn't have trusted you."

"I didn't shoot anything down."

"Not you personally. Your army. Your government."

"It's not my government, either. I'm Mexican."

"Whatever."

"Where did they shoot you down?"

"In the back."

"I mean, where? Like, somewhere around here?"

"How would I know?" Gus said. "I wasn't at the controls. I was monitoring communications. That's my specialty. Languages. I'm good with words. I was on the radio."

"I like words," I said.

"Good for you," Gus said. He sighed and looked at me. "I like words, too. And I guess it was some place close by here. Where they shot us down. It was like they had it planned. They shot us down and we crashed, and they were right there to pick us up. And it didn't take them long to get us to the place where you found me." Gus said. " Gus nibbled on the lemon and must have liked it better than the tomato. He ate the whole thing, peel and all.

It was getting dark. "Come on," I said. "We better go."

Act IV Scene 4

Sometime around 1975, I heard this song on the radio, "Midnight Rider," by the Allman Brothers. I wasn't so much into rock and roll, but this song was weird. It took me back to the night of July 7th, 1947, riding across New Mexico with Gus on my bike.

I've got to run, to keep from hiding.
And I'm bound, to keep on riding.
I've got one more, silver dollar.

But I'm not gonna let 'em catch me, no.
Not gonna let 'em catch the midnight rider.

I told you I like riding, especially in the mountains, especially on winding roads, and most especially, at night. I might not have been much of a thinker, but I did my best thinking on that bike. And that night I had a lot to think about. There was some moon. Not full, but more than half. Enough to be pretty. I stopped at a gas station outside of Ruidoso to get a coffee. I thought I'd ask around if people coming up from the south had complained about roadblocks or anything. I told Gus, "Wait here," and I went in, got a coffee, and chatted up the night clerk. He probably figured I was dodging cops, but he was like, sixteen and dropped out of school. He was cool. No roadblocks that he'd heard about. I got a second cup and gave him a five-dollar tip.

When I came out, I couldn't find Gus anywhere. I almost had a heart attack. But then he came running around the side of the building. I looked at him and he said, "I had to urinate."

I looked at him.

"*Orinar?*" he asked.

"We usually do that in toilets," I said. I pointed at the signs.

"I didn't think that was a good idea."

I took a sip of my coffee.

"What's that?" Gus asked.

"Coffee."

"Is it good?"

"It's okay," I said.

"You drink this coffee for food?"

"I drink it to stay awake."

"I see."

I took another sip.

Gus was looking at me. "Your kind sleeps a lot," he said.

"Sometimes. Sometimes not at all."

"What is it like, this sleeping?"

"It can be nice," I said. Sometimes we dream. Do you ever sleep?"

"Not in the way that you do."

"What is dreaming?"

I thought about that. "Dreaming is like being in another world where the rules don't apply."

Gus looked puzzled. "You go to another world where rules don't apply? What world? What rules?"

"I didn't say we went to another world. I said it was *like* another world. There are no rules. Things change in our dreams. Impossible things can happen. People long dead come back. We can fly. We see things a different way. It's kind of strange."

Gus looked at me like I was making this us. "All your kind goes to this place?"

"Yes," I said. I took another sip of coffee. "But it's not a real place. It's just something that happens in our heads."

"How do you know that?" Gus asked.

"Where else would it be?" I replied. "I go to bed at night and get up in the morning in the same place. Where would I go? It's just dreaming. Something our mind does."

Gus shook his head, then asked, "Was that boiled?"

I thought about telling Gus it was complicated, but I said, "Yes." It was easier that way.

"Could I have a sip?"

"Aren't you worried that it might be poison?"

"If you can drink it, I doubt if it would kill me."

I gave him the cup and he took a sip, wrinkled his face, then took another."

"I didn't put much sugar in it."

"It tastes okay," he said. "Kind of warm and funny feeling." He drank the rest of it and wiped his mouth with the back of his hand. "You know, I probably won't make it back to my ship. But if I do, I will be the first of my kind to have walked on your planet, ridden on your motorcycle machine, eaten your tomatoes and lemons, and drank your coffee."

"You'll be famous," I said.

"We don't do things like become famous," Gus said. "The group is more important than the individual. But our kind will want to know what it was like. I could tell them. Tomatoes are not so good, lemons are okay, but the coffee is pretty interesting. Could I have another?"

I went back inside and got two more coffees. I didn't leave another big tip. When I came out, I asked Gus, "What do you call your kind in your language?"

Gus cleared his throat, took a very deep breath, and began to make that slow, rumbling music I heard on the army base. But then he stopped and I looked back and the clerk was standing in the doorway looking at us. "We better go," I said. So we finished our coffee and left.

Outside of El Paso I pulled over and pointed out to Gus the thin, dark line of the river that split the two cities and made the border between America and Mexico. Even the lights in the cities were different—they were brighter in America.

"So that's Juarez," Gus said. "Where's the radio?"

"There," I said, pointing. "That tower down there."

"Then we can go now!"

"No way," I said. "I can't think straight. I'm not dealing with bridges and guards and shit tonight. I gotta go home and rest a little while."

"And dream?"

"Maybe," I said. A look of what I might call uncertainty crossed Gus' face.

"And my wife's gonna kill me. I been gone like, five days."

"Kill you? What is it with you people and killing? You're always killing one another. She's going to kill you for being gone a few days?"

"I didn't mean that *literally*," I said. "It was a joke." But even as I said this, I wondered what Maria would think of my companion.

Gus must have been thinking the same thing. "So you have a mate?"

"Yes."

"I do not wish to frighten your mate. I can find another way."

"I don't think that's such a good idea. I'll take you, but I have to sleep a few hours first. There's lots of places around my house where I can hide you. It's probably the best place to hide that I know of. And it would be very dangerous for you to cross into Mexico without my help."

Gus looked at the tower as if considering his options. We had both gotten off of the motorcycle to stretch our legs.

"I don't see how," he said.

I patted the seat and said, "Trust me. Come on." He came to me. I picked him up like a child and set him on the seat behind me. "We'll be okay," I said.

Act IV Scene 5

Even though I'm growing older, I still like to try new things. If I go to a restaurant, I might see my favorite dish on the menu, but I am as likely to try something new as to eat something familiar. Unless, of course, I am feeling nostalgic. I go to bookstores and pick up books by writers I have never heard of. I like listening to new and different kinds of music. Of course, Latin rhythms are still my favorites, and like most people, I like music from my youth the best. But would it surprise you to learn that one of the songs that most affected me was the Patti Smith version of "Smells Like Teen Spirit"? I had heard that Kurt Cobain and Nirvana were very popular, and I had my opinions about what people call *grunge*. But I realized one day that I had these negative opinions and I had never listened to the music at all. So one day I got on YouTube and started listening to various grunge songs. When I hit "Smells Like Teen Spirit," something broke inside of me. I listened to that song over and over and over again. I think I know why Kurt Cobain killed himself. He didn't say so in words. But if you listen to the music, you can hear it just the same. Pain. Confusion. Despair.

I have probably been insane much of my life. I know that now. I'm not asking for sympathy. It's just a statement of fact. If anything, I'd like to think that sharing what coping skills I developed might someday help somebody else who needs it. Somebody who wakes up every day asking: What happened? Why did it happen? and Why does it keep happening to me? I think maybe twice in my life I probably should have been institutionalized. I know that after finding my mother's dead body, there should have been someone or something to take better care of me. I was a child. Maybe what the old priest said was true. Maybe God *was* looking out for me. It didn't feel like it at the time, but I survived. And then there was the night I came home with Gus.

Riding is fun but, like riding a horse, it's also work. I'd been up almost twenty-four hours. In that time I had broken into an army base, killed a man, escaped with an alien, and then ridden two hundred plus miles in the dark. You could say I was tired. I rolled the bike into the shed by the side of the house and then arched my back, tried to work the kinks out.

Gus was looking left and right in the almost total darkness of the orchard. "You live here?" he asked.

"Shhhh," I said. I still wasn't sure where I was going to put him, or how I would explain him to Maria if she saw him. Is it even possible to explain a little green man? I leaned against the wall by the front door and closed my eyes. I was waiting a light to come on. Maria must have heard the bike. It was quiet in the orchard and she was a light sleeper. But nobody stirred. I pointed to the shed. "Stay there," I said. "Let me get Maria settled and I'll find a place for you. You want some more water?"

"Boiled," Gus said. "Coffee would be even better, if you have any."

"I'll see," I said. I tried the door. It was unlocked. Maria was always careless like that. When I'd scold her for not locking the door, she'd shrug and say, *Quién más podría venir aquí?* Who would come here? I slipped off my shoes. I opened the door quietly. It was black inside. I didn't want to turn on the lights if I could help it. I took off my watch, left my wallet and keys on the counter by the sink. I turned on the water and washed my hands and face. The water felt good. I felt for the table in the dark and found it, used it to steer toward the bedroom, but in the middle of the room I tripped and fell over a chair. There was a chair turned over on the floor. I waited for Maria to give me hell— surely the noise woke her. But there was nothing and the anxiety hit me like a truck. I felt the wall for the light switch. Maria hung from a rafter in the ceiling. For the second time in my life, the world was a blank stare.

I must have cried out. Or perhaps Gus heard me fall. Either way, he was by my side. We stood side by side and looked at her. "Did you kill her?" he asked.

"Yes" I said.

For just one moment Gus looked at me, mouth open. A shadow of doubt crossed his little triangular face. He was probably recollecting our conversations. I had insisted on coming home to see her. Gus knew I didn't kill her. "What is it with you people?" he asked. "You run out of others and you kill yourselves?" He looked at me, and all I saw was disgust in his eyes. But then his expression softened and I saw something else. Pity. Or perhaps *compassion* is a better word. He reached out and with four long, thin fingers, took my hand and held it.

What I was thinking in that moment was how perfect and beautiful Maria was, and how sad it was to see her with her neck stretched to breaking and face almost black. Maria had done this quite cleverly. She stood on the chair, placed the noose around her neck, then cinched her hands into another loop that passed around her waist and between her legs. It was like the knot Don Pablo's men used on Michaelo. There would be no turning back, no prolonging the agony, no grasping at the knot that choked the life from her body. She had only to tip the chair over. "I hope it was quick," I said.

I said, once, that as a child something broke in me—something that was supposed to feel, or to tell me what to feel. So if I was thinking how beautiful Maria was, what I was feeling was that blank stare thing. It was like waiting for something I knew should be there, but wasn't. I should have felt grief, but I felt only admiration for her beauty.

"Don't you know," Gus said, "that this is wrong?"

"I know," I said, though I wonder if we were speaking of the same thing.

"Come out of here," he said.

I switched off the light.

Outside it was dark and hot. Dry Texas heat. The faintest breeze stirred in the orchard. The sound of a billion leaves was like the sound of a distant ocean, the billion endless washing frictions of ebb and flow that speak to us of light and air and stone and water and make the beach restless and reflective.

I know that you want to know what happened that night. What Gus said to calm me. I wish I remembered the events in an orderly way so that I could make a proper narrative—a story to entertain you. But I'm afraid that of the chaos that was my mind—the hallucination that became my reality for a while that night—I can thread no narrative. In retrospect, the way Gus listened, the way he spoke soothingly to me, was the kindest thing anyone has ever done for me. Later I would come to wish that Gus had been my friend for longer than a few days. I recall only bits and pieces of this odd conversation that was just enough to save my life, even though at the time, I did not want my life saved, nor think it worth saving.

Gus pulled me outside, pushed me against the wall, then pulled on my arm until I sat dumbly down. He sat down beside me, clutched my arm like a child might cling to a parent. I could feel the pointed angle of his cheek digging into my bicep. "She is here," Gus said. "You do not have to grieve overmuch for her. She is watching from a better place."

"You believe in heaven?" I said.

"Not in the way that your religions describe, though in their odd way, they sometimes hit closer to the truth than you would think."

"I don't understand."

"Time is a property of the physical world," Gus said, "the one you and I occupy right now. Time is the sequence of events or changes in the physical world. It is a record of movement. But there are other worlds beyond the boundaries of this world, and in those worlds there is no physical matter; hence, no movement, hence, no time. At death we leave this world, but we can no more end our existence than we could begin it. In that sense, there exists what you might call heaven. You might say," he said, taking a moment to consider his words, "you might say that it is like *dreaming*. Maria is there now. She can see you. She would tell you much if she could, but she must trust—as you and I will someday trust—that those left behind will come to understand. She meant you no harm, Pablo. She could not take the pain. She only wanted the suffering to end." He searched my face. "Do you understand? This is something that you and I and all living things share. Our existence is painful. We all seek release from that pain."

"Is there a hell?"

Gus shook his head. "A long time ago our kind settled the debate about the nature of God. We made a list of God's attributes. Even your kind has a list of qualities you call Godly or God-like. Things like love, honesty, kindness, compassion, forgiveness, trust, understanding. All these good things. And then there is the notion of infinity—of God as infinite in both spatial and temporal bounds. Do you understand?"

I shook my head.

"Our kind determined that the only God worth following would be a God of infinite love and infinite forgiveness. God has better things to do than torture dead souls forever. If we don't learn our lessons in this life, then we come back and try again."

"So your kind doesn't die?'

"Of course we die." He paused. "Our kind does not measure time according to the orbit of your planet around your star. Our time, and our ways of dealing with time are much different from yours. We will die, but we also believe we will be reborn. I think your kind is less certain of that."

"Is there a God?"

"Oh, yes," Gus said. "There is, though God's existence makes as little sense to us as our lives would make to those insects calling to us from the darkness. There is a God. We just don't try to understand too much. We trust that what we don't know we couldn't understand, and that we will learn more at the proper time. I believe your kind would call that *faith*."

"Does God watch over your kind, Gus?"

"I can't answer that, Pablo. Sometimes it feels that way. Sometimes not. Sometimes good things happen. Sometimes bad. Sometimes the best intentions go wrong. And sometimes things that start out wrong end up right. Is this up to God? Or does it depend on how we react to adversity. Or to success, for that matter? Perhaps some things just happen and we look for meaning where there is none. Who knows? Perhaps someday we will know the answer for certain."

"Do you go to church?"

"Our kind does not meet in churches to talk about what we already know. Our service to one another is our service to God. For us, any place is a place of worship, and all places are what you might call sacred. Your kind worships by the repetition of rituals as though words could magically transform. Our kind knows that words are important, but we value actions more than intentions, what is done more than what is promised." He sighed. "This knowledge is free. It is available to anyone. You might say that this enlightenment is God's gift to us all. Perhaps that is the one way we could know for sure that He looks out for us—we learn to be kind to one another. There have always been those among your kind who have known this. We know that. It is one of the things that attracted us to you. These men and women, they knew to pass along what they learned. The problem is that others of your kind lust for power, and use these words to secure their own positions, their own destinies. Sometimes they twist the words to their own ends. And even when sincere, it's difficult to pass this knowledge along. The idea, for example, that one should *love one's brother as himself* often raises more questions than it answers. It requires thought to understand, and honesty and humility to put into practice. It requires faith. It is far easier to create rules to deal with situations than it is to think through the situation and then act. And what if one's actions are wrong? Or what if one's actions are right, but for some reason, things still don't work out? What then? How does one handle the uncertainty, the guilt, and the fear? So the enlightened ones attract followers who vie for succession and become leaders of organizations that generate rules and explanations and expectations.

"These organizations, even if well-intentioned, try to make simple what can never be made simple, try to codify what can never be codified. They try to short cut short what cannot be abridged. And these organizations acquire properties and take on lives and objectives of their own. Worse, they all-too-often compete with one another, even violently. So to answer your question, Our kind long ago abandoned these organizations. They were part of our evolution, but are not practical, permanent solutions. And yet, our faith remains strong. Perhaps it even grew stronger. We have no organization to substitute for our own faith and decision-making. Your kind claims to believe in God because of *exceptions* to natural laws. Our kind believes because of the invariable *consistency* of those same laws. Your kind practices in the expectation of reward or the fear of punishment. Our kind practices in the pure celebration of goodness. Your kind sees a conflict between science and religion. Our kind sees science as the study of the nature of God. Our religion, such as it is, is the right application of what knowledge we gain.

"I'm not saying, Pablo, that our way is better than yours in a moral sense. It is another step on the same path. Perhaps a little more advanced, but not better in a judgmental way. More effective, perhaps. We once felt as you feel, acted as you act. It almost killed us. This is one reason we came to you. We wanted to help. We have a saying among our kind: 'Before you accomplish the solution, you must first suffer the problem.' Your kind, Pablo, has problems that you must solve, and soon. We're not certain that you even recognize them, but if you do not face these realities, your kind will not survive. You have less time to act than you think."

Sometime in the night, I asked Gus if he was afraid of death.

"Of course I am," he replied.

"Then why did you come here if it might kill you?"

He patted my arm. "Because it was my duty, and because I was judged as having strong qualifications for this encounter. Courage," Gus said, "is not the absence of fear. It is the resolution to do what is right and necessary in the presence of one's fears."

"But you feel pain?"

"Yes."

"Physical and emotional?"

Gus considered this question. To the east the sky lightened just enough to make out the tops of the trees. "Yes," Gus said at length. "We feel physical pain. I also feel what you call emotional pain."

"Do you miss your wife?"

"We do not mate or reproduce in the same way that you do."

"How . . . "

"How do we reproduce?" Gus laughed. "Your kind might not understand. Perhaps the closest analogy I have are your ant colonies. Do you know much about ants?"

"No."

"At various times in our lives," Gus said, "we begin to have these growths on our skin. After a time, we must withdraw from our normal activities, as these growths become, how should I say, *inconvenient*. And we must safeguard our health. You might say this is our *time of the month*. When these growths mature, we break them off and place them in tanks of water. They gestate there. They develop into a water-dwelling stage. For several years they will swim, but then their bodies secrete a kind of shell and the young enter a third stage of life in which they incubate as a kind of egg. They emerge from that state as small but fully-formed adults, and they join the colony."

"Colony?"

"Yes. Our kind lives in colonies. Our social evolution is complete. You would find, if your kind cared to investigate, that by far the largest volume of life on your planet is that which has undergone social evolution. Your kind is a bit of a puzzle to us. All of the advanced kinds that we have encountered in the universe—all of them—are socially evolved. Some more so than ours. But all of us have this quality in common—that we are as or more concerned about others of our kind than we are for ourselves. Your kind is stuck somewhere in between. You are strong physically. Perhaps that is your undoing. You do not have to rely completely on others to survive. You laud individuality over your sense community. You value rights more than responsibilities. You create heroes, gods, myths. I believe your word for this is ego. Your nation, for example, this so-called United States, has a document called the *Bill of Rights*. It is a virtuous document. But what happened to your *Bill of Responsibilities?* Most species in the universe see their individual obligations to one another as more important than others' obligations to the individual."

"So you have a home?"

"Of course I have a home."

"But you have no wife?"

"Not in the sense that your kind has husbands and wives to reproduce. But I do have many dear friends and I care deeply about them. Enjoy their company. And, yes, I miss them. And for that, I experience emotional pain."

"Gus," I asked, "Am I your friend?"

"Yes," Gus said. He squeezed my arm. "You are my friend."

"Gus?"

"Yes."

"What's your home like?"

"Do you mean my home, as in planet, or my home, as in where I live?"

"Both."

"My planet is very hot compared to yours, and there is not so much gravity as you have here. And it is very wet and green with plants. There are many forms of life such as insects and warm-blooded creatures. There is lots of ocean, and much less landmass than your planet has. Most of the life on our planet is in the water. We live in colonies—kind of like your cities, only more organized. Land is valuable because there is so little of it, for this we see land as belonging to all of us. We do not see land as something that one of us can own, and we know we have to take care of it. We plan its use. We work very hard to keep it beautiful. And we take care of all of the kinds of life on our planet. We did not make that land or any of the life forms that share it with us. If we are the highest form of life on our planet, we see it as our responsibility to care for all the others, even at our own inconvenience. We see that as our duty to God. We take care of the creatures that, like us, are part of God's creation and evolving just like we evolved. Who knows? In a thousand million years, they might be just like us. At least, in the ways that matter.

"As for my home, in our society we provide comfortable living for all of our kind. I share a room with five of my friends. We have time to work and time to relax. We do not sleep in the same way that you do. I am curious to know

127

more about this dreaming. I would like to try that, if I could. If I live, I will research this more. I am not aware of any other kinds who dream as you describe. There may be more to this than you think.

"We like good food. We listen to music a lot and we love to sing and compose long, intricate passages of song. Our songs can last for hours. We search for life in the universe just as your kind might someday. One of the things we listen for is music. Music is a sure sign of intelligence. We also like colors and painting. And we make statues and sculptures. And among other kinds, there are art forms you have not even dreamed of. Could not imagine without, say, the ability to sense geomagnetic lines."

"Does your kind ever kill?"

Gus looked at me and tilted his head slightly to his right. He looked like he thought he misunderstood my question.

"Very, very rarely will we ever kill anything. I won't say never. But if it happened then it would be the result of a choice where we concluded that the killing was the lesser of two harms."

"But you have crime, right? All of you can't be saints? Surely you have criminals?"

"Yes," Gus said. "There are times when one or more of us may be criminal. It's not common but it happens."

"So what do you do?"

"We are very sad when this happens."

"No. I mean, What do you do? To the criminal."

"We don't do anything to them."

"So you don't have courts or police or prisons?"

"We have the means to settling disputes, if that's what you mean. And we have, among our division of labor, some who are assigned to maintain civic order. But we don't have prisons like your kind. Frankly, we don't think much of your system."

"Why?"

"Because if a being has committed some wrong, if they have a problem with their values or practices, the last thing they need is to be confined with others who are similarly afflicted. Think, for a moment. If you had a piece of your fruit, like your lemons, and one of them was rotting, would placing it with more rotten lemons make it well?"

"No," I said.

"So if one of our kind has this problem, we isolate them and have professionals work with them to help them resolve their issues. We don't place them in the company of others like them who might reinforce their illness. But, like I said, we have a very strong social instinct, so this kind of thing is very rare. And we don't glorify that kind of behavior like your kind does."

"What do you do for work?"

Gus laughed. "At home, I'm a teacher."

"So you have schools?"

"Of course!"

"What do you teach?"

"I specialize in languages and language acquisition."

"I like languages, too," I said. "I wished I could have gone to school."

"So why don't you?" Gus asked.

"It's complicated. How," I asked, "are you able to travel so far? Is it frightening? How long were you traveling to get here?"

"You would not understand our machines," Gus said. "It is far, but the physical distance is not so important as you think. There are more ways to travel than you can yet imagine."

I must have looked puzzled because Gus continued. "Your kind has airplanes."

"Yes," I said.

"Do you know how they fly?"

"They have wings and wheels and engines."

"Do you know how a wing works?"

I shook my head.

Gus made something like a C shape with his hand, but horizontal. "The shape of the wing creates lift," he said. "Because the wing is curved, the air through which it passes must travel further to go over the top of the wing than it does to go under it. This makes the air above act as though it were less dense—as though it weighed less. This effect is called lift. Do you understand?"

"No," I said.

"It doesn't matter. The point is that you fly by using shape to create lift. Someday your engineers may discover other ways to use shape to overcome some difficult engineering problems. If you don't kill yourselves off, you will figure this out, as dozens of other kinds have figured it out before you. It is like physics—natural law."

"Are we going to kill ourselves off?" I asked.

Gus looked at me. "Was that a bad choice of words?" he said. "What I mean is that your kind is so strange. You have so much to like and so much intelligence. You have a lot of physical prowess, but your social development is so . . . so weak. Every kind that we have encountered, all of us, we all studied what you call nuclear physics. We learned about the elements, and the powers that bind matter together. We all learned how to harness that power."

"You are talking about atom bombs?" I said.

"Every kind we have encountered learned about this power. But not one of them—not one—ever dreamed of using that power for destruction. Your . . . kind . . . your kind seems to value destruction above all else. You have so much to like. Why are you so invested in killing? Even your own kind? Why are you so bent on destroying it all? I fear you will kill yourselves off. That's why we came to help, but I don't think we can do this again." He looked at me for a long time.

"Promise me something, Pablo."

"What is that?"

"Promise me that you will never kill again."

"I promise," I said. In that moment, would have promised him anything.

He patted my arm and said, "Thank you."

After that, I must have slept at least a little. An hour. Perhaps a little more.

Act IV Scene 6

Apparition: the appearance of a heavenly being on earth.
Mystery: An event that cannot be understood through human
        experience or reasoning.
Incredulity: The deliberate refusal to accept the truth.

I have told you that I do not believe that you will believe my story. I can't blame you. Who would believe such a tale? That in just a few hours I snuck onto a military base, killed a soldier, rescued a being from another planet, and came home to find my wife dead by suicide—who would believe it? And yet everyday billions of people on our planet set out to live their daily lives according to mythologies equally strange, if not stranger, and do so with the utmost gravity, even severity. At least my story has not violated any of the laws of physics. Except, perhaps, for the part about the space ship. I'm not too sure about that. But in 1900 nobody had flown; television, our own space travel, lithium batteries, LED lights, and the internet were all the stuff of science fiction. So who knows? We're at least moving in that direction. And nobody in my story walked on water, called down fire from heaven, parted an ocean, or flew through the air with a magic hammer.

My own reaction to all of this was that, for the second time in my life, I was not capable of functioning as a human being. So you may perhaps forgive me if my account of my conversation with Gus is incomplete, and perhaps out-of-order. I have spent many years in contemplation of those few hours we spent together, and have tried to piece together as much as I can remember of the questions I think most people would like to hear answered. If the effort is poor, please forgive me. I've done the best that I could under difficult circumstances.

I did not dream. I awoke, startled, the light in my eyes, the pain in my back and neck from sleeping sitting up, the sudden rush of memories. Sunlight filtered through the trees. It looked like seven, perhaps even eight A.M. Gus sprawled on the ground not far from me. I got up. "Gus," I called. I ran to his side. "Gus?"

He opened his eyes but said nothing.

"Gus?"

"Water," he said. "But if you can't go in there..." he gestured with his eyes toward the house.

I boiled the water and made coffee. I also found a grapefruit and a suicide note. I read the note while the water cooled. When I came outside, Gus had crawled into the shed to get shade from the sun.

"I'm dying," he said. "If there is something you must do here, I understand. I don't want you to get into any trouble. But if I die, please bury me where nobody will know. I think that would be best for all concerned."

I gave him the water and the grapefruit, and a cup of coffee. This time I put more sugar in it. "I'll take you to Mexico." I said. "If you can make it. I can leave now. There is nothing I can do here, and I can't stay."

Gus drank some of the water and all of the coffee. "I like this stuff," he said. He looked at the grapefruit. "What is this?"

"A big lemon," I replied.

He bit into it carefully. "Not bad," he said. "Do you have any more coffee?" After a second cup he said, "I feel a bit better. I think I can make it if you take me now."

Gus looked much worse in the daylight than in the dark. I retouched his skin with the shoe polish but he would never pass for human. People might not notice if we blasted by on a motorcycle at seventy-five, but we'd never make it across the bridge. Especially if anybody was looking for him. I thought about this while we drank our coffee.

We crossed the river in New Mexico and then turned south toward Mexico, following a dirt farm road until it ended in a cotton field. We crossed the no-man's-land of the border south of Mt. Cristo Rey. In the desert there were only two things that could go wrong. The first was that we might encounter the border police, which was not all that likely, but could happen. Even if we did, they were not likely to worry about people crossing illegally *into* Mexico. They might think we were weird, but they wouldn't stop us. Unless they were looking for us. The second (and most likely) was that we might damage my motorcycle. If we did, we'd have to walk and I wasn't sure Gus would make it. But that was a risk we'd have to take. I'd just have to try not to lay the bike down. And there was an added benefit to this route: the transmitting tower was on a mountain southwest of Juarez. Once we crossed into Mexico, we were practically there. I was worried for Gus, though. He was sick. He had difficulty holding on to me as we rode.

But we made it okay—I only laid the Indian down once—and the damage to the chrome was not all that bad. It could be fixed. Gus could not.

Once in Mexico we found roads again. First there were footpaths, but I could handle the bike on them. Except for one place, a steep climb up an arroyo where the path was loose sand and stone. That was where I laid the bike down. I had to gun it up on my own and come back and carry Gus. He was mostly okay. He'd cut his forehead, though. He had green blood. And I found that he'd lost his John Deere cap somewhere along the way. I tore a strip off my tee shirt and wrapped the cut on his head. He looked pretty bad. He looked like an alien dressed up like a farm worker.

After the footpaths were dirt roads that led to Juarez. The city would have paved roads, but we turned off and rode up the hill to the transmission tower.

Before we could even bang on the door a man opened up and came outside. "*No puede usted leer el letrero*?" he asked. Can't you read the sign?

I stuck the .45 in his face and said, "Listen, motherfucker, we need the transmitter."

His hands shot up over his head. "*Adelante*," he said. Come in.

I pushed him inside and we faced a wall lined with gray steel cabinets dotted with dials and lights and meters. In one corner sat a desk and chair with its own little gray steel box of dials and lights and meters. He also had an orange thermos and a burrito and a telephone.

"*Necesitamos un micrófono*," I said. We need a microphone.

"I don't have one," the engineer replied.

I cocked the pistol.

"You can shoot me all you want, *pendejo*, but I still won't have a microphone. This is a *transmitter*. All I have is the tower and the feed from the studio. The studio has the microphones."

"Where's the studio?"

"Fuck if I know. I just started last week."
I pointed the pistol at him and he made a face at me.

"I know," I said. "I can shoot all I want but you still won't know where the studio is."

"I think," he said, "that it's on Avenida Reforma. But I'm not sure. When they hired me I filled out the paperwork at an office on Juarez Avenue."

"Okay," I said. "Do you have a phone?"

The engineer nodded toward the desk.

I ripped the phone out of the wall and gave it to Gus. I also took the burrito and the thermos. "What's this," Gus asked, looking at the thermos.

"Breakfast," I replied. "And coffee."

Outside I told Gus not to worry. I knew who knew where the studio was. I could have gone to see Don Pablo. He would have known. But Don Pablo would have asked questions I wasn't ready to answer. Instead I went to see Armando the printer. He directed us to the studio, which was on Avenido Reforma. We roared off on the bike, and down the road and out-of-sight I told Gus to throw the phone away. I ate the burrito, but Gus kept the coffee.

By the time we reached the studio, Gus could barely stand. The place itself was a long, low, redbrick, one-story building with a flat roof and windows that ran almost the whole front of the building. It took up almost half the block. I carried Gus into the office and was promptly ordered out by a gray-headed old secretary who spoke so loudly and with such authority that I feared she would call the police. For the next five minutes I walked up and down the sidewalk in a panic. Then I borrowed a handcart from an open-air vegetable market next door and placed Gus in a cardboard box labeled DOLE. I wheeled him that way around a corner and to the alley behind the building. There we found a back door with a man leaning against the wall smoking a cigarette. I told him, "*Regístrate aquí para la entrega.*" Sign here for the delivery.

"*Tómelo dentro,*" he replied. Take it inside. He jerked his thumb at the door and in we went.

There was a bracket bolted to the door that was made to hold a two-by-four and bar the door from the inside. The board was standing in the corner. I put the board in the bracket and wheeled Gus down the hall and into a room that looked like a warehouse. It was packed with boxes of equipment and stacks of spare furniture. There was another door out and it led down another hallway. This second hallway took us right into the studio. We heard the music before we saw the band.

Inside the studio a short, baldheaded Mexican man in a gray business suit was directing a show. There was a sound board behind him with an engineer at the controls. As we came into the room behind them, their backs were to us. A six-piece band with four singers was performing. All of them were Negroes. And behind them, stood another couple of dozen people—mostly Negroes: friends, family, and girlfriends of the musicians.

The band was a kind of country swing band and the singers were singing a song called "Across the Alley from the Alamo." It was a popular song that year. The band, as the expression was, was jumping, and the fans were all rocking. Even the director was swaying and tapping his feet and bouncing in time with the music. He turned around once and grinned at the engineer, but paid no attention to me.

The sound engineer was a big, fat Anglo in a cowboy hat and dark glasses. He was chewing gum and watching the dials on the sound board. He didn't seem interested in the music at all. He blew a big, fat pink bubble. He also paid no attention to me until I jerked the headphones off his head and stuck my pistol into his kidney. "Be very careful and do exactly what my friend tells you to do," I said. "Don't make a sound. Got it? Don't say anything to anybody." I cocked the pistol for emphasis.

He looked back at me with this big bubble of gum in the middle of his face and a *what-the-fuck* expression in his eyes, then nodded. I don't know what scared him more. Me with the pistol, or Gus standing in the DOLE box with a strip of white and green cloth tied around his head.

Gus climbed out of the box and looked at the pistol in my hand and said, "You promised not to kill anybody, remember?"

The engineer spit the gum and I nudged him with the pistol.

"Just tell him what you need," I hissed to Gus, "and let me take care of this asshole."

"But you promised!"

"Just do it! And hurry. You're dying, remember?"

"Stop the broadcast," Gus said.

"Don't tell them!" I added. "Don't disturb them. Let them sing, just turn the broadcast off."

The engineer looked from Gus to me and back to Gus.

Gus nodded.

The engineer unplugged a cable from his control panel. The music played on in the studio. He said, "Okay. It's off."

"I need a microphone," Gus said.

"He needs a microphone," I said. I nudged the engineer with the pistol and he handed Gus a big, clunky, stainless steel thing that weighted as much as a soup kettle.

"Plug it in," I said.

"What are you trying to do?" the engineer asked.

"What's your name?" I asked.

"Scotty," he replied. He was big fucker. When he turned around to look at me I saw that he had a white goatee. Kind of a pre-Beatnik thing. I remembered seeing him in Don Pablo's bar and I'm pretty sure I looked familiar to him, too. Scotty was easy to spot. He was that big. But he was trying to place me, too.

"I'm going to plug you, Scotty, right here in the studio, right in the fucking gut. That's what I'm doing if you don't plug this fucking microphone in right now," I said. "Got it?"

Scotty plugged the microphone in.

"Turn the power up," Gus said.

"Turn it up," I said.

"It is already up," Scotty said.

"I have to talk to my friends," Gus said. "They're a long distance away."

"He has to talk to his friends," I said. I jabbed Scotty with the pistol again. "They're a long way away. Do it."

He reached for a dial and turned it all the way up. I swear I could feel the electricity in the hair on my arms.

Gus tapped the microphone with his finger. "You are sure this is on?" Scotty nodded.

"If it isn't," I said, "I'll make you wish you were dead."

"They'll hear you at the north pole," Scottie said.

"Good," I said. "Now just look straight ahead and act natural."

Scotty looked straight ahead and probably wondered how to act natural with a gun jammed in his kidney.

I looked at Gus. Something like doubt crossed his face. He looked at me and began that long, slow music-like sound like I had heard at the base in Roswell.

No sooner had he started singing than the music stopped. The friends and station manager clapped and whistled.

Gus looked at me.

I jabbed at Scotty's kidney and said, "Get them singing again."

"Yeah, baby!" he shouted. "You guys are rockin' now!" He made a rolling gesture with his left hand and a thumbs-up with his right. The manager turned and looked at him funny. "Let's light it up with another one, huh?" Scotty shouted. "Whadaya say to that? Huh? If you got the money, honey, we got the time!"

The band struck up "When You Were Sweet Sixteen." It was another popular song. Scotty turned up the volume in the room.

Gus went back to singing his own song into the microphone, but a minute later he shook his head. "I need quiet. I think they will not hear me over this other music."

"Fuck," I said. I nudged Scotty's kidney with the pistol. "You got somewhere quiet?"

He pointed. "We got a sound booth."

To our right was a little booth about a quarter the size of the main studio. I have no idea what you would use it for. A news broadcast? An interview? A reading? But it had glass windows and a glass door. "It's quiet in there?"

Scotty nodded.

I looked at the booth and I looked at all the people in the room. With the pistol, it was easy to persuade Scotty and the station manager and band and their friends and family to all go into the little booth *for just a few minutes*. It was crowded, and they looked a little bewildered, and a few of them tried to hand me their wallets, but nobody argued with me and I didn't take their money. I shut them inside and they had to jam together like it was an elevator. But they fit and then they all stood looking out at us.

Gus looked at me like I was never going to get it. "I meant that maybe *we* could go in the booth."

"Whatever," I said. "You said you wanted quiet. It's quiet. So sing already."

Gus sang into his microphone in the now-silent studio. The only interruption we had was when the man smoking the cigarette—the man we had locked outside—came in from the front office with the gray-headed secretary. She looked even madder. We stuffed them in the booth, too.

When Gus was done, we made a break for the motorcycle.

"Where now?" I asked.

"Back to the antenna," Gus said.

"Will they come?" I asked.

"I hope so," he replied.

And we raced the hell out of there, leaving the secretary, Scotty, the director, the band, the singers, and the friends all staring after us like they'd just met a space alien or something.

They came. I can tell you they came, and I can tell you the details, but I can't explain the physics. I wish I could. I've had many years to remember this day and I've formed my own theory, but who knows? Nobody explained it to me. Gus was weak and sick and not talking much. And we hurried like the devil was on our tail.

I imagine that Gus knew the others would monitor the radios. He said they had a plan. They heard his call and could pinpoint the source of the transmission. I suspect that Gus told them to pick him up at the tower, but he didn't explain that to me. That would be the easiest thing. At the time it seemed like a miracle, but today you can use GPS and cell towers for just about anything. If I can find a Starbucks on Google Maps, I doubt it was difficult for them to find the most powerful radio broadcast in North America.

And they must have been listening, and maybe even watching, for no sooner did we arrive than the ship dived down a like bolt of silver lightning to hover inches above the ground. A door appeared in the side of the ship. I say *appeared* because nothing mechanical moved. The opening appeared where none had been and two beings so identical to Gus that I could not have told them apart ran to us. I was standing by the motorcycle supporting Gus. The two took Gus, doing their best to avoid touching me, and rushed back to the opening. But Gus cried out and they stopped. Gus shook loose and looked at me, his eyes large and (I swear) a little watery. He still clutched the orange thermos. He waved with his free hand and said, "Thank you, Pablo," but there was something else he wanted to say. I saw that.

I watched this in disbelief, stunned by the iron lightning that swooped from the sky to stop inches above the ground. I haven't even started to think about the door that opened from nothing, the green men that rushed to Gus, or anything else that had happened in the past thirty-six or so hours. "*De nada*, Gus," I replied. It was nothing. A stupid thing to say, but I spoke out of habit. It was not what I was thinking.

"Pablo," Gus said, his voice weak, "will *you* be all right?"

At that moment I had no idea what all right might look like. I still had blood under my fingernails from the soldier whose throat I slit. My wife's body was hanging from a rafter in the kitchen. I was going to have to tell Don Pablo that I had failed. And beside those little things, my entire reality, such as I knew it, had evaporated. I had not told Gus about the other side of dreams—nightmares. Gus said he would like to dream, but I hope that if he does, he will not experience what I felt that afternoon. "Sure," I said, "I'll be all right."

136

The two pulled on Gus's arms but he hung back and looked at me. "Pablo..."

My mouth was dry. There was so much I wanted to say to Gus.

Gus said something to the others and they replied in their strange, musical language. One of them called and a third came out and walked straight to me. He pressed into my hand a small clear pouch that I would today instantly recognize as a tiny Ziplock bag. Inside were two small white pills.

"If you get sick after I've gone," Gus called, "take one. With water. If it doesn't work in twelve hours, take the other."

"One?"

"One," Gus said. "We don't think it will hurt you. We haven't tested it, of course, but it was part of our plan if one of you should become contaminated by us."

"Okay," I said.

"I got my coffee." Gus lifted the thermos and smiled.

"I see," I said.

Gus looked at me and then at the two supporting him. "Pablo " he said. But then he didn't say. "Good-bye, and thank you. *No te olivdes tu promesa,*" he added, speaking Spanish, perhaps for emphasis. Don't forget your promise.

"I won't," I said. And then, just before they went inside. I said, "Gus—will you come back someday?"

They stopped again and he turned. "No," he said. He shook his head. "We will not come back." He looked at me with something like sadness in his eyes. "Your kind," he said, his breathing labored, "we would have helped you. We *came* to help you. But you are too dangerous. I don't know if you can be helped. I fear that you will kill yourselves off."

"I'm sorry," I said.

"Not *you* personally," Gus said. "I mean your kind."

"I know," I said.

"*You're* kind of interesting," Gus said. "I wish we had more time together. I'll miss you."

The transmission tower where we stood was surrounded by a fence, and at night they kept a watchdog on the grounds to keep people away. The dog, presuming there was one, must have been chained somewhere. Perhaps around back. I never saw it, but there was a bright yellow sign by the front gate that read CUIDADO CON EL PERRO in large black letters. BEWARE OF THE DOG. It showed the growling face of a mean dog, just to make certain that any trespasser was forewarned. Even one who could not read. Gus pointed at the sign. "We are going to put one of those out there," he pointed up, "so that should any others pass this way, they will know what you are like."

"Gus," I said.

He looked at me.

"Gus—" I said, but I couldn't say. "Did any of the others ever come? I mean, before you?"

Gus looked uncertain. "I don't know." He shrugged. "Perhaps."

"Gus?"

"Yes?"

"Were you watching us long?"

"In your time, for a while. But not so long in ours."

One of the creatures said something to Gus. It looked like *We have to hurry*.

Gus waved once more, then they turned and went inside. The opening closed. The ship was again a smooth, seamless silver metal. In an instant it streaked upwards and they were gone. There was no noise, no rocket, no visible engine. But a column of vapor marked the trail where they streaked skyward. And far above, very high in the sky, a still, round, orb of cloud appeared and lingered long after the ship was gone. I stood for several minutes looking after it before I saw the engineer standing in the doorway, his mouth wide open, his hands limp by his sides. He looked like he had seen a spaceship or something.

Act V Scene 1

I went to see Don Pablo and I expected to die. To tell you the truth, I didn't care if I did. And Don Pablo was expecting me. I could tell that right away. He probably had people out looking for me. Perhaps he was even worried about me. More likely he was worried about his business, but perhaps worried about me, too. I'd like to think so. He would have put the word out to watch for me. I bet the guards on the bridge were watching for me. By then I'm sure Don Pablo knew that I was in Juarez. Someone would have seen me. Armando would have sent word. So there was nothing else for me to do but to go and see Don Pablo—*to face the music* as they say. I had no idea what to tell him. The truth? That would go over really well.

Don Pablo was at his table. It was mid-afternoon. He watched me closely as I approached. I must have looked terrible. I was numb inside, exhausted. He signaled for me right away. I came to the table and sat down. The bar girl brought us a pitcher of beer and poured two glasses full. I saw a newspaper by Don Pablo's elbow. *The El Paso Times*. Don Pablo didn't read English. I wondered who was reading to him. As soon as the bar girl was gone Don Pablo leaned forward and grabbed my arm. "What happened?" he hissed. "What went wrong?"

I took a deep breath. "Everything."

Don Pablo glared at me. His face flushed red. He gripped my arm so hard it hurt.

"It is a long story," I said.

"I said delicately! *Delicately*. Did you have to kill them all?"

I stared at him. "Kill them all?"

He pushed the paper at me and I took it. It was folded to the fourth page and I picked out the article right away. "Soldiers Die in Fiery Crash."

I read, Don Pablo talked. "In the paper," Don Pablo said, "they call it an accident. They say the car went off the road, but . . . you killed him. Yes? Them. There were four of them. The soldiers. Did you shoot them all? Or just him? But they didn't mention you. Why would they? They wouldn't want people to know that their soldiers could be hunted down and killed like that."

The article was simple. Four soldiers died when a car drove over a cliff on a road outside of Ruidoso. One of them was Sergeant Varney Hall. The names of the others meant nothing to me. "He's dead," I said. It was a situation I would ponder for years.

"And three others. A butcher's job. Shit, I'm afraid to cross the border now." Don Pablo let go of my arm and leaned back in his chair, drained his beer and snapped his fingers for another. "But you got him." He shook his head and looked at the barmaid already refilling his glass. "I'll say that for you. When I send you out to do a job, you do it. I only wish it had been quieter. I don't need problems with the army." He withdrew an envelope from his inside coat pocket and handed it to me.

I took the envelope and stuffed it into the pocket of my jeans without opening it. But what I remember the most about that moment was the look in Don Pablo's eyes. It took a moment to register. I had known Don Pablo since I was a little boy, but I wasn't a boy now. For the first time in my life, Don Pablo was uncomfortable in my presence. I wondered if he was worried about the army causing him trouble, or the thought that I had just murdered four men.

"Don Pablo," I said.

"Eh?" he replied.

"It has been a long couple of days."

"I bet it has. Where did you find him?"

"He was on the base. There was something... he didn't want... he couldn't come off. He was on duty."

"But you got him. And his friends." Don Pablo grunted. "That will scare the hell out of Nixon."

"Don Pablo?"

"Yes?"

"I need to take some time off. Would you mind if I went away for a while? A lot has happened, Don Pablo."

Don Pablo took a long drink and set his glass down carefully. He looked at me. "I think laying low would be a good idea. For a while. Where do you propose to go?"

"I don't know. I need some time. Don Pablo..."

"Yes?"

"When I came back home, Maria was dead."

Don Pablo blinked in surprise.

"She hanged herself, Don Pablo. In the kitchen. I can't go home. The authorities will be looking for me."

Don Pablo took this in.

"I have always been loyal to you," I said. "You have been very good to me and I will not forget it."

"Go," Don Pablo said. "When you are ready to come back, you know where to find me." He took out his wallet and withdrew another stack of U.S. notes. He stood as I stood, and he pressed the money into my hand. I finished my beer and walked away. I had no way of knowing at the time, but this was the last time I would see Don Pablo. Odd, to wish now that I had said a better good bye, even to a man like him. Why is it that we bond with those who have abused us?

Act V Scene 2

Let me elaborate on my theory for just a moment. The US government knows that there is other life in the universe. Gus and his friends had been watching for a while. They knew that soon we humans would develop our technology to the point to where they would be found out. They had to act soon, and they were genuinely concerned with helping us. So they contacted someone in Washington. Here's where it gets tricky. Nobody knows who they contacted, or what the original instructions were. But an appointment was made, probably to meet at White Sands, which is remote as can be and close to Holloman Air Force Base. In the climate of the cold war, the military perceived an opportunity to gain access to new technology, potentially even new weapons. At the very least, they feared that this technology or these weapons might fall into the hands of the Russians. I can understand how they might fear that. So they shot down what has come to be known as a flying saucer. Whether by accident or design, somebody fired on Gus's ship. But the ship didn't crash right away. It escaped, but could not navigate well. The pilot, Gus's brother, was injured. They crashed outside of Roswell. It was recovered and the ship and Gus escaped *with the aid of a mysterious man who appeared from nowhere in a stolen Colonel's uniform and might be a Russian spy*. To this day the government doesn't know and doesn't say.

The knowledge that the government obtained was so important, and the way of life they were sworn to protect so threatened by these events, that everyone who had any knowledge whatsoever of the operation—its success and its significant failure—anyone with even remote knowledge of this, was killed. They died in car crashes and plane crashes. They died of diseases and allergic reactions. Electrocution. Drowning. Industrial accidents. Avalanches and drownings. They committed suicide. They fell down elevator shafts. They vanished without trace. Clerks, soldiers, MPs, x-ray technicians, radar operators, pilots, drivers, and surgeons, all of them. The only ones trusted with this knowledge were a small inner circle of generals and politicians—men who they knew would carry this secret with them to the grave.

Today the government still scans the skies for signs of life, but true to his word, Gus and his kind never returned. As for the rest—the wreckage and the ranchers and the weather balloons—all of this that you read on the internet, this is the hoax.

I did not kill Sergeant Varney Hall. Even the soldier whose throat I cut will have a certificate attesting that his death was due to some natural cause. The only reason that I am alive today and can tell this story is that—so far as they know—I was never there. Even weirder, the only witness to all this is Pablo Barela, a man *who never really existed*. And after July 8, 1947, the man who didn't exist, *ceased to exist*. For when I left Don Pablo's hotel, I returned to Armando's print shop and picked up the new IDs he prepared for me. And that night when I crossed the bridge to America, I bore the name of Pablo Zapata. Paul the Shoemaker. It was an inside joke on Armando's part.

What was it Gus said? That among his kind, names change, lengthen over time? So my identity changed. Again. In time, I would come to see this as being reborn, after a fashion. But to be reborn, one must first die. And that death was painful.

There is a term today for the shock, depression, even insanity, that follows serious trauma. They call it *post-traumatic stress disorder*. One survives the event, but in the aftermath experiences the pain. It is like the old saying, It is not the fall that kills you, but hitting the ground. You could say that, after all this, I hit bottom. For the second time in my life, I set out on the road. But unlike my childhood, I had a destination.

I abandoned my motorcycle in the alley behind Don Pablo's hotel and tossed my pistol into a garbage can. I walked across the bridge into El Paso and followed the railroad tracks east to the switching yard. I caught a train that night and late the next day I climbed off in San Antonio. In just a short time I found myself across the street from the Alamo. Out of curiosity I searched all around but found no alley, no pinto pony, no Navajo. No sign that there had ever been such things. The words of the song came back to me and I remembered that they had walked carelessly along a railroad track and been killed. The song reminded me of Gus and I was drawn to him in a way that I have never felt drawn to a human being. Not Maria. Not even Don Pablo. I wondered where Gus was at that exact moment and whether he could look down from above and see me. I wondered if he cared, and yet, I knew that for some reason, he did. They must have feelings, right? Gus grieved for his brother. And though Gus was ill, surely his kind prepared for that. He said they had a plan. He had to be alright.

I found a room for the night in a wino hotel downtown. It was a rotten, cockroach-infested old firetrap, but the room was cheap and the air was so bad I could have smoked for free just breathing. And I was not feeling well. My head hurt, my stomach was sour, and I felt fluid in my lungs. Even my bones ached. I took one of Gus's pills and went back to sleep.

I woke the next morning and felt much better. I ate eggs and beans and toast in a little restaurant downtown. When I left the restaurant, I passed a construction site where men were excavating in advance of putting up a building. A man called to me, "*Buscas empleo*?" Are you looking for work?

I shook my head.

He looked surprised. I think he was not used to being refused. Especially by drifters. "*Pagamos todos los días*." We pay every day, he said. He was a tall man, a gringo, and he wore a silver steel helmet. He walked over to the fence and offered me a cigarette.

"*Yo no fumo*," I said. I don't smoke.

He lit the cigarette and pointed back at the men digging. "*Necessito buenos trabajadores*." I need good workers.

"I speak English," I said.

"I'm shorthanded today," he continued. "I'd put another dozen men to work if I could find 'em. Tell you the truth, you'd be doing me a favor. I'll give you four dollars a day, and we got gloves for your hands. Hell, I'll even buy your lunch if you ain't got any."

It had never occurred to me—the thought of working for someone because they needed something done. I did not need the money. There were five hundred dollars in the envelope Don Pablo gave me, and he put two hundred more in my hand when I left. But I was doing nothing urgent. The day was twenty-four hours long and it didn't matter how I passed it. "Okay," I said.

I suppose if I worked as a laborer all my life, I would know a great deal about the types of soil, and which methods work best to manipulate it into position. I suppose my muscles would become like iron wires and the skin of my hand like the bark of a tree. But the first time you dig, even with gloves, the skin comes off your hands and your arms ache like they will fall off with the next movement, and you think you have learned all there is to know about digging in the first five minutes.

On the other hand, there was something comforting and familiar about the pain, and I was drawn to it: notching a groove in the ground for some pipe or another, advancing at a snail's pace through the heat of the morning until at noon everybody laid down their tools and ate lunch, then slept until three. At three we picked up our picks and shovels and went back at it until nearly nine. The boss bought me rice and beans and tortillas for lunch. There was plenty of water. All of the workers were Mexican. All the bosses were Anglo. The bosses cursed the Mexicans and the Mexicans laughed off the insults and then spit and swore under their breath as they worked.

Ants, Gus said, were social creatures. Socially evolved. Ants dug in the dirt. I liked digging. With a shovel in my hand and a line in front of me, my life had purpose. It might not seem like much, but after all I had just been through, it was the best I could come up with. It was all I had.

I took a different room that night. The room wasn't much better than the first, but I drank myself to sleep, lying alone in my bed and counting the cockroaches that crossed the opposite wall. In the morning I woke up and returned to the jobsite. I worked four days and then it was Sunday. On Sunday there was no work.

I liked working. I had shined shoes and done this and that for years, but I had never labored with a shovel. But I did not want to stay in San Antonio. I hitchhiked to Houston. In Houston a man shouted to me from a machine shop. His name was Arnold and he needed someone to grind the welds flat on parts that he was making for forklifts. It was mindless, tedious, hard work. I liked it. In Beaumont I drilled holes in lengths of pipe. In Lake Charles I scoured barnacles off the hull of a tugboat. In Lafayette I ran a machine that sealed the lids on cans of stewed tomatoes. Slitch, pop. Slitch, pop. Slitch, pop. Twelve hours a day of that. In Baton Rouge I was in a shipyard again grinding new welds flat on the factory deck of a fish processor. By now I learned that if you were Mexican and walking down the road, people figured you were looking for work and were willing to pay you a few dollars a day for your labor. The expression today is *under the table*. There were no taxes and no insurance. You would work a day or a week and then leave, or if the work ran out, be told when to return.

Some of the workers were friendly. Others grim and silent. I was of the opinion that the talkative ones came to America to support families back home. They chatted because they missed their families. Sometimes they rented homes and brought their families from Mexico or Guatemala or El Salvador or Nicaragua. Honduras. Belize. Costa Rica. The grim and silent ones, I suspected, were on the run from something. The law maybe. Debts. Enemies. Who knows? They had nothing but each other. They stuck together in little groups.

I liked the talkative ones but said nothing and stuck to nobody. I drank myself to sleep every night. Every morning I woke hoping only to lose myself in the pain work promised. My muscles tightened and my blisters crusted over, but the ache in my heart was there every morning like the ocean or the wind or the sun. And it was all this that I carried now—the blood, the anger, the pain. Filo. Maria. The soldier in the clinic. The fact that my entire belief system— such as it was—had been turned upside down. I was afraid the weight of it all was going to kill me. Those who live by the sword, Father Sheehy said. Or perhaps, I was afraid that I would not die, would never die, and my penitence was to carry this pain around forever. Crime and punishment.

Act V Scene 3

The architecture is French, not Spanish. The structures are white stone, not red brick or adobe. St. Louis Cathedral is much larger than Sacred Heart Church. And in all of New Orleans, and certainly in the French Quarter, it might be the easiest building to find. How hard can it be to find a priest? I had only to ask to be directed to the church and a hallway and an office where I saw an old familiar sign: STUDY. I knocked and the door swung open. Father Sheehy blinked for a second before he smiled, stood up, and grasped my hand. "Pablito," he said, "I've been expecting you." And hearing this, I burst into tears.

After I regained my composure Father Sheehy led me out of the church and to the open air market where he stopped and bought a baguette and a basket of ripe strawberries. Then we walked to the river and south along the levy until we reached a pile of boulders.

It had been ten years since we last spoke, but Father Sheehy looked much, much older. He was thin now, his face creased, and he bent slightly at the waist and limped when he walked. His hair had gone all white. His mouth was pinched and there were fine lines etched at the corners, veins showing in his cheeks. He handed me the strawberries and broke the loaf in half, gave me half, and then he munched on bread until I passed him the strawberries. All this time I said nothing, nor had he spoken to me. After I finished my bread I said, "You asked me once what I would do if I found that my life had been a mistake?"

He nodded. "And what have you found, Pablito?"

"That it was."

"What happened, Pablito?"

"Do you believe in miracles?"

"I don't just *believe* in miracles, Pablito, I depend on them."

"I mean like people walking on water and fires that don't burn out. Stories that people tell about things that happened. I need to know, father, are these things real?"

For the second time Father Sheehy said, "Pablito, what happened?"

"It doesn't matter," I said.

He took a strawberry and ate it, looked at me as if he could see into my heart. "How long has it been since you've been to confession?"

"I've never been to confession, Father, unless my mother took me when I was very small. Or unless you count our time talking together."

"Perhaps it is time, then."

"What would it change, this confession?"

"Confession changes many things, Pablito. Perhaps everything."

"It can't change what happened."

"It can change the way you *feel* about what happened, and that's important. And it can change the way God feels about what happened. That's

144

the most important thing of all. To be forgiven, one must first admit one's mistakes."

"If God has all power, doesn't he already know what happened?"

"Of course he does."

"Then wouldn't he already know how I feel about things?"

"He knows that, too. Your confession is about your honesty and willingness. It is a statement that your faith is greater than your fear. There is no way to make that statement except to confess."

"What if I told you that everything we believe is wrong? Me. You. All of us. What then?"

Father Sheehy touched his chin with his thumb. "Pablito, what have you done?"

"I haven't done anything, Father. Or maybe I have. It doesn't matter."

"Something has changed in you."

"I asked if you believe in miracles."

"And I do."

"What is a miracle?"

"A miracle is something that happens that cannot be explained by natural law."

"Have you ever seen one of these miracles?"

"What are you talking about, Pablito?" There was urgency in the priest's voice. "What happened?"

"I asked if you had seen one of these miracles. With your own eyes? Have you?"

"Not with my own eyes, but—"

"Do you know anyone who has?"

"*Has* what, Pablito?"

"The church talks about miracles, Father! About saints and angels and things like . . . like . . . like walking on water and fires that burn forever . . . things we can't explain."

"People rising from the dead."

"Yes, people rising from the dead. Do you know even one person who has seen any of these miracles?"

Father Sheehy stood up. "No, Pablito, I don't know anyone who has seen these things "

"Then how do you know they really happened?"

"These are Articles of Faith, Pablito."

I looked at him.

"Do you know what that means, *Article of Faith?*"

I shook my head.

"It means that we accept the testimony of trustworthy men and women who have seen and recorded these events. It means we accept them and we don't ask questions."

I was thinking about what Gus had said about some men who had glimpsed these truths, and how they tried to pass it on to others, but that the message changed, maybe through our imperfections, perhaps through misunderstandings, or perhaps these other men and women had their own goals in mind, or that the organizations they created to perpetuate these teaching themselves took on lives of their own. What was it he said? They did the best they could with what they had?

Father Sheehy took a deep breath and looked up at the sky. "Pablo," he said, "people come to the church looking for answers. It's one of the things I most admire about people—that they ask questions. Sometimes I think that's what the Bible means when it says man is made in God's image—that we alone of all creation ask these questions about life. A dog doesn't ask how to be a dog but a man asks how to be a man. But at the same time, we have to understand our place in things. Do you know what humility is, Pablo?"

"No."

"Humility means knowing one's place. Humiliation is what happens when we are put in our place. It's one thing for people to ask questions, but another to demand answers. Would we even understand the answer if it were given us? I think that what matters is not that we ask questions, but why we ask questions. Are we asking questions to grow, or are we asking to keep from growing? To keep from doing what we know is right? Or worse, to continue doing what we know is wrong? And sometimes, Pablo, there are no answers. Sometimes we have to accept what happens without question." Father Sheehy looked alarmed. He bent down over me and took me by the shoulders. His grip was strong. "What happened Pablito? Why won't you tell me? What have you seen?"

"It doesn't matter, Father. Even if I told you, you wouldn't believe me."

"I might," he said.

"No. I only came because I had to know if you believed in miracles, and because you told me once that I should remember that I am not alone. Right now, I feel very alone."

Father Sheehy relaxed his hand on my shoulder. "You are only as alone as you choose to be, Pablito. I also told you that I saw a struggle inside you between light and darkness, and that I didn't know which would win. To be alone, Pablo, is the best way I know of for the darkness to overwhelm us. This is why believers congregate together. This is why God gave us the Church."

"Then tell me, Father, why there are hermits and saints and monks who seek solitude?"

Father Sheehy squinted at me.

"You told me, Father, that if I wanted to make a new life for myself, that God would forgive a small lie."

"I believe that he would."

"Would he forgive something bigger?"

Father Sheehy sat back down beside me. He took a deep breath and said, "You know, Pablito, God loves every one of us. He loves us so much that sent his Son to die for us so that by having faith in Him, we can be forgiven anything. We have only to ask."

"Are you saying," I asked, "that God killed his own Son?"

"In a manner of speaking, yes. His Son also chose to die."

"What is it with you people?" I said.

"What?"

"I killed Filo," I said.

Father Sheehy stared at me.

"Later on, I married his sister. And then I killed her, too. Not with my hands, Father, but with my actions. I killed what we had. I killed her love for me. And when that was gone, she killed herself."

Father Sheehy watched me, motionless and silent.

"But now something happened and I know better. Only, now I don't know what to do, Father, and there's nobody else I can talk to."

"Are the police after you, Pablo?"

"No," I said. "Nobody knows. Maria hanged herself. Even she did not know about Filo, or if she knew, she never said. As for Filo, he tried to kill me. He almost did but I escaped. That was kind of a miracle. He betrayed the whole gang. That started a war. A lot of people got killed because of Filo. Don Pablo caught him and sent me to kill him. I think he thought that I would enjoy my revenge. But I did not want revenge. I didn't. Now I would rather I died in his place. But at the time, there was no way out for him. Probably not for me, either. I stabbed him in the heart, Father, and I buried him in the desert. I wished it was different, but I can't go back and change that. And now I have promised that I will never kill again, but I need to know if I can be forgiven."

Father Sheehy motioned that I should follow him. The sun was setting and the sky fading to a deep red. One of the famous paddlewheel ships was passing by on the river. There were tourists there on the deck, and a brass band playing a hopped-up version of "There is Rest for the Weary." It was a popular song back then. The boat sounded two blasts on its horn.

"This is not," Father Sheehy said, "the first murder confession I have heard. There is little you could say that would shock me."

"Okay."

"Only God can search your heart and determine whether to forgive or punish. I suspect that you carry around a great deal of guilt, Pablo. Perhaps God sees this and sought you out for whatever experience you claim. All I can say is that if you call on Him in faith, and you seek forgiveness in His church, and you make confession and follow the instructions the confessor gives you, then you have nothing to fear."

"Filo didn't have a crippled brother."

Father Sheehy looked at me. "What?"

"You told me he had a brother and he asked you to help him. But there was no brother. He was lying to you. He used you, the same as he used me."

Father Sheehy shrugged. "It doesn't matter," he said. "He was just a boy."

"I just thought that if you knew, you might not think so badly of me."

"I don't think badly of you, Pablo. You, too, were just a boy. An orphan at that. I believe you did the best you could with what you had to work with."

"Then you don't hate me?"

"No, Pablo. I can only love you, and to the best of my human ability, forgive you. And if I can do this, imperfect human that I am, how much better can God forgive you? You have only to ask."

"I wish that it was that simple."

"It is that simple," he said.

"No, it isn't."

Father Sheehy held me in his gaze for several minutes, then we turned and walked on. The street was filling up with tourists. It was evening and they were headed out for a night of eating and drinking and music and whatever. Juarez, New Orleans, it's the same the whole world over.

"What are you going to do, Pablo?"

"I don't know," I said. "I don't know what I can do. I don't know if I even want to keep on doing."

"Come," Father Sheehy said. We were walking back south down Decatur Street. We neared Jackson Square and I could see the cathedral. Father Sheehy pulled me into the Café Du Monde. We found a table. A waiter came. Father Sheehy ordered two café au laits and two baskets of beignets.

The coffee was hot and we sweetened it with powdered sugar. Gus, I thought, would have liked it. The beignets were sizzling, right out of the fryer, and we dusted them with powdered sugar, too, and ate them before they cooled, all six of them.

When we finished the beignets, Father Sheehy ordered more coffee, and when it came he said, "My family came from Scotland, Pablo. Do you know where Scotland is?"

I shook my head, No.

"It is a small country north of England. It's much like Scandinavia—cold in the winter, and the summers are short. Where I come from, most of the people mine coal. In the winter, it is dark. The miners go to work early in the morning and it's dark, and they come out at night and it's dark. They can go months in the winter and not see the sun. It's no way to live, Pablito.

"And it's difficult to make a living. The people are poor. I was the youngest of three sons. My father made it clear he was going to leave what little he had to my oldest brother, Hamish. A cottage, a little land. My middle brother, Boyd, moved to Glascow. He apprenticed to a machinist and works in a factory. I wanted an education, Pablo. Maybe that's why I'm sympathetic to young people with no opportunity. How could I afford school?

"None of my family had ever been to school. They were old-fashioned, Pablo. Rustic and plain. My father wanted nothing more than meat on his table and a fire in the hearth. And there is nothing wrong with that. But young people, Pablo, they always find fault with their parents. I know you're an orphan and can't imagine that, but this is how it is. Every generation despises the one that came before. So I hated my father for his simple ways. I hated him for his lack of education and ambition. I hated him for all the things he couldn't give me.

"In Scotland there were three ways to obtain an education. If your father was wealthy, he sent you to the university. Mine was not. If you distinguished yourself in school there were government scholarships or patrons who might support you. I did not. The only other option was the church. When you enter the priesthood, you enter into college. The path to becoming a Jesuit takes many, many years. That was why I became a priest, Pablo. I wanted an education. My father forced me to withdraw from school to work in the mines. I was fourteen. I ran away from home and I found refuge in the church. So you see, Pablo, you're not the only boy in the world who's had troubles.

"But there was something else," he said. "I did not know it then, I'm not even certain that I could have seen it had it been shown me, but underlying my desire for education was something else. Pablo, I became a priest because I wanted to *help* people. That was why I was teaching Filo, and that was why I taught you. So would it surprise you to know, Pablo, that I do not agree with every teaching of the church?"

This startled me and I searched the old priest's face for a lie.

"No, Pablo, those who seek knowledge are driven by questions, and with those questions comes the propensity to doubt. All men of faith wrestle with doubts. Perhaps that is why some of them—as you pointed out—seek solitude as hermits. But even those who repudiate faith wrestle with doubts, and the louder they protest against faith, the stronger (I suspect) is their longing for the answers that faith provides. Perhaps, Pablo, this is what I saw in you in those last few months we studied together."

"That I had doubts?"

"No, Pablo. That you wanted to help people."

I shook my head. "I never helped anyone, Father. I think that most of my life I have only harmed others."

"You bought Filo shoes. You sought to protect him from me. That was helping."

"I stabbed Filo in the heart."

"You acted as anyone would given the circumstances of your upbringing."

"Then what good have I done, Father?"

"You came to me to learn to read and write. You came for an education.

And I can tell that you have continued to study on your own. That's three more good things, and every other good thing that you do will be the result of those. You are not the same boy that you were. Now you ask me what to do with this knowledge. You can do many good things if you choose, Pablo. You wish that certain things hadn't happened? You cannot change the past, but you can change how you feel about your past. You can use these things to make recompense for what wrongs you have done. Helping others, Pablo, will ease your pain."

"I cannot repay those I have harmed the most, Father, though I wish that I could."

And then Father Sheehy said the strangest thing. "You are thinking only of this plane of existence, Pablo. Our Lord said not to store up treasures for ourselves in this world, but rather, to store up treasures for ourselves in heaven. You can transform the harm you have done, but it will take time, and faith, and you will wrestle with your doubts. But if this thing that has happened to you is real, then you will be all right. But only you can answer that. Do you know why I brought you here, Pablo, to this café?"

I shook my head.

"Because on the bad days, I have to remind myself that there are good things in this world, too, like coffee and beignets, and that God wants me to enjoy them. Life is about balance, Pablo. Help others with their suffering. But when all you see is suffering, and the suffering is too much for you to bear, remember to do something nice for yourself. Keep your strength up, Pablo."

Father Sheehy reached out and touched my arm. "I was certain that I would see you again before I go. And I'm glad you came now. Next week I sail for Europe. They will send me to Germany, or Poland, or somewhere where they need priests more than here. I don't expect that I will see you again."

"How hard can it be to find a priest?" I asked.

"Probably not hard, Pablo," he said, "but first you have to know where to look. And for today, only God knows where that will be. But at the risk of being sentimental, Pablo, if you remember our conversations, I shall always be with you."

Act V Scene 4

Once I wondered whether there were good people in the world. Now I know that there are. I've met a few of them. Others I admire through the pages of books or from television or newspapers. The testimony of trustworthy men and women. I especially appreciate their patience and faith and the gentleness and compassion with which they navigate (or navigated) life. Some of these are or were religious leaders. Others just ordinary people. Perhaps I should say extraordinary, although I believe they would dismiss that adjective. Would it surprise you to know that among those I admire are Mahatma Gandhi, Leo Tolstoy, Cesar Chavez, Martin Luther King, Mother Teresa, Aung San Suu Kyi, and Tenzin Gyatso? Maybe that's not what you'd expect from a shoeshine boy. But why not? Can't a shoeshine boy acquire values?

I also respect and admire my wife. But the two who influenced me most I knew only for a short period of time. I knew Father Sheehy for two years, and Gus for less than two full days. But as Father Sheehy suggested, I have carried their words with me ever since, and in that way I still feel their presence. And their words have been for me like a key. They unlocked a door to understanding many things.

I wish I could say that I lived up to the priest's admonition to help others, but I am a man, not a saint. What does it mean to do good? It is one of those complex things like Gus talked about. Gus, on the other hand, made me promise only one thing: not to kill! By comparison, that was easy. But if one can do *one* easy thing, is it that difficult to stretch the easy thing into another, or into something only a tiny bit more difficult? For instance, if I were not to kill someone, would it become a bit easier, say, not to beat the crap out of them, even if they deserved it? And from there, perhaps to a state of being where I could control my tongue? And from there, to control my anger, even in the secret and silent spaces of my heart? So if I made any progress at all, it was incremental, at best. And there were setbacks all along the way.

For the next seventeen years I lived the life of what they call an illegal alien, walking, riding, hitchhiking, hopping trains from place-to-place. I tended grapefruit orchards in Florida and onion fields in Georgia. I worked in shipyards in Mississippi until they ran all the illegals out, and then I returned to New Orleans for a time, where there was always a restaurant that needed a cook, a dishwasher, or a busboy. There was always someone with a room or a bed to let, and in restaurants you never starve (although I have to admit, I tired of chicken necks and gravy over rice).

There were women on the road and in the camps. Sometimes they traveled with their families, sometimes with female companions, sometimes they were with men, and if they were alone they were seldom alone for long. So there was always companionship to be had, if I wanted company. Several times, when I spent time with just one woman, I found, for a while, that the spark I thought had died still burned faintly somewhere deep inside me.

I craved love, even if I pretended that I didn't. I wanted a home. But these torrid and tempestuous affairs never last, and I kept my reputation as an independent man; a brooding, sullen, silent man. I read all the time, and was often teased for my habit of reading. It was not something that mostly illiterate laborers admired. Perhaps they were jealous. Perhaps it reminded them of their own lack of opportunities. One thing for certain: my ability to read and write and speak English served me well, and I used my skill to help others. When my fellow workers needed help with English, they came to me. I read contracts, and translated leases. I negotiated purchases, even explained some small legal matters. Things like this.

Only once did I ever see anyone I knew from my former life—a man who showed up one day to harvest onions outside of Visalia, Georgia. I recognized him from the bars in Juarez, though he did not recognize me. I quit that afternoon and left Georgia that night. Another time I heard some people around a burn barrel talking about me. I had come up from behind them and they didn't know I was standing just outside the circle of light. Somebody said that I ran with the gangs back in Mexico. He said I was a hit man. Maybe somebody I didn't remember recognized me.

I don't know which will drive people away faster—having a reputation as a hit man or being caught reading books like *Song of the Open Road*. "Why are you reading this?" somebody asked. What could I tell them? Because Whitman would have known what it was like to walk from Torreón to Juarez, or from Birmingham to Chattanooga? That he would have enjoyed a walk like that? That he might have understood my pain?

The world is full of people, but to the gringos I'm an alien, to the Mexicans I'm a freak. The only people I understood, and who I thought might understand me, populated the pages of the books I read. And so on paydays, when everybody else loaded up on food and liquor and cheap, glittering jewelry and shoes and clothes they did not need, I stalked the aisles of second-hand bookstores. I graduated from the Hardy Boys and Nancy Drew to Cervantes and Steinbeck, Hemingway and Sinclair Lewis. I read every book I could get my hands on including old textbooks about literature. I read the jackets on the books and the authors' biographies. I read to find other books they wrote, or books they liked, or books and authors who influenced them.

I'm not saying I didn't drink. I did. But I read, too. I'd read for a while and then drink myself to sleep. That was my life. Working and reading and drinking. One thing bothered me, though. The more I drank, the less I enjoyed reading. Sometimes I'd wake up and find a marker in a book, and not remember a word I'd read. That bothered me.

Only once in those years was I ever tempted to break my promise to Gus. I was cooking in a restaurant in Oklahoma City. I had been sleeping with a married waitress named Sonia. She worked at the same place. Her husband did not have a job. They shared a trailer with a half-dozen other illegals. When her husband found out about us he beat her black and blue. When I saw her at work the next day, I quit my job, slipped a filet knife into my belt, and went to the trailer. His name was Manny and he was sitting on the front steps drinking a Coors when I pulled up. I got out of the car and he stood up and I flattened him. There were two other men in the house and they came out in time to see Manny try to stand up and me flatten him again. They came down the steps but I took

Manny by the throat and pulled the knife. "I've done it before," I said. "It's nothing to me now. I'll cut his throat, then yours."

They looked at me.

"Go ahead," I said. "Call the cops. Let them take us all to prison."

I had broken Manny's nose and his jaw. He was trying to pry my hand from his throat but I was so angry I could hold with one hand what he could not pry off with two. "Listen, *pendejo*," I said, poking him under his left eye with the knife and drawing blood, "If you had a job and took care of your woman, she wouldn't look for love anywhere else, *comprende*? So when you get out of the hospital, and she's gone, and you start over, think about doing better next time, eh?" I cut the tendons in his thumbs to make sure he didn't hurt Sonia again—and to give him something to remember me by.

I took Sonia to Wyoming and we lived together almost three years. I went to work as a grinder in a machine shop. She worked breakfast and lunch shifts in restaurant downtown. My boss was a cowboy type named Leonard Fitchbinder. We all called him "Bitchfinder" behind his back, but he was a good guy. He drove a white Cadillac convertible with the top down except when it rained or snowed. He hired a lot of drifters and Mexicans and whatnot. He had a few Germans working for him, and in the post war years, that was a big deal. He even had a Russian. I don't know how the Russian got to America, and he didn't say.

Bitchfinder didn't pay all that much, but on Fridays he'd bring a couple of cases of beer to the shop and he'd drink all night with us. He wasn't like a lot of the people I worked for. Sure, he was exploiting us. But if a man got hurt on the job, Bitchfinder took him to the hospital and paid the bill. And if a man's kids got sick, Bitchfinder paid the doctor's bill. If somebody's car broke down and they were having trouble getting to work, either one of the mechanics at the shop fixed it, or a few extra bucks might show up on somebody's paycheck. Hell, I once found Bitchfinder under the hood of my old Ford, changing out the carburetor. He was a good guy. So I wasn't too mad when I found out he took a liking to Sonia. I suppose I could have made a scene, but for what? He could offer her a lot more than I ever could, and it's not like I hadn't done my share of messing around. Maybe I was just getting older, or maybe it was one of those *progress in small increments* things. I didn't even get mad. Besides, my car ran better than ever. Maybe that was why he fixed my carburetor. I left Wyoming as winter was about to set in. I drove all night just ahead of a storm. I drove all the way to California.

Act V Scene 5

There was a lot of talk about California in the early 60's, but I'd never been there. Maybe that's why I finally went. It was kind of a scene. Especially around San Francisco. And there were a lot of Mexicans living there, and they had been there for generations, just like in Texas. But until I got to California, I'd never heard the word *Chicano*. Many Mexicans used this new name for themselves, but there was some dispute about its meanings and origin, and who could properly call themselves Chicano. I came from Mexico and even though I'd lived, by now, most of my life in America, I still thought of myself as Mexican. But there were Mexicans or Latinos or Hispanicos who had lived their entire lives in America, who spoke better English than Spanish (or even no Spanish at all). They wanted to differentiate themselves from the Mexicans who came north every year to pick beans and harvest grapes, and who sometimes—like me—stayed if they found a place in the shadows. I think the word Chicano came, at least at first, to mean those people like me who were neither here nor there. We were not Mexican, but we were not American, either. We were aliens in both places. Later on, when anger spilled over into rebellion, and the word *Chicano* became cool, many people, even Latinos from other Spanish-speaking countries, co-opted the word for their own identities.

So in the winter of 1964 I was in San Francisco. I found the cheapest of all rooms from a man who wasn't particular who he rented to. I had the room in the daytime. Somebody else had it at night. How's that for doubling your profit? There was a sink in the room to wash in and a toilet that didn't work down the hall. I never saw the sheets clean the whole time I stayed there, which wasn't all that long.

I worked in a restaurant for a while—that's the easiest job to find—and then I worked in a tire shop until a jack slipped and chopped the tip off the middle finger of my left hand. I crushed it under the rim of a '57 Chevy. That was no fun. Part of the deal at the tire shop was that I got to sleep in a shipping container in a weedy lot behind the shop. The minute I couldn't work, I was out of a place to live. They also didn't pay me. They acted like it was my fault. Yeah, the rim was busted. But that didn't mean I had to buy a new one.
The shop foreman bandaged my hand. He did that just before the owner and his buddy showed up told me to clear out. I slept in Golden Gate Park for a few nights. I drank a lot of wine to dull the pain, and another bum gave me some little pink pills he had in his pocket. I had to take all of them, but they did the job. While I was there, another homeless man told me that the grape-growers down south were desperate for help and would pay $1.25 a day for labor. He had a flyer with some names and phone numbers, a little map. I figured I could cut grapes all right with a hand-and-a-half, so the next day, I hitchhiked south. That was in September, 1965.

It was nighttime when I reached Delano. I got some tacos and beer downtown, then lugged my gear to the vineyards out west of town and up in the hills. I didn't even reach the place in the flyer before I found a job. I was just walking up the road. There was a big burn barrel in the middle of the road where the entry to this vineyard turned off the highway. A couple of men with shotguns sat in folding chairs playing cards and drinking coffee. I knew right away something wasn't right, but before I could say anything the men were up and asking if I'd come to pick grapes, and like a fool, I said, "Yes." One of the men walked me down the road to a little camp where thirty or forty workers had pitched tents. I should have known better, but I was about half-stoned from the beer. *Maybe it's just different out here*, I thought.

I slept on the ground, wrapped in a blanket, and used my duffel bag as a pillow. In the morning the boss hammered on a bucket and woke us up at sunrise. They fed us coffee and cornbread and beans and everybody ate in a rush. We piled into the back of an old flatbed truck and they hauled us out to the vines and we went to work. I didn't have a good knife—just my old switchblade—and the foreman didn't like that I had but one good hand. So instead of picking, he put me to emptying baskets and told me I damn well better keep up or he'd have a new helper the next morning. Each basket had a number and each worker had three or four baskets. My job was to take the full baskets and then run from wherever they were cutting back to the truck, which was at the end of the row. I had to call out the basket number to the foreman, empty the baskets, then run back to where I had collected them and leave them there. The baskets were wicker and I could carry two in each hand and one more hung in the crook of my elbows. There were ten or fifteen pounds of grapes in each basket and, if the workers were at the far end of the row, sometimes I had to run a couple of hundred yards. The ground was rocky and rough and I hadn't made three trips before I got my feet tangled up in some old baling wire and fell. I spilled all the grapes and I crushed two of the baskets. After that the workers were pissed at me, too. They got paid by the day, but they also had to fill a certain number of baskets. If the foreman thought the baskets were anything but heaping full he only counted them as half. Worse, when I fell, I smashed my hand pretty good, and started bleeding again and aching something terrible.

There was no way I could keep up. Every up-and-down I got further and further behind. When the workers had to wait on me to bring empty baskets, they cursed me. "What the hell?" I said. "Take a break." But they didn't want breaks. When you're living on a $1.25 a day, you don't have any savings to fall back on. You got no way to relax. Hell, I thought, I made more money shining shoes.

There was an old woman in the group who carried a big bucket of water and a ladle to drink it with. She went around from picker to picker with the water. By ten in the morning it was ninety in the shade and there wasn't any shade. We ran out of water and the old woman walked back to the camp for more. That took her an hour. So when it got real hot, we had no water. Later another truck came by with more cornbread and beans and we knocked off for lunch and to lay under the vines until two or so. I could barely move and nobody wanted to talk to me. They were all mad that I was so slow.

I was forty-three years old. Up to then I'd always been able to do things, you know. I could run, work, fight, fuck all night. I sometimes worked thirty-six, forty-eight hours on end. I sometimes worked two jobs—a day job and a night job. I had felt contempt for people who couldn't work like I did, but that fall I learned what it meant to grow old. I knew that I couldn't work like I did forever. There was no way. Life catches up with you. All the old hurts, they come back. I thought of all the old people I had worked with. I tried to do nice things for them. I wanted to make sure they had the easiest jobs and enough food to eat and a good place to sleep. When I ran a crew, I wanted to make sure that my people were okay. But not everybody was like that. This place sure wasn't.

I looked at the old woman and realized that she was, what? Sixty? Sixty-five? And all the workers a few years younger than her were just holding on, just trying to make it through another day, another season, hoping against hope that somehow, someway, they would make enough money to buy a house, start a business, find a real job, to settle down and live a normal life. The family members, at least, helped each other the best they could. Gus would have said they were working for the common good. The rest, like me, what did we have going for us? What did we have to offer but our blood one day at a time? What chance did we have?

I'd had a house, once, and a wife, and a pretty comfortable life. And all I had to do to get it was to run a little dope, break a few laws, and kill a few people who probably deserved it anyway. Now I was doing supposedly honest work, and I could barely feed myself. *What is wrong with you people?* I wondered.

I knew the Ten Commandments—I remembered this from *Catechism for Youth*—and that Thou Shalt Not Kill was one of these, and that Thou Shalt Not Steal was another, and that I was supposed, little-by-little, to move in the direction of doing good. It was a short step from not killing to not stealing, but according what I had learned they were equally wrong in God's eyes, and there were eight other of these things, or at least, other things that I was supposed to learn to do, or not to do. But how can you do good when only the bad is rewarded? Was this the "wrestling" that Father Sheehy said would happen?

We didn't stop until almost nine P.M. Long before that I quit running. I could barely walk. I could carry one basket in each hand. My arms were killing me. The foreman was mad. The pickers were mad.

The truck was loaded. There was no place to put any more grapes. No room for us, either. The truck left for town and we stumbled back to camp in the dark, exhausted. When I got there two goons with shotguns met me and said, "Come with us" and walked me out to the front gate. One of them gave me a dollar. They fired me.

I looked at the bill in my hand and said, "You promised me a buck twenty-five a day."

"And you got it," he said. "But we charge you a quarter for your meals and your tent."

"I had two meals!" I shouted. "Beans and cornbread, not even any meat! And nobody gave me a tent! I slept on the fucking ground!"

The goons chambered shells. "Get lost," the first said.

"You can't work for shit," the other one said, but you might make okay fertilizer."

And then a voice behind me said, "You're not going to shoot anyone, Karl."

The goons looked past me and I turned. Stepping out of the dark behind me was an Anglo priest, and flanking him a Chicano man and woman. They must have been watching from the field across the road. "Give him his money," the priest said. "Or I'll shut this place down. I'll block the road until your grapes rot."

For a moment, nobody said anything. Then the man the priest called Karl took a quarter from his pocket and flipped it high into the air. It plopped on the road in front of me. When I bent over to pick it up, he kicked me in the ass and flattened me. They laughed.

The priest and the man with him helped me to my feet. "*Vamanos*," the priest said. Let's go. We started to walk but the woman stayed behind and unleashed a torrent or profanity at the guards beginning with "You motherfuckers" and ending with "straight to hell."

The other Chicano went back and pulled her away. "*Calmese*, Dolores," he said. Cool it.

Act V Scene 6

I had worked long hours, gone hungry, been fired more times than I could count. I'd been cheated of my pay, robbed at gunpoint, lied to, lied about, defrauded, you-name-it. But for some reason, this time really hurt. Maybe it's because I was getting older. Maybe it was because winter was coming and I had lost part of a finger and my hand was fucked up, and for the first time in a long time I was worried about surviving. Maybe because it all happened so fast. Maybe I was just sick of it all—the whole thing—life, people. I thought about Gus. "What is wrong you people?" he asked. Why are we so intent on hurting one another? Why? Why do we treat each other like this? Why didn't they just pay me and let me go? Did twenty-five cents mean that much to them? They

157

weren't going to keep that quarter because they needed it. They were going to keep it precisely because *they didn't* and *I did*. And that's just wrong.

The goons were still laughing about kicking me, the way I fell face first into the dirt. The priest had an arm around me and supported me. The woman had grabbed my duffel bag but the other man took it from her and slung it over his shoulder. They walked behind us. "I'm Donald McDonnell," the priest said. "We've got a camp a few miles down the road. Do you think you can make it, or should I send for a motorcycle?"

"I can make it," I said. I shook loose from him. "Here," I said to the man behind me. "I'll take my bag."

The man was short and stocky, broad-shouldered, and the Indian in his blood showed through. High cheekbones. A broad, smiling face. Straight black hair. He had the look of a man who knew hard work. He also had the warmest smile I have ever seen on another human being. You had only to look at this man to know he was the best friend you were ever going to make. He stuck out his hand to me and said, "Cesar Chavez."

The camp down the road didn't look much different from the camp where I'd spent the night the night before. Bigger, maybe. And cleaner. There might have been a hundred people there. There were plenty of tents and lots of campfires. Some of the tents were just tarps hung over ropes and staked into the ground. They might keep the rain off for a while, if it wasn't too windy, but they weren't going to keep anybody warm. There were a few trailers, too, and one old yellow school bus. They led me to the middle of the camp and an old woman appeared with a big plate of beans and cornbread. The beans, at least, had a taste of pork, even if I couldn't find any meat.

"*No tengo una cuchara*," she said. I don't have a spoon.

"*Yo tengo*," I said. I have. But when I looked in my duffel bag, my knife and spoon and fork were all gone. Also my blanket and a raincoat I'd had. "*Hijola!*" I said. Son-of-a-bitch.

"What's wrong?" Chavez asked.

"They stole some of my things."

Chavez said something to the woman and she went away. A minute later she was back and handed me a spoon and fork. She also gave me a grocery bag with a wool blanket, a plain white tee shirt, some socks, a rubber raincoat. It wasn't much, but it was something. It looked like something Chavez and the priest had prepared, and I wondered how many people turned up with nothing. Did all the growers treat their workers like they treated me?

"Don't worry," Chavez said. He squatted down in front of me. "This shit happens all the time."

"You speak English," I said.

"Of course," he replied. "I don't like to talk it in front of the ranchers. Sometimes they forget that I can and they let something slip."

"What is this place?" I asked.

"Welcome to the United Farmworkers. We're on strike for better wages and conditions."

I'm not stupid. I had read plenty about unions and organizers and strikes and such. I'd read *The Jungle* and *The Grapes of Wrath*. But I had actually never met an organizer before. You didn't get a lot of them in places like Florida, Georgia, Louisiana, Mississippi, and Oklahoma. But you heard plenty from the bosses about how much trouble they'd bring. Let me tell you, there was no word more hated, no sound that struck more fear into the heart of a shop owner or shipyard boss or ranch foreman than *union*. To hear them tell it, the ground practically bled communists. And there was nothing, including hanging, that they wouldn't do to shut things down if even the rumor of an organizer floated around. And here I was, face-to-face with one. I liked it.

Father McDonnell went off to one of the trailers but Chavez stayed with me. He took a stick and was drawing something in the dirt. I had the impression he was thinking and it occurred to me he might be making a map.

McDonnell came back with a nurse in a white dress. He pointed at me and she knelt down beside me and said, "You mind if I take a look at that?'

It took me a few seconds to realize that she meant my hand. I was cradling the plate in the crook of my left arm and shoveling the rice and beans into my mouth with the spoon in my right hand. In the campfire light I realized that my hand was a mess. Blood and grape juice and dirt. The old, torn bandage. The whole thing look pretty bad. And it was throbbing, too. Had been since I fell that morning. "It looks worse than it feels," I said.

The nurse started to unwrap the bandage but then made a face and said, "Let me go get my bag," and left.

Chavez was making a map. He pointed at a place in the dirt with the end of his stick. "We're here," he said. He traced a line a little ways. "And the Dempsey place—where you worked—it's right here." He tapped the stick in the dirt.

I could barely see in the firelight, but I nodded.

"The road you came down, it leads to the house and the shop and the warehouse and the camp. Now the house is way back here," he said, pointing in the dirt with the stick, "but the shop and the warehouse are right here." He tapped at a different place in the dirt. "And the camp," he said, tracing a line, "Is right here, on the other side of the road. It's about as far from the house as you can get, right?"

Again I nodded.

"Tomorrow," he said, "we're going to go in there and get your stuff back."

"Hey," I said. "It's no big deal. I can—"

"Actually, it is a big deal. What? You think this is just about you? You think you're the only worker they've abused? You know what those fuckers were paying before we went on strike? You know what they were paying?" The light was shining in Chavez's eyes now, the glittering reflection of the campfire between us. And his voice was catching fire, too. The minute Chavez raised his voice everybody looked up, and in just a few seconds there was a crowd around us.

"Eighty god-damned cents a day, that's what they were paying. And kids under fifteen got *forty*. You think you can live on that? You think you can feed a family, keep them in clothes, send them to school, take them to the doctor on *eighty cents a day*?"

"Hell no!" somebody shouted.

Chavez shifted to Spanish so they could all follow. "And where do you think those tents, blankets, pots and pans and knives and forks and things came from?" he asked. "The things in the camp? The things they *charged you* for using?"

"From us!" a half-dozen people shouted at once.

"Damn right from us," he said. "And tomorrow we're going in there and get them back. And when we leave, we're taking all his workers with us." He shifted back to English. "Fuck Dempsey and his grapes!"

And yet, as angry as I was, and as much as I liked this Chavez fellow, what I was thinking was, And here we go again. What's wrong with you people? There's going to be a riot and people are going to die.

The nurse pushed her way through the crowd and knelt down beside me. She took my arm and studied the bandage, but said to Chavez, "Don't get carried away."

"*No armarse un lio*," Chavez said to the workers. Literally it means, Don't arm a mess. Figuratively it means not to let things get out of hand.

"Nobody gets hurt," the nurse said. She took out a pair of surgical scissors and worked one blade under my bandage.

"*Nadie se hace daño!*" Chavez shouted.

"You cannot defeat violence with violence," the nurse said.

"*No se puede derrotar a la violencia con violencia*," Chavez shouted.

Then nurse looked up at me and smiled softly. My name's Phoebe," she said. Then, to Chavez, "You can only defeat violence with kindness." Looking back at my hand, she very gently cut the bandage away.

"*Sólo se puede derrotar a la violencia con amabilidad*," Chavez said.

I looked at Phoebe and she looked at me. I looked into her eyes and in that instant my heart melted like butter in the fire. At that same moment, she cut through the bandage and the wrapping fell away. She looked down at my hand and her expression froze; the pale, blood-soaked, swollen flesh, the missing, discolored tip of my finger.

"Mildness and self-control will sap their will to resist," Chavez continued, still speaking in Spanish. "We will return evil for evil to nobody. Anybody can love a friend. Our obligation is to love even our enemies. Through our determination, and the power of kindness, they will come to understand."

I looked up at Chavez, his face glowing in the blazing light of the campfire, his eyes, it seemed to me, flames of passion and truth. This was not what I expected. Here was someone advocating non-violence. Why had I never heard anyone speak like this before? And what would Gus think of this?

"We've got to get you to a hospital *right now*," Phoebe said. "*Ahora*."

"No," I said. "Really, I'm all right. I just need some antibiotics and painkillers."

Some days are just like that, aren't they? I meet this woman and am struck instantly in love. I hear someone say something I should have known but somehow missed my entire life. I'm not sure which I wanted most: to sit by the fire with Phoebe holding my hand, or to hear Cesar Chavez talk about change through non-violence. There is an expression in America, *I would give my left hand* for this or that. And in my case, I would have. Literally. Right then and there. Almost did.

But Phoebe got McDonnell, and he found some Chicano with the oldest motorcycle I have ever seen—it didn't even have seats, just a big blanket folded and tied with rope to the frame, and the three of us—the owner, the priest, and me—rode into Delano and the Catholic hospital there, and they stuck a needle in my palm and drained from my swollen hand about a pint of the worst smelling yellow shit I have ever seen. And then there were antibiotics, and pain killers, and the doctor scolded me about the dangers of gangrene, and all I could think about was how I wanted them to hurry up and finish so I could get back to the camp.

But I wasn't going back to the camp. They admitted me on the spot. Father McDonnell arranged that. I had a fever of 101 and they were worried about something called *sepsis*. It was worse, they said, than losing my hand to gangrene. It could kill me.

"Die from an infected finger?" I said. "That sounds pretty far-fetched."

"You betcha," the doctor said. His name was Roberto. He was a Chicano, too. That's probably why he was working graveyard shift at a third-rate hospital in small town in the middle of nowhere. But he was a nice guy and it was sort of cool to see a Mexican doctor, even if I didn't think he was very good.

"You don't believe me, ask them." He was scraping away infected skin from my finger, but he pointed with his chin at the room across the hall. There was a Mexican family in the room, nine or ten people, all holding candles and surrounding a bed. They were praying silently. The priest was with them.

"What's over there?" I asked.

"Little girl cut her foot on some barbed wire awhile back. Didn't tell anybody. Foot got infected. Gangrenous. They were workers. Couldn't afford to see a doctor. We cut it off last week, but we were too late. Infection got into the leg. We cut that off below the knee, but now she's got sepsis. It's in her blood. If she lives through the night we'll cut the rest of the leg off tomorrow. If she lives.

But I don't think she'll make it. The priest just gave her Last Rites." He paused and looked out the door at the scene across the hall. "And I'm not too sure about your hand, either. So, yes, you need to stay the night."

I wasn't too keen on the idea of losing my hand. In my bag I kept an empty tin of *El Oso* shoe polish. It's like a shrine to what past I have. In the tin I kept a few things that I had collected over the years, things that I did not wish to part with. A blue marble I picked up in the desert on my way to Juarez. A ticket stub from the 1938 Sun Bowl. A small silver crucifix I found at the bullring. An 1835 dime that a crazy drunk gave me for a shoeshine. A postage stamp sized black-and-white photo of Maria. A plastic bag with a little white pill.

After Dr. Roberto was gone, I pulled the IV from my arm and got out of bed. I dug through my bag until I found the tin and then I took out the little white pill. I lay under the covers clutching the pill and fighting off sleep and wondered if it would still work its magic. I had carried that pill for seventeen years in case of emergency, but Gus hadn't said anything about how long it might last. I was too dumb to know anything about shelf life. If somebody gave you a pill it was a pill. Like money, in a year or twenty it would be the same. The first pill might have saved my life once, a long time ago. Gus said I might need a second, but I hadn't, not yet, anyway. I thought about my hand for a long time. Hard to work with just one. But then I thought about the little girl across the hall. Hard to be a little girl with no leg, either. She, at least, had a future. What did I have?

So in the dark hours of the early morning, when the staff dozed and even the girl's mother, sitting by the bed, lay her head on the mattress and slept, I crept to the girl's bedside and gently shook her shoulder until she awoke. "*Es hora de que su medicamento*," I whispered. Time to take your medicine.

The girl could barely move. Her eyelids fluttered. She opened her mouth just a crack, but didn't speak. I put the pill on her tongue and held a cup of water to her lips. She sipped and swallowed and closed her eyes. For a moment I watched her chest rise and fall, looked at the place under the sheets where her right foot should have been. Then I slipped back across the hall and barely made it into bed before one of the nurses turned up and scolded me for pulling out the IV. I was so tired I don't even remember her putting it back.

That night I dreamed of silver boxes that fell softly, fluttering like leaves from the sky, and leaving trails of cold fog wherever they floated. In my dream, the fog trails transformed into handwriting, and the words were written across the sky in pearlescent white, but the writing was in a language that I did not know, and I cried because the script itself was so beautiful, and I cried because I could not read the message, even though I was certain it came from Maria.

Act V Scene 7

In the morning I awoke thinking about my dream and about Chavez and Father McDonnell and Phoebe. But I was still messed up from the morphine they gave me. I'd read somewhere about morphine and opium dreams, but I had never taken any of those things before. The feeling was weird. I kind of liked it.

As the fog in my brain lifted, I became aware that there was a lot of noise downstairs. That struck me as odd for a hospital. It didn't sound right. I tried to get up but I had forgotten the IV in my arm and it hurt like hell when I yanked on it. I pulled it out and climbed out of bed. I felt sick to my stomach. I steadied myself by the bed, then walked slowly to the door. I felt cold and my legs were weak. I looked down the hall. There were two nurses standing in front of the nurses' station. They were looking away from me towards the elevator and the main stairway. That's where the noise was coming from—from downstairs. There was lot of shouting, like a riot or something. I slipped down to the other end of the hall where there was a fire exit. I was still unsteady on my feet but I made it down to the first floor. That was where the ER and the main lobby were.

There must have been a hundred people milling around and shouting in front of the ER desk. There was blood everywhere. At least a dozen people—all Chicanos—lay on their backs in the hallway or sat dazed in chairs in the lobby. Some had been beaten, others looked like they had been shot or slashed or stabbed. And there were two distinct groups squared off around the ER desk and the entry to the ER. One group was police and Anglos—the grape growers or their goons. I was standing behind them. The other group was all farm workers. They were on the far side, beyond the police and Anglos. The hospital staff had fled and watched from behind the thick glass walls that separated the front office from the rest of the ER treatment rooms.

I searched the crowd to see if Cesar and Phoebe and the priest were okay. I couldn't make out the faces—I guess my vision was messed up from the morphine—and I panicked. I stumbled down the last few steps and almost fell. I ran headlong into the sonofabitch who'd kicked me the night before. Karl. I don't think he recognized me, but he shoved me against the wall just the same. I wanted to slug him but I wanted to see the injured more. I wanted to know that Chavez was all right, that his woman, Helen, was all right, that Father McDonnell was all right, and most of all, that Phoebe was all right. Half the workers in the hospital were men and women I had worked with the day before. They paid me no attention at all. I saw the old grandmother—the one who had served us water. She was sitting on the floor cradling her head. But she had been bandaged. I was sure Phoebe had done that. Who else was there? The old woman recognized me. I pushed my way through the crowd and knelt in front of her. "What happened?" I asked.

"*Ellos sabían*," she said. They knew. "*Alguien les dijo*." Someone told them.

"But what happened?"

She looked at me and her eyes narrowed. "*Eras tu?*" Was it you?

I shook my head and then showed her my arm, now wrapped to the elbow in a clean white bandage.

She said, "*De noche, todos los gatos son pardos*." Literally it means, At night, all cats are brown. Figuratively it means, Who knows the truth? She put her hands to her face and sobbed.

The room was crazy. Both sides were shouting, raising fists. The police waved clubs and tried to arrest the Chicanos, but the Chicanos refused to be handcuffed. When the cops grabbed one, three or four wrestled him or her away. There were too many of them for the police to manhandle. The Chicanos were shouting that the injured should be treated right away, but the grape growers blocked the door to the ER and demanded that the protestors be arrested first.

I looked at the men and women lying on the floor, the crying children clinging to parents, the police, the goons, the anger on all the faces, the blood. I looked at all this and then everything got very faint and far away. The blood pounded in my ears. I remembered an evening a long time ago when I opened a door to find a half-dozen men with ax handles and knives, and I remembered that when I ran for the back door, there was no escape. I remembered a weird ringing sound as the iron bar met my skull. I remembered lying on my back tasting blood and steel and straw and dust while the lights and faces above me turned like a kaleidoscope. I remembered lying on the ground and trying to form the words to ask, Why?

The next thing I knew I had a policeman jammed against the wall and was choking him with his own baton while two others tried in vain to pull me away. I was shouting over and over, "What is the matter with you people? They're hurt! They're bleeding! Help them now and arrest them later!" And then the whole room went quiet. Even the policeman behind me with his night stick raised to hit me had frozen. A single flash bulb struck like lightning.

Father McDonnell stood in the hallway. "Let him go, Pablo," he said. "We will not fight them. We will not resist them. Let them arrest us. If we bleed to death in jail, so be it. There is a heaven for those who die in worship of the living God, and a hell for those who take the lives of others. God will judge and we will not resist them. Let him go, Pablo."

And like that, it was over. McDonnell had that kind of presence. Even his enemies listened to him. Chavez, too. I've thought about this for a long time now: these men, the principles that guided them. They were sought out by influential people. They had powerful friends. Yet they did not accomplish anything through violence. Rather, they accomplished things through the power of their convictions; their willingness even to die for what they believed—but their equal willingness *not to kill* for what they knew to be right. This was how they accomplished so much for so many. It was a miracle. And I saw it with my own eyes.

McDonnell knew where the police station was. No doubt he had planned for this contingency. Silently and swiftly the workers gathered the injured and began to file out, following the priest and leading the police towards the city hall and the police station. Already the cops were having second thoughts and the Chief of Police was *just-a-minute-here* running after McDonnell, and the grape grower bosses were running after him to make sure he did arrest the whole crowd of them—even the injured. Even I got in line but the nurses and doctors were coming out of the ER and one of them spied me in my hospital gown and grabbed me and whisked me into the elevator and out-of-sight. Probably a good thing, as I can think of at least one cop who would have liked to have got me alone in a cell for a few minutes to explain to me what happens to people who choke cops with their own Billy clubs.

And I probably would have been fine except for two things. One was the AP reporter and photographer covering the disturbance. The photographer snapped a lovely photo of me jacking that cop up against the wall. And the other was that Father McDonnell called me Pablo. As in, "Migrant Worker Pablo Zapata Assaults Cop in Hospital Riot." The article went out by wire and made all the major papers.

The next morning, at 8:00 A.M. on the button, a tall, skinny, bearded Chicano biker appeared in the doorway of the ward room where I was sleeping another morphine-abetted sleep. He looked around the room, asked for Pablo Zapata, and one of the patients directed him to me. I woke to find him tapping me on the shoulder with an envelope.

I knew he was a biker, though for the first few seconds I struggled to sort dream from reality. He wore black jeans, black motorcycle boots, a red bandana, a red tee shirt, and a black leather vest with the words Bandidos MC emblazoned in an arc on a patch over his heart.

"Pablo Zapata," he said.

"Who's asking?"

"I have a message from Don Pablo."

"Don Pablo?" I asked.

"Don Pablo."

"You know Don Pablo?"

"That's not important. Don Pablo says to tell you he never forgets a friend and he still considers you a friend. He says to clear out right now. Get out. Here. He said to give you this." He flipped the envelope onto my chest.

I looked at the envelope, then at the man standing by my bed. "I'm in the hospital," I said. I know it was kind of obvious, but my mind was doped up and I wasn't thinking clearly.

"I know where you are," the man said. "A lot of people know where you are. Don Pablo says to clear out. If I were you, I'd clear out right now."

"Right now?"

"This minute."

"Why?"

"I don't know, and it's not my business. I got paid to give you a message." He shrugged. "I gave you the message."

He turned to go but I called to him, "Hey, who are you?"

He looked at me like I was stupid. "A friend of a friend of a friend and that's all you get. This guy must like you 'cause he went to a lot of trouble to get you this message. If I were you, I'd clear out right now."

"Can I have a ride?" I asked.

"Not on your life," he said. And he walked out.

I opened the envelope. Inside was $500 in twenty dollar bills. Five minutes later, I skipped out by the stairs at the end of the hall and headed for the highway.

Act V Scene 8

By dusk I was in Las Vegas. I slept under a plastic tarp I picked up on the highway out west of town. The next day I hitched a ride to Salt Lake City. By the time I reached Salt Lake my hand was killing me—it was like somebody was sticking a hot knife in it over and over again—but I was afraid to go to a hospital. I kicked open the back door of a pharmacy downtown and stole all the antibiotics I could find. I felt bad about stealing, but what else I could do? I didn't want to lose my hand, and I didn't want to die.

What frightened me most was wondering how Don Pablo had found me. I didn't yet know about the photograph and the newspaper article. So the message scared the daylights me. Run, he said, but from what? I thought I left my past behind. But is that possible? Maybe Gus was right about time and dimensions and names. Maybe we carry our whole history with us no matter what. Just because I don't see it doesn't mean it isn't there.

I took a handful of the antibiotics and washed them down with a bottle of cheap wine. I woke up in the morning with a hangover, but my hand felt a bit better. I ate a burrito for breakfast and walked around downtown.

There were lots of Mexicans in Salt Lake, but none of them wanted anything to do with me. It was the only place I've ever been where people didn't ask if I wanted work. Eventually, I started asking around about jobs, places to stay, but nobody knew anything, nobody was talking. I don't know what the problem was. I was suddenly paranoid that everybody everywhere knew who I was and why I was running. Only I didn't know why I was running. It was like a nightmare. Was it tattooed on my forehead? That evening I got a box of tacos and a six pack of beer. I walked around wondering what was going on. I took the rest of the antibiotics and threw the pill bottles away, just in case the cops decided to shake me down. And sure enough, ten minutes later, they did. Thank God I was clean.

Looking back now, I wonder why I didn't just follow Chavez and the others. If somebody was looking for me, fine. If they wanted me dead, fine. If they wanted me in jail, fine. I suppose I had plenty of reasons to run. But at that moment, in the hospital room with the biker, the thought didn't come to me to stick around and face the consequences. Not yet. Perhaps, as Father Sheehy might say, God was looking after me.

I thought I was pretty brave, to grab a cop in a riot and pin him to the wall. Even if I didn't know what I was doing at the time. In the photo I look crazy. So is that real courage? Or was I just overcome by rage and fear? Wouldn't real courage be to overcome those emotions, rather than succumb to them?

I did, however, find a great second-hand book store in Salt Lake, and one book caught my eye: *Non-Violent Resistance* by Mahatma Gandhi. I picked it up and started reading and liked it so much that I bought two more of Gandhi's books: his autobiography, which he called *The Story of My Experiments with Truth*, and a book called *Third Class in Indian Railways*. I bought that because I had hopped so many trains, I wanted to see how you wrote a book about it.

That night I gave up on Salt Lake and walked down to the freight yard. I found a train headed east. We went straight up into the mountains and right into the first big winter storm. It was hell. Total whiteout. Worse, something must have happened to the railroad track—a landslide, snowdrifts, something. We holed up in a box canyon half-in half-out of a tunnel, and I was a day and half in the snow without food, water, or warm clothes. I thought I was going to die. At least I got to read Gandhi.

Just when I was going to find the engineer to beg for help, the train lurched forward and I almost didn't catch my boxcar. It was the only one unlocked on the train. That would have been bad—getting left behind like that. I would have frozen to death. But I caught the car, though I had a rough time climbing into it as I ran alongside, what with my hand an all. But I made it, and the next morning I woke up hungry and freezing in the rail yards in Denver.

The first thing I did was to find a diner. I ate two orders of bacon and eggs and hash browns and toast. I read a newspaper. It was a few days old. That's when I saw my photo. Quite a shock to see my picture in the paper, especially when I didn't know it was there. It didn't help my paranoia, either. I read the article. They tried to make it sound like the workers were violent, and I felt bad about that. According to the press, the grape growers were taking care of their workers while the organizers were exploiting them.

I wanted to explain that I wasn't an organizer, hadn't been part of the morning raid—that I was there by accident—but somehow I knew that Chavez and Phoebe and the others knew that I didn't mean to cause any trouble. The article didn't say anything about the workers volunteering to be arrested, the ones beaten and bleeding on the floor, nothing like that. And the papers wouldn't give a shit why I was there.

To the best of my knowledge, I had never been in the news. Not by name, anyway. I also couldn't remember *ever* having my photo taken. Even those old Texas drivers' licenses didn't have photos. Not back then. The photos came later.

I drank coffee until the second-hand stores opened and then I bought a jacket and gloves and a knit cap. I walked around. I was on Colfax Street, and it was pretty seedy and run-down. There wasn't much going on. It was cold as hell, and snowing. I think it was a Saturday, and everybody who could was staying warm at home. It didn't matter what I ate or put on, where I stood, I couldn't get warm. I started up a wet cough and I felt like shit. No strength. I found a room in a rundown hotel and bought a bottle of wine. This'll warm me up, I thought. I drank the wine and went to bed.

Act V Scene 9

I woke up in a hospital. The hotel clerk found me when I didn't answer his knock. I guess he really wanted his bill paid. So he found me and called an ambulance. The ambulance took me to the hospital and they kept me in the ER until dark. Then they kicked me out. I was so sick I wished I'd died. The worst part was, somebody stole all my money. The hotel clerk seemed more likely than the ambulance crew, but who knows? No use arguing about it. I spent the night huddled over a steam grate.

The next morning I found a job as a dishwasher, but my hand was killing me. I'd only lost the first joint of the middle finger on my left hand, but the infection had screwed up the nerves in all my fingers. My whole hand was weak. It went numb all the time, and when it wasn't numb it was fire hot or prickling with electricity or stabbing pain. It was no fun, and no matter how I tried, I broke too many dishes. I just couldn't hold on to them. The restaurant fired me.

That was the worst winter of my life. If I'd died it would have been a relief. My mind was black with depression. It seemed like I could do nothing right. I couldn't afford a room. I lived in flop houses and shared rooms with four, five, six guys. Mattresses on the floor, not even beds. I wound up in something called a shooting gallery. It was the first time I met real junkies. All the drugs I had carried across the border and I never took to them. But one night I asked one of the guys why he did heroin and he asked me, "Have you ever done morphine?"

Or course I had.

"Same thing," he said.

I don't know why I never made the connection. I tried it. At first I sniffed it, then I smoked it with some pot. Finally I shot up with a borrowed rig. I can't say I liked being high, but I liked that it took away the pain. It did that.

I got work as a day laborer scraping snow and ice from a parking lot. It was hard work but I could drink all day. Nobody gave a shit. My hand was even worse in the cold. It would be numb all day and then burn all night. At night I got fucked up. It was the only way I could sleep.

I came home payday and that night the junkies rolled me for what cash I had. I'm lucky they didn't kill me. I was smoking a joint with them and the lights went out. Not the electric lights. My lights. Somebody knocked me over the head with something. I woke up in an alley across town wrapped in a carpet and buried under three inches of snow. It took me half an hour to get loose from the carpet. I wonder if they thought I was dead.

I made a tent out of the carpet and slept in it. I woke up sick again. This time it was pneumonia *and* heroin withdrawals. I had never had that before, and hope I never have it again.

I like the word irony. It means when things are the opposite of what you expect, except that it's not like some ordinary mistake or random outcome. With irony, there's a kind of meaning. There's a lesson. It had been eighteen years since I promised Gus that I wouldn't kill anybody, since I'd promised Father Sheehy that I would try to do some good in the world. With those promises came this little voice that said just one more thing, just one more thing, just one more thing, don't fight, don't steal, don't tell lies, and all these little things were supposed to add up to my being (or at least *trying to become*) a good person. And I had wanted to be a good person. Really.

But when I was a boy I had become some kind of a gangster, and I had all the money and food and clothes, and guns, and jewelry, and things I wanted. I had cars and trucks and a new motorcycle, a house, a wife, a girlfriend. People worked for me. Then I tried to live a good life and wound up sick and starving, living on the streets with nothing. I lost everything. Even my old tin of *El Oso* shoe polish with my dime and crucifix and marble and the ticket stub to the Sun Bowl. I lost everything. *What kind of fucked up world is this?* I wondered. Ironic, that's what kind of fucked up world this is. But who was I to complain? Those who live by the sword... And I had done my share of damage. I was ready to give up.

I went to the E.R. and nobody would talk to me. I was just another bum taking up space. At least it was warm. I was getting sicker by the hour. I was there almost twelve hours before I saw a nurse. They wouldn't waste a doctor on me. The nurse was a man, Charlie. He was tall and thin and long-haired. You were starting to see more and more people like that, even in places like Denver. Charlie checked me out and gave me a little bottle of antibiotics and told me to stay warm and drink lots of fluids but no wine. Chicken soup was good, he said. So were oranges.

I told him I'd got rolled and had no job and no money.

"Tough break," he said.

"Can't you do anything for me?" I asked. "A bed? Something to eat? Anything? "

Charlie shook his head. He was writing notes on a clipboard.

"You're going to kick me out," I said, "just like that?"

"Just like that," he said. He snapped a finger for emphasis and turned to go, but stopped at the door and looked back at me. I think he was wondering if I was like the rest of the trash that blew in with every snowstorm. "You can get a bed at the Mission," he said.

"The mission?"

"Yeah, you know."

I didn't know. "Have you ever slept at the mission?" I asked.

Charlie looked at me. "Or you could do what all the other dope heads do," he said.

"What's that?"

"Get arrested. We don't admit homeless people unless they are really, really, really sick. Like dying. But if you get sick in jail, the county will send you back and we have to take you. But don't commit a felony. Those stick with you. Just do some misdemeanor. Break a window or something."

Then he left and I went out to the waiting room and broke a window and sat down to wait for the cops. While I was waiting Charlie came by and saw what I did. He came right to me and bent down and hissed in my ear, "I didn't mean *here*."

"Sorry," I said. I got up and looked around. "Do I have to go break another one someplace else?"

"No," he said. "Somebody will call the cops. Probably already have. But don't tell anybody I told you to do it. I could lose my job."

The cops took me to jail and I was so sick I could hardly stand. Even the other prisoners didn't want me around. I was coughing and hacking and spitting. I was drenched with sweat and then shook with chills. I was so out of it I shit my pants. The guys in the holding tank started banging on the door and shouting, "Get this loser outta here!"

The cops didn't want me around anymore than the prisoners. I was two hours in the holding tank before they processed me. They didn't ask if I could read or write. Mexican. Homeless. Junkie. They sent this old cop to fill out the forms for me. His name was Scoville. I sat down at a desk in front of him while he read me the questions and typed in my answers.

Scoville was a white-haired old geezer who looked like he was ten years past retiring and two weeks short of dying. Fat face, fat neck, fat belly, fat red hands. He had a frog face. Big lines by his mouth. A chin down to here. Wrinkles. And he chain-smoked camel no-filters.

"Name?" he said.

"Pablo."

"Full name."

"Pablo."

"Your full fucking name, Pablo."

"Ortega," I said. It was the first thing that came to mind.

"Age."

"Forty-two.

He said, "Say you're thirty-nine."

"Why should I say I'm thirty-nine?" I asked.

"It's better that way," he said.

"But I'm not thirty-nine," I said.

"And my money says you're not Pablo Ortega, either, but who gives a shit? Here you can be anybody you want to be and any age I tell you to be. Within reason. Suit yourself, but its better if you're thirty-nine."

"Okay," I said. "I'm thirty-nine."

"And you were born in?"

"Nineteen twenty-three," I said.

The cop stopped typing and rubbed his eyes. "Stupid Mexican," he said. He wrote 1926.

There were some other questions. Identification. *None.* Outstanding warrants. *Not that I know of.* Drug use. *Yes.* What? *I said yes.* I mean what drugs, numbnuts. *All of them.* More eye rubbing. Home address. *None.* Family. *None.* Next of kin. *None.* Job. *None.* Education. *None.* Bank account. *None.* He inventoried my possessions. *None.*

"You're a real charmer," he said. "I don't need ask if you got a girlfriend."

I thought about telling him to fuck off but I didn't say it.

Scoville ripped the paper out of the typewriter and pointed to a line at the bottom, "Sign here." I signed and he said, "Wait."

I was in fucking jail. Where was I gonna go? And he called *me* stupid? Half an hour later he was back. Five minutes after that they loaded me in an ambulance and carted me back to the hospital.

Act VI Scene 1

It was my third morning in the hospital and I was finally feeling a bit better. I was looking out the window at the sun shining down on the flat part of Denver, the east side. It had warmed up a bit. The snow was melting and the wind blew out of the south. It looked okay enough that I wasn't terrified about getting out. I was thinking it might be a good idea to leave if I could get away with it. I didn't know whether the cops would come back for me or what. Nobody said anything about that.

I was thinking about Father Sheehy telling me that God might forgive little white lies if I said them for a good purpose. I was wondering if breaking a window to get into the hospital was something like one of those little lies, or if I was just being selfish. If I had real faith, would I just lay down and die?

The hospital food—people might complain about it—but I tell you, it was a whole lot better than the nothing I would have been eating out on the streets. I might have even gained some weight. They even gave me an orange every day, though I didn't see Charlie again.

So I was lying in bed after breakfast, and I was feeling better, and this young man and woman came into the ward with a nurse and she pointed at me and the man and woman came to my bed, one on each side, and the man said, "Pablo Ortega?" The man was average height and he wore his hair in what they called a Beatle cut. He wore thick glasses in black plastic frames. He had a thin moustache, too, and later on, when I met Ringo Starr, I thought they looked a lot alike. Except for the glasses.

The woman was a bit taller. She had platinum blond hair, almost white. She wore a simple cotton blouse with some red and green embroidery across the top and a long blue cotton dress that fell all the way to her sandals. It looked like something the whores might have worn back at Don Pablo's hotel, back in the old days, but it was all the fashion back then. She wore glasses, too, but the lenses were small and pink, and the frames were of gold colored wire.

They both carried leather briefcases, his black, hers brown. I wondered who Pablo Ortega was and what they might want with him. They looked at me funny and then I remembered that I was Pablo Ortega. If they hadn't said it, I would have forgotten. "That's me," I said.

"Good," the man said. He held out his hand and I shook it. "My name is Herman Stoltzheimer and this is my co-worker, Melanie Freisenhofer. We're graduate students at the University of Denver and we're from the SLED Program. Have you ever heard of the SLED Program?" He did not wait for me to tell him that I had not heard of the SLED Program. He continued with barely enough pause to inhale. He sounded like a used car salesman. "The SLED Program is SLED stands for Saving Lives Through Education. It's a program of education for minor offenders," he said.

"Minor offenders with a history of drug use," Melanie added.

"Minor offenders with a history of drug use," Herman said.

"But by minor we don't mean, *minor*. I mean, minor as in *underage*. We work with *adult* offenders," Melanie said.

"Adult offenders, but *minor* offenses."

"As in misdemeanors."

"Do you know what a misdemeanor is?" Herman asked.

I shook my head. If I wasn't confused already, these two were getting me there in a hurry. I was kind of hoping they would leave.

"A misdemeanor is a minor offense."

"As in *not very important*," Melanie added.

"Well they're all important," Herman said. He glared at Melanie. "But what we mean is that nobody got hurt like a knifing or a shooting or a fight or a robbery or something like that."

"Some robberies are misdemeanors," Melanie said. She sounded sulky.

"But what we're really concerned with," Herman said, looking at a piece of paper that looked suspiciously like the one I had signed a few days ago in jail, the one Scoville had typed up, "what we're really concerned with is drug use."

"You want me to teach you how to use drugs?" I asked.

"No, Mr. Ortega," Herman said. "We want to help you to stop using drugs."

"Okay," I said. That didn't sound difficult. How hard can it be to <u>not do</u> something?

He looked at the paper again. "It says here you're thirty-nine, is that correct?"

I shut my eyes and said a silent prayer that God might forgive me. "Yes," I said.

"That's good because our program only takes people up to the age of thirty-nine."

"So if you were forty or more," Melanie said, "we couldn't take you."

"Where are you taking me?" I asked.

"We're not taking you anywhere," Herman said.

"But she just said you were taking me someplace."

"What Miss Freisenhofer means, Mr. Ortega, is that we can take you *into our program*."

I looked at Herman and Melanie and wondered if a circus was missing a few clowns.

"What I mean," Melanie said, "is that we can help you get an education."

"And with an education, you can get a better job."

"And if you get a better job--"

"*And* an education."

"*And* an education. If you get an education and a better job, maybe you won't want to do drugs anymore. That's our goal."

"The SLED Program goal."

"To help you get an education and a job."

"And to not do drugs anymore."

I thought about this, and in spite of their best efforts, I thought I understood what they were saying. I got the *send me to school* part. But I couldn't believe it. Who would send an old Mexican like me to school? "Do you mean you'll send me to school?" I asked.

"That's exactly what we mean," Herman said.

"Exactly," Melanie added.

"And how much does it cost?" I said. "I don't have no money or nothing."

"It doesn't cost anything," Herman said. "That's the best part."

"In fact," Melanie added, "We'll *pay* you to go to school."

"You'll *pay* me?"

"Well, not exactly *pay*, Mr. Ortega. What Miss Freisenhofer means is that—"

"Mr. Stoltzheimer, would you please stop telling me what I mean."

"What Miss Freisenhofer means is that we will pay all of your school expenses."

"And we'll pay for you for a place to stay."

"And a place to stay."

"We'll also find you a daytime job," Melanie said.

"A daytime job. But there's also a small allowance for personal items."

"Yes, a monthly allowance for personal items."

"And a grant at intake to help you with necessities like clothes and shoes and things like this," Herman said.

"A hundred and fifty dollars," Melanie said.

"A hundred and fifty dollars," Herman echoed.

"So you *could* say that we will pay you to go to school," Melanie said, folding her arms triumphantly.

"After a fashion, I suppose you could," Herman said. He adjusted his glasses and then opened his briefcase and took out some papers. "So if you want to join the SLED Program, all you have to do, Mr. Ortega, is sign right here." He pointed at a line on the paper.

Act VI Scene 2

The University of Denver was on the southeast side of town, and it was a pretty nice area. This was the rich part of town, and all I had to do to live there was take some drugs, commit a misdemeanor, and tell a few lies. I like irony.

They drove me from the hospital in a university van. They put me in a small apartment off campus that I shared with three other men who, like me, had all been in jail for minor offenses and had a history of drug use. But unlike me, these three really were long-time drug users. And I was the only Chicano. They were hippie types, all three of them. Bill, Bob, and Larry. They were also way younger than me. We were the first ones in this new program.

My first morning there I met with a couple of professors. There was Dr. Alderman, a psychologist, and Dr. Ackerman, a psychiatrist. There was a couple of other professors there, too, but I don't remember their names or what they did. They talked to me for a while as a group, and then I met alone with Dr. Ackerman and he asked me a lot of questions about my upbringing and where I was from and how long I had been in America and what kinds of fantasies I had at night. Things like that. I thought he was weird and maybe I should say something to the others about this.

In the afternoon Melanie showed up without Herman and said she was going to give me my grant money and take me shopping. She took me to a St. Vincent de Paul thrift store and I got some jeans and good shoes, some underwear, tee shirts, some flannel shirts, a wool cap with ear muffs, another jacket, a scarf, some socks. All that stuff you need. But I never saw any of the money. She just paid for things and kept the receipts.

Later she took me to the university clinic and I got a medical exam. They said I still had a touch of pneumonia and should take antibiotics for another week. They also said the idiots at the public hospital had prescribed the wrong antibiotics and it was a wonder they hadn't killed me. Melanie took me to dinner, and that night I slept in a clean bed in a warm room I only shared with one person. It was like heaven.

The next morning Herman came to see me and we had a cup of coffee and some donuts and then went to the building where the Psychology Department was. There they gave me some more tests. These were easier than the ones the other day. There was some reading, some math, some questions about science and history and geography. Things like that. They even had me write a one-page essay paper to answer the question: What Would a Perfect World Look Like?

That was the last thing, the essay. I thought for quite a while about that. I thought about what Gus had said about the way other kinds in the universe cooperated more than competed with one another. I also thought about what I just read about Gandhi, and having respect for one another. I wrote: *In a perfect world, people would think more about others and less of themselves. They would care for one another. They would respect one another. They would not be afraid of their differences, but rather, would appreciate their similarities and celebrate their differences. The way to accomplish this is through respect based on shared experiences. For instance, Mahatma Gandhi suggested that the leaders of India be required to travel in third-class rail cars. By experiencing for themselves what the average Indian was forced to endure, they would change their policies to be more compassionate.*

There was a lot more, but this was the main point. I had never written an essay before. I had read lots, but I had never really thought about writing, other than the conversations I had with myself in my head. I mean, who would care what I had to say? I thought I did a pretty good job, for my first essay.

In the morning, Herman came by and took me to Denny's for breakfast. We had bacon and eggs and toast and coffee. Afterwards he introduced me to the manager, Mr. Statler, and said I was going to be the morning-shift dishwasher starting the next day. That was the job the program arranged for me. I was to work from five A.M. to eleven A.M. After that, Herman said, I would eat lunch and then come to the school and take some classes in the afternoon. In the evening I would study and have appointments with psychiatrists and psychologists and such. And there was something else called AA and NA. They were supposed to help me adjust to life without drugs and alcohol. That's what Herman said, anyway.

But when we got back to the campus something was wrong. Everybody was waiting for me. The professors, Melanie, the psychologists, all of them. They took Herman aside and me straightaway into this room with a long table. They all sat down and looked at me. I was just standing there by the door. Then Dr. Ackerman came in with Herman and my test results. He asked me to sit down.

"Am I in trouble?" I asked.

"No," Dr. Ackerman said. "You're not in trouble. We just need to ask you a few questions." He looked at my test papers. He seemed to be thinking. After a few minutes, he said, "Here in the math section, Mr. Ortega, on question seven, you selected "unknown" as your answer. Can you tell me why you did that?"

"Maybe," I said, "because I didn't know the answer." There was a round of muffled laughter and I felt embarrassed. "But there were a lot of questions," I added, "and I really can't remember them all. Can you read me the question?"

"The question is: Define a slope parallel to a slope where x equals 7."

"That's messed up," I said. More laughter. "I mean, you can't have a slope with one number on the x-axis. You have to have a y-axis, too. If you don't know that number you can't make a line. And if you don't have a line, there is no slope."

Dr. Ackerman leaned back in his chair. "I see," he said. He pulled another paper from the stack and read a little bit. "What can you tell me about the Louisiana Purchase?"

I had to think about this for a minute. I worried that if I got something really wrong they might be mad at me. I didn't want to insult their country. And I sure didn't want to get fired from the program during my first week. "It was in 1803," I said.

"Yes, and... "

"Between the U.S. and France, I think."

"Yes, it was France. What else can you tell me about it?"

I was starting to sweat. I didn't think it would be this hard. The test the other day was just A-B-C or D. All I had to do was think about it and remember and then check the box. It wasn't so difficult. I could eliminate some of the answers and make a good guess if I didn't know for sure. "The main thing the U.S. wanted," I said, "was New Orleans. It's on the river and they knew it would be an important seaport. If you go there today you can see all the ships. It's really busy, the river. I've been there, so I know. But there was a lot of arguing about this land in Europe. The King of Spain said it was his, and the King of France said it was his. But Napoleon made the King of Spain sign it over. So James Monroe and Robert Livingston went to France and bought it. They got a pretty good deal, if I remember right. I think they paid about seventeen cents an acre for a whole bunch of land. A little more than eight hundred thousand square miles. A square mile is 640 acres. It's much of the middle part of America today. Even Denver was part of it, I think. The Alaska Purchase was not as big but it was maybe worth more money. Did I get it right?"

Dr. Ackerman looked around and the professors shrugged. "I think you got it right," he said. "Would you mind telling us what's the difference between igneous rock and metamorphic?"

By now I was really sweating. I knew I did something wrong but I had no idea what. "Have you ever dug through metamorphic rock?" I asked.

Dr. Ackerman shook his head. "I can't say that I have."

"Well, if you did," I said, "you wouldn't have to ask."

Everybody laughed and I looked around. I've been in a room full of men who wanted to kill me, but I'd have traded them for these guys in a heartbeat. I was trying to remember all the doors and hallways in case I had to make a run for it.

"But specifically," Dr. Ackerman said, "what is the difference between the two?"

"All rocks start out as igneous," I said. "Except maybe the little bit that comes along from someplace else like meteors and comets and such. But the rest of it is all igneous. But that gets worn down and it becomes sedimentary. Either that, or it gets put under heat and pressure and becomes something else. That's what they mean by metamorphic. But either igneous or sedimentary rock can be changed. For instance, if you put enough pressure on limestone, it becomes marble. Metamorphic rock can't be changed like that. It has to wear away or get remelted."

Nobody was laughing now. Nobody said a word.

"I never had to work in any marble quarries," I said. "But I worked a rock crusher once outside of Stone Mountain, Georgia. And let me tell you, that granite is a sonofabitch."

Dr. Ackerman shuffled some more papers. At length he came to my essay. He looked at it for a moment, then sighed. "Pablo," he said, "you don't mind if I call you Pablo, do you?"

"I don't mind."

"Pablo, I've been teaching here at the University of Denver for thirty-four years."

"Okay."

"According to your intake, you've never been to school."

I wanted to tell Dr. Ackerman that there were different kinds of schools, and many ways to learn. But he had been teaching college for thirty-four years and I had never taken a class. Who was I to tell him anything? "I never went to school," I said.

"Then how did you learn to read and write?"

"A priest taught me."

"A priest taught you?"

"Yes, sir," I said. "Father Sheehy. I think he's in Poland now. Or Eastern Europe someplace. I saw him a few years ago when I was in New Orleans. In 1947. That was the last time I saw him. He said they were sending him back where all the priests had been killed. But it shouldn't be hard to find him if you want to ask. I'm sure somebody in the church would know."

Dr. Ackerman looked down at my essay. "Have you actually read *Third Class in Indian Railways*?"

I nodded.

"Pablo. When you were arrested you had nothing. You didn't even have a change of clothes."

"I got robbed," I said. "Somebody took my stuff."

"Are you telling me that somebody stole your copy of *Third Class in Indian Railways*?"

"Yes, sir."

Dr. Ackerman looked at Melanie and said, "Will you...?"

Melanie looked at me and nodded and I had the feeling that something had been decided a long time ago and without including me. A conspiracy, I think they call it. I got up and we went out in the hallway. Before I could say anything Melanie said, "They think you cheated on the exam, but I don't think you did. Did you?"

"How would I do that?" I asked. I was so stupid I wouldn't even know how to cheat. Was I missing something?

"They think somebody helped you. Somebody gave you the answers. They think you got that essay from another student. Took it from somebody. Did you?'

"I broke a window to get into jail so they could put me in the hospital, but I'm no thief."

Melanie squeezed my arm. "Come on," she said. "I'll buy you a cup of coffee."

I stopped. "Does this mean I won't get to go to school?"

"I don't know," she said.

"But what's the problem? Didn't I pass? I thought I did okay. I did the best I could."

"Pablo," she said. "You scored about ninety percent."

"That's not good enough?"

"We expect people coming into in the SLED program to score about twenty-five. The minimum to get in is ten."

That afternoon they gave me all the tests again. This time they put some people to watch me. I was pretty nervous. I felt like this test was harder than the first one. But I went through it anyway, feeling worse and sweating more as the afternoon wore on. I was in a little room and there was a window and it was hot even though I could see a storm was blowing in from the north. It started to snow, hard, and I could tell it was going to be a real blizzard. It was the kind of afternoon where everybody wants to quit work and go home early. I was wondering where I would sleep that night if they put me out.

Two professors watched me take the test. They didn't want students to do it. Or trust them, one. From time to time Dr. Ackerman came down and looked in, just to make sure I was still working and being watched.

I came to the last question. Another essay. It said: *Write one page about an important event that changed your life.* I looked at the question and couldn't believe it. What was I supposed to write about? My mother? Don Pablo? Filo? Maria? Gus? Would anybody believe any of it? If they didn't like my essay about Mahatma Gandhi, they sure wouldn't like anything else I had to say.

I broke my pencil. The men watching me looked up. I just had in my hand and it snapped. I didn't even know I was squeezing it that hard. Maybe this was what was wrong with me. I had no idea what normal people would write about. The time I Baked Cookies and Burned Them. What I Learned When I Broke my Arm on the Trampoline. My Grandfather Got Cancer. I don't know what other people think or feel or how or why they do what they do. I don't know anything. Sometimes I feel like Gus must have felt. *What is wrong with you people?* How strange we must have looked to him—him the little man with photosynthetic skin and green blood and bumps that grew into things that fell off and then lived in the water. He liked lemons. He got over being afraid on my motorcycle. He said they liked music. He liked our coffee.

I wrote: *If we knew how anything was going to change our lives we would be seeing the future and that's impossible, except maybe in some other dimension, or in science fiction, and that's not real. Things happen and we respond to them. How do we know what is or isn't important? How do we know what to do? Sometimes we do and sometimes we don't. When we don't we blame everybody else for our mistakes. When we do we take all the credit.*

People see what they want to see, and ignore the rest. And they lie all the time to make themselves feel better. But what do I know? Nothing. I'm just a stupid Mexican and I don't know anything and you don't want to hear about it. Especially from me. my name is pancho i live on a rancho i work for two pesos a day. i visit my lucy i play with her pussy she takes my two pesos away. I handed the paper to the professors and went for a walk in the snow. Fuck'em if they didn't like it.

Act VI Scene 3

I got home to find that Larry had come home drunk and beat the shit out of Bob. He beat Bob up and then broke all the windows in the house. The cops came and took Larry back to jail. I shared a room with Bob. He had two black eyes and a split lip. He was really upset, and Dr. Alderman and him were sitting at the kitchen table talking. There was a repair crew replacing the glass. Bill and I went out for burgers and he told me about it. He was pretty glad that Larry was gone. He said Larry had been stealing things, you know, like food out of the fridge, coins, things like that. Nothing big. It was just annoying. So Bob accused Larry of eating his Peanut Butter Cups and Larry went crazy—just like that—and beat him up. I was glad I wasn't there. I had seen stuff like that get really bad in the camps. Somebody might get knifed or something. That kind of thing happens a lot more than you would think. Gandhi would say this is a natural consequence of poverty. I think it's just fucked up.

Nobody at the college said anything to me all weekend. The snow piled up a foot deep and I was glad that I didn't have to sleep out in it. I found a used bookstore but I didn't have any money to spare. I was just standing there reading. The owner watched me. He knew I was just trying to stay out of the cold, but he was nice about it. He told me he had a case of books in the back that were water damaged and I could have a few if I wanted. I had nothing else to do, and I was grateful, so I went through the box and picked out a couple that looked good. I got a copy of *Pickwick Papers* that was only missing a few pages, a book with no cover about the Australian Army in World War I, and a copy of *Hamlet*.

Hamlet was hard to read—there were a lot of words I didn't know—but I still found it interesting. There was this young prince, not much more than a teenager, really, and he's not sure if he's having a hallucination or seeing a ghost. It's his father's ghost he thinks he sees. And it tells Hamlet that he was murdered by his brother. His brother then married the queen and become the king. I've seen stuff like that in the camps, too. Except for the king and queen part. But like I said, things have a way of getting out of hand. But I liked the part about how confused Hamlet was. He pretends to be crazy, but then, I was wondering, wouldn't you have to be crazy to pretend to be crazy? So maybe he was crazy after all. Anyway, the King, his uncle, sends Hamlet to England with these two fake friends who have a letter to the King of England telling him to kill Hamlet. But Hamlet finds the letter and changes it to get his friends killed, instead. Then he comes back and gets in a sword fight and they all die.

It was a pretty good story. I wished the author had made up his mind whether to write a story or write poetry, though. He was pretty good at both, but still, I thought it was a bad idea to mix them up together in one book. I thought it was interesting, however, how he divided the book into Acts and Scenes. I had never seen that before. It was different from the usual chapters, or even the chapter and verse that you find in the Bible. I thought he was pretty clever to think of that. I said right then that if I ever wrote a book, that's what I was going to do.

Before I left I asked the guy how he got the water damage. I was just making conversation. "Fucking pipes here are for shit," he said. "I got a toilet that overflows all the time. There's always something leaking." He looked at me. "You know anything about plumbing?"

I found a hardware store and spent the rest of the day fixing things. The guts on his toilet. A drain and trap under the sink. Gaskets. You know what I mean.

The owner's name was John. He told me he used to be a professor but he got sick of the whole thing and quit to "devote his life to literature." That and somebody named Dean didn't like him screwing the undergraduates. I liked the part about being devoted to literature. It sounded like a happy marriage. I liked the other part, too, about the undergraduates. That sounded pretty interesting, too, but it didn't sound like it would lead to a happy marriage.

John wanted to pay me but I didn't want to take his money. "I wasn't doing nothing anyway," I said. "It was kind of fun." I liked working.

"Are you nuts?" he said. "You got any idea what a plumber would have charged me for all that?" I had no idea. John gave me a ten and told me I could have all the books I wanted.

I laughed and told him I would take *all* the books he had and he said he didn't mean all of them, not literally, but if I wanted a book every now and then I could have one, and I could borrow anything so long as I brought it back in good condition.

I asked him how he could make a living running a store like that and he said he couldn't, that he actually made his living selling dope to college kids, that the store was just a front.

I told him I knew how that was because I used to do something like that a long time ago. "I make more money selling grass than I made as a professor," he said, though I doubted that. Still, it was nice to make a friend in the book business, and he told all his friends that he knew a really good handyman, and I made a lot of extra money that way.

Act VI Scene 4

I was supposed to start work Monday morning but Herman came to the house early and said that I had to see the judge that morning instead. "Am I in trouble?" I asked. I was still thinking about the test I screwed up.

"No," Herman said. "It's about your misdemeanor."

I had forgot all about that. I said I didn't want to get in trouble with my boss on my new job but Herman said my boss had already been told and it was more important that I not get in trouble with the judge. We took the bus downtown.

We sat in the court for only a few minutes when the judge called my name. I stood up and a bunch of other people stood up, too. Evidently the SLED Program sent a lawyer from the university to represent me. And the university sent some people, too. I think they were there to explain to the judge what they were doing, just in case the judge had any questions.

The judge was an old red-faced guy with white hair and glasses that kept slipping down his nose. He didn't seem like he cared. He looked like he'd spent the weekend in one of Don Pablo's cantinas. The courtroom was full of people and it was really noisy. There was babies crying in their mother's arms. There was lawyers talking with their clients. There was cops coming and going. Doors opening and closing. People all the time interrupted the goings-on to *Sign this* or *Have a look at this* or *Do you know anything about this?* and then the judge would be even more distracted than he already was.

The judge listened to the lawyer for about fifteen seconds and banged his hammer and said, "Case continued." He signed a paper and that was that.

We drove back to the campus in a car with one of the guys from the university. He let us off behind the Psychology Hall and we went upstairs to the same meeting room. The room was full of people again. Now I knew I was in trouble. I felt about as bad as a man can feel.

I liked the idea of going to school. I liked it a lot. It hurts to be so close to your dream and then watch it slip away. Maybe this was even worse. I didn't even dream of school until Herman and Melanie came along.

I had John's ten dollars in my pocket so I wasn't flat broke. And I had eaten breakfast and slept in a real bed, so I didn't feel too bad. I was mostly over the pneumonia, too. I couldn't understand what I had done to get in trouble. Maybe it was God getting even with me for lying about my age. I thought about Filo and I remembered the look in his eyes when he saw me. He knew how his story was going to end, and I knew how mine was going to end, too. I would rather have had the judge just send me back to jail. Oh, well, I thought. Nothing to do but to man up and take it. No use even being mad about it. Kind of like when Sonia ran off with Bitchfinder. I went into the room and looked around.

Ackerman, Alderman, and Melanie were there, and most of the others from the previous Friday. There were some others who looked like students. I hadn't seen them before. Ackerman pointed to a chair and I sat down. He held my test papers but he wasn't looking at them. He laid them on the table in front of him and said, "Mr. Ortega, you didn't perform quite as well on this test as you did on your first one."

"Does this mean I don't get to go to school?" I asked.

"No," he said. "that's not what it means at all. It's just that, when we conceived of this program we anticipated that our participants would score somewhere between ten and twenty-five percent. We have prepared a program that begins about fifth or sixth grade level and is geared to taking students up through the GED. Do you know what the GED is?"

I thought about how SLED stood for Saving Lives Through Education and I wondered what GED might be. I ran through a whole list of G-words but nothing came up. "I don't know," I said. "Growing Up Through Education?"

He looked at me. "No, it stands for Graduate Equivalency Diploma. It means you have covered all the things you would have learned in high school and you qualify for a better job, or to get into college. It's a test for men and women who, for whatever reason, never finished high school."

"Like me?" I asked.

"Like you," Ackerman said. "The problem is that you'll have no trouble passing the GRE."

"GED," Alderman said.

"Right. The GED. You scored in the upper 80s across the board. Everything but the essay. You failed that." He looked at me and scowled. "Still, all-in-all, it's remarkable considering that you say you never spent a day in your life in school."

"There are many kinds of schools," I said. "But you didn't ask me about that."

"You're right," Dr. Ackerman said. "And I should have. We knew that one day we would encounter a student like you. We just weren't expecting that so soon. We want expand our program to send our participants to Junior College—eventually. But we haven't finalized the arrangements. We only have four participants, you know."

"Three," Alderman said.

"Three."

"So does that mean I can't go to school?"

"No, Mr. Ortega," Dr. Ackerman said. "We're going to send you to Arapahoe Junior College. We *want* you to go to school. And we'll make the arrangements right away. But first, you have to take the real GED exam. That shouldn't be a problem for you." Dr. Ackerman looked down at my test papers and then back up at me. "And I apologize for doubting that you wrote that essay about Gandhi. It's just—" he broke off. "It's just that you don't expect a homeless and unemployed jail inmate to have read Gandhi."

"But sir," I said, "Wasn't Gandhi himself a homeless, unemployed jail inmate?"

Dr. Ackerman smiled and nodded. "He most certainly was, Mr. Ortega. And I appreciate your reminding us of that. But on the essay that you write for the GED—lose the sarcasm."

That night, Herman and Melanie took me out for ice cream even though it was freezing out. There was a place called Baskin Robbins and they had thirty-one flavors. I thought that was incredible. I had seen their stores in California, but I had never eaten in one. It was like heaven.

Act VI Scene 5

On Tuesday I got up early and went to work. Mr. Statler wasn't there. The manager in the mornings was named Ivan. He was a big guy with black hair and a round face, a neck so thick it bent his ears outwards. Ivan explained to me how to wash dishes and got just about everything wrong. After he left I forget everything he told me and did what I wanted. I would say never tell a Mexican how to wash dishes, but I don't want to sound racist. But I think we're just born knowing. I had to be really careful. My hand was better, but still not a hundred percent. But I did fine. After a few weeks Ivan said I was the best dishwasher they ever had and he wished he could put me on nights. Not long after that, he started bringing the new dishwashers to me so I could train them.

A week later I took my GED and the next week I found out that I passed. Melanie came by the apartment and told me. She also had a little blue card for me. It had my name and a number on it. It was called a Social Security card.

"Does this make me a citizen?" I asked.

She laughed. "No," she said, "but you have to have one to work in the U.S."

I had worked in the U.S. since I was six and never seen one of these cards.

"Take care of it," Melanie said.

"You bet I will," I replied. The first thing I did was to make six copies of it. Then I went down and had it framed and I hung it on the wall by my bed like it was one of Maria's saints. I also went to John's bookstore and got a book on Social Security and another one on citizenship.

John had a Lebanese friend who ran a kebab shop down the street. He told me his friend needed some light fixtures changed out and a new vent fan installed over the stove. He asked if I could help him. I said that I could and that night I made another twenty dollars.

I couldn't start school right away. I had to wait for spring quarter, and that started in March. Until then I worked in the mornings, and in the afternoons I read or worked with a tutor in the writing center. The tutor was named Leslie and she was in her fifties and little fat, but really nice. She showed me how to cite things in the text and how to write a Works Cited Page. She made me pay attention that I was writing in something called the *active voice*, though I never quite figured out what that was. And she told me never to use semi colons. She said people almost always use them wrong and there were only two times to use semi-colons correctly: one was to attach something called a dependent clause to a complete sentence, and the other was to make a list of lists if the lists have items in them that are separated by commas. I still remember what she said. If anybody is actually reading this, you can check for yourself. If you count carefully, you will find twenty-five semi-colons up to now, and I am pretty sure I got all of them right. There's one I'm not too sure of. I think it is a dependent clause. I hope so. I think Leslie would be proud of me. She really didn't like semi-colons.

Around the end of February I started getting scared about school and stuff. I mentioned this to Dr. Alderman in our weekly meeting and he suggested that, since I had my afternoons free, I sit in on some classes. "You mean I can do that?" I said. "I can just go into a class and sit down?" I was wondering why I hadn't thought of doing that on my own a long time ago. Kind of like the library in El Paso.

He looked at me funny. "Well, it's not like *taking* the class," he said. "You can't ask questions or take tests, and you won't get a grade or credit for the course. But you can learn something about how college works, and it might make you feel a little more comfortable when you start at Arapahoe."

I was still hesitant. I thought he was pulling my leg.

"I'll talk to Herman for you," he said.

For the next few afternoons I followed Herman around to his classes. He was a graduate student and it didn't seem to me like he did all that much. His classes only met once or twice a week, and for only an hour or two. There weren't many students in the classes and all they did was talk about books and articles and experiments and things. I never actually saw them do anything. And there weren't any tests or quizzes, although the professor kept reminding them something about a term paper. I had to look it up to see what that meant because I was too shy to ask Herman. I thought it was like a test essay, you know, write something about your favorite term. Something like that. I would have written about irony. But then I found out that a term paper referred to a major work written during a period of time in a school. The students had to write one or two papers every quarter. This has to be bullshit, I thought. It's way too easy.

I went to some classes on my own, too, and Melanie took me to a couple. I looked at all these people and decided that my problem was that I didn't know anything at all about being a student. I knew lots of useless information, but I didn't know what it meant to use this in a classroom. I needed to have some kind of common experience if I was going to understand students and college. I thought it would help if I tried to look like other students and talk like them and be as much like them as I could. I had this idea that if I did that, I might finally understand. So I took some of the money I made doing odd jobs and I bought some more jeans and sweaters and things so I would look more like a student.

At the apartment we got a new roommate. His name was Ben and he was skinny and had a lot of scratchy home-made tattoos all over. He looked sad all the time and I didn't like him. I was glad he shared the room with Bill.

Act VI Scene 6

I started classes for real in mid-March of 1966. I had to take the bus to Littleton. That's where the Arapahoe Junior College was. Is. Back then it was located in an old high school downtown. The old high school had moved to a new building, and the city donated the old building to start this junior college. It didn't look at all like the university in Denver. The university in Denver was big with lots trees and nice old buildings. This was just an old school on a street full of run down bars and restaurants and second-hand stores and pawn shops. Right away I knew what it was: the school for Mexicans. And there were some Mexicans there. But there were some Anglos, too, and even a few Negros. Apparently this was the school they sent all the losers to. An equal opportunity school for losers. I was pissed about that for about ten minutes.

My first class was something called Freshman Composition. I went in, sat down, and fell in love. Not with the class. Nobody likes freshman writing. With the teacher. Miss Elisa Prieto. The minute she walked in I knew she was the one. She was short and dark with long hair, slim hips, beautiful full lips, wide brown eyes, and a smile from here to here. I knew she was the girl for me. The only thing I couldn't figure out was why she went up to the front instead of sitting down with the rest of us. Then I got it. She was the teacher. Until then I had never met a Mexican teacher, or even thought that there were any, except, maybe, back in Mexico. Wow, I thought.

Miss Prieto told us that we were going to write a short paper every week and revise it for something called a portfolio. Our first paper was to tell her what we wanted to do with our education. After that, I never heard another word she said. Listening to her talk was like listening to music, and my mind focused on one thing: What paper could I write that would make Miss Prieto fall in love with me?

I went home that night and sat down at the kitchen table and wrote: *I want to be a teacher with my education. I want to go out into the migrant camps and teach the little kids how to write and stuff. I think that being a teacher is the best job.* There was a lot more and it was just as bad. I was nervous, I think. I wanted to impress Miss Prieto, and I thought the way to do that was to tell her I wanted to be a teacher like her. I would establish common ground and then she would want to talk to me.

A few days later she gave me my paper back. She didn't give me a grade but she did talk about writing in the active voice and using an outline to organize my thinking and not using slang expressions like "and stuff." I think she said something about run-on sentences, too.

Our composition class met on Monday, Wednesday, and Friday. I had another class after that. Algebra. That was just numbers, and numbers are easy. Math is about rules and the first thing you have to know is that there is either a right answer or there is no answer at all. Unless you just get the answer wrong. But if you are careful with your operations, that shouldn't happen. Best of all, in our class, the teacher said all our problems had right answers. All we had to do was find them. So by process of elimination, that made things easier right there. There would not be any tricky questions.

In English there are just as many (if not more) rules, but you never know if you get anything right. People either like it or they don't. The word for this is subjective. You write something and then somebody who knows nothing about you has to decide what you were trying to do and whether you did it or not. It sounds kind of fishy to me. But maybe I'm just suspicious because I had that bad experience with my first essay—the one about Gandhi.

In Algebra there are rules and you get it right or you don't. The word for this is objective. But at least in math you can prove your answer.

On Tuesdays and Thursdays I had biology and psychology. Biology was pretty easy. We just looked at slides and stuff, memorized Latin names for things. The professor talked a lot about the different kinds of life. She reminded me of Gus, only she wasn't green.

Psychology was more difficult, but only because of all the big words they used. I wondered what the authors of the book were hiding from? Most of what they said was pretty simple, but they used all these fancy words to make it sound more complicated. As soon as we read about *complexes* I knew what their problem was. But I liked psychology. I didn't know that the world was full of people asking the same kinds of question as I was: Why is everybody so fucked up? Unfortunately, psychology is more like English than algebra. There were lots of theories, but not so many answers. As for proving things—forget it.

My second composition assignment was to write a paper where I expressed an opinion and backed it up with three facts. I wrote another paper about how important it was to be a teacher. My three facts were that people needed teachers to learn things, that being a teacher paid well, and that people couldn't learn things without teachers. Miss Prieto wrote on my paper, *Come see me in my office.* I tell you, I was walking on air.

Unfortunately, Miss Prieto didn't like my essay. She had it out on her desk waiting for when I got there. In fact, when I got to her office, she told me she was a little worried about me. "I'm a little worried about you," she said. It was the first words out of her mouth. I wondered what it was about my essays that pissed people off. She said to wait there and she went out and came back with a man she introduced to me as Dr. Crawfurd. He was the college president. He was a middle-aged man with dark hair. He wore a bow tie. He didn't say much.

"Listen," Miss Prieto said, "I'm getting kind of a bad vibe from you already. I just want to be clear about something, okay?"

"Okay," I said.

"You don't have to impress me *as a person* with your writing. Just write what you really feel. My job is to teach you to write and that means telling you what you do well, which at this point isn't very much, and to tell you what you can do better, which right now means almost everything. But especially it means to stop slobbering all over me. Just take the class, write your papers, and get on with your life. Do you understand?"

By coincidence, we had started our psychology class talking about child psychology. Maybe that was a good place to start, so to speak, at the beginning. But I had just finished reading an article by John Bowlby about Attachment Theory. Attachment Theory talks about how children, especially children who have been abused or institutionalized, develop different kinds of relationships with people they perceive as care givers. This, in turn, gives rise to different behaviors known as *patterns*. According to Bowlby, there are four patterns: secure, anxious-ambivalent, anxious-avoidant (which are all organized behaviors), and disorganized (which is plain old disorganized). It was clear to me that Miss Prieto was anxious to avoid me. The only question was, Why? It was easier to tell her that I understood than to ask her to explain why she felt like she did about me. "I understand," I said.

"Okay," she said. "Here's your paper."

I made an F.

Outside her office, Dr. Crawfurd patted me on the shoulder. "She's a looker, all right," he said, "but a real hell-cat, that one. I'd stay away from her for a while. Let her cool down a bit." Then he went off whistling down the hall.

I went home and spent all night revising the paper.

A few weeks later I went back to Miss Prieto's office. I hate to say it was springtime and I had spring fever, but it was springtime and I had spring fever. The grass was getting green and there were flowers popping up all over. There might be another late snow, but I knew that winter was going to end soon and I was feeling pretty good about things. And lonely. I was doing extra work almost every weekend and I was sure somebody was going to ask me where I got the money for all my new shirts and stuff. But nobody had. Not yet, anyways.

So I went to see Miss Prieto and I stood in the doorway until she looked up and said, "Oh. What do *you* want?"

"Miss Prieto," I said. "If I make an A in your class, will you go out to dinner with me? Just once? Please? If I can't make you laugh I'll never ask you again. I promise."

She looked at me like she'd stepped in something smelly on the sidewalk. "Listen," she said, "I ought to throw you out of my class right now."

"But you won't, Miss Prieto. I know you won't. I can tell you're not that kind of a person. I know I'm not much, but I read your Master's Thesis and I know you grew up in the camps, and I'm just like you only different. That's probably why you want to avoid me."

Never let anybody tell you that research isn't a useful skill.

"Different?" she said. "Do you mean different as in, Just-got-out-of-jail different? Or how about, In a drug-treatment program different? Or different as in, Who-in-the-hell-really-are-you, Mr. Ortega? I can research, too, you know."

"Okay," I said. "So you know I been to jail, but I only went there once for a few hours, and that was because they wouldn't put me in the hospital unless I committed some misdemeanor and went to jail first. Then they said they'd take me. It was either that or die. You know how that is. I bet half the people you grew up with are just like that, or had something like that happen."

"So what about the drugs then?"

"I never did much drugs. A little. Just enough to get strung out once but that was all."

Miss Prieto looked like she might scream.

This wasn't working out like I wanted it to. "I don't want nothing to do with drugs," I said. "I never did like them. I only told them that in jail because I thought that was what they wanted to hear. And if I hadn't told them that then I wouldn't have got into this SLED Program and got into school. I never got the chance to go to school before. And now I got the chance, but I—" I stopped.

"You *what*, Mr. Ortega?"

"I—it's just—" I looked at her. She was so beautiful it hurt to look. "It's just… Miss Prieto, nobody really knows me. Nobody. And I never met anybody like you before, you know. You're smart and pretty and nice. I want to be like that, too. And I just thought if I could spend some time with you, I could learn more how to be like you, you know? How to be the right kind of person.

"I didn't even have camps to grow up in, Miss Prieto. I grew up on the streets. My mother was dead. I never knew my father. I just had to make out the best I could. And my whole life I've looked at people like you and wondered how you did it. I don't know how to be around people, Miss Prieto. When I'm with people all I can think about is being alone, and when I'm alone, all I want is to be around people. I don't know what's wrong with me, but I'm trying to work through it.

"But I really *do* like you. You're smart and you're pretty. And I might even understand why you're afraid of me, or just don't like me. I could see that. I'm sure you could do better than me. But I'm not stupid, Miss Prieto. I'm kind of smart, in a weird way. I've just never been to school. I got no education. And I just thought if I could raise my grade to an A, maybe you might go out to one dinner with me just one time. That would mean a lot to me. Kind of like a challenge, or a goal. Give me something to work for, you know. Something to keep me studying when I what I want to do is sleep or watch TV."

Miss Prieto sat at the desk with her lips pressed tight and a red pen clutched in her right hand like a steak knife. She was grading papers. I could tell by all the marks on the page in front of her. She said, "So now you tell me that you lied to the hospital, you lied to the police, and you lied to the SLED Program, but *I'm* supposed to believe you? Thanks a lot, Mr. Ortega. Is there anything else you lied about?"

"I'm not really thirty-nine, either," I said. "This old cop, Scoville, he told me to say I was thirty-nine. He said it was better that way. I didn't know why. I'm really forty-two, but I did what he told me. And if I hadn't, I couldn't have got into the SLED Program. But please don't tell nobody "

"Anybody."

"Anybody. They might kick me out. I didn't mean nothing by it."

"Anything," Miss Prieto said.

"Anything," I said. "But if it helps any, I'm in pretty good shape for a forty-two-year old. Except for my hand." I showed her my hand. "But it's getting better."

She sighed and looked at me like I was hopeless. I think she was trying to figure out the quickest way to get me out of her office.

"Look," I said. "If you grew up in the camps, you must have known a thousand guys just like me. And none of them were any good. But we're all people, Miss Prieto. We all deserve a chance. We're *supposed* to get better. We're *supposed* to help each other. I couldn't blame you for not liking me. Hell, half the time, I don't even like me. But at least I'm trying to do something about it. When I was picking grapes at Delano—"

"You were at Delano?"

"Yeah I was at Delano. Have you ever been there?"

She hesitated. "I grew up in Delano."

"Okay," I said. "So you know the place. See—we have something in common! So when I was at Delano I met these guys, Chavez and Father McDonnell. They kept saying that people can change, and that the only way to—"

Miss Prieto's eyes opened wide. "You worked with Cesar Chavez and Father McDonnell?"

"Yeah, a little. Do you know them?"

"I thought you said you read my thesis. Or were you lying about that, too?"

"I read it," I said. "At least, most of it."

"I knew McDonnell," she said. "We also lived for a while in *Sal Si Puedes*. He built a church there. We used to go on Sundays. Sometimes that crazy fool would get everybody up in the middle of the night for a service." Suddenly she looked at me and her eyes narrowed. "You're bullshitting me, aren't you? You read that in my thesis and now you want to talk about it because you think you can get close to me that way, right? You sonofa—"

"No!" I said. "I was working at this vineyard and they threw me out because my hand was fucked up. Then these goons didn't want to pay me. I started to argue with them and these two guys and this girl come out of the shadows and say, "Give him his money," and they did. They kicked me, but they gave me my quarter. That was a lot of money to me right then. I didn't have much."

"Two guys and a girl?"

"Yeah. Father McDonnell, Chavez, and this woman named Dolores."

"Dolores Huerta?"

"Yeah, I suppose."

Miss Prieto looked skeptical. "What does Father McDonnell look like?"

"He's tall and dark-haired and skinny. He's got a big nose and big ears and a deep voice. If you know him, ask him. He'd remember me. I was the guy in the hospital. The guy in the picture in the paper."

Miss Prieto sat up straight. "That was *you*? The guy choking the policeman?"

"Yeah, that was me. But Father McDonnell wasn't too happy with me. He's the one who told me about Gandhi and non-violence. I wasn't supposed to fight with the cops. Everybody else just walked off to jail, but I was in the hospital already so they wouldn't let me leave. But I would've gone if I could have."

Miss Prieto sank back in her chair and then looked at her watch. "Shit," she said. "I got a class that started two minutes ago." She stood up and gathered a folder and some books.

"So will you?" I asked.

"Will I what?" she said as she pushed past me to the door.

"Will you go out to dinner with me if I make an A in your class?"

She stood in the hallway, keys in hand, waiting for me to come out so she could lock the door behind me. "It's against school rules for faculty and students to date," she said. I came out and she locked the door and walked away. But she stopped a few steps down the hall and looked back. "That was really you—the guy in the paper?"

I nodded.

"And you really know Father McDonnell and Cesar Chavez?"

"Ask them," I said.

She frowned. "*After* the class is finished, *after* all the grades are submitted, *if* you make an A, *which* I doubt you can, but *if* you make an A, I'll meet you for *one* cup of coffee across the street. *One* time only. Provided that you don't ask me again, and you don't take any more classes with me after this. Okay?"

"Okay," I said.

I took classes that summer and the next fall, winter, and spring. In December of 1967 I graduated from Arapahoe Junior College with straight A's. I was also the first graduate from the SLED Program. Neither Bill nor Bob nor Larry made it, but that's another story. Dr. Ackerman and Dr. Alderman put on a big celebration for me. Herman and Melanie came. The Dean of the Psychology Department came. The President of the University of Denver was there, too. He said they were all very proud of me. I got my picture taken with him. He talked about how wonderful the SLED Program was and how education could do so much to make the world better. He also had a special present for me: a scholarship to the University of Denver. In January of 1968, I went to work on my Bachelor's Degree in Psychology. And best of all, on Valentine's Day of that year, I married Elisa Prieto.

Act VI Scene 7

I hate to tell things out of order, but I'm like that. In fact, most Chicanos are like that. We go by what is more important first, rather than straight linear time like most Anglos do. I used to feel bad about that, but now I'm kind of proud of it. To me, it makes more sense. What's important is what's important, not what happened first.

So I told you that I met Ringo Starr. I also told you that neither Bill nor Bob made it through the SLED Program. This is how all that happened. None of these things are that big of a deal by themselves, but the whole thing together became very important for what happened a few weeks after I graduated from Arapahoe Junior College.

Remember how I said that Larry and Bob got into a fight and Larry went back to jail? They got into that fight because Larry accused Bob of stealing some of his stuff. After that, we got a new roommate. His name was Ben. Ben was the sad guy with all the scratchy tattoos.

It wasn't too long after this that Bill and Bob began to complain again that somebody was stealing in the house. It was just little stuff. Coins. Food. A shirt. Stupid stuff. But one day I found that I was missing ten dollars from the money I made doing odd jobs. I thought maybe I had just miscounted, but I'm pretty good with numbers, so I wondered about that.

Eventually Bill convinced Bob that he had seen Ben with some of Bob's things, and Bob got pissed off at Ben and punched him. That was that. Bob went back to jail and Ben got kicked out of the program. I don't think he went to jail. Nobody found any of Bob's stuff on him. But I think he had other problems, too. Like, I think maybe he was still smoking some dope on the side or something.

So it was in the summertime and Elisa and I were dating. We went to church every Sunday. I didn't much like going to church, but it was important to Elisa, so I went with her. It made her happy. And I think she thought the better of me for it. After church, we walked over to the Pioneer Monument Fountain where there was a good taco stand. We'd eat soft chicken tacos and talk and sometimes sing. There was a lot of good music back then, and sometimes musicians would hang out in the square and jam just for fun. I remember me and Elisa singing "California Dreaming." That was one of our favorites. So this one day we were talking and eating tacos and I looked down and saw something glittering in a crack in the pavement. I don't know why, but I felt it was important to find out what it was. Just curious, I suppose. It took me a little while to pry it out.

What it was a really big diamond set in a gold ring. How it fell in like that I can't imagine, but it did, diamond side up. That's what I saw. The diamond. And it was really, really big. In fact, it was so big I was sure it was a fake. I didn't even think twice about it. Except that when I looked at the inside of the band, there a little tiny inscription: to Mo from Richie.

I don't know much about jewelry. I never owned anything worth worrying about. Not even my little crucifix. Certainly not that blue marble. But I sort of wondered why somebody would put an inscription on a cheap ring with a fake diamond. I tried the ring on Elisa's finger but it was too big. She was the one who started wondering about the diamond. It bothered her enough that she got up and found a coke bottle scratched the glass. She said that meant it was a real diamond.

I have no idea what a diamond that big is worth, but I knew it was a lot. Enough that people would know I had no business with it. If anybody found me with that stone, I'd have been in trouble for sure. And all this talk about stealing in the house made me nervous. So I knew right away I had to return it. But how?

The longer I held it the more panicked I got and the more trouble I imagined myself getting into. What if somebody had just lost it and the cops were looking for it *right then*? How would I explain that I had it? Even if Elisa was a college teacher and said she was with me, in my experience, nobody believes Mexicans anyway.

So we were walking down the street and there was this big luxury hotel called the Brown Palace. That was where all the really rich people stayed when they visited Denver. Elisa suggested that if I was really that uncomfortable, that

I go in and give it the manager. She said he would know how to get it back to its owner. So I did. The manager came out and I showed him the ring and told him that I had found it in the park and wanted to give it back to the owner. You should have seen the look on his face!

It turns out that the Beatles spent two nights in Denver in 1964. They played a concert up north at a place called Red Rocks and stayed at the Brown Palace. Ringo (whose real name was Richard) had given the ring to his girlfriend (and soon to be wife), Maureen. He called her Mo. She called him Richie. She always claimed that the ring was stolen from the hotel, but nobody ever caught the thief. Then I walked in with the ring.

The hotel manager was very excited. He wanted to take down my name. I didn't want to give it. I didn't think it was important who turned it in. But he wanted to know where I found it and what the circumstance was because, evidently, some other guests lost things, too, and he said the police or insurance company might want to talk more to me. That really spooked me and I was sure the cops would come after me. But Elisa said that I had nothing to hide so eventually I gave them my name, address, and phone number, and we left.

A few weeks later I got a call from the hotel asking if I could stop by for a few minutes that Friday evening. Once again I was sure that I was in some kind of trouble and didn't want to go, but Elisa said they would probably give us a dinner or a free night's stay or something. She said it would be nice and we should go.

When we got there the manager took us up to the eighth floor. You had to have a special key just to make the elevator open on the eighth floor. He took us down the hall to a room and knocked on the door. The door opened and man stood there looking at us.

Elisa elbowed me and said, "Do you know who this is?"

"Yeah," I said. "Herman. What are you doing here?"

Everybody laughed and Ringo, without missing a beat, said, "That's the other half of the invasion." Everybody laughed again. I had no idea what he was talking about.

Ringo offered us some wine or champagne, but I wasn't allowed to drink any alcohol. That was part of the SLED Program, too. They didn't want us to drink because they said it would trigger our addiction. I had a Seven-Up instead, and a little bit of a sandwich.

Ringo told me he gave the ring to his girlfriend before she was his wife, and was very sorry to have lost it. He thanked me for returning it and then he gave me an envelope. I told him I didn't want anything, I was just trying to do what was right, but Ringo said he made more money in a night than I made in a year, and it was his way of thanking me. He said he was sure I could put it to good use. We got our picture taken together and then we left. He seemed like a nice guy. And he really looked just like Herman Stoltzheimer. It makes you wonder about people. Or their parents, anyway.

Outside the hotel I opened the envelope. There was a thousand dollars inside. Let me tell you, when you are a student, and *especially* a poor, broke Mexican student, a thousand dollars goes a long way. But you know what I did with that money? I put it in a savings account. It was my first legal bank account in America.

But the real kicker is this: later that month things *really* started disappearing in our apartment. By then we had two new roommates, Glen and Ramon. Ramon told me that Bill kept telling them that they had problems with stealing ever since I came to the house. He told me Bill said to keep an eye on me. A few days later I came home to find the apartment in a big uproar. Dr. Alderman was there, Herman was there, the cops were there. Evidently Glen went through my stuff and found some things of his. Bill had told him he saw me in their room earlier that week. Glen was going to kick my ass but Ramon, bless his heart, called Dr. Alderman, and Dr. Alderman called the police.

They searched us all. For a little while I thought I was going to jail, but then Elisa came over—she was bringing me a framed copy of the picture of me and Ringo Starr—and she told Dr. Alderman about the ring and the hotel and all that. She even had the photo and Ringo's thank you note right there. The police called the hotel and the manager told them it was true. I turned in a ring that was worth *half a million dollars*. Who do you think the cops believed after that? Dr. Ackerman kicked Bill out of the program and we never had any more trouble with stealing. Never let it be said that honesty doesn't pay.

Act VI Scene 8

So when I graduated from the SLED Program they threw a big party and the University President shook my hand and I got a scholarship to the University of Denver. It was a big deal and there was a reporter there and he took my picture for the newspaper and asked me to say a few words. I really didn't have much to say except to thank the university for the chance to have a better life. I was always kind of guarded. I was also anxious about having my picture taken. I hadn't had much luck with that, but I didn't know how to ask them not to. Instead I kept my mouth shut.

Sure enough, a few weeks later I came home from class to find two FBI agents sitting on the couch. They were pretty ordinary looking guys. About my age. Blue suits. Shiny black shoes. Short hair. Shaved. Not fat, not skinny. They stood up when I walked in. They showed me their FBI identification. "Pablo Barela?" one asked. The minute I heard that name I knew I was in trouble.

Gus said many things that I did not understand, still do not understand. He said that time is the orderly sequence of events in this dimension and that time is a property of this dimension. I think he meant that outside of this dimension, things might happen in different ways. Or perhaps they have a different way of seeing what we experience. Maybe in some other dimension, they can see everything—past, present, even the future. I don't know. Ask a physicist. Stephen Hawking might know.

Anyway, we think that things happen and the past is gone, but it has a weird way of coming back around to haunt us. Sometimes it's *fantastic* or *fabulous*. Sometimes it is *ironic*. There's another word I learned in psychology for these weird coincidences that happen: *synchronicity*. It's something seemingly random that happens but that has meaning in our lives. There's a big debate about whether these things, these events we take for signs or messages, come from inside of us or outside of us. Are they something we create? Or are they something that the universe sends to us as a warning or a reward, or even a punishment for what we have done? Do they have meaning on their own, as in a *purpose*? Or do we just find some meaning based on our experience? You think you leave it all behind you, but maybe in some other dimension, it's all just sitting there for anybody to see. You should have seen the look on Elisa's face when I answered to another name.

"I used to be Pablo Barela," I said.

"Yes, we know," one of the detectives said. He held up a copy of my arrest record from the Denver jail. It had my fingerprints. "We also found your fingerprints in a hospital in Delano, California, but you were gone before we got there."

"What's this all about?" Elisa said.

"I don't know," I told her. I said to the agents, "What can I do for you?"

"You used to rent a house on Stevens Street in El Paso, am I correct? Across the street from the cemetery? You rented from a man named" he looked down at his notes, "Winegardner?"

"Yes," I said. "I did."

He looked at his notes again. "And this would have been sometime in about 1939, right?"

"What's this all about?" Elisa asked again.

"Yes," I said. "I rented that house in 1939."

"Are you in some kind of trouble?" Elisa asked. Without waiting for me to answer she turned to the agents and said, "Is Pablo under some kind of suspicion? Are you trying to question him without an attorney? Because if you are, nothing he says will be admissible in court."

"We just have a few questions, Ms. Ortega," the second agent said. "This isn't a formal questioning, though we might have grounds on the basis of immigration status to bring Mr. Barela in if he doesn't want to cooperate."

Elisa turned to me and said, "Pablo, don't talk to these men. Let them take you in if they think they can get away with it."

"It's all right," I said. "I've done nothing wrong." To the agents I said,

"Would you like some coffee or tea or something?"

"No thank you," the first agent said.

I turned to Elisa and said, "Would you make me a cup of coffee?" but she crossed her arms and stood her ground. I knew that look. The coffee would wait.

"I lived there for about a year," I said. "I was sixteen in 1939. What's going on?"

"A few years ago," the agent continued, "El Paso Natural Gas ran a pipeline through the neighborhood. When they were digging, they uncovered skeletal remains in the backyard of a house at 611 Stevens. The coroner determined that the remains were those of an unidentified Native American male who died of a gunshot wound that could not have been self-inflicted. They estimate he was somewhere between thirteen and twenty years of age and that he died sometime between 1934 and 1944. Since this was brought to the FBI's attention, we've been checking out the former owner and all of the former tenants. So you could say these are just some routine questions about an unusual event."

"Are you talking about a murder?" Elisa said.

"We didn't say *murder*," the second agent said, looking up at her. "We only said we were asking if Pablo knew anything about a body that was found in the back yard of a house he once rented."

The first agent took a deep breath and added, "It was also brought to our attention that at the time, Pablo had no visible means of support—no regular employment that we know of—that could give him the income to do things like, for example, pay rent."

"And," the other agent continued, "when we talked to Mr. Winegardner—he's dead now, by-the-way, but when we interviewed him in 1952 "

"When the body was found," the first agent said.

"When the body was found," the second continued, "Winegardner recalled under oath that Mr. Barela—"

"As Mr. Ortega used to be known," the first agent said.

"As he used to be known. But Mr. Barela disappeared in the middle of the night without giving notice. And we thought that, also, was a little bit—shall we say—curious."

"I left the key on the counter," I said.

"Well that explains everything," the second agent said.

"And then there's the matter of your first wife."

Elisa's jaw dropped. She looked like she'd just been shot. "Your *wife*?" Elisa said. I had never said anything to her about being married before.

"Maria Barela," the first agent said.

"She was found hanging in the kitchen of a home in Canutillo rented by Pablo Barela. That was in July of 1947," the second agent said.

"She left a note," I said.

"Yes," the second agent said. "We know. We have your fingerprints on the note, and from the house, and from a number of items found in the house." He opened a manila envelope and spread out some Polaroid color snapshots. I looked at the photos. I had to reach down and spread them out to see. One of them was of my old shoeshine box. I hadn't thought about that box in years.

"Your toolbox?" the first agent said.

"Yes," I replied.

"And the landlord," the first agent said, reading again from his notes, "a Mr. Perkins, he also mentioned under oath that you disappeared in the middle of the night, so to speak."

"Seems to be a habit of yours," the second agent said.

"Leaving bodies behind in the middle of the night," said the first.

"Pablo," Elisa said, "Don't say *anything* to these men. I'm calling Dr. Alderman *right now*."

"I'm not in that program any more, Elisa," I said. "So I doubt if Dr. Alderman would do anything."

She went to the phone anyway.

I said, "The body in the backyard is a boy named Oscar. He was a Tarahumara from down in Central Chihuahua."

"And how did you know this boy, Oscar," the first agent said.

"He used to work for me," I said.

"And what did he do?" the second agent said.

"And what did *you* do?" the first said right after him.

"He shined shoes and sold things. Gum. Cigarettes. Magazines. Combs. Things like this. He used to carve little figures, too, animals and people. He was in downtown El Paso out in front of the Hilton. I did that too, for a while," I said. "And then I had some other boys working for me."

Both of the agents took out pens and started taking notes.

"Alderman's on his way," Elisa said. "Will you please stop talking, at least until he gets here."

"I haven't done anything," I said.

"That doesn't matter," Elisa said.

"This is just an informal session," the first agent said. "But Mr. Barela—Ortega—doesn't have to answer any questions he doesn't want to answer."

"You *do* have the right to have an attorney present during questioning," the second agent said. "I should tell you that. And anything you say could be used against you."

"I thought you said this wasn't questioning," Elisa said.

"It's informal," the first agent said.

"But it's still questioning," added the second. To me he said, "And what did you say *you* did?"

"I looked after the boys who worked for me."

"Looked after them?"

"I got them the things they needed. And I protected them."

"I see," the first agent said. "And they paid you for this protection?"

"They did," I said. "Every night. And I never had any trouble with any of them. Except one," I said. "And that wasn't Oscar."

The agents looked at each other.

"Listen," I said. I suddenly had the feeling I was skating on pretty thin ice. I remembered something I learned in a sociology class about how systems take on a life and purpose of their own. You'd think cops are there to solve crimes but sometimes there's more to it than that; their own advancement and promotion, for instance. Promises made to others for things like *closure* or *revenge*. Crooked cops might cover things up for other people. I realized that this was why Don Pablo had sent a biker to warn me. He must have known that the cops were asking around about me. And it probably wasn't just my interests he was looking after. I consider you a friend, he had said, Don Pablo always remembers his friends. He also never forgot his enemies, and I had seen firsthand what happened to people who crossed Don Pablo.

I got up and went to the window. I really wanted that cup of coffee, but Elisa hadn't moved. In fact, she placed herself between me and the FBI agents, as if she could prevent their even touching me. "I can tell you the whole story," I said. "I don't think I've done anything wrong. At least, not anything that you can prosecute me for thirty years after the events. And I think you really want to know what happened so you can close the book on this, am I right?"

The agents said "Of course" at the same time.

"But the problem is that there is somebody else involved, and while I'm not afraid of you, I am very afraid of what that person would say if he knew I was talking to you, do you get my drift?"

"For the love of God!" Elisa shouted, "Can't you just shut the fuck up for a few minutes until Alderman gets here?"

"Elisa!" I said, "It's okay." I meant that I hadn't done anything wrong.

She shouted back at me, "This is *not* what okay looks like!"

"Maybe you better wait," the first agent said.

"Can you just go make that coffee now?" I asked Elisa. "Please. I could really, really use a cup of coffee."

Elisa stomped off to the kitchen.

"You're cops," I said. "Do you know much about El Paso and Juarez?"

"A little," the second agent said. "That's the office we work out of."

"So you know what happened in Juarez in the summer of 1939?"

"Would this have anything to do with a gang war?" he asked.

I nodded.

"Perhaps a man by the name of Pablo Dominguez?"

"Do you mean Don Pablo?"

"Don Pablo," he said. "That's the man I had in mind."

I took a deep breath. "And how is Don Pablo these days?" I asked.

The agents leaned back in the couch and looked at one another. Then the first agent said, "Have you been in touch with Don Pablo recently?"

I shook my head. "I haven't spoken to him in years."

"And when was the last time you heard from Don Pablo?" the second agent asked.

"You know the answer to that," I said.

"Delano, California? 1965?" he asked.

"That's right," I said.

"He told you we were looking for you?"

I nodded. "He told me to run. He didn't say why, but when Don Pablo tells you to do something, you do it or else. Now do you understand why I say I have to be careful?"

"Would it make you feel any better," the second agent said, "if we told you that Don Pablo was dead?"

I was stunned. "Do you mean that, or are you trying to trick me?"

"We don't have to trick you," the first agent said. He shrugged. "If we wanted to arrest you, we could. You're in the country illegally."

"Improper disposal of a dead body," the second agent said. "Failure to render aid. Contributing to the delinquency. Conspiracy. There are probably a hundred things we could charge you with. Income tax evasion. I don't believe you paid income tax on that protection money you said took from your shoeshine boys."

"We just want to know what happened and why there was a body buried in the backyard at 611 Stevens," the first continued. "Especially when there was a for-christ's-sake cemetery right across the street."

"How did he die?" I asked.

"Just like he lived," the first agent said. "We think it was quick."

The second said, "Some gangsters from central Mexico grabbed him off the street in a dispute about smuggling routes. Nobody ever found a body. We just presume," he said. "That's one reason we asked if you'd been in touch with him. But we think he's dead."

"Okay," I said. I was thinking about the ranch out in the middle of no place. Mexico is full of places like that. A chair, a rail, some wire, a knife, an iron bar, some fire, something. Poor Don Pablo. Whatever it was, you can bet it wasn't quick. I wondered how he took it, but inside I knew. *Get your filthy hands off me you pieces of shit. The best part of you ran down your mothers' legs. Do you know who I am? I'm gonna make you wish you had never been born.* That's what Don Pablo would have said. What is it they say, Everything that you do comes back to you? Those who live by the sword…

Right then Dr. Alderman pulled up. He screeched to a stop in front of the house and sprinted to the door. "What the hell's going on here?" he asked.

Elisa came in from the kitchen with the coffee.

"Dr. Alderman," I said, "I want to thank you for everything you've done for me. Can I tell you a story about how poor Mexicans grow up?"

Gandhi said that people were only free when they practiced rigorous honesty. Gus said that we liked to hide from the truth and believe whatever lies we thought would make our lives more convenient, or at least, more bearable. I knew that someday I would have to tell my story. I suppose I also knew that someday it would come back to haunt me. We hope that we can bury things so they won't resurface. But it doesn't work out like that. At least, it didn't for me. In a way, I was glad to get a few things off my chest. What was it Father Sheehy asked? Had I ever been to confession? So I told them how I met Don Pablo and how I came to El Paso and what I did to survive as a boy. And I hoped that when I told them they would understand that I didn't kill Oscar, and why I couldn't have said anything to the authorities. I mean, Oscar was dead so we buried him. What else could we have done? I didn't know any better, and even if I did, I was in house full of gangsters. What could I have done differently?

But, of course, I had killed somebody. Two somebodies, to be exact. And I was blamed for even more, but I didn't talk about that. What could I have said to explain that away? There is no statute of limitations on murder. But they weren't asking me about the man in the blacksmith's shop, or Filo, or Don Elias' driver, or the soldier in the clinic, or Varney Hall and his pals.

Instead I told them about my fractured skull and how Oscar saved my life. I told them how I told Oscar to take me home, but Oscar thought I meant Juarez and we got to Don Pablo's hotel just in time to save Don Pablo's life, and how we hid him out at my house, and how Oscar died in the backyard because he never said and nobody thought to ask if he was hurt. And under the circumstances, what else could we have done? I wasn't running the show. I was just a shoeshine boy.

The agents drank their coffee and listened, and when I was done they looked at each other and then at me. "That's quite a story," the first agent said.

I had the feeling they didn't believe a word of it.

"Very impressive," said the second. I was pretty sure from the way he looked at me that they'd been asking questions for a while, and probably knew some of the events, but not the order, not what was important, and not the hows and whys of things. I suspect, too, that they knew more about me than what they were saying. Who knows? Maybe that's just my fear talking? My guilt. But they didn't catch me in any lies. What could they do?

"And as for my first wife," I said, "she hung herself because she thought I was having an affair. And she left a note, and there was nothing I could do about that, either. I loved her and I ran away because—because I went crazy for a while. So are you going to take me to jail?" I asked. "Because if you are, I'll go."

"No," the first agent said. "We told you this was just informal questioning. We just wanted to hear from you what happened. You're probably the only man alive on the planet who really knows."

"If we need anything else," the second agent said, "we'll be in touch." They stood up and set their cups on the coffee table.

"We'll be in touch," said the first.

They left cards.

When they were gone, Dr. Alderman said. "Wow. That was a fabulous story. I had no idea. You should write all that down someday."

"Will you take my scholarship away?" I asked.

"No," he said. "You graduated from the program. You earned your scholarship. Why would we take it away? You might not have told us *everything,* but to your credit, we didn't ask, now did we? Frankly, considering all you've been through," he paused, "I think it's pretty remarkable and I'm proud to shake your hand. This is precisely the kind of success story we envisioned when we conceived of the SLED Program. Though I have to admit, if we'd known the whole thing, we might not have let you in."

And about then, Elisa, who had walked off when the agents got up to go, came out of the bedroom with a suitcase. "I'm going to stay the night with a friend," she said. And she left.

After she was gone Dr. Alderman asked, "Are you okay?"

I shook my head. "This is not what okay looks like."

Elisa would come back—eventually. She was Catholic and we were married, and that's what Catholic girls do. For a while she talked about getting an annulment, but she never did. But our relationship was never the same. I think it was just too much of a shock for her. And we had our difficulties. Sometimes the differences were so black-and-white that it was like being from another planet. And from the beginning her instincts warned her about me. That had to hurt.

Sometimes I wonder if relationships happen because we are in love, or whether we just see what we want to see and ignore the rest.

It was several months before Elisa came home. Even after she came back, she often spent weekends, even whole weeks, with this relative or that, this friend or that. She began to travel more to conferences and things. She picked up an extra class and taught at night.

I had my own studies to lose myself in. I was working on a degree in Psychology. And you know how hard school can be.

Dr. Alderman helped me a lot. When I was in the SLED Program, he came to our house four nights a week and spent time with one of us one-on-one. He made time for me, even though he had classes to teach and other things to do, even other students in the SLED Program. I think he wanted to make sure I was all right. But like I said, that might not be all about me. He had written some articles about the SLED Program, so there was its reputation to consider. And he needed to keep the grant money coming. Sometimes things happen for reasons that have nothing to do with what you wish they did. I wish I could say he really liked me. Maybe he did. Maybe he just didn't want to lose his project's biggest success story. Who knows? Maybe he had a side bet with Dr. Ackerman about whether I would make it all.

At any rate, sometimes Dr. Alderman or Dr. Ackerman would take me with him to interview potential participants. Sometimes they would ask my opinion about things, or ask me to do little things like help with paperwork or so forth. Dr. Alderman even arranged for me to have what they called an internship so that I made a little extra money working at the university. That always helps.

One day we were getting coffee after talking to an inmate at the jail, and Dr. Alderman asked me what I wanted to do when I got out of college. I hate to admit to being stupid, but to tell you the truth, I had no idea. I didn't want to go back to washing dishes, that's for sure. Even though I had a standing offer from Denny's.

"Have you ever thought about graduate school?" he asked.

"No," I replied.

"You should think about applying," he said.

I was thinking that this meant I wasn't getting this college stuff and that maybe I needed more than the usual four years. But then again, lots of my classmates were talking about what kind of jobs they wanted. In psychology, people either go into research or they go into counseling. Research is interesting, but it doesn't really help people. Theories might be useful on some level, but they aren't answers. Counselors might not offer big-picture answers, but at least they help people solve practical problems. It's a little more objective. "Maybe I could go into counseling," I said.

"I think you'd be good at that," he replied.

One more thing. A little thing. I kept the cards that the FBI agents left on my table. One day I wrote them a letter. I asked if they still had my old shoeshine box, and if so, could I please have it back—if they were done with it. I said it had sentimental value, and if they didn't need it for evidence or something, could they please send it to me. I even offered to pay the postage. A few weeks later, it came in the mail.

Act VI Scene 9

Just after I started at the University of Denver, a letter arrived from a lawyer named C. Gordon Beasley in Phoenix, Arizona, asking if I had a brother named Marco Perez and, if so, did I wish to see him? There was a photograph and the minute I saw it I knew that Marco Perez was my brother. Beasley said I should reply as soon as possible.

I had thought about my brother lots over the years, even talked with Dr. Alderman and Elisa about looking for him. It never occurred to me that Marco might look for me.

The good news was that I was going to see my brother. The bad news was in the *as soon as possible* thing. Marco was in Eyman Prison, in Florence, Arizona. That's where they do the executions. He was on death row for murder. I called Beasley and we arranged a meeting at the prison at two P.M. on the second Friday in March.

We met in a special room for death row inmates. They aren't allowed hardly any visitors and can't be alone with anyone, even their lawyers. This was a five by seven concrete cell with iron-barred doors on each end, a cement table with two small benches in the middle. Nothing else in the room. Not a thing.

I came in first. I was not allowed to bring anything—no gifts, no papers, nothing. I was strip-searched before the visit to make certain there was no contraband or weapons. I was escorted in and two guards watched me the entire time. At two-ten a guard appeared at the opposite door with my brother.

Forty years is a long time to wait. Time can do a lot to a man. Half a lifetime. I was in college. My brother was on death row. I had done lots of things but hadn't been caught for any of them. My brother got nailed for shooting a gas station attendant in a robbery. I was working on a Bachelor's Degree in Psychology. He was set to be executed as soon as the Supreme Court okayed executions again. If you didn't know my story, you would not look at me and know what I knew that afternoon—that it could just as easily be me in chains and an orange jumpsuit. Of the two of us, Marco's future was more certain than mine. I would have gladly traded with him, but not for that reason.

My hair was trimmed, my clothes neat, I did not smoke, bore no tattoos. My brother was not so tall as me, but wiry and thin. His hair was black and he wore it long and shaggy, like younger people did back then. His face was grizzled with short, angry beard. Tattoos encircled his neck and flowed like blue and green rivers down his arms. The tattoos themselves could not cover the scars on his hands and face—scars that hinted of knives and fists that flashed in the night, of footsteps that echoed down dark alleys on the jungle side of town. But his most startling feature—and most recognizable—was his eyes. Marco's eyes were so dark and round and sad, and they were overshadowed by dark, heavy brows like rain clouds. Even in this gray prison, this concrete cell, this time forty years removed from our parting, I remembered my brother's eyes. My little brother. Life is hard and I should have sheltered him from it. And what had I done? But the smile on his face—boy, that was something to see. My brother.

We leaned across the table and I took him in my arms—his hands were chained to his waist and to his feet, and he shook in my arms for some time before he twisted away and sat down, bent his head and brushed the back of his right hand across his face. Our conversation was all in Spanish.

"I always knew I would find you," he said. "And I knew you would be doing well when I did. I knew I'd be proud of you."

"How did you find me?" I asked.

"The paper," he replied.

"The paper?"

"You won a scholarship. Imagine—my brother going to college."

"What paper?"

"*Nuevo Mission*. It's out of California someplace. They got it here in the library. Not much else to do, you know. They keep me in solitary. But I been looking for you. I knew I'd find you. I knew that someday I'd see your picture in the paper, and when I did, it would be for something good. And knowing that gave me something to live for all those years."

"Oh, Marco," I said, "I wish we'd found each other sooner."

Marco learned back and shrugged, his chains jingling. "It doesn't matter," he said. "I'm just glad I got the chance to see you. I wanted to say thank you before—you know."

"Thank me? For what?"

"You saved my life, Pablo. Don't you remember?"

I shook my head. "I don't remember saving you, Marco."

"Oh, yes," Marco said, nodding. "The night our mother... you were fighting with that man. He pulled you out of the box and you started fighting with him. You shouted at me to run away. That's what you said. 'Run away!' So I did."

I closed my eyes. I remembered the man but I couldn't remember fighting with him. I remember him dragging me out of the box and beating the crap out of me.

"He was beating the crap out of me," I said. "He hauled me out of the box and beat the hell out of me."

Marco nodded. "Yes, he was beating you. I was there, remember? But you were fighting with him. I was just standing in the box scared out of my wits, and you were fighting with him. He was hitting you but you wouldn't let him go. You kept shouting at me, 'Run, Marco! Run! Run away!' and so I did. I climbed out of the box and I ran down the road as fast as I could. I ran all the way to town. I found a cantina and a policeman and I told him to come. I took him by the arm and begged him. I told him a man was beating my brother, but you know how cops are." Marco looked around suddenly, his eyes lighting on the guard standing by the door, behind him and slightly to his right.

Marco looked down, then back at me. "The cop—he didn't want to be bothered. There's always somebody somewhere beating somebody's brother. I had to cry and scream until finally he got up and came with me—just to shut me up, I think. But by the time we got back to the house you were gone and our mother..."

I was stunned. "*You came back*?" Why hadn't I thought of this at the time? How different our lives would have been. But at the time, all I could think was that the man took my brother, and I don't know which felt worse: believing that he had, or finding out that he hadn't.

"We came back," Marco said. "I only wish I could have run faster, or argued better. I wish we had come back in time to find you. But you were gone and our mother was dead. Pablo, we looked everywhere for you. The whole town. People looked for days. The cops. The neighbors. They looked everywhere. We were sure he took you. They caught him, you know, but he said he didn't take you. All these years I hoped you got away. I was sure you would. I wanted to ask you what happened. Where did he take you? How did you get away?"

"They caught him?"

"Yeah, they caught him. He was a local fuck-up. Kind of a gangster, you know." Marco grunted and looked away. They tried him for killing our mother and kidnapping you, but they only convicted him of the murder. They put him in prison for a while. Later on, when he got out, he came back. I cut his throat, Pablo. But before I killed him I cut off his—"

"I don't want to know," I said. "I don't want to hear any more about killing. I'm tired of all this killing, Marco. There's too much. I wish it would stop."

We looked at each other.

"So what happened to you?" he asked. "How did you get away?"

"Nothing happened," I said. He put me back in the box and locked it. After I got out, I thought he took you. I was so frightened and ashamed, I couldn't think right, so I ran away. I walked all the way to Juarez and lived there for a while, then I came to America."

I looked at Marco. He was smiling. There were tears in his eyes. I think he was thinking of the story they tell all the time in Mexico, even if it's rarely true. *Mexican makes good in America.* "Marco," I said, my voice dropping to a whisper.

He looked at me.

"Did you really look for me?"

"The whole city looked for you. It was like you vanished into thin air."

"But Marco—all these years—all these years I felt so bad for leaving you."

"But you didn't leave me," he said. "You saved my life."

Was that possible? Or was Marco just believing what he wanted to believe? "What did you do?" I asked.

"They put me in an orphanage," he said.

"Where?"

"In Torreón. That's where we come from, remember? Just outside of

Torreón. It wasn't bad, Pablo. Some nuns ran the place and I had a real bed. And I didn't have to share it with but a few other kids, and there wasn't even many bedbugs." He laughed. "And they fed me, and I went to school and everything. If I got into any trouble back then, it was just little stuff. The kind of things kids do, you know? Stealing fruit. Smoking. Drinking when we could get beer or tequila. A little fighting here or there. You know how kids are. But when I saw... after I... well, that was the first time I went to prison. I was sixteen I think." He shrugged. "After that well, once you get started... " Marco opened his hands in a gesture of helplessness and shrugged, "... it don't seem like there's no way out, is there?"

"No," I said. "It doesn't."

"It would take a miracle," Marco said. He looked down at his hands traced the line of a scar that ran from the middle joint of his thumb all the way to his wrist. "But you found a way out, Pablo. I knew you would."

"I didn't escape," I said. "He locked me in the box and then set the house on fire. I screamed and screamed. After a while, I rocked the box onto its side and the lid came open. I got out and found our mother dead and you gone. I thought, all these years, that *he* took *you*. I felt so bad I just ran off into the desert. I should have died, but somehow I made it to Juarez."

"That's not what I meant," Marco said. "You made it out, you know, to America," Marco said, "and now look at you." He leaned forward. "They said in the article you have a wife?"

"We got married in February. She's a teacher at the college I went to."

"And you're going to be a legal citizen, too?"

"That's what they say. There's paperwork. I've started it." I smiled. "It is different, I tell you. I don't know what I'll do if I can walk down the street like everybody else. I don't know how that will feel."

"I bet it will feel great," Marco said. He whistled softly through his teeth. "My brother the U.S. citizen. And in college, too."

We stared at each other, and I had the feeling that there was something more to this visit than Marco cheering for me, or thanking me for saving his life. If I saved his life. I didn't remember it that way.

"Someday," Marco said, "when you're walking in the park with your wife and your kids, I want you to take a minutes just to enjoy being there just for me, Pablo. For all the times we should have had but never got. Will you do that for me, Pablo?"

"I'll do that," I said. "That'll be easy."

"There's one more thing."

"I'm not killing anybody," I said.

"No, no." Marco shook his head. "I don't want you to kill nobody. I killed the man just like they said, and some others they don't know about. I'm getting what I deserve. But Pablo," Marco looked back at the guard, then up at me again, "I have a son, back in Torreón "

"A son?" I sat straight up. "I have a nephew? Family?"

"His mother doesn't like me very much," Marco said, "and she's pretty much kept him away from me these past few years. Before . . . you know. Before they . . . I wanted to ask . . ."

"You want me to see your son?"

Marco leaned forward close to me and his eyes were wet. I saw, then, for the first time, that Marco had small blue tears tattooed from the corner of his eyes and down his cheek. It was the first time I ever saw that kind of tattoo, though I would see them more often as they became fashionable.

Marco's voice turned gruff and he said, "She won't have nothing to do with me, you know. She's a good girl, Luisa is. And my boy, Pablo—we named him after you!—he's a good kid. And you! You're going to be a big hero back home when you go back. The missing boy is found! And, look how well he's done for himself! Going to college and everything. I bet they're already talking about it. I can't be the only one who saw.

"She'll see you, Pablo. For Pablito's sake. She'll want him to know his whole family didn't turn out bad. Will you look after him for me, Pablo? Maybe send him a little something every now and then? Maybe you can tell him a few lies about me. Tell him his old man wasn't all bad. And maybe, if you do, he won't turn out like me. Will you do that for me, Pablo?"

This was in 1968. The U.S. was in a big fight about capital punishment. Executions were suspended. A lot of people hoped that all death sentences would be commuted. But Marco didn't want his sentence commuted. What was it he said—"I'm getting what I deserve?" And there was something else he said, something that didn't hit me until later. Something about knowing he would find me doing well gave him something to live for. A week after I saw him, Marco hung himself. When Beasley called to tell me, my first thought was, *Please, God, not again.* What is wrong with you people? Maybe solitary does that. I wouldn't want my brother locked up in a box. We had enough of that a long time ago. The death penalty resumed in Arizona in 1976, so I guess it didn't matter.

I told you that I liked the word, *irony*. There wasn't much difference between Marco and me. I wonder how much difference there is between any of us. I think we all, every one of us, has an Oscar buried in our backyard. Some people get caught, some people don't. Some people are lucky. Some people aren't. It just takes time for these things to work out. Those who live by the sword, Father Sheehy said.

I never told Marco that I was not the man he thought I was. He could have known. Surely some gossip about Pablo the Shoeshine Boy reached Torreón. Especially if Marco was running with the gangs. Perhaps he never made the connection. People see what they want to see and ignore the rest. And that applies to me, as well.

Act VI Scene 10

In the spring of 1969 I graduated from the University of Denver with a Bachelor's Degree in Psychology and an almost perfect 4.0 G.P.A. I had one picky creative writing teacher who gave me a 3.8. When I went to his office and asked what I would have to do to earn a 4.0, he said a perfect score was for a perfect paper, and he had never seen a perfect paper, and he had never given a 4.0. I took his class again and he gave me a 3.9. He said that my work was way overly imaginative and I relied too much on profanity and slang. He also said I needed to work on writing in the active voice, to learn punctuation, eliminate repetition and fragments and run-ons, and I should run right at the conflict. Whatever that means. I told you, this writing stuff is all subjective. He said I should stick to essays, but he still gave me an A.

Dr. Alderman suggested that I apply to several graduate programs, and that these should include a variety of schools both geographically and in terms of quality. But he said that being Hispanic and having good grades, I would probably have my pick of offers. He was right. I decided to go to U.C. Berkeley. Berkeley's a good school. And the Bay Area was kind of cool back in the '60's.

Elisa was kind of warming back up to me. Slowly. I think the idea that I got into Berkeley helped. It was starting to look like I might have a future. And the FBI hadn't come around asking about any more cold case murders. That kind of things builds trust. I mean, if the FBI trusts you, why shouldn't she, right? So the idea was that I would move to Berkeley and find a place, and she would look for work in the junior colleges in the Bay Area. She'd join me in the spring or summer.

I rented a room on Euclid, up near the Rose Garden. I thought it was a nice area and it would be a nice surprise for Elisa. It was close to the university, and I figured I'd find an apartment nearby when Elisa joined me. She would like the old houses and the garden. We could go walking there in the evenings.

The lady I rented the room from was Mrs. Woolley. She was a widow with this beautiful old white house. It was what they called Victorian style. It was two stories tall, wood, with lots of pretty carvings and woodwork around the windows, high pitched roofs, a round tower like a castle. Considering some of the places I'd slept, it was like heaven. It was like living in a fairy tale.

Mrs. Woolley rented rooms to students. I don't think she needed the money. I think she just did it to be nice. Or maybe she felt better with other people in the house. Who knows? She lived downstairs and there were three rooms upstairs. We—the tenants—shared an upstairs kitchen and a bath. And we ran errands for Mrs. Woolley—bought groceries and stuff. Got her prescriptions filled. Things like that. There was also an old coach house in the back yard. She had fixed that up into a cottage and rented it out, too. I took one of the upstairs rooms, but you can imagine my surprise when, on my second morning there, I walked outside and ran right into Phoebe. Of all the people.

I was going out to look for a grocery store and she was coming back from the grocery store. I could tell by the bag of groceries she carried. She was wearing this beautiful long blue almost-sheer hippie sun dress with a white cotton blouse and a big, wide straw hat with a big, blue African bride flower and a sprig of lavender in the band. And she was barefoot. She looked like she stepped right out of the pages of a magazine. "Hey," I said. I hadn't recognized her just yet. "Where's the good groceries around here?"

Phoebe pointed down the road and said, "There are two stores that way. The good one's a block past the other. It's got organic produce, if you're into organics."

That was when I recognized her. "Phoebe," I said.

She looked at me.

"Do you remember me?"

She shook her head.

I held up my left hand.

She said, "Did we have a class together?"

"You saved my hand. You put me in the hospital."

She said, "I'm a nurse. I'm sorry, but I don't remember every hand I save. I wish I did."

"This was down in Delano. I'd just got fired from a vineyard. My first day. I had my hand in a wrap."

"Oh," she said. Her face brightened. Then she said, "You're the guy who got his picture in the paper!" She sort of frowned as she remembered. "You know how much trouble that picture caused us?"

"You know how much trouble that picture caused *me*?"

She looked at me kind of blankly.

I thought about telling her about Don Pablo and the FBI, but then I thought that might not be such a good idea. "I'm sorry," I said. "I didn't mean to cause anybody any trouble. It was just a little overwhelming that day, what with the riot downstairs and all. And they had me doped up on morphine, so I wasn't thinking to clear."

Phoebe looked at me kind of skeptically, but she smiled, I think to be polite.

"But, hey," I said, "You guys taught me about Gandhi and non-violence. A few days later I bought *Non-Violent Resistance* and *The Story of My Experiments with Truth* and *Third Class in Indian Railways* and read them when I was stuck in boxcar in a blizzard in Colorado."

Phoebe looked at me, then at the cottage, then back at me. She shifted the bag of groceries from her left arm to her right and opened the gate.

I sighed. This wasn't going like I wanted it to. Why was it so difficult talking to women? "And a few weeks after that—" I almost said, *when I got out of jail in Denver*, but I bit my tongue just in time, " I wrote an essay about Gandhi. He got me into college."

"Gandhi got you into college?"

"Well, not Gandhi *personally*. But the essay *about* Gandhi. That got me into college. Once they decided that I really wrote it. So in a way, I could say that you got me into college because you turned me on to Gandhi. Anyway, I earned my B.A. at the University of Denver, and now I'm starting grad school at Berkeley. I'm studying child psychology."

"Psychology's cool," Phoebe said.

"I want to be a counselor. I want to help people. Especially kids."

"Really?"

"Really," I said.

"Wow," she said. "So how are you? That hand heal up okay?"

"It did," I said, even though it really hadn't. Not perfectly. I still got numb spells and prickly spells, and sometimes my finger still hurt for no reason at all that I could tell. "It got better. You know, if it hadn't been for you, I would have lost it. So thank you for that, too." Phoebe looked at me. She was standing in the back yard and I was leaning on the fence across from her. Then it dawned on me. "You live here?" I said. I was more of a statement than a question.

She nodded. "Yes."

"You're not going to believe this," I said, "but so do I."

You know where this story goes. Phoebe asked if I wanted some juice or tea and I said okay. She led me into the little cottage and it looked like the home I had always dreamed of, right down to the pictures of the saints on the wall.

Phoebe was the only tenant who wasn't a student. She met Mrs. Woolley a year or so earlier when Mrs. Woolley was in the hospital for something or another and Phoebe helped take care of her. Phoebe was going through a bad divorce. Phoebe took extra good care of Mrs. Woolley and Mrs. Woolley offered Phoebe a place to stay. Phoebe told me all of this over something called oolong. I didn't ask what it was but it tasted like tea. "So what happened to you?" she asked. "Why'd you disappear like that?"

I told her that I used to run with a gang down in Juarez, and about the message I got from Don Pablo, and how that led me to Salt Lake and then Denver, that I'd read, all three books by Gandhi while stuck in the snow and almost freezing to death, that I wrote the essay about Gandhi for the SLED Program and they didn't believe I wrote it. But I told her how I really liked Gandhi now, and wished more people could be like him.

Walking in Rose Garden Park Phoebe told me that she was still in nursing school when we met, but she graduated the next year and now she was something called a Nurse Practitioner, though she still worked as an R.N. She did her other stuff on the side. She said that she spent as much time as she could volunteering in the camps and helping farm workers. She'd been a farm worker herself for a while, when she was little. She and her family had come north from Morelia, in Michoacán State, in Mexico. She said she was just a baby when they left. She said she didn't remember Mexico, though she'd never forget her first years in the U.S.A. But her family made it. They did okay. They had got citizenship a long time ago and now they ran a nursery and a greenhouse outside of Modesto.

Over lunch I told Phoebe about college but I omitted the part about Elisa for the time being. I told her about my crazy roommates and about meeting Ringo Starr. She thought that was cool and she wanted to know if I liked music because she had some friends who, as she put it, "tour with the dead." I wasn't sure I wanted anything to do with people who traveled with the dead, but she invited me to meet some of them, anyway, so I said okay.

That afternoon, riding the bus into San Francisco, she told me what it was like to work in a women's clinic and all the things she did to try to keep from going crazy from all the abuse she saw. She liked flowers and music and photography. She played the guitar and sang a little, but everybody in San Francisco played something and sang, at least back then. She did yoga in the park every morning that she could, and was learning to meditate. She said psychologists should pay more attention to Eastern philosophies and Oriental medicine, and I agreed with her.

That night we went to Haight-Asbury. We ate Indian food in an old house that had been converted into something called a bistro—the first time I had ever eaten *murgh tikka masala* (it tasted like spicy chicken) or been in a bistro (it was just like a restaurant only fancier). Then we went to somebody's house to listen to a jam with Jerry Garcia and Merle Saunders and some other musicians I didn't know. Phoebe thought it was cool that I didn't drink. She drank a little wine, but said she'd seen too many problems caused by drugs and alcohol.

Very late that night she lit incense and candles and we showered together and then I made love to her on a waterbed. Remember waterbeds? I'm not surprised they didn't make it, but it was still nice to sleep with Phoebe on one, once I got used to the waves.

Two weeks later I wrote to Elisa that our marriage was over. I said I was sorry. I said that she was right about me. I told her that when she called me into her office that day and chewed me out for flirting with her, that I had formed some opinions about her, and I let those opinions guide our relationship all this time, but that I was wrong about them. I said I didn't think badly of her. That wasn't it at all. But when I first met her, and she wanted nothing to do with me, I thought she was exhibiting the anxious-avoidant pattern of Attachment Theory. Now I said, I thought that she was right and I was wrong. She was right to avoid me and I was the one with the attachment problems. I was probably just plain disorganized and might never get over it. But either way, I said, our marriage was over.

Elisa wrote me back a one-word reply. *Asshole.*

I liked the simplicity of her answer. Sometimes the simplest answers are the best.

Phoebe and I married in June of 1971, right after I earned my Master's Degree. Jerry Garcia played at our wedding, but it wasn't like a real show. Our kids saw Jerry in our photo album and freaked out. Who would believe that? But hey, he was a Chicano. *A bro.*

I went to work that following August as a guidance counselor at Sonora High School, which is as close to heaven as I think you can get without a spaceship. Sonora—not the school! We had a son and a daughter, and both our kids went to the university, too, though Marco went to Stanford and Helena went to UCLA. They're both married and have kids of their own. Five grandkids in all. Marco writes computer code and makes more money than God. Helena is a doctor, and she does pretty okay, too.

Even my nephew, Pablito, came to America and lived with us for a while. He didn't like high school, but he got his G.E.D. and went to Sonora Community College. He got his two-year degree just like I did. But he didn't go on to the university. He got married instead and became an air-con tech. He lives up in Sacramento, and he's a good kid, too. I told him lots of stories about his father, and what it was like growing up poor in Mexico. I left out some of the bad stuff. The hardest part, though, was to tell him the truth.

Sometimes good people make bad choices. I told him that was what happened to my brother, his dad. Pablito had a touch of that, too, but he's okay now. I love him like a second son, and Marco would be very proud. I mean, after all, his Pablito made it in America, too.

Phoebe worked at the Tuolumne County Hospital and sometimes chipped in at the Behavioral Health Center. I even did a little work on the side with Behavioral Health, especially if they were really busy or had Spanish-speaking clients who needed help. We bought a little house out west of town with a beautiful view of the mountains, and even got a little summer place on Don Pedro Reservoir, out past Chinese Camp. I liked the name, Don Pedro. Once in a while I'd slip up and call it Don Pablo Reservoir and people would look at me like I was crazy. Maybe they're right.

But the best part is that from August of 1971 until June of 1998 I was a counselor at Sonora High School. Twenty-seven years. They made me retire in '98 because I turned seventy-two. Of course, my *real* age was seventy-five, but they didn't know that. I had never got my paperwork changed from when that cop, Scoville, wrote down that I was thirty-nine. It got into my Social Security records and everything. Oh, well. Sometimes I think God gave me back a few of my wasted years. I was glad I could put them to good use.

Over the years, I got to help a lot of kids who might have turned our like Oscar or Filo or Marco or me. Well, maybe I didn't turn out so bad, but you know what I mean. I sure could have. Did for a while. And while Sonora isn't a bad place to grow up as, say, *Sal Si Puedes* or Compton or Oakland or South L.A., we have our share of troubled kids. And in the summers Phoebe and the kids and I drove out to the camps, or visited some of these rough neighborhoods, and Phoebe donated her vacation time volunteering as a nurse for low income families, and I talked to the kids who were in trouble. We did that because we were both grateful to have a better life, but also to help our kids to grow up and care about others, and they do. And we wanted them to know where their people came from, so they might better appreciate what they have and how they came to have it. We also wanted them to know what might happen if they didn't take care of it.

Sometimes the local cops came and took me to jail—to talk to kids they picked up! I was always nervous when cops showed up outside my house, even after all those years. I might have helped some of those kids. Others—who knows? You do the best you can and leave the rest up to God. I don't think any of them was the worse for talking to me.

And it was funny to talk to these kids—in school, in the camps, in jail, wherever—and they'd see me with my nice clothes with my hair neatly trimmed, and they'd notice things like my watch or my wedding ring or my sunglasses or (later on) my laptop and phone. They'd know about my wife and kids and the car we drove. And they'd know from all that I had a good job and a nice house, and many of those kids didn't have much, if anything. And sometimes they'd say to me, "What do you know about trouble?"

What could I tell them? That I knew what it was like to get fucked up the ass? That I knew what it was like to sleep out under the stars or eat out of garbage cans? That I know how a heart muscle cinches when you stick a knife into it? That I walked into the kitchen and found my wife hanging? To be down and out on the streets of Denver? Juarez? To be twice almost murdered and left to die? No, there was way too many things I couldn't tell them. And who would have believed it if I had? Mostly, all I could do was listen.

Fortunately, one of the things people need most is somebody to listen to their troubles, and one of the requirements to be a good counselor is to be a good listener. Most of the time, I think, people already know what to do. They just want to be heard. Don Pablo called me his quiet one. I had a professor once who said, "Everybody learns to talk, but nobody learns to listen." So I listened to these kids talk and I might not say anything. But I think that just by listening, they knew at least one person cared. Sometimes, just like Father Sheehy asked me, I asked them, "*But what would happen if...?*" I didn't have to answer the question. Maybe the best thing I could do was to get the kids thinking, or give them a little hope, to get them to see that they have alternatives to whatever behavior was hurting them. Once in a while, even now, one of those kids writes a letter, or calls, or emails, and says what they are up to, and that they are doing good. Well. That always makes me feel good. Once in a while, one even says thank you.

One more thing. One afternoon, while I was still in school and Phoebe and I were living together but not yet married, she came home from work and told me that the funniest thing happened at work.

I was sitting at the kitchen table drinking a glass of fresh lemonade Phoebe had made that morning and writing a paper about schizotypal personality disorder. The assignment was to write about a personality disorder that we thought didn't affect us and then explain why it didn't affect us. People with schizotypal personality disorder may hold odd beliefs such as believing in magic or conspiracy theories or odd notions of religion. They're eccentric. They also often report unusual perceptual experiences, but not extreme hallucinations or psychosis. They frequently link their odd beliefs to these experiences. They also usually report negative self-image or low self-esteem, and problems with relationships. "So what happened?" I asked.

Phoebe said, "Do you remember being in the hospital in Delano? Do you remember a girl there who lost a leg? You probably didn't know her, but I treated her in the camp and saw her later at the hospital. I think you were there about the same time. Poor thing, she almost died. She'd cut her foot on some barbed wire or something and it got infected. Gangrene. Sepsis. Father McDonnell gave her her last rites." Phoebe grunted. "But she survived. She came into the clinic today. She was getting fitted for a new leg and she recognized me. So we got to talking and she told me the strangest story. She said that she had been in and out of consciousness most of the night that night, but she remembered Father McDonnell whispering and she remembered her family praying and lighting candles. But she said that in the middle of the night an angel came and gave her a drink of magic water and she knew the minute she saw that angel that she was going to be all right. And she was. The next morning she was better. She recovered—it was like a miracle. A few days later she was out of the hospital, and they didn't even have to amputate the rest of her leg. Funny how people have these experiences, isn't it? So now she's all religious, but she's a sweet girl and I'm happy for her. Anyway, she's almost twenty now, and she wants to run in a race in few months. She asked if I wanted to train with her. She gave me her number."

Phoebe left her purse and keys and things on the table, and went off to the kitchen to make some tea. Beside the keys was a torn strip of paper. On the paper was written: Maria, 431-7747. I looked at the last four numbers. Some things, Father Sheehy said, you just don't question.

I'm glad the girl is all right. Really. But I wonder which explanation would be harder to believe. That an angel gave her a magic pill that cured her infection, or that a gangster from Mexico gave her a pill that a space alien gave him. There's a billion people on the planet will believe the first. Not very many, if any, would believe the second.

So now you're asking, *What's the point?* What's the point of this whole story?

The point is that a long time ago my mother was murdered, my brother lost, my life transformed from difficult to nightmarish. I said that at that moment it was like a bullet passed through that place in my heart that registered feelings. From that moment I would not feel what I should have felt, or know what others felt, or relate to their feelings. You might have described me as schizoid, with overtones of antisocial or avoidant behavior (though sometimes these symptomatic behaviors overlap). However it begins, people like me are almost invariably condemned to suffer and die alone.

In time I would learn that this type of disassociation is a survival mechanism. When we are overwhelmed, our bodies bury those feelings. Or try to bury them, though they may manifest at inappropriate times or in inappropriate ways. But somehow, someway, a kind of miracle happened for me, too. Or many miracles, for I, also, did not die. Even my suffering was relieved.

Someone once told me that I would not think my way into a new way of living, but I might live my way into a new way of thinking. Knowledge is experiential. And, to a certain extent, so are our feelings. Over time, the feeling of alienation evaporated. I became comfortable in school, at work, at home, with my wife, with myself, with some friends, even with God. I felt okay because okay was what I was *supposed* to feel—*exactly* what normal people would feel in that situation. And I understood, too, that much of the confusion I felt when I was younger was not because I was crazy. Not to feel anything—that would be crazy. I was a normal person undergoing a crazy experience. The confusion, pain, alienation, fear, all of that, was *exactly what I was supposed to feel.* One of the definitions of sanity is to feel the correct emotion at the correct time. And what I felt was, at the time, correct. I was a sane person experiencing a crazy life. I just didn't know it.

Some of this I learned from my mentors, some of this I learned in school. Knowing that I was not crazy helped me to feel better about myself. So as I began to relax, I also began to better understand what other people were feeling, and I could identify with them. Not perfectly, but better. But to the end, the people I best identified with, and the people I helped the most, were the people like me—the people who lived on the edge and suffered. Especially kids. With these, I could make something good out of something bad—using the lessons of my past to help them shape better futures. The point is: I learned how to be human. I learned how to feel.

Epilogue

At the beginning of this memoir, I suggested that you might ask, Why are you telling me this? All those years I was haunted by my past. How many lives did I live? How many names had I had? How many people do I know who've died? And above all, I was haunted by a few days that I spent with Gus.

My angel. He was so simple and logical and real. He told me so much that somehow I came away with something like hope. What if people could learn to cooperate? What if we could focus on our similarities and set aside (or perhaps even celebrate?) our differences? *What would happen if... ?*

But what could I say? What could I do to make anything better for anybody else? I wanted to do that on a big scale, but I was just a poor shoeshine boy. Nobody wanted to hear what I had to say. And who would believe any of it? Especially the part about Gus. So this latter part of my life I focused on the little things—what I could do, rather than what I couldn't. You could say I was most interested in *practice* than *theory*. And now I come to the end of my life. And it should be a good end, and I should feel good, and I should die in my bed, happy and fulfilled, surrounded by my family and friends. But life doesn't always work out like we want, now does it?

So a few weeks ago Phoebe got an email from her cousin, Teresa, about a big family reunion in Morelia. She wanted to go and she wanted me to come with her. Many of her relations she hadn't seen in, what, eighty-something years? She thought it would be fun.

But I haven't been feeling all that well lately. I'm ninety-three. I still get around pretty good for an old guy, but the thought of driving up to Sacramento, of flying to LA and changing planes to Mexico City, and changing planes *again* to fly to Morelia—it just felt like too much. But Phoebe really wanted to go. We could break the trip up, she said. Stay a few nights in Frisco. Eat out in Chinatown. We could stay a few nights in Mexico City, too. But I didn't want to go. I guess, like most old people, I can get pretty stubborn.

So Marco drove over from Frisco for the weekend and took Phoebe back with him, and she flew to Mexico City, and then Morelia, and she called me from Teresa's house and said it was nice and she was having a good time and would I say hello to her family? So I said hello.

And the next morning she emailed me that she had another cousin she remembered from when she was a little girl, Carmen, and Carmen lived in Mazatlán, and she was going to ride all the way to Mazatlán by a bus by herself, and Phoebe didn't think it was a good idea for Carmen to ride alone, so she was going to ride with her, and would I please consider flying to Mazatlán and meeting them there? Mazatlán is nice. A beach resort. We could spend a few days on the water, she said, and then we could fly home together.

So I got up and read the email and wrote back that I really didn't want to fly and I wished she'd just fly home like she'd planned. But by then, Phoebe was already gone.

It's a long trip to Mazatlán. First you go west to Guadalajara, then you drive north up the coast. It's an all-day thing. So I wasn't too worried when I went to bed and hadn't heard from her. I go to bed early, anyway. But when there was still no word in the morning, and I couldn't get a signal on Phoebe's cell phone, I started to worry.

I called Teresa in Morelia. "Haven't you heard?" she said. "The bus went missing."

"How does a bus go missing?" I asked.

"Who knows?" she said. "This is Mexico."

I guess in Mexico, busses go missing.

I called the number she gave for Carmen in Mazatlán. No answer. And I don't know how to say this, but I just knew. For the third time in my life, the world was a blank stare. Sometimes there is just nothing.

It took them three days to find the bus. Whoever took it burned it in an abandoned quarry about a hundred kilometers off its route. Who took it? When? Where? Why? What happened to the passengers? Nobody saw anything. Nobody heard anything. Nobody found anything. Nobody knew anything. Just a burned-out bus left in the middle of no place.

If I listen, I can hear Phoebe whispering to her cousin in her own quiet, confident way that it's going to be all right, just like she did when she saw how fucked up my hand was, or when I confessed to her I was married, or when she told me she was pregnant, or when Marco broke his leg playing football, or when the school district told me they had a retirement policy. Forty-seven years she's been by my side telling me things were going to be all right, and she hasn't been wrong yet. She probably held her cousin's hand. She might have even tried to talk sense into the heads of whatever thugs robbed everybody. I imagine that when the end came, she prayed. She was like that. I hope it was quick. What is wrong with you people?

So it's February of 2016 and it's 5:00 in the morning and I'm sitting in our little kitchen with a cup of coffee long gone cold. Marco and Helena and Pablito have come to stay with me for a little while. They're asleep. We're waiting, but the authorities don't know anything, or aren't saying if they do. These things happen in Mexico, they say. People disappear. Hell, these things happen all over. India. Africa. Iraq. Syria. Pretty much everywhere.

I once told an FBI agent that I thought nobody cared when people disappeared, but he said it would surprise you, that usually somebody somewhere did care, even when you thought that nobody noticed.

I'd like to ask whoever did this if there was really anything on the bus that was worth killing thirty-one people to take. Especially two old ladies over eighty. What do you get? A little money? Some jewelry? A few cell phones? They would have given them to you. I'm sure you didn't have to fight to take them. And most of these people took the damn bus because they couldn't afford to fucking fly. They didn't have all that much to begin with. And if you think about it, neither do the one's they leave behind.

At the beginning of this book I said that I spent my whole life learning how to feel, and the irony was that I had succeeded. Now you know why. I learned to feel and feeling isn't something I want right now. I spent my whole life learning how to love, and when I did I set myself up to have my heart broken. But that's still not why I wrote all this down.

The last half my life I worked to try to undo all the bad things that I did in the first half, and now it feels once again like my past is knocking at my door. I thought I could leave it behind, but find that I carry it with me. I can change my name, and I might even change how I feel about my history, but my past is still my past and I cannot change the facts. Is this what I get for killing Filo? For killing that soldier? For making Maria's life so miserable that she killed herself?

I've never told anyone what happened in Roswell. Who would believe me? But I listened to what Gus said and I promised that I would never kill again, and I am proud to say that I kept that promise. In fact, I've built on it. I learned to do honest work. I got an education. I did everything that I could to try to make this world a better place for my having been here. Until this past week, I had no regrets.

Over the years I've read many conspiracy theories about UFOs. I remember a book from the early 70's, *Chariots of the Gods*. And there have been tons of movies. *ET, Terminator, Alien, Predator, Close Encounters of the Third Kind, Star Trek, Star Wars, Contact*, and so forth. What I find interesting is that in all of these, humans are portrayed as saviors of the universe. We dwell on the summit of the evolutionary mountain. We claim that we are brave, intelligent, and moral, when, in fact, we are none of those things. We play make believe. We see what we want to see and disregard the rest. We bury our heads in the sand and pray that somehow, someway it will work out in the end. I think sometimes it's like that speech in *Network* when Peter Finch goes crazy on the air and starts shouting "Please, at least leave us alone in our living rooms. Let me have my toaster and my TV and my steel-belted radials and I won't say anything. Just leave us alone." People remember the "mad as hell" part of that monologue, but nobody gets mad anymore. In the sixties, people got mad. In the sixties, people wanted to change things, and I thought for a little while that we might. But we didn't. Now everybody just wants to hide. In psychology, we call this denial. At worst we call it *delusional*, if not *psychotic*.

But can we hide? We slaughter each other at unprecedented rates. Millions and millions every year. And not just humans, whatever species stands in our way. Whole species! There are six billion of us on the planet and we're choking in our own excrement, but we don't have sense enough to plan our societies so that we can live within the means our environment provides. And all the while we claim to love and follow the dictates of a loving God while we shit all over his creation. Jesus said that not a sparrow falls but that our Heavenly Father knows. And weeps. But who pays attention to that anymore?

Gus said his kind believed in a supreme being, not because of exceptions to the laws of nature, but because of the very *consistency* of those laws. So what happens today? Men and women of the spirit repudiate science and men and women of science belittle the spirit. Men and women of different faiths vilify the men of science as though scientists had the power to destroy faith. Men and women of faith ignore our present life and tell us that what matters is the life that comes next. In turn, the men and women of science glorify intellect above the compassion that we should hold in our hearts because, after all, they say, *we are responsible to our shareholders*. And they focus entirely on the here and now, but ignore what we leave behind for future generations.

But who is responsible for us? The things of the spirit cannot be measured in microns and milliliters and grams and light years, but they are just as important as the things that can. Knowledge is power, but power without conscience is the most corrupting force in the universe. We are all in this together. *What would happen if* we acted like that was true?

All my life I carried this knowledge around, and I have not been able to make anything better. All I have done since the day I set forth to cross a desert on my bare feet was to feel like an alien among my own kind and a stranger in the world to which I was born. But who am I to change anything? I'm just a shoeshine boy. The world had Jesus and we killed him. The world had Gandhi, the Kennedys, and Martin Luther King, and countless others who stood up and said, "What would happen if...?" Have you read the Sermon on the Mount? Living a good life is not that difficult. What's difficult is living like we do.

And that's why I am sharing this with you. Phoebe is gone and I'll be gone soon enough. I don't want what I know to die with me. Let them kill me if they want. What difference will it make?

I've often wondered if Gus is still out there watching. I wish he was, but I suspect he did as he said. Somewhere beyond the bounds of our solar system floats a beacon with a message for who or whatever passes by. DANGER: BAD DOG. They're done with us. And who could blame them? We're on our own now. As a species, it's sink or swim.

I said I have one regret, and I do. Gus said there was no heaven, not a physical place like we teach in our religions. But he said there were worlds where the inhabitants thought more of others than they did of themselves, worlds with as much health and prosperity as the inhabitants could engineer in a spirit of cooperation and harmony. He said there were worlds where the advanced beings treated all life with respect. He said there were places where all were happy and kind. I'd like to see that. All those years ago, when I watched Gus step through a hole in the side of his space ship, he looked at me, and I looked at him, and I think there was one thing both of us wanted to but could not say. I wish that that hot afternoon in July I had been able to call out the words that caught in my throat: *Take me with you.*